Praise for *A Secret Cornish Summer*

'I LOVED *A Secret Cornish Summer* . . .
Gloriously uplifting and unashamedly warm-hearted!'
Faith Hogan

'A lovely summery read, full of secrets and hope.
A smashing slice of life in a seaside town, the perfect place
to draw a line in the sand and for new beginnings.'
Jo Thomas

'Escapism at its very best, what a book!
The most wonderful setting, lovely characters and oozing
with heart and hope – I adored it.'
Milly Johnson

'The whole thing was so captivating, and I loved that there
were secrets peppered and hinted at throughout. *A Secret
Cornish Summer* is a blissful story full of sunshine,
secrets and Phillipa's trademark romance.'
Cressida McLaughlin

'Sunshine, secrets and a stunning setting make this the
perfect summer read!'
Heidi Swain

Praise for Phillipa Ashley

'Sheer joy.'
Katie Fforde

'Will make you laugh and cry.'
Miranda Dickinson

'Filled with warm and likeable characters. Great fun!'
Jill Mansell

'Within moments you'll feel like you're at the Cornish seaside, gazing out on the waves, cream tea in hand. The ultimate summer reading escape!'
***Yours* Magazine**

'Full of genuine warmth and quirky characters.'
Woman's Own

'Serious escapism . . . like a big warm hug.'
Popsugar

'Romantic and life-affirming.'
Woman's Weekly

'A feel-good read for summer.'
The Sun

'Charming.'
Publisher's Weekly

PHILLIPA ASHLEY is a *Sunday Times*, Amazon and Audible best-selling author of uplifting romantic fiction. After studying English at Oxford University, she worked as a copywriter and journalist before turning her hand to writing.

Her debut novel, *Decent Exposure*, won the Romantic Novelists' Association New Writers Award and was filmed as a Lifetime TV movie, *12 Men of Christmas*, starring Kristin Chenoweth and Josh Hopkins.

Since then, her novels have sold well over a million copies and been translated into numerous languages.

Phillipa lives in an English village with her husband, has a grown-up daughter and loves nothing better than walking the Lake District hills and swimming in Cornish coves.

@PhillipaAshley

Also by Phillipa Ashley

The Cornish Café Series
Summer at the Cornish Café
Christmas at the Cornish Café
Confetti at the Cornish Café

The Little Cornish Isles Series
Christmas on the Little Cornish Isles: The Driftwood Inn
Spring on the Little Cornish Isles: The Flower Farm
Summer on the Little Cornish Isles: The Starfish Studio

The Porthmellow Series
A Perfect Cornish Summer
A Perfect Cornish Christmas
A Perfect Cornish Escape

The Falford Series
An Endless Cornish Summer
A Special Cornish Christmas
A Golden Cornish Summer

A Surprise Christmas Wedding
The Christmas Holiday

A Secret Cornish Summer

Phillipa Ashley

avon.

Published by AVON
A division of HarperCollins*Publishers*
1 London Bridge Street
London SE1 9GF

www.harpercollins.co.uk

HarperCollins*Publishers*
Macken House
39/40 Mayor Street Upper
Dublin 1
D01 C9W8

A Paperback Original 2023
1
First published in Great Britain by HarperCollins*Publishers* 2023

A catalogue copy of this book is available from the British Library.

ISBN: 978-0-00-849435-3

This novel is entirely a work of fiction. The names, characters and incidents portrayed in it are the work of the author's imagination. Any resemblance to actual persons, living or dead, events or localities is entirely coincidental.

Typeset in Birka by Palimpsest Book Production Limited, Falkirk, Stirlingshire
Printed and bound in the UK using 100% renewable electricity at CPI Group (UK) Ltd

MIX
Paper | Supporting
responsible forestry
FSC™ C007454

This book is produced from independently certified FSC™ paper
to ensure responsible forest management.

For more information visit: www.harpercollins.co.uk/green

To John
Happy Birthday
ILY forever xx

Chapter One

'*Eden! There's a strange young man in the garden!*'

*E*den paused, midway through filling a paper bag with coffee beans. When necessary, her Granny Iris had a voice that could penetrate a nuclear bunker. It easily carried through the open door of the outbuilding behind Lighthouse Cottages. Once a store for oil for the lighthouse generator, it was now the home of her roastery business.

'*Eden!*'

With a wry smile, Eden sealed the bag and wiped her hands on a paper towel. She'd been hard at work since six-thirty that morning, roasting and filling bags with the fragrant beans. Some were for customers, but most would be used in her café, the Lighthouse Coffee Container.

She certainly needed a break and even if she hadn't, Iris was obviously too worked up about this 'strange young man' to allow Eden to carry on with her work.

'Coming, Granny!'

She emerged from the shadow of the roastery into the

bright May day, to find her grandmother, Iris, leaning on her walking stick in a pool of sunshine.

'Hurry up,' Iris said, clearly itching to hurry back to the gardens that fronted Lighthouse Cottages. 'You *have* to see him.'

'It's probably just the garden centre man come to deliver Mum's compost,' Eden said, bemused as to why this 'strange young man' had got her granny so worked up.

Iris snorted. 'It's not the garden centre man. I'm not so decrepit that I can't tell an attractive young chap from one who spends every spare minute propping up the bar at the Shipwright's!'

Wincing at the volume of the conversation, Eden followed her grandmother around the side of the row of four cottages, each of whose small front gardens was separated by a neat box hedge.

'Shh, Granny. He might hear you.'

'I doubt it, not with that whale music playing. Anyway, he's probably on the wacky baccy.'

'Granny!'

'I know about these things. I wasn't averse to the odd spliff in the sixties, you know.'

Eden gave up trying to quiet her grandmother. Whoever this strange young man was – holiday guest, hippy or lost camper – he probably wouldn't stay long once he'd discovered that his neighbours were even stranger than he was.

It never ceased to amaze Eden how fast her grandmother could move if she wanted to. She was practically skipping towards the fence, almost as speedily as if she'd spotted a special offer on her favourite jeans in Marks & Spencer. She certainly didn't seem to need the stick and, for a moment, Eden forgot she would be ninety later that summer.

As they entered the garden of Wolf Rock, where Eden lived

with her mother, she spotted Iris's book abandoned on the garden table.

'Come on!' her grandmother urged Eden in a stage whisper. 'You can see him through the gap in the fence.'

'That's spying,' Eden murmured, cringing again.

Ignoring her, Iris perched on the stone bench that was sited to make the most of the sea view from the garden. Located on a finger of land jutting into the Atlantic, the cottages enjoyed a dramatic vista over the Cornish coast, with the Lizard Peninsular to the east and Land's End to the west.

Hartstone Lighthouse itself was still operational, though the adjacent cottages – once home to the keepers and their families – were now privately owned. Only the Carricks were full-time residents. The other three were holiday lets, managed by Eden's mum Sally.

Iris lived in a bungalow in Penzance but loved to visit the cottages, where she had once lived herself as the wife of a lighthouse keeper. With its vista over the sea, the bench was her number one favourite seat and, today, the gap in the hedge also gave a clear view into the neighbouring garden.

Gently, Eden caught Iris's arm. 'Granny, we really oughtn't to spy on this man.'

'Well, I think it's our duty.'

Eden had to smile at the wicked gleam in her granny's eye. 'OK, I'll take a look but only if we do it *discreetly*.'

'Of course,' said Iris, lowering her voice. 'I'll sit here while you sneak a look through the hedge. He won't hear you with that weird racket going on.'

It wasn't a racket, Eden thought. It was quite a soothing piece of music, with tinkling bells and pan pipes. Not her thing, but it could be a lot worse.

'Go on then,' Iris whispered, urging Eden with a wave of her hand.

I so should not be doing this, Eden thought, sinking to her knees on the small patch of lawn. What if this man caught them? How embarrassing to be found watching him through a hedge. It would look creepy at best.

The turf was damp under her knees and there was a loud miaow at her side. She looked down and saw the family cat staring up with accusing, yellow eyes. Eden put her fingers to her lips. 'Shh . . . not now, Sardine,' she murmured, although if the 'strange young man' hadn't heard her grandmother, he was hardly likely to be put off by a ginger cat. Eden tried to stroke Sardine's back but he dodged her caress and wandered off towards the doorway into Wolf Rock, his tail twitching in disdain.

With the music drifting over her head, Eden parted the leaves in the hedge and—

'*Oh!*'

'Told you!' Iris said with a hiss of triumph.

Cursing her exclamation, Eden let out her breath of surprise as quietly as she could although the 'strange young man' didn't seem to have registered the presence of anyone else. He seemed oblivious to everything around him.

Well, he was certainly *young*, not far off her own thirty-three years, and as for strange . . . by Iris's standards, possibly. He certainly didn't look like most of the guests who normally rented the neighbouring cottage for their holidays.

'Longships' was a two-bedroom rental and was almost exclusively occupied by couples or small families. Their activities were mostly confined to reading in the small, walled garden, or barbecues on summer evenings. Most of them were reasonably behaved, although at odd times rows would break out, and the music would become very loud and definitely not soothing – usually after too much of the local cider had been consumed.

Eden had never, ever seen one of its occupants standing on his head, wearing only a pair of orange Speedos.

She had to admit that her curiosity was piqued. Even upside down, it was obvious he kept in shape. Well, you had to keep in shape to hold a headstand for that long, she supposed. Surely, he was going to wobble and collapse on the grass at any moment?

There was barely a tremor. He must have a core of steel and in fact, from the tanned torso with its six-pack, that was obvious. His toned, muscular legs were perfectly aligned, the feet arched and toes pointing skywards. He reminded Eden of a lighthouse, with its base – his head – rooted into the rock, the tower tapering up to the clouds, built to withstand anything the Atlantic seas could hurl at it.

At lightning speed, the man deftly returned to all fours, sprang up and was on his way to the fence. Eden shot backwards, lost balance and fell onto her bum.

'Oh God, I think he's seen us!'

She scrabbled to get up off the lawn.

'Want a hand, love?' Iris held out her hand.

'No, I'm f-fine. Not fine. How could I be fine when I've been outed as a Peeping Tom?!'

She stood up, brushing grass off her shorts.

'*Morning.*'

The strange young man was peering over the fence. 'I hope I haven't disturbed you.'

Beside her, Iris seemed mesmerised, and Eden could hardly blame her granny.

He certainly looked even better the right way up. His dark-blond hair almost brushed his bare shoulders and his emerald-green gaze swept over Eden, whose cheeks felt as hot as a freshly brewed espresso.

This was so not her: blushing and fumbling in front of some bloke. No one fazed her these days and certainly no man – no matter how attractive or charming or seemingly nice – would ever get within a hundred feet of her heart again. Not after Simon. Oh no.

'Do we look disturbed?' she said, more crossly than she'd intended.

'Well . . .'

'Actually, don't answer that,' Eden muttered. 'I was looking for my – um – earring on the lawn, actually.'

'Have you found it?' the 'strange young man' asked with amused politeness.

'No. It must be in the roastery.'

The stud in the corner of his eyebrow wiggled. Eden liked it; she had a nose stud herself. 'The roastery?' he echoed.

'The coffee roastery,' Iris said, staring at him in awe. 'The Lighthouse Coffee Container is Eden's own business. Best coffee in Cornwall.' Pride swelled in her voice. 'You won't find better in London.'

'I'm sure I won't.' He had an interested gleam in his striking eyes. 'And you roast it here?'

Eden was about to go all modest and bashful, but changed her mind. 'I do. We do,' she corrected, keen to get into the habit of referring to the business as if she had a large team of staff. 'We're committed to making it the best it can be,' she said, hoping she didn't sound like a politician. 'The beans are from sustainable cooperatives in Colombia and Guatemala.'

'Arrive on a sailing ship, they do,' said Iris.

'You ship your coffee by sail?'

'Some of it is shipped by sail cargo from Colombia,' Eden said, encouraged by the admiring tone. She was quietly proud of the way she'd built up her little café business from scratch over the past few years after a nightmare experience that had virtually wiped out her finances and totally destroyed her confidence.

'I'm not a huge coffee drinker, but if they're organically sourced and eco-friendly, then I'll definitely try them. Do you sell direct from the roastery?'

'No,' said Eden.

'Yes, she does,' cut in Iris.

'Not as a rule, Granny,' Eden insisted, not wanting the 'strange young man' to expect any kind of special treatment just because he could do a headstand and not look ridiculous in Speedos. 'I have a café at a campsite near Land's End. You can't miss it because it's housed in a shipping container.'

'A shipping container? Actually, I think I passed it on my way here last night. It's blue and yellow, isn't it?'

'That's the one,' Eden said, pleased that a stranger had noticed the business.

'I'm Levan, by the way,' he said, offering a tanned hand over the hedge.

Eden shook his hand, firmly but briefly. He was wearing a silver skull ring on his little finger, which was warm from the sun and glinted in its rays.

'I'm Eden Carrick and this is my grandmother, Iris.'

Iris couldn't take her eyes off him. 'I'll shake your hand when I don't have to reach over that hedge, if you don't mind,' she said breathily, from the bench.

Levan smiled warmly. 'I'll look forward to it, Iris.'

'Eden will sell you some beans, though,' she chirped up, never one to miss a sales opportunity. 'In fact, you should have some in the welcome pack in your cottage and you'll find a grinder on the worktop. I've one in my bungalow, too. I love a decent cup of coffee. Can't be doing with instant rubbish.' She shuddered and Eden glowed inside. Her gran was brilliant. Sometimes infuriating, but mostly brilliant.

'I did see the grinder but, sadly, there was no welcome pack.'

'Oh?' Iris pulled a face. 'That'll be the fault of the bloke who's doing the changeovers while Sally is on holiday. She's my daughter-in-law, Eden's mother, and she's the property manager for all the Lighthouse holiday cottages. You'll be seeing her. I'm surprised she hasn't told us we have a new guest. I expect she will when she's back.'

Eden let her granny talk, trying not to stare at Levan and his orange Speedos and the way he kept pushing his tousled blond hair out of his eyes.

'Well, I'm sure I will be seeing a lot more of you,' he said. 'But not because Sally will be cleaning my cottage. I'm not renting it, you see. I've bought it.'

'That's not possible,' Eden blurted out.

A second or two of silence ticked by before Iris said, '*Bought* it? Are you sure?'

'I am sure. I completed on it yesterday afternoon. Moved in this morning.'

'Where's your stuff?' Eden asked, then realised, too late, how rude that sounded.

'I bought it furnished and I don't have much stuff. What I have fitted in the truck.'

'But – but we haven't heard anything about Longships being sold,' Eden said, her shock overcoming her manners. How could Levan possibly be going to be living there permanently? Did that mean he'd be doing his half-naked yoga every day, right under her nose?

'The Yarrows would have told us,' Iris declared. 'They would have told Sally and she hasn't said anything.'

'She may not know,' said Levan gently, as if breaking bad news to a pair of children. 'The agent said that the Yarrows wanted to keep the sale very discreet. The admin of it was getting too much for them and their daughter doesn't want the place so they decided the time was right. I don't think they wanted to upset the neighbours or want people to think they were cashing in. They asked me to keep it to myself. I'm sorry.'

'Mum will be upset.'

'Maybe she does know and hasn't told us because she's on holiday,' said Iris. 'And folk can be funny, Eden. We hardly ever saw the Yarrows and they'd no duty to let us know.' She sighed.

'Yes, you're right, but even so . . .'

'They might have warned you that a weird new neighbour was moving in?' he replied, deadpan.

'I don't think you're weird,' said Iris.

Raising her eyebrows at this outright fib, Eden managed to say, 'Welcome to Lighthouse Cottages.'

Iris now seemed ready to give him a warm reception. 'It'll be lovely to have a proper neighbour rather than a bunch of strangers moving in and out all the time, won't it, love?' she said to Eden. 'Or the place being empty half the time in the winter.'

Eden's reply – not that she'd formulated one – was prevented by a loud miaow from the other side of the hedge.

'Oh, a marmalade cat. I love cats.' Levan crouched down to stroke Sardine who, much to Eden's surprise, allowed himself to be rubbed between the ears for all of ten seconds before rolling onto his back and purring. *Just you try and touch his tum, though*, thought Eden wickedly. *You'll see how friendly he is . . .*

Levan laughed. 'Ah, now, I won't stroke your belly, mate. I know what'll happen if I do.'

'You've had cats, then?' Iris said, clearly impressed by every aspect of him.

Eden was also impressed that Sardine was so entranced by this new neighbour. He was no lap cat, that was for sure.

'When I was young, at my parents'. Not lately.'

Iris nodded sagely. 'Landlord wouldn't allow it, I expect? We can't have pets in my sheltered housing place. Not that I need one when I can borrow Sardine.' She laughed. 'Now you can have a share in him, too.'

Sardine was surely not going to agree to that, thought Eden, but the cat answered by rubbing himself against Levan's muscular calves and purring like a drill.

'So, what brings you to this part of Cornwall, Levan?' Iris asked. 'Escaping the city?'

'Escaping?' he echoed.

'I meant a fresh start. You sound as if you're from London.'

'Granny . . . we mustn't make assumptions,' Eden said, cringing at Iris's directness.

'That's OK. I have lived in London,' he said. 'And it is a fresh start. Kind of. I'm here for my job.'

'Something interesting?' Iris said, and Eden despaired.

However, Levan seemed not to be offended. 'The opposite, actually. I work in IT, some of which I can do from home,' he said. 'Pretty boring if I'm honest.'

Iris nodded sagely, though Eden would have liked a few more details and for once wished her grandmother would continue with her nosiness.

'It's a nice name, Levan,' Iris said. 'A saint's name.'

He laughed. 'Oh, I'm no saint.'

Iris chuckled. 'I'm glad to hear it. Saints are boring. Can't stand these holier-than-thou types,' she added with relish.

'That's definitely not me.' Levan captured both of them with a warm smile and a sweeping glance. 'Well, it was great to meet you. I'm sure we'll be seeing each other over the garden hedge again later. Maybe under it too. Eh?'

'We can hardly avoid it,' said Eden, her cheeks glowing again at the realisation Levan had spotted them spying on him.

'No. Well, I must finish my yoga session before my Zoom meeting,' he said, then caught Eden's eye. A frown spread over his handsome face. 'Erm, by the way,' he said. 'Is it possible your missing earring might actually be in your ear?'

Instinctively, Eden's hand went to her lobe, where both silver hoops were firmly in place.

'These are. It was another one I'd lost,' she said with a smile. 'Enjoy the rest of your yoga session. I have orders to fulfil.'

'You work too hard,' said Iris, settling into her seat. 'I think I'll stay here and enjoy the view a while longer.'

Chapter Two

Eden worked for the rest of the morning in the roastery, though it was Levan and not coffee that was on her mind for much of it.

At lunchtime, Iris appeared in the doorway with a glass of iced lemonade. 'Come and have a bite to eat, love. You look hot and bothered.'

'Thanks, Granny.' She accepted the glass, enjoying the feeling of the condensation against her palms. The homemade lemonade was sharp but just sweet enough.

'I've made some ham salad sandwiches with French mustard,' Iris said.

'Sounds delicious, like your lemonade.'

'We can drink it in the garden.'

'I think I'd rather stay inside.'

'Why?' asked Iris. 'Levan's not out there doing his downward dogs, if that's what you're worried about.'

'Why would I be worried about him?' Eden said in as casual a tone as she could muster. 'I hadn't given him a second thought. You seemed *very* taken with him, though, Granny.'

With a snort, Iris peered at her over her specs. 'Me? I'm only interested as to how he came to move next door without us knowing,' she said, then sighed deeply. ''Tis peculiar and I'm surprised your mum hadn't found out from the cottage company.'

They crossed the yard to the back of Wolf Rock, whose kitchen door stood wide open to allow the breeze through. With the gardens to the front, the rear of Lighthouse Cottages shared a neat paved communal yard that was scattered with benches and flower tubs. Hartstone Lighthouse itself was situated on the western side. Eden's roastery occupied one of the lighthouse complex's former storerooms.

'Maybe she did know,' Eden said, adjusting her pace to Iris's. 'Maybe they emailed her while she's been in Spain. You know how strict she is about not looking at her email on holiday.'

'She's a lot better than I am. I can't keep off my tablet for more than an hour,' said Iris. 'And WhatsApp's pinging all the time with you lot and my groups. I have to mute some of them, or they'd drive me nuts, interrupting my book.'

Eden smiled. She herself was as addicted to her tech as anyone but her mother had the balance right.

'What are you reading at the moment?'

'*The Mayor of Casterbridge.*' Iris wrinkled her nose. 'It's the "Classic Choice" at my book club. It was Diane Robinson's idea and I've had to skim-read to the end. Talk about depressing! I want something that I can't put down rather than want to fling in the bin.'

'Sounds awful.' Smiling, Eden let Iris enter the kitchen ahead of her, thinking what a wonderful woman her granny was. However, Iris's book group was rapidly superseded in her mind by Levan again.

'It shouldn't be such a shock that the Yarrows have sold Longships,' she mused. 'It's not as if we've ever been their actual neighbours. I don't think I've seen any of them here for a couple of years.'

Iris sat down at the kitchen table. The kitchen's thick stone walls kept it cool in summer and cosy in winter. 'The Yarrows might have been embarrassed to tell us they were selling. We had an assistant keeper's family like that. You know, not long after we were first married when your grandad was doing his first stint on a tower lighthouse in Devon. We were all living in the Lighthouse Cottages. She was nice as pie and friendly with us all, then her husband came off his tour of duty. The next morning when we woke up, they'd gone.'

'Just like that?' Eden said, while washing her hands at the sink.

'Yes. Not a word of goodbye. Vanished in a puff of smoke, almost. I heard later that the husband couldn't stand another two months on the tower so they'd sneaked off in the night. The accommodation came with the job so they had to leave and I think they were too ashamed to face anyone.'

As ever, when she heard Iris tell the story, Eden knew exactly how that family might have felt. It was a very hard and lonely life, being a lighthouse keeper – or the family of one. Her late father, Roger, had found it challenging at times and she'd heard him and her mother talk often about the toll it had taken on some of the families.

Eden herself had been a 'lighthouse child' and had grown up in the cottage. Her father and her grandfather had been in the service, both rising to the post of Principal Keeper. Both Iris and Eden's mum had been known as 'Mrs PK'. Then, when

Eden was around six, the lighthouse had been automated and her father had been made redundant.

She had vague memories of him coming home one day to tell them that he would never 'have to go away again' and her mum crying with relief that 'he'd never be on that bloody evil tower again'. Her dad had been around forty at the time.

He'd got a job with a friend who did general maintenance and he and her mum had taken the chance to buy Wolf Rock Cottage from the lighthouse authority. Eden had thought everything would then settle down into an idyllic pattern, but it wasn't to be.

Unbeknown to her, the years of lighthouse life, chain smoking and stress had taken its toll. A few years later, her father had a heart attack lifting some heavy timber at work and died instantly. Eden had been at school at the time and after that she'd had no male role model in her life. She'd sometimes wondered if that had affected her choice in men – and not for the better.

How distressing that Levan's arrival had sparked off these thoughts again. Change did that, though. Eden was in the throes of deciding whether to expand the business, and not sleeping as well as she might. Now, a new neighbour had arrived in unusual circumstances and shaken an already less-than-stable apple cart.

Just wait until Morwenna heard about him, Eden thought, imagining the look on her best friend's face when she got to meet the mysterious Levan.

While Iris popped to the bathroom, Eden arranged the sandwiches on a tray with some extra salad and found a bag of crisps. She was often too busy to stop for lunch but Iris was staying over in Sally's room for a few days while her mum was away, and she was determined to make the most of the time with her grandmother.

The cottage was now her home, possibly forever, but it hadn't always been that way. After Eden had left school, she'd gone to catering college in Penzance and then to work in London, where she'd lived with a friend until she'd met Simon.

At the age of thirty-three, she'd never meant to return to Lighthouse Cottages – not permanently. Anyway. She'd never thought she'd *have* to return, in order to have a roof over her head and be able to feed herself.

But that was where Simon had left her: homeless, broke and heartbroken.

She could not and would not forgive him as long as she lived – and she would never ever fall for a handsome face again, however charming its owner might seem.

She took the tray into the cottage sitting room, where the bare hearth was brightened with a vase of tulips and late narcissi from her mother's beloved garden. Their fragrance tinged the air.

Iris came back from the downstairs bathroom and saw the sandwiches and salad.

'Oh, lovely, I do love a nice plump onion.' She held a spring onion aloft. 'Oh, I meant to tell you, the postman came this morning.'

What relevance the onion had to the postman, Eden couldn't fathom and didn't want to know. However, she now noticed the envelopes and circulars on the side table next to her grandmother. 'Anything exciting?' she said with an eye-roll.

'Bills for your mum. Junk mail and a seed catalogue. An eye test reminder for you, by the looks of it.'

'I can't wait.'

'There was this, too,' Iris said, putting down the onion and reaching for the mail. She found an envelope from the bottom and tossed it onto the sofa next to Eden.

It had a handwritten address, in neat, attractive writing of the kind you usually saw in films: carefully crafted, unlike the dashed-off scrawl that most people used on envelopes.

Eden stopped, midway through chewing a tomato.

'Are you all right, love?' Iris asked.

She swallowed before answering. 'Yeah.'

'Do you know who it's from?' Iris asked.

'Looks like an old college mate,' Eden said evenly. 'In fact, I'm sure it is.'

'There's juice on your chin, love,' said Iris. 'Here, have a tissue.'

Iris handed her a Kleenex.

'Thanks, Gran.' Eden dabbed her chin, hoping Iris wouldn't notice that her hands were still slightly shaky. She'd lied to her grandmother: that letter wasn't from an old mate, but from someone who had *never* been a friend to Eden.

'So, what do you think about our new neighbour?' Iris asked, then took a bite out of her sandwich.

With difficulty, Eden wrestled her thoughts from the letter and replied, 'Can't really say. Been too busy to think about him.'

'Really?' Iris said innocently. 'Well, *I* keep thinking about him. He reminded me of someone . . .'

'Oh, yes?' Eden said, her interest piqued. 'Someone we know?'

'Oh, no!' Iris said, seeming wistful. 'Not anyone *you* know.'

Yet someone Iris herself had known? 'Well, *who*, Granny? You've got me intrigued now! Do say!'

Iris waved a hand. 'Just a character in a book. No one *real*. You'll probably think I'm bonkers, but he reminds me of the Merman of Porthgwarra, from that old myths and legends book you used to love.'

'I remember the story,' Eden said, scouring her mind to recall the illustration. 'Not the picture, though. It's the one about the merman who came onto land and fell for a young woman in the village, isn't it? It didn't end well.'

'None of these tales ever do,' Iris said. 'In this one, the merman lured her to sea and she was never heard of again.'

'Yes, I remember, but was he doing yoga in his Speedos?'

Iris giggled. 'I don't think he had any Speedos on. He had a fish tail, from what I recall.'

Despite her trepidation over the letter, Eden had to smile at her granny's fascination with their new neighbour. 'So, why did Levan remind of you the merman?'

'Oh, I don't know. Maybe it was his blond hair. They mention it in the story. "Hair like corn, eyes like the emerald of a sea pool".'

'Well, he is blond, I give you that, but he might bleach it like most of the surfers.'

'Looks natural to me,' Iris said.

Privately, Eden agreed. Levan's mane was quite a dark blond, with honey and caramel tones that went well with his all-over tan and, admittedly, beautiful eyes. She herself had chestnut hair cut in what her gran called a 'pixie crop' – which didn't quite fit with the 'beautiful village maiden' vibe.

'His hair may be natural, but I'm pretty sure he's no merman,' she said, feeling that the romanticisation of their neighbour had gone far enough. 'Unless mermen have taken to doing "boring" stuff on computers all day.'

Refusing a slice of cake after her sandwich, Eden told her gran she had to go back to work and hurried back to the roastery, shoving the letter in the pocket of her dungarees while her gran was washing up.

However, she couldn't settle. She knew Iris would have a nap after lunch so there was little danger of her coming out to the roastery again. Eden had instantly recognised her ex's handwriting on the envelope and didn't want to worry her gran by sharing that fact. It was fortunate Iris didn't seem to have recognised it herself.

One option was to throw the envelope straight in the bin, or burn it, but Eden knew she had to read it. OK, she didn't *have* to, but she *needed* to and she wanted to read it somewhere in the open, under a big sky, not in her home or place of work.

She didn't want Simon contaminating the new life she'd built and she didn't want to be caught crying.

She knew just the place where no one would find her.

Away from the tourist hotspots, there were still places where you might walk for half an hour and see almost no one. Most people didn't venture away from the car park to the beach, whereas Eden knew every inch of the headland around the lighthouse.

It was a glorious May day, so beautiful as to have you pinching yourself in disbelief that a sea could be that shade of aquamarine, or that so many bluebells and wild garlic could grow in one place – or that those shadows in the water really were basking sharks. The photos of the area she posted on Instagram had no need of filters.

On the flip side, they didn't show the reality of living in 'paradise' – it was becoming almost impossible to afford your own home or rent a place.

Eden never thought she'd find herself in that position, not with a degree and years of experience as a manager in some decent bars and restaurants. Her life had taken a very sharp and unexpected turn and she was only just steering herself back on course.

The split rock lay ahead, on the tip of the headland but just out of sight.

She made her way through a 'rabbit run' in the bracken, its bright green fronds just starting to uncurl. Ahead lay a place that had been her sanctuary and secret since she'd been a girl, roaming free around the lighthouse. Even when she'd been with school friends or other lighthouse kids, she'd never shown it to them.

Her father, Roger, had shown it to her and his father – Grandad Walter – had revealed it to *him*, handing down the secret from generation to generation.

There it was, a pink granite stone rising just above the heathland on the very edge of the cliff. From a distance, it looked like any other of the million granite boulders littering the cliffs or rising from the ground, split and sculpted.

Yet Eden knew its secret.

Being careful of the spiky gorse, she slipped through the narrowest of the paths and made her way to the stone. Close up it was eight feet high and finally revealed its secret: a cleft that bisected it. When she was little, she liked to think a giant had chopped it in two with his axe. Now she knew that it was the elements: water, wind, a rare frost that had sculpted it. Nothing supernatural; only nature.

It was big enough for her to slip through sideways and out the other side onto a rocky platform, which in turn was big enough to sit, read and picnic on: her own private balcony overlooking the treacherous reef that had wrecked so many vessels.

She was hemmed in on all sides by clumps of pink thrift and golden gorse, a hint of its coconut scent floating on the breeze. Below her, the cliff fell away to a rocky shoreline that continued under the water to the treacherous reef which Hartstone Lighthouse had been built to warn against.

Finally, Eden felt secluded enough to look at the letter again, even if another glance at the handwriting was enough to stir up feelings of bitterness, anger and betrayal that she'd thought she'd finally managed to put a lid on.

So careful, so neat and appealing. In a bloody fountain pen, too! Who wrote with a fountain pen these days? Yet she also remembered a time when she'd thought it was sophisticated, and in keeping with the tailored suits and shiny shoes he favoured. He'd seemed driven and sexy to her, ready to work all the hours to give them a good life.

Eden curled her lip at her own gullibility. Oh, the days when she'd been so naïve as to judge a man by his footwear . . . it seemed ridiculous now.

Slipping her nail under the flap, she worked her finger underneath and ripped the top open. Cursing his name out loud, she pulled the sheet of paper out. It would be the usual total crap. How could it be anything else?

Dear Eden,
 I'm not sure if you'll even read this and to be honest

'Ha!' she burst out. 'Simon, you wouldn't know "honest" if it turned up on your bloody doorstep in a big box labelled "Honest". This will be good. I just know it!' she declared.

She read on.

> to be honest, I don't expect you to read it. It's very
> likely to have gone straight into the dustbin and I can
> hardly blame you, but on the off-chance you do read
> it, I hope you'll keep an open mind.

'What?' She snorted. 'Like our marriage?'

Her exclamation startled a pair of choughs, who flew into the air with a flash of their red legs, cawing their eerie '*chow chow*' cry.

'Sorry,' Eden said to the rare birds. 'You don't need me disturbing you from your courting. You've enough problems to contend with. That's what Simon does to people – you, any creature – you see. He leaves a trail of destruction wherever he goes. He's even got me talking to myself,' she said. 'Because if I don't say how I feel to you, I might tell the people who truly love me and it will only upset them all over again.'

Eden clamped her lips together, aware that not even the choughs could hear her now. There was only the low rumble of the waves breaking on the reef a hundred feet below her perch.

With a sigh, she returned to Simon's letter.

> You'll know I'm out now, back in civilised society.
> I've got a job; it's not much but with Mum and Dad's
> help, I've managed to keep on the straight and narrow
> for the past six months. I'm living in their home office
> in the bottom of their garden. It's a glorified shed really,
> but at least it doesn't have bars. Ha.

He'd added a hand-drawn smiley.

Eden wasn't laughing.

> Anyway, that's the good news. The bad news is, I've not been feeling well lately. Tired and rundown. I thought it was prison life but apparently it's potentially some kind of male problem.
>
> I don't expect sympathy, but I thought that as my wife, you should know.

'I'm not your wife, Simon. We're divorced and if you'd had your way, I would only have been *one* of your wives.'

> Now, don't be alarmed, it might be treatable and manageable even if it can't be cured. I thought you would want to know in case you want to get in touch. I'm truly sorry for what I put you through and I know I can never make it up. I won't bother you again, but if you do want to speak to me or write, you know Mum and Dad's address and phone number.
>
> Yours,
> Simon

Eden sat back and took a deep, calming breath. He must be lying. This must be another of his scams. Nothing was beyond a man who'd had two mistresses, one of whom he'd proposed to, all while being married to her. A man who'd said his 'dearest wish' was to have a family with her, and when she'd got pregnant had left her and emptied their bank accounts of almost every penny they'd saved.

She threw the letter down in disgust then grabbed it before

it was whisked off the cliff by a gust of wind. She might need it one day . . . why, she didn't really know. Maybe as evidence for some future harm he might do her?

'I won't, though,' she said quietly. 'Because whether this story is true or not, I am never letting you near my life again.' She raised her voice and called out over the waves. 'You will never hurt me again, Simon! *Never*!'

Chapter Three

'Hello. Are you OK?'

Eden almost jumped out of her skin when she saw Levan silhouetted in the cleft in the rock. Already on edge after the letter, her heart was beating nineteen to the dozen.

He emerged from the shadows, a worried frown on his face. '*Are* you OK?' he repeated.

Eden was robbed of words momentarily, still shocked by his materialising in *her* place. She was about to ask what he was doing there, but it was self-evident from the shorts and running vest, and the sweat glistening on his arms and chest.

'Yes. Fine. I was startled, that's all.'

'Sorry, I didn't mean to scare you . . . I took a track through the bracken that I hoped led to that beach down there. Obviously it only leads to the cliff edge and then I hung back because I heard voices. Or rather a voice – yours – and you sounded upset and as if you were having words with someone. A man. And I was worried that he might be hassling you.'

'No!' she burst out. 'I don't need you charging to the rescue.'

He held up his hands and turned away to leave. 'OK. I'll leave you to it.'

'No. No, wait. Please,' Eden added, regretting her impulsive outburst.

To her relief, he didn't seem offended, and waited.

'It's only Simon,' she said as calmly as she could manage. 'He's my ex.'

Levan's attention shifted uneasily to the cliff edge. 'This Simon was *here* with you?'

'Oh, not in person!' Eden hurried to clarify. 'Only in spirit.' She sighed. 'Which is bad enough, but don't worry. I haven't done away with him.'

He blew out a breath. 'That's a relief.'

'Occasionally, I'd like to though,' she said wryly.

His eyebrows rose. 'Maybe it's good he wasn't here, then.'

'Yes . . . well, I wouldn't actually harm him,' Eden insisted, embarrassed and feeling she was digging an ever-deeper hole for herself. 'Not physically. I don't want him to be hurt or ill, just . . .'

Levan didn't reply, simply listened. She had a feeling he was good at it, a sympathetic ear . . . which worried her.

'We didn't part on good terms.' She stuffed the letter in her dungaree pocket. 'And he wrote to me today and it's not great timing. In fact, I'd rather not hear from him at all.'

'I see. Well, at least I don't have to worry about you pushing him off a cliff.'

'No.' She tried to force a smile to lighten the atmosphere, but was struck by a horrible thought. 'How much of my ranting did you overhear?'

'Some,' he said evenly. 'Sorry, I could hardly fail to, but I didn't want to intrude.'

'Until you thought I might have done something crazy?'

There was a glint in those emerald eyes. 'Anyone can do crazy things if they're pushed far enough.'

Eden thought before answering. 'Maybe, but no one pushed Simon into . . . doing what he did and ending up in prison.'

'In *prison*?' Levan echoed, with genuine shock in his voice.

'Yes, in prison. He served eighteen months, which wasn't long enough for what he did to me,' she said.

'You're not saying he was violent?' Levan said sharply, as if angry on her behalf – if she was honest, angrier than she'd expect a stranger to be.

'Not physically, though you could say he was emotionally abusive if being a serial liar and a fraudster counts. If hurting someone and not caring if you ruin their life counts . . .' Eden stopped, trembling and already regretting revealing even more of her personal life to him.

'I'm so sorry you've had to go through this. He sounds like a piece of work,' Levan replied.

'Thanks, but you don't need to apologise on his behalf. Simon isn't your problem and he shouldn't be mine any longer. Now,' she said briskly, eager to end the conversation as quickly as possible. 'I really have to go back to work. I only came out here to read Simon's letter in privacy.'

'Which I invaded,' he said with a grimace. 'I'm sorry for intruding. I'll go away.' Once more, he turned to slip away through the rocky fissure, but Eden felt she couldn't let him leave without a few more words of explanation.

'Thanks, but – please hang on a moment. I honestly didn't mean to be rude. Thanks for your concern, but I am fine. I will be fine, and I'd appreciate you not telling Granny about this. Or Mum, when she gets back. I don't even want them to know Simon's been in touch. It will only worry them, and they've had enough of that to last a lifetime.'

With a brisk nod, he finally left her standing in the sunlight, the waves breaking below, the gulls crying. Tilting her head back, she stared up at the sky, wishing that for just one day, she could be that bird and take flight, soar above the land and free herself of her past.

She'd told their new neighbour far more than she should have or wanted to, but she hadn't told him everything: not the cruellest blow of all; the reason why her bitterness towards Simon was so deep and corrosive.

Chapter Four

After his encounter with Eden on the cliff path, Levan jogged home, trying to process Eden's revelation that her ex had been jailed and ruined her life.

It had rocked him in more ways than one and he could tell she regretted having told him even that much about her private life. She'd only done so because he'd caught her at a vulnerable moment. Effectively, he'd cornered her in her place of sanctuary and, even though he knew for a fact she had greater problems than him, he felt guilty.

As Iris had apparently sensed, he'd come here hoping for a fresh start but mere days had gone by and he'd already been reminded that the past could not be ignored so readily.

Back at Longships Cottage, he spent the rest of the afternoon rearranging his possessions and making sure the office was set up to his liking. After finally falling asleep to the waves breaking on the rocks, he woke early and worked most of the day before the siren call of his surroundings proved too tempting to resist any longer.

A 10k run along the cliffs took him to tiny coves and across wild headlands, with ridiculous views. Several times, he had to stop and simply look and listen; savouring a freedom that was impossible to put a price on.

With the sun at his back, he picked up the pace on the homeward route and arrived, sweaty and hot, at the lighthouse where he paused to catch his breath.

He spotted Eden, Iris and a woman he presumed was Sally Carrick, Eden's mother, walking from the parking area by the side of the cottages to the garden gate of Wolf Rock.

He wasn't far away but realised that they were too distracted to notice him, so he slipped into the shadows created by the lighthouse wall, catching his breath, keen not to interrupt them. However, his position meant that he could hear most of their conversation. With no one else around, and excited to be together again, they clearly felt no need to keep their voices down. Levan smiled, despite the guilt he felt at listening in. The warmth of their relationship was clear.

He knew that what he should have done was walk around the lighthouse and go into Longships by the back door, but his curiosity to observe their reunion got the better of him.

'Hello, Sally!' Iris declared. 'You look well! I'm glad to have you home, though.'

'It's lovely to be home,' Sally replied, embracing Iris and giving her a peck on the cheek.

Sally held the gate open for Eden to wheel a suitcase into the front garden. 'Thanks, love,' she said to her daughter. 'I really do appreciate you picking me up.'

'We didn't want you paying out for a taxi from Newquay or trying to get the bus, after flying all this way,' said Eden.

'It's great to be chauffeured after a long journey.' Sally stretched her arms over her head.

She was a tall, elegant woman, who, in contrast to her daughter, had long blonde hair, caught up on top of her head with a clip, and she looked tanned.

As he watched, Sardine sauntered out from the hedge to add his own welcome.

'Hello, rogue!' Sally said, stooping to stroke him. 'Have you behaved?'

'He brought in a live mouse,' said Eden, sounding disgusted. 'I managed to set it free but I don't know if it survived.'

'Oh, Sardine, you naughty boy,' Sally declared, although her tone held more pride than censure.

Unrepentant, Sardine strolled off towards the cottage.

Sally tugged her cardigan around her.

Iris gave her a sympathetic look. 'Bet it seems chilly here after Spain.'

That accounted for the tan, thought Levan.

Sally laughed. 'I'm sure I'll get used to it, Iris.'

'I bet you'd love a proper cuppa. Both of you.'

'Thanks, Granny,' Eden said.

'Everything OK here while I've been away?' Sally asked. 'No problems with guests? Shouldn't have been with Nikita in charge.'

Levan strained his ears for Iris's reply.

'There's only one cottage occupied. It's been very quiet unless you count next door of course . . .' she said. 'We have a new neighbour.'

'A guest?' Sally said.

'No, he's bought the place.'

He heard a gasp. 'Bought it? The Yarrows never said anything.'

'Apparently, they wanted to keep it quiet.'

'I have no idea why – though I'll admit, they were never super friendly. Who is this neighbour? You said it was a "he"? Some retired birdwatcher or lighthouse fan fulfilling a boyhood dream?' There was amusement in Sally's voice.

Iris cackled. 'No! He's a handsome young chap. Fit, too. Likes doing yoga in the garden in his pants. Doesn't he, Eden?'

'He seems to keep pretty fit,' Eden said – at least, that's what Levan thought she'd said. It could just as easily have been: 'He seems to be a bit of a tit.'

'What's he doing down here?' Sally said far more clearly.

'We don't know yet but we plan to find out, don't we, Eden?'

'I'm not going to pry, Gran!' Eden exclaimed. 'He does something in IT,' she added. 'I don't know any more than that, and besides, it's his business.'

'Hmm. Maybe, but I must meet him,' Sally said. 'Shame he won't be needing any property management, but I'm with your gran on this: I'd like to know more about someone who'll be living next door for the foreseeable.'

Levan waited for Eden to reply but she said: 'I'll get your duty-free from the van, Mum. You go inside and put the kettle on.'

With that, the older Carrick women went into the cottage while Eden walked off to the car. Levan slipped around the rear of the lighthouse to enter Longships via the kitchen door, as he should have done in the first place. He hadn't heard anything *bad* about himself, but it was clear his new neighbours were intrigued by him and wanted to know more.

Eden had seemed the least interested, which was a good thing. A very good thing.

He went home and showered, before heading upstairs to

do 'something boring' on the computer in the spare room of Longships Cottage, now set up as his home office.

The only sounds were the cry of gulls and the breaking of waves on the rocks below the cliff through the open window. He hadn't wanted to work downstairs in case of the inevitable visits from his new neighbours. However, when he was in the office, he liked to keep the door open. He'd had enough closed ones to last a lifetime.

The room housed his desktop, two screens and an array of other IT hardware you wouldn't find in your average high street tech store. It had arrived by van the day before.

He'd said that he didn't have many possessions and that much was partly true. Much of the appeal of the place was that, as a former holiday home, it came fully furnished with everything from the duvets to a coffee grinder, as Iris Carrick had pointed out.

It was part of a row of four, of which Wolf Rock – owned by the Carricks – was the largest. The one on the other side of Levan's – Pendeen – was a holiday cottage, currently vacant.

They were all whitewashed, with green-painted woodwork and doors, like the lighthouse itself and its adjacent outbuildings, one of which apparently Eden used for her coffee roastery. There were two more ex-keepers' cottages on the far side of the lighthouse, which were also holiday lets.

Hartstone was a land lighthouse, where the keepers had lived and worked, rotating shifts between six men and their families. It was still operational, although the fog horn had been discontinued a decade ago.

All of this had been imparted to Levan by the estate agent, when he'd spoken to her on the phone. He'd known very little about the place before the sale, which had gone through about as fast as a sale ever can. He hadn't bothered with a survey and had paid cash, but it had hardly been a risk, he'd thought.

It pained him to have had to tell a white lie to someone like Iris, a decent, kind and friendly woman who had lived through a world war and a pandemic. Ditto, her granddaughter – he stopped and sighed. He so wished his neighbours hadn't been friendly, pleasant and, in Eden's case, bright, sparky and very attractive. From the cute haircut and dolphin tatt to the denim dungarees and 'no prisoners' attitude, in other circumstances he'd have loved to get to know her much better.

He'd probably already got too near for comfort – and their own safety.

Why had he had to ask her if she was OK on the cliff? Why had he ventured into her private space? She'd been visibly upset when she'd told him about her husband, and she'd also clearly regretted telling him anything.

'You idiot, Levan. You total prat.' Cursing himself under his breath, he abandoned the screen, having spent the past five minutes staring at it, thinking of Eden and berating himself.

Instead, he went to the window and drank in the view over the Atlantic. The lighthouse from which the cottage took its name was just out of view. So treacherous was this coastline, it had needed three lighthouses to guard it . . .

Below, he spotted Iris sitting on a small plastic seat, pulling a few weeds from the paved patio with a long-handled tool.

Eden was out of sight, doubtless at work in her roastery. Was that the faint aroma of coffee on the breeze? Was he imagining it?

He heaved a sigh.

Why fret about a little white lie: he'd have to tell a whole lot more before the summer was out. Lying was his raison d'etre these days.

He actually knew the Yarrows – or rather, knew *of* them. They were old university friends of his mate, Dion, for whom Levan now worked as an IT 'contractor'. On the surface, Dion ran a computer security company, and had a list of customers who were household names in the telecoms industry. It was not exactly a secret, if you cared to look, that half-a-dozen of these companies had operations in the far west of Cornwall. They were the landing stations for dozens of undersea cables that snaked their way all over the globe.

And Land's End, obviously, was not only the end of the country, but the start of it. Ever since the first undersea cable had been laid from Cornwall, this remote part of Britain with its toe in the Atlantic had become a hub of global communications.

But few people were even interested in that. Most would have nodded off before he'd got as far as the end of the phrase 'a global telecommunications network'. The locals, he'd been informed, either didn't know or didn't care that the smart new barn in a farmer's field transported all the financial data between New York and London stock exchanges. Or that the shuttered cottage down a quiet lane could be the place where information was gathered from unfriendly states by the security services.

The fact that Cornwall had secrets hidden beneath its granite, concealed in ramshackle sheds and beneath its azure waters, was lost on the sunbathers. They lay on the golden sands, oblivious to the priceless information passing beneath their feet – all those trillion-dollar deals whizzing across the Atlantic in a tiny fraction of a second. All those shadowy transactions that could be so easily intercepted if anyone wanted to.

It was Levan's job to make sure that they weren't intercepted by the wrong people, and occasionally that the shadowy transactions were intercepted by the right people.

So in one way he'd spoken the truth: he was involved in 'boring IT stuff', although the fact that he was working for the security services, even if indirectly, would have been considered the opposite of boring by most people.

It was work that he needed to try his best to keep secret. He therefore had a very good reason for being economical with the truth, even with decent people like the Carricks.

However, his other secret was different. It was one he felt compelled to keep, just to try and rebuild his life after a moment of madness that had brought it crashing down.

A moment he still would not change, no matter what the cost.

Chapter Five

Eden didn't have to wait long for her mother to meet Levan. The next morning, she and Sally bumped into him when they were both unloading cleaning supplies and linen from her car for one of the cottage changeovers.

Levan strolled out of his cottage wearing jeans, a hoodie and a warm smile that brightened up the dull, cool morning. He lifted a hand in greeting but seemed hellbent on heading to his car – but Eden's mum had other ideas.

'Morning!' she called out with a wave.

Eden couldn't see the look on his face, but he did turn round and walk over to them so he couldn't have wanted to avoid them too badly.

'Good morning,' he said with a smile that was friendly enough.

'I'm Sally, Eden's mother. I don't want to keep you but I thought I should introduce myself as you've already met the rest of the family.'

'Yes, I've met Iris – and Sardine,' he added, as the cat wound himself around his jean-clad legs, purring loudly.

'Morning,' said Eden, marvelling again how Sardine had become so friendly with Levan, so fast.

'Morning,' he said in return and she wondered if he was regretting hearing her private business as much as she now regretted sharing it.

'I was just popping out to the supermarket,' he said, clearly hinting that he was ready to end the conversation.

However, Sally had other ideas.

'I wasn't expecting to return home to a new neighbour,' she said, changing the subject smoothly. 'Eden tells me you've bought Longships. We'd no idea it was even for sale.'

'So I gather. Like I told Eden and Iris, it was all done in rather a hurry.' His tone was still polite but perhaps, Eden sensed, a little edgy with impatience to be gone.

Sally lifted an enquiring eyebrow. 'An impulse purchase, then?'

Eden cringed.

'Aren't they the best kind?' he returned, *smooth as butter,* thought Eden. He'd answered a question with a question, thereby avoiding the need to answer. He seemed very unruffled; not exactly a charmer . . . simply well-mannered.

'True.'

'Mum, would you like me to carry this stuff into the cottage before I go back to *work*?' Eden said pointedly. 'I need to pack up the new batches for the café tomorrow.'

'No, don't worry. I'll take it. Well, I expect we're all busy people, so I shan't keep you from your shopping now.'

Levan smiled, possibly in relief. 'I'm just getting used to a twenty-minute drive to buy some dinner.'

'Yes, it's quite isolated here but you'll get used to it.'

'I'm sure I will.'

'Talking of food,' Sally added suddenly, 'I wondered if you wanted to come round for Sunday lunch next weekend?'

'A week on Sunday?' He hesitated, and Eden wondered if he now was trying to come up with an excuse. 'I – er—'

'It's not compulsory, but Iris will be here and it would be lovely to welcome you properly and get to know each other a bit better.'

He smiled, and politeness seemed to win over his reticence. 'It would be lovely to meet Iris properly. Thank you.'

'One-ish?' her mother said, beaming up at him. 'You know where to find us.'

'I'll try not to get lost,' he joked, before walking away to the car park.

Eden watched him drive up the hill away from Hartstone before rounding on her mother. 'Next Sunday when Gran's here? Mum, we hardly know him.'

'Which is exactly why we should take the chance to find out more about him,' Sally said firmly. 'He seemed perfectly happy with the invitation.'

'He could hardly say no, could he, with us living next door? He's a captive audience.'

Her mother shook her head, a little exasperated. 'It's lunch, not *Mastermind*. I promise not to give him a grilling.'

'Oh, *really*?'

Sally eyed her shrewdly. 'Don't you want to know more about him?'

'Not particularly. He might be the kind of guy who likes to be on his own,' Eden muttered.

'Eden.' Her mother's tone stopped her from walking away.

'Are you sure that everything is all right? Has anything happened while I've been away? Only you've seemed quieter than usual since I've been back.'

Hesitating, Eden wondered if she should tell her mum that Simon had written – she still hadn't made up her mind on how to respond or even if she should. Definitely not a call, and absolutely not a visit – not even a text . . . Maybe an email?

She shuddered. Her instincts told her to ignore him.

'Everything's fine.' She touched her mother's hand. 'I've been working long hours to prepare for the café season. I really need to take on some extra help.'

'I can pop over on my days off if you can't find anyone else.'

'Thanks, Mum. I know you'll always be there if I need you but you've a full-time job. I've already had a word with Courtney about it. I think he might agree to do more shifts.'

Courtney was Eden's casual help, and great with the customers. He already had a bar job but Eden knew he wasn't happy and might be willing to jump ship to the Coffee Container.

'Good. You can't run the roastery and the café on your own once the school holidays come. It'll be crazy.'

'Well, now I've got a steady customer base for the coffee, I can invest in more staff.'

Her mother smiled. 'I am so proud of you, Eden. I was proud of you anyway, but after what you've been through with Simon, I'm thrilled for you. Not many people could get up and start all over again.'

'I didn't have much choice,' she said. 'God knows where I'd be without you and Granny helping me out. The little I had left after Simon cleaned out our accounts would never have covered all the equipment and the container space.'

Sally put her arm around her. 'I was glad to help and I knew you'd make a success of anything you turned your mind to.'

Eden laughed at her mum's blind faith in her abilities, but it did mean a lot. Sinking the last of her funds and some of her family's savings into her own business had been a huge risk, even though she adored being her own boss, but her mother was right: it was more than paying off. 'I have a beautiful place to live, and a brilliant family around me. A lot of people don't have that.'

Sally shook her head. 'Even so, I'm still angry that Simon robbed you of your opportunities. I can never forgive him for that.'

Eden sighed. 'I've had to let it go, but I'm wiser now. No one will ever con me the way he did.'

'No . . . but remember. Not everyone is a Simon. There are some good people in the world, even good men. That's one of the things I can never forgive that snake for: making us suspicious of everyone.'

'Not everyone. Joe is a good man. Ravi too,' said Eden, citing the names of her baker friend and his partner. They were two of the kindest, loveliest men – humans – she'd ever known.

'Yes . . . it's why I want to discover more about this Levan. Better the devil you know, I say. Even if you aren't interested, I want to know exactly why he must have given up a home and job in wherever he's from to come and live in the back of beyond.'

'Maybe we'll find out more on Sunday,' Eden said, with a smile.

She headed back to work. Her conversation with her mother had decided her; she wouldn't tell anyone else about Simon's letter and, for now, she wouldn't respond. As for Levan, her mother was wrong. Eden was as keen to know why Levan was at Lighthouse Cottages as her mum. She was just better at hiding it.

Although she believed he hadn't meant to, she regretted that Levan had invaded her private space and found her secret refuge. It didn't feel quite so safe and special any more. Worse, she regretted telling him about Simon, and her feelings towards him. If he hadn't come across her when she was angry and vulnerable, she never would have said anything.

Well, it was too late now – and a warning to be more guarded in the future. He'd so easily coaxed out of her things she didn't even want to share with her nearest and dearest.

However, no matter what she'd said to him about wanting her ex-husband out of her life forever, she knew she'd have to find out if what Simon had claimed was true.

Chapter Six

'Ow!'

Levan heard Eden's squeak of pain from the car park. He'd been out to his car for his sports bag when he'd spotted her trying to drag one of several large sacks in the direction of the roastery.

She stood up, wincing and holding her back before setting her face in a determined grimace and grabbing the sack as if it were a grizzly bear that needed to be wrestled into submission.

After their conversation the previous day, he wondered if she might find it more painful to accept his help than struggle with the heavy load. However, the sight of her grunting as she tried to haul the coffee sack along the ground decided him.

He jogged over. 'Here, let me help.'

She stopped, pink in the face with exertion but smiling politely. 'There's no need, I'm fine.'

'I'm sure you are, but wouldn't it be quicker and easier with two?'

Doubt crossed her face until she finally nodded. 'Yeah . . . thanks. I'm a bit pissed off to be honest. The delivery people normally bring them inside on a trolley but this guy must be new. I'd popped to the bathroom and when I came out, I just found them dumped here, with the delivery note underneath.'

Levan tried to lift one. 'Jeez, they weigh a ton!'

'Forty kilos, to be precise. I can just about drag them inside.'

'What about the radical idea of us shifting them together?' he suggested.

She eyed him a little suspiciously before rewarding him with a brief smile. 'Thanks, because I can't leave them out here. They're blocking the parking area.'

Together, Levan and Eden lifted a sack, watched by Sardine who was washing himself in a pool of sunlight.

'Where do you want them?' he panted as they approached the door.

'T-to the left of the entrance, p-please, by the table.'

Together, they carried the first bag inside. Eden might be slight, thought Levan, but she was very strong. Coffee roasting was clearly a physical job. Hot too, he assumed, spotting the shiny roaster with its metal hopper. The fragrant aroma filled his senses, making him twitchy for some caffeine even though he wasn't a massive coffee drinker.

'You don't lift these bags into that hopper, do you?'

She burst out laughing. 'I'd have to be an Olympic weightlifting champion to do that! No, I only roast five kilos at a time.'

Levan laughed. 'Phew . . .'

Once all the bags were in, they paused to catch their breath. He couldn't help thinking how sexy Eden looked, her hair now ruffled and her face rosy from the effort.

With difficulty, he dragged his gaze from her face to the bags they'd moved inside. 'Are these the beans that have been shipped by sail?'

'No, unfortunately. The sailboat coffee sold out almost immediately and I haven't been able to get any more since then. Two of the bags are from Ethiopia, one's from Guatemala. It's all single-origin or high-quality blends from small producers.' There was a glow of pride in her voice.

'How do you choose the beans?'

'From ethical enterprises. Many of them are collectives owned and run by women. It's not just about tasting the coffee, what's in the cup – it's about how that coffee got here, how it was grown and who produced it.' She smiled. 'Coffee production is dominated by male growers and plantation owners, even though seventy percent of the people actually working in it are women. So that's why I try to buy most of my coffee from smaller female owner-producers. It's not the easy route but . . .'

Her dark-brown eyes fired a challenge at him. Perhaps she was expecting cynicism.

'What *is* the "easy route"?' he asked, holding that provocative gaze. 'Is it choosing to do something that makes life easy for you while turning a blind eye to the effects on someone else? Taking the path of least resistance? I'd rather try the hard way and fail than live with regret.' He checked himself and turned a sunny smile back on her.

'I know what you mean. It was a risk to start this business. After years of serving – and drinking – coffee in London cafés and bars, I thought I'd have a go myself.'

'And make a better job of it?'

Just for a moment, she didn't seem to know how to reply,

then seemed to collect herself. 'Like I say, I'd rather try to do the right thing than the easy thing, even if it means I'll never be rich. My customers seem to like that way of thinking, too.'

'Who are your customers?' he asked.

'Well, I use most of it in my own café, of course, but I also sell to bars, cafés and delis in the west of the county. I've started a small website that enables people to order beans and ground coffee online and collect it from the container so they can drink my roasts at home.' Her voice was animated. 'We do speciality hot chocolate, teas, muffins and cakes, too.'

His eyes widened. 'Don't say you bake as well as do all the coffee roasting and run the café?'

She laughed out loud. 'You must be joking. I'm no Mary Berry. All the cakes are delivered by a friend who lives in the valley. He's the baker. Believe me, you wouldn't want to eat one of my scones. Unless you want to play stone skimming with them.'

'I dunno. I like the idea of some scone skimming . . .' He took in the roaster and the laptop on the table, curious as to its precise part in the process. 'So this is where the magic happens?'

'It's more hard work than magic. Rest of the time I'm roasting, bagging up beans or doing admin.'

'It must get warm in here, but the smell is fantastic.'

'It is, though I've become so used to it that sometimes I hardly notice. Would you like a little tour?' she added, almost shyly.

Levan was taken by surprise and felt he was being given access to her private world again. 'I'd like that,' he found himself saying, then reminded himself to keep things businesslike in case she thought he might have other ideas. 'Though I'm sure you're far too busy,' he added briskly.

'Right now, I am,' she said. 'I need to get this lot into the roaster so I can stock up at the café.'

He was determined to tread carefully with Eden – and to keep an eye on himself to make sure that he was never getting too close to her. He was only chatting, though, what harm could that do?

'I've been – er – wondering how you make sure you get the exact roast you need?' he said, guessing she'd be happy answering questions about her business.

She smiled. 'Come over to the table and take a look.'

With obvious passion in her voice, she guided him through the computer program she used to set the timings and control the heat levels at different stages of the process.

'It's surprisingly easy to ruin it,' she said. 'Even with a computer to help. It's all about stopping the process at exactly the right moment.'

He was intrigued. Obviously he'd known tech was involved but it hadn't really occurred to him just how much. In his mind's eye he'd imagined some hipster crouched over the roaster like a medieval alchemist, but there was clearly a lot more science to it than that. Then again, he hadn't been in a lot of artisan coffee bars of late.

Proudly, she showed off the shiny steel roaster.

'It only takes a few minutes but it's down to experience to decide when to kill the process and open the door. That's the key to a perfect roast.'

'What happens if it goes wrong?'

She rolled her eyes. 'I waste an expensive batch of coffee. When you roast the beans, the sugars caramelise, you see. If you leave them too long, they go oily and you end up with the kind of bitter stuff you often find in big chains.' She shuddered.

'You don't want that.'

'Absolutely not! It's why I roast my own beans when I possibly can. I was fed up of drinking rubbish coffee.'

'I hadn't realised that it was all so complex.'

'Oh, that's just a tiny part of it,' she said, her voice swelling with enthusiasm. 'Look . . . I just finished a batch earlier. If you're not too busy, do you fancy a coffee?'

'Do you have time?'

'It's work.' There was a gleam in her eye. 'I'd like to try out a new roast on you. If you're happy to be a guinea pig, that is.'

'Me?' he exclaimed in surprise. 'Help in a coffee tasting?' He wanted to say yes, but remembered just in time that he wasn't supposed to be getting even more involved. He rearranged his face into a more detached expression. 'I'm probably the wrong person to ask.'

'Oh,' she said, her buoyant mood obviously sinking. 'If it's not your thing.'

Levan felt churlish and, anyway, he was finding it hard to resist the chance to spend just a little longer with her. After a few more moments' pause, he gave in to the temptation. 'I'm always happy to try something new.'

'If you're sure?' she said, hesitantly.

'I am. Let's go for it.'

He was rewarded with a grin and was struck by what a different woman Eden was now, from the distressed soul he'd come across on the cliff edge. *Possibly playing a part*, he thought, but he wasn't going to push her.

She led him to a small area at the side of the roastery with a basic kitchen with counter, sink and crockery.

'A proper cupping session would have the beans laid out for the buyers and a strict protocol to follow.'

'Sounds serious,' Levan said.

'Oh, it is. Deadly serious. I'm just going to make two different types in the cafetieres, and we can sip them. You don't have to spoon it up and slurp.'

'I'm relieved to hear it.'

She laughed. 'Won't be long.'

Soon the aroma of freshly brewed coffee filled the warm air. Eden filled four espresso cups with the dark liquid – two for her and two for him.

'One of these is a guest blend from the Guatemalan collective and one is the usual Colombian roast,' she explained.

He sipped the first coffee. 'Hmm. Smooth, fragrant.'

'Take your time. Think about the finish. That's the aftertaste.'

He sipped again and waited a moment after he'd swallowed the coffee.

'Does it leave a lingering effect on your tongue?' she said.

It was a few seconds before he could reply, having been unable to banish the wholly unbidden image of Eden's tongue lingering in his own mouth. Eden, however, seemed perfectly serious.

'Um. It's ever so slightly bitter – but not in a bad way,' he added hastily.

A small, satisfied smile appeared on her lips. He'd obviously said the right thing. Phew.

'Now this.' She offered him another tasting cup.

Levan inhaled the aroma before sipping the new one. 'Hmm. That's definitely fruitier and a little sweeter. Reminds me of berries . . .' He laughed. 'I sound like a wine sommelier but, really, I'm making all of this up!'

'That's fine. You don't need to be an expert, just enjoy a decent cup of coffee. There's no wrong answer.' She smiled. 'So, which is your favourite? Please be honest. If you had to choose one to drink for the rest of your life.'

'Like I said, I'm no afficionado but I like good coffee. And these are both good but if I had to choose one to take to a desert island, it would be . . .' He pointed at the second cup. 'This one.'

She punched the air in triumph. 'Yes!'

'Wow. You seem pleased? Did I pass the test?'

'It wasn't a test, but you did go for the new Guatemalan roast.'

'Great . . . but I hope you won't buy a load of it in on my say-so.'

'Don't worry, I shall try it out on some of my regulars as well as Granny and Mum. I'd never make a commitment like that on the word of a stranger.'

'Oh.' Levan composed his face into a crestfallen look.

'However, you *have* made a small but meaningful contribution to my decision,' she said solemnly.

He fought back laughter. 'I'm glad to hear it.'

Sardine wandered in and brushed against Levan's legs, purring.

He stooped to stroke the cat's back but Sardine scooted off.

'He's such a tease. Comes up for some fuss then runs away if you try to touch him.'

'He goes his own way,' Levan said, spotting Sardine hiding between two coffee sacks, his eyes glowing watchfully. 'And no one can say anything because he's a cat and that's what cats do.'

She laughed. 'And Sardine *always* does what he wants.'

'Don't we all, in the end?' he said meeting her eyes, which were both beautiful and challenging. The challenge for him was to tear himself away, yet he was as drawn to her as iron filings to a magnet. Their work was done and he now had no excuse to stay. This was the moment to thank her for the coffee and say he should be getting back to work or going for a run or – anything to restore the distance between them.

He especially didn't want their time to end while she was in her element, relaxed and at ease.

'So, this is part of Hartstone Lighthouse?' he blurted out simply for something to say. 'Is it open to the public?'

Eden's eyes widened as if she was as surprised as he that he'd continued the conversation. 'Um. No, but occasionally special interest groups are allowed to send a small group tour. Historical societies, lighthouse enthusiasts.'

'Lighthouse enthusiasts? That's a thing?'

She chuckled. 'It is. They fall for the whole romance of lighthouse keepers and their families. Not that there is much romance about it. We aren't professional guides either, more custodians. We're too busy to be leading tour groups, but we do have the keys.'

'And you *have* lived the actual lifestyle. Who better to talk to people about the reality of living here?'

'Ah, but they don't have to *live* here. I could tell you some tales . . .'

He loved the glitter of enthusiasm in her eyes. She'd lit up when she'd spoken about her business and even more so when she'd started talking about her family and the history of

Hartstone. There was an inner glow to Eden Carrick that attracted him like a moth to a flame. It was dangerous . . .

'Actually,' she said, cutting into his thoughts, 'that door over there leads into the lighthouse. It was a way in from the storeroom here.'

Peering into the shadows, he spotted a wooden door set deep into the wall. It looked about six inches thick, with a padlock and bolts on the outside. Despite the warmth, he shivered and rubbed his forearms without even thinking.

She frowned. 'Are you cold?'

'No. No . . .'

'Could be prickly heat? It's humid in here.'

'More likely an allergy . . .' he murmured, transfixed by the door.

'Oh? What are you allergic to?'

'Not much, but some things can bring me out in hives.' Tearing his eyes away from the door, Levan said, 'It's sure to be the humidity, like you say.'

His joke hid the turmoil inside him. That locked and bolted door had set images rampaging through his mind . . . sounds, too. Violence, fear, despair . . . screams and crying . . . He fought to crush them.

'Levan . . .'

'Yes?' He whipped around to find her staring at him, her arms wrapped around her body. He recognised the stance of defence.

'What we talked about the other day – about Simon. Can we forget that ever happened? I shouldn't have burdened you with my private problems and, to be honest, I'd rather forget I opened the letter at all.'

In other words, Levan thought, he shouldn't have been there to hear them.

'Of course we can forget it,' he said with a smile. 'Consider it done.'

'Good. Thanks.' Eden scraped up a smile, but it was clear the atmosphere had changed. 'And thanks for trying the coffee. I guess I'd better stop messing about and do some real work.'

This time, the hint for him to leave was unmistakeable. On cue, his Apple Watch pinged and a glance told him he needed to respond quickly.

'Work?' she said.

'Yeah. Thanks for the coffee. Good luck with the new blend.'

She nodded and he made himself scarce, relieved and regretful to step out of the dark warmth of Eden's world and into the light.

Levan's thoughts had calmed a little by the time he got back to his laptop. He spent an hour dealing with a work call from the data centre, which turned out to be a technical issue he could easily fix, and then one from Dion, fishing for information on how he was getting on in his new home.

'OK. Fine. The cottage is cool. In every way.'

'Broadband good?' he joked.

Levan laughed. 'You know very well it is with the extra booster kit I've installed.'

'How are your neighbours? The Yarrows told me that the Carrick family are a decent bunch. They felt bad about not saying goodbye.'

'I think the Carricks were disappointed not to have been informed but the older lady, Iris, seemed OK with it. They're a lighthouse family and they've seen a lot of people come and go in their lives.'

'You've met the whole family, then?' Dion's interest was clearly piqued.

'Yes. Iris and her daughter-in-law Sally, and the granddaughter,' he added, keeping his voice casual, while the image of a tousled Eden sprang into his mind. '*Does it leave a lingering effect on your tongue?*' Her words came back to him, arousing very pleasant sensations.

'Well, it's good for you to interact with the locals,' Dion said. 'Better than stirring up gossip as a reclusive loner. When I come down for this meeting at Jackdaw Farm next week, shall we go for a pint and a pasty afterwards?'

'Definitely . . .' Out of his bedroom window, Levan saw Eden walking from the coast path towards the lighthouse, phone clamped to her ear. She'd changed into cut-off shorts that showed off her long, tanned legs. Feeling guilty for his thoughts, he turned away from the window. 'That would be great,' he murmured.

'On that note, have you tried any of the pubs yet? Can you recommend a place to get a good pint?'

'No, haven't sampled the local hostelries yet,' he said. He stopped himself from adding, 'But I could tell you where to get a great cup of coffee.'

Chapter Seven

'And these are genuine arabica beans from Guatemala? I *will* be able to tell, you know. I've been to several cuppings and was told I have a highly developed palate.'

Great. A coffee snob. Eden gritted her teeth as the customer droned on. Coffee connoisseurs helped to keep her in business, but instinct told her this guy was going to be a pain. It was Saturday morning, and she'd just served the breakfast crowd from the campsite. This guy had turned up in a Lexus, and taken up two of her precious customer parking spaces.

'When I was working in Melbourne, the choice blew my mind,' he went on, while Eden set about grinding a fresh supply of the new roast especially for his drink. 'The Aussies may not be the most refined of people but they're positively evangelical about great coffee.'

With an inward sigh, Eden pressed the grinder to drown out the man, while shouting, 'Oh, really?' as he wittered away.

The man droned on about the coffee shop that he and his

colleagues – on a year's secondment from a London law firm – had frequented every day.

'Of course, we spent an absolute fortune,' he said, with a smirk. 'Probably kept the place in business for a whole bloody year and we were experts by the time we came home. The place has probably gone bust now we're gone!'

Probably put out the bunting and popped the champagne, more like. Eden made interested noises, seeing her forced smile reflected in the coffee machine.

She added his cappuccino to the rest of his order. 'There you go. Hope you enjoy.'

The man sniggered. 'If it passes muster with the rest of the gang, I might possibly be back again. We're here for a week.'

'Lucky me,' Eden muttered, turning away to grab a cup sleeve.

'Sorry?' He was frowning at her and his eyes reminded her of a weasel's.

'I said, lucky you, sir; the forecast is great. Now, can I tempt you to some of these cinnamon rolls? They're from an artisan baker friend. He uses Cornish milled flour . . . they've won a Great Taste Award.'

The customer was only too happy to try the rolls. Over his shoulder, Eden tried not to meet the eye of a strawberry-blonde woman in a white cowboy hat who'd just arrived and was making a rude gesture that indicated the customer was a 'dickhead'.

'Here are your pastries, sir.' Eden handed them over, determinedly focusing on the customer. She did not need Morwenna Smith's visual commentary while she was trying to be polite.

The man finally left, clutching his tray of coffees and a bag of Joe's cinnamon rolls. Eden hoped his vehicle had plenty of cupholders as it sped off, spraying up gravel.

Stepping up the ramp inside the container, Morwenna heaved a deep sigh. Eden hadn't seen her for a couple of weeks, as Morwenna had been away, which meant her friend was unaware about developments with Levan and Simon. Her ex's letter was still hidden away in the glove box of her van.

'What a plonker. You have the patience of a saint. I couldn't deal with the public.'

Eden rolled her eyes. 'You're a photographer, Morwenna. You *do* deal with the public.'

'Rarely these days, thank God. I stick to inanimate objects. Welcome hampers and balcony furniture don't talk back.' She grinned. 'Any chance of a coffee? Instant will do.'

'You're barred,' Eden said. 'The usual?'

'A double. I need it.'

'Busy morning?'

'Totally manic. First job was one of those seaside palaces near Zennor. Glass from floor to ceiling, heats up like a bloody greenhouse. Window cleaning costs alone would cover my electric bill for the year and anyone on the coast path could see you on the loo if you wanted them to. I think it lets for ten grand a week in the summer.'

Eden gasped.

'Then I went to a "basement conversion" on the moors. Farmer converted it from the cellar and told me blatantly he was looking to "cash in on the staycation boom". It had one very high window overlooking the cow yard and "rustic art" his son had made from old tractor parts.'

'Jeez. Were you able to make it look good?'

'I took a lot of flowers with me and turned on every light in the place. Though it would take the royal florist and an arc lamp to make that place look remotely fit for a holiday. More like Wormwood Scrubs . . . Oh, hello . . .' Morwenna mouthed a 'Wow' at Eden.

It was immediately obvious who'd caught her attention from the white van that had parked by the hedge and decanted its driver.

Dressed in jeans, Levan strolled across the gravel, his white linen shirt stirring in the sea breeze, his work boots disturbing puffs of dust. With his long stride and blond mane tugged back in a ponytail, he reminded Eden of a friendly lion. Then she reminded herself that lions were never friendly.

'Now, who is *that*?' If Morwenna had had a fan, she would have deployed it. Her eyes had lit up like Sardine's when the Dreamies tin came out of the cupboard.

'I'm afraid he's our new neighbour,' Eden said in a low voice.

'Neighbour!' Morwenna telegraphed astonishment with her eyes but the conversation ended abruptly when Levan's boots rang out on the ramp and he joined them at the counter.

'Hello,' Eden said brightly.

His keen eyes took in the neat container with its white-painted walls and chrome equipment as if he was impressed. 'Hi there,' he said. 'I was passing and I saw you were open so I thought I'd call in. See if my roast made it onto the menu.'

'The Guatemalan blend did,' Eden said, amused that he'd taken ownership of her new roast.

Morwenna pounced. 'What's this – you've been roasting coffee with Eden?'

'No,' said Eden swiftly. 'Levan has been tasting it and giving his opinion. Once.'

'Wow. Eden trusts your opinion on coffee? She doesn't even trust mine and I've known her since she was four.'

Morwenna flicked her hair back, which was a sure sign she was trying to catch Levan's attention. Which was fine because Eden was trying to avoid it.

'She did say that she wouldn't be unduly influenced by what I thought,' said Levan.

'Your opinion concurred with what the rest of the taste panel concluded,' Eden replied.

Morwenna squeaked in mock shock. 'What taste panel? You didn't invite me.'

Eden shot her a look. 'You were away.'

'So, who *was* on this taste panel?' Morwenna asked, innocently.

Levan stood by, shaking with suppressed laughter.

'Various people. Mum, Granny, Joe . . .' Eden stopped, unable to name anyone else because that was the sum total of the taste panel. 'You just had that roast in your espresso,' she added to distract her friend.

'Mmm and it was delicious.' She turned her gaze to Levan. 'You have impeccable taste – um – Levan?'

He shook his head. 'I'm no coffee afficionado. It was sheer luck, but I wouldn't mind sampling the finished article.'

'Wouldn't we all?' Morwenna didn't wear false eyelashes but if she had, she'd have fluttered them at him.

'Cappuccino, espresso, flat white?' Eden threw at Levan. 'I wouldn't want to keep you from your work.'

'I've been to work. I'm on my way back to the lighthouse, actually,' he said. 'And I'd like a cappuccino, please.'

With Morwenna keeping up the conversation behind her

back, Eden set to work on making his drink, straining her ears to hear over the gurgles of the coffee machine.

In reply to Morwenna's question about where he worked, he gave a similar answer to the one he'd given Eden. 'Dull IT stuff, mostly working from home.'

'You're on your way back from work this morning, though,' Eden couldn't help saying.

'Yes, had to pop into the data centre up the road.'

'At Jackdaw Farm?' Eden said. 'The place with the shutters on the side of the road?'

Levan met her gaze. 'Yes.'

'The one owned by Universal Telecoms?'

'That's the one,' he said. 'You know it?'

'Joe's partner did some work on the farm there. He said the farmer had leased it to a telecoms company. It's where one of the undersea Internet cables lands, isn't it?'

Levan raised an eyebrow. 'You're well informed.'

'We have lived here all our lives,' Eden said stiffly, a little miffed that he seemed surprised she knew her own backyard. He also hadn't answered her question.

Morwenna wrinkled her nose in disgust, indicating that she had no interest in Levan's geeky job or the delights of undersea cables.

'So, Levan, you moved into Longships?' she said, with another flick of her locks. Her earrings bobbed excitedly.

'Yes, right next door to Eden.'

'Have you moved here with your family?' Morwenna added, white teeth flashing.

Eden put the espresso shot into the machine while she frothed the hot milk. The machine gurgled away cheerfully while Morwenna interrogated Levan.

'No, I'm on my own,' he said.

'Oh, I see. Oh well, at least you won't be lonely with Eden and her mum next door.'

Eden swirled the milk jug, dismayed that living with her mum did make her sound like a teenager.

'No, I certainly won't be that. That smells great, by the way,' he said as an aside to Eden.

Eden deployed her best customer-friendly voice. 'Thank you very much.'

Morwenna ploughed on. 'You'll have plenty of visitors, I'm sure, Levan. Friends – relations.'

This was exactly what Eden herself had tried to winkle out of him, so she could hardly criticise Morwenna.

'It depends if I invite them,' he said with an enigmatic smile

'Here you go. One Special House Roast cappuccino,' Eden said, pushing the sustainable paper cup forward.

'Thank you. I can't wait.'

Eden flashed her most customer-friendly grin. 'Would you like anything with it, sir?'

Morwenna snorted.

'Pastries, I mean. Muffins or cakes . . .' Eden gabbled, feeling her cheeks flush and wincing as Morwenna's eyes turned into saucers.

'Not today, thanks. I had a good breakfast and I want to go for a run when I get home. Another time, definitely.' He collected his cup. 'See you back at the lighthouse.'

'I'm sure you will,' Eden murmured. 'Have a good day.'

'You, too. Both of you.'

Clutching his drink, he strolled back to his van and drove off smoothly onto the lane that led to home. Morwenna waved and Levan responded with a hand out of the driver's window.

The moment he'd driven off, Eden braced herself for the inevitable explosion from Morwenna.

'Bloody hell! You kept him quiet!'

'You were away!' Eden protested.

'You could have messaged me. Sent me a picture.'

'Spied on him, you mean? No, I couldn't, and anyway, why would I think it worth bothering you with random pics of the bloke next door while you were on a work trip?'

'Because the bloke next door is hotter than a thousand suns. He's absolutely the sexiest straight man in the whole of West Penwith.'

Eden smirked. 'Well, the bar's not that terribly high at the moment, is it?'

Morwenna tutted dramatically. 'You really are very, very cynical, my dear friend. Genuinely, if you aren't the slightest bit interested, then I wouldn't mind . . .'

Morwenna was tall, slim and coolness personified. In black jeans, a grey T-shirt, biker boots and aviators, she might have sashayed straight from the front row of a London fashion launch via the set of *Top Gun*.

If Levan was as free as he seemed, and was going to fall for anyone, Morwenna was it. And as Morwenna had a proven track record of never getting her heart broken before she broke someone else's, Eden could be sure she was safe from any romantic complications with Levan.

Basically, Morwenna would see him for the summer – he might last until October if he was lucky – and then gently dump him and move on.

Unlike Eden herself, who fell for very few men, but very hard when she did, with the most painful of landings.

She swore loudly. 'I heard from Simon the other day.'

Morwenna swore very creatively. 'You didn't? How does he have the nerve!' Her eyes narrowed suspiciously. 'What does the snake want?'

'He claims he's got something life-threatening – he's hinted it's a male thing so I'm worried it might be cancer – and says he wants to make his peace just in case his treatment doesn't work.'

Morwenna covered her face with her hands. 'He's lying, of course?' she said through her fingers.

Eden shrugged. 'I don't know, and that's the problem.'

'No, it's his problem. Not yours. I mean, I'm sorry if it's true. More so for his mum and dad than him, frankly, but you'd cut all connection with him. You owe him nothing, while *he* still owes you two hundred grand.'

'Yes but . . . I was married to him for over two years so I must have loved him once. If he's terminally ill, I can't ignore that. I could never live with myself if . . . I can't stand him, Wenna, and I hate what he's done. I don't love him, but how can I ignore a dying man?'

'*If* he's dying. Personally, I don't believe a word of it. Whatever he says he's got, I'd want to see proof – hear proof from his consultant. I'd want to check with them in person, too.'

Morwenna flashed her a wicked grin and glanced at her phone. 'Jeez. Is that the time? I have to go. I've got a job for a local magazine. A new fish restaurant in Newlyn.'

'Sounds good.'

'But it won't smell good. You know I'm a veggie and I can't stand the stench of fish. I'll have to hold my breath.' She mimed a gag and Eden burst out laughing. 'I might set all the lobsters free, too.'

Ponytail flying, Morwenna sped off in her soft-top Mini, leaving Eden with mixed feelings.

No matter how much she protested, Morwenna always cheered her up but today she had confronted Eden with some uncomfortable truths.

They were very different people but her friend had always been there for her. Morwenna had offered her a home in her own small flat when Eden had had to come back to Cornwall. Even though Eden had known there wasn't room and moved into Wolf Rock, she appreciated the gesture. Morwenna had picked her up when she was down, listened to her moans about Simon and – lately – urged her to start her life again.

Eden was very glad she hadn't let on to Morwenna that Levan had overheard some of the letter, and that she'd told him about Simon. Her friend would read far too much into that. She still regretted it, even if she was warming to her new neighbour a little. OK, make that a lot – physically at least – and at least Levan hadn't been in jail for fraud and deception. As far as she knew . . .

Her phone rang and she answered it with the sunniest voice she could muster. It was a team of builders doing up a farmhouse. They wanted eight coffees and pastries and would be along to collect them in ten minutes. Eden set to work. She was very lucky to have a business, a home, the best family in the world and friends like Morwenna.

People you could trust and rely on were more precious than any amount of riches.

Chapter Eight

'Is this some kind of joke?' Dion said, pointing at the sign above the pub door with his one remaining hand. He'd lost most of his left arm below the elbow after a close encounter with a booby-trapped radio set in Afghanistan.

'It has decent reviews on TripAdvisor,' Levan said, 'and its claim to fame – um – seemed appropriate.'

Levan read the sign aloud in a dramatic tone:

The Last Chance Saloon.
Your final chance to get a pint before Newfoundland.

Dion slapped him on the back. 'Relax, buddy. This isn't your last chance. I'm always here for you, whatever has happened or might happen.'

Levan raised a laconic eyebrow, though he was deeply touched by his comrade's support and loyalty. He owed Dion so much; he was one of the very few people not to have deserted him when everything in his life had imploded. Although Dion had ceased to serve on the front line after being wounded, he'd taken a back office posting with the Royal Signals, the army's communications specialists.

That was where Levan had first met him, almost a decade previously. At the time, Levan had been a lieutenant in the Signals, while Dion was a more senior officer in another department.

They were both very much civilians now, although their experiences in the military had cast a deep shadow over both their lives.

'Are you trying to hint that I should buy the first round?' Levan said.

'No, I'm hinting you buy all the rounds.' Dion slapped Levan's back again. 'Come on. The smell of those pasties is driving me nuts.'

Levan had to agree. The aroma of pub food combined with malt and hops was almost as good as the coffee scents from Eden's roastery. With a menu of specials including locally caught fish and chips and homemade pies and pasties, Levan could hardly wait.

The food matched the pub: nothing fancy and very much of its place. The clientele looked like permanent fixtures, as much a part of the inn as the flagged floors or the settle in the hearth. Their ancestors had probably propped up the bar, too.

The Last Chance Saloon claimed to be a sixteenth-century building and Levan could well believe it. Both he and Dion had to duck under the granite lintel at the entrance, and again to avoid the oak beam between the corridor and bar itself. There were beams everywhere, blackened by age and woodsmoke though the hearth was now empty.

On this dull early June evening, the lights were on in the

pub, as so little sunlight penetrated the diamond-paned windows set in walls at least a foot thick. Lamplight showed faded framed photographs of seafarers standing by lifeboats, or people on tandems completing journeys from John o' Groats to Land's End. So much history. So many memories.

Dion found a space in a dimly lit corner while Levan ordered the drinks. A pint of Atlantic for himself and a low-alcohol beer for Dion, who was driving him home then staying over with another colleague near St Ives. They perused the menu, but talk took over. Not about work: all those discussions had taken place earlier in the data centre.

'How's it really going?'

'OK. Much better. What you said earlier about interacting with the locals. Dion, these are genuine people. Salt of the earth you might say, as far as possible. I don't want to stray from the path of truth any more than necessary.'

'You don't have to stray from it at all, mate.'

'No, but I do have to hold something back.'

'As far as work is concerned, of course you must. As far as your personal life goes, well . . . I can't tell you what to do, but I'd be discreet for now. You wanted a fresh start. This is it. Don't overcomplicate things. Settle in for a while.'

'Yes.'

Dion sipped his drink. 'That's *if* you stay.'

'I bought the house, Dion – and while I'm grateful for the opportunity and it's what I want to do, I don't have that many options.' Levan took a large swig of his pint. 'I'm not going back. There's nothing for me now.'

Dion nodded. 'I'm pleased to hear you want to make a go of it. I'd half worried you'd get down here, realise it was the end of the earth and start hankering after the scent of burning rubber on the M25 and someone's arse in your face on the Tube.'

'Believe me, there were times I hankered after both those things in the past few years, but not now. I've never been a city boy. I love the peace and quiet here. I went for a run earlier and I didn't see a human for a whole hour.'

'You wait until August, when you can't get an inch of space on the beach and the roads are snarled up.' Dion reached for the menus. 'Now, can we order a dessert as well as the pasties? I fancy this apple crumble and custard. Good job I'm not watching my weight.' He patted his belly and Levan rolled his eyes.

Apple crumble and custard and a pint in the pub. What a privilege that was. A luxury – and Levan was going to enjoy it.

Some time later, Dion's spoon clattered into the dish. 'Do you think anyone would mind if I licked the bowl?'

Levan laughed and was scooping the last morsel into his mouth when Eden walked into the pub with a man.

An inch or so taller than Levan, the man had movie star looks and chiselled features. Levan took an instant dislike to him especially when he put his arm around Eden's back and kissed her on the cheek. The guy walked straight up to the bar, while Eden disappeared in the direction of the pub toilets. She didn't seem to have noticed him sitting in a secluded booth.

'Hello. Earth to Levan.'

'Sorry?'

'What's so interesting, as if I hadn't worked it out?' Dion asked. 'Know those two, do you?'

'The woman is my new neighbour, Eden. Never seen him before though.'

'Boyfriend?'

'She hasn't mentioned one . . . and from the little we've said, she didn't give the impression she was looking.'

'Maybe she changed her mind. He looks like something from a Marvel movie.'

'Who? Captain America?'

Dion chuckled. 'He could be, and I don't blame you for looking at her. She's eye-catching. Reminds me of a pixie.'

Levan grimaced.

'In a good way,' Dion clarified. 'Cute hair, very pretty. Elfin . . .'

'Elfin?' Levan snorted. 'You should see her shift a forty-kilo coffee sack.'

'What? You're joking?'

'Only half-joking. She runs a café near here and roasts her own coffee at the lighthouse. I helped her shift a delivery the other day. She can take care of herself, and not just physically. There's no father around from what I can gather, just the three women. She and her mum and the granny are a steely lot.' Levan left out the details about Simon.

Dion's eyes gleamed with interest. 'They've clearly made an impression on you.'

He felt uncomfortable talking about Eden when she was effectively in the same building. 'Shall we have another drink?'

Levan was at the bar, paying for the food and ordering another pint, when Eden came back into the room, this time spotting him instantly. Her chiselled companion was by the pool table chatting to some locals.

Her mouth opened in an O of surprise when she saw him. 'Hello,' she said warily.

'Hi.'

69

'You found the local, then?'

'Hard to miss, being the last pub in England.'

Chiselled Hunk approached and slipped an arm around Eden's shoulders. 'Are you going to introduce us?' he said in a rich Cornish accent.

Eden smiled. 'Of course. Joe, this is Levan, our new neighbour at Lighthouse Cottages. This is Joe, who runs the bakery that supplies all my cakes – and half the bakes and pasties in this part of Cornwall.'

Levan smiled, hoping Joe was merely a business colleague, then felt cross with himself for even caring.

'Shall we go and order?' Eden said to Joe. 'I'm starving.'

Taking the hint, Levan went back to the corner, where Dion was on his phone. Or pretending to be because he'd obviously witnessed the chat between Levan, Eden and Joe.

'Boyfriend?' Dion raised an enquiring eyebrow. 'Or just interested? Could be a first date.'

Levan watched Eden and Joe laughing at the bar, their heads almost touching. Eden had given the impression she wasn't interested in any man after her experience with her ex, but she might not have meant it. She might have been trying to throw him – and anyone he might gossip to – off the scent.

'Maybe. Not sure,' he said, refocusing on his pint.

Dion gave a cheerful grin. 'Well, if he is, you've no chance, mate.'

Chapter Nine

Come Sunday, Eden was laying the dining table when Levan announced his arrival through the open front door with an appreciative sigh. He was clutching two bottles wrapped in paper and wearing faded jeans and a polo shirt that showed off the muscles in his arms.

'That smells good!' he said. 'I brought a bottle of wine. Well, two. I wasn't sure whether you preferred red or white.'

'Both,' said Iris, emerging from the kitchen with a tea towel in her hands.

Secretly impressed by his good taste, not to mention his biceps, Eden took the bottles. 'Thank you. The white will be perfect for the prawn cocktail we have for starters. Very retro,' she said with a laugh that sounded more nervous than she liked. She'd been on edge overnight, lying awake telling herself not to be on edge. It was Sunday lunch with a neighbour . . . not the least bit significant.

'The prawns are local,' she added, determined to give him a warm welcome, even if she had mixed feelings about him being invited at all.

'Sounds great to me.'

'There's beef for main course . . .' Sally walked in and suddenly put her hand to her mouth. 'I never thought to ask if you eat meat!'

'Don't worry, I do, and roast beef will be perfect.'

'That's a relief,' said Iris. 'With the yoga and whale music, you could have been a vegan.'

Eden squirmed a little, but Levan broke into a grin. 'The three don't necessarily go together – not in my case, anyway.'

'Good, because you'd have been eating lettuce and summer pudding,' Iris said.

'There are worse things in life.'

Eden exchanged a smile with him. 'I'll pop the white in the fridge and help Mum.'

She came back from the kitchen to find her grandmother sitting in the garden, chatting to Levan about her life as a lighthouse keeper's wife.

'Have you always lived at Hartstone, Iris?'

'Oh no. When we were first married, Walter was stationed on the Bishop Rock and we had to have council accommodation. That was in the fifties. He was a SAK then, the lowest of the low.'

'SAK?'

'Supernumerary Assistant Keeper,' Eden explained, setting down a tray on the table with three gin and tonics and the beer Levan had chosen as his pre-lunch drink. 'Junior lighthouse keeper. You could be sent anywhere for the first couple of years.'

'And how they moved Walter all over the place,' Iris said, taking her drink with a nod of thanks for Eden. 'Didn't know if either of us would stick at it, then. Thought we'd made a huge mistake. Not with each other,' she added quickly. 'The job.'

'It sounds a very tough kind of life.' Levan took his beer from the tray. 'Thanks.' His eyes flashed gratitude at Eden and she tried not to be transfixed by them.

He tipped the bottle to his lips.

'Wouldn't you like a glass?' Iris said in a tone of wonder.

'The bottle's fine, thanks,' said Levan.

Iris pulled a face. 'If you say so. I can never understand why people don't want a glass. Imagine if I started necking gin out of the bottle in the lounge at the flats.'

'Oh, I dunno, I think it would be pretty funny.'

Iris smirked. 'Maybe I'll try it then . . .' Then she grew more serious. 'Eden's right about being an SAK, though. Roger – Eden's dad – went through the same process. The lighthouse owners shunted you from one posting to another. Never knew where you'd be. Over the years, with my dad and Roger's service, I've lived at Cromer, Eddystone, Pendeen . . . just after we married, he was six months on the Bishop – off the Isles of Scilly. The tower lighthouse there used to shake when the seas were big.'

Levan grimaced. 'That sounds terrifying.'

'Walter was scared at first; he said you'd be mad if you weren't and that's what kept you safe. You could never let down your guard for a moment if you were outside the tower on the set-off.'

Eden caught Levan's look of confusion. 'The set-off is the landing area on a tower lighthouse. The place where supplies and relief keepers are landed.'

'Literally, sometimes,' Iris declared. 'They used to have to winch you onto it by rope from the boat.'

'My dad was almost washed off the rocks one day,' Eden said. 'I just about remember him telling us when he came home. He was fishing and it was a beautiful, calm day but out of nowhere, he said, the seas boiled up and knocked him off his feet. He would have been sucked into the water if his mate hadn't managed to grab his hand.' She rubbed her arms. 'It still gives me goosebumps to think about it.'

While Eden was talking, Sally had re-joined them in the garden. She squeezed her eyes shut briefly. 'I had nightmares after he told me about it. I almost wish he hadn't said anything.'

'They kept that story from me for years,' Iris muttered.

Sally patted her hand. 'Because we knew it would worry you.'

'It would have. I hated thinking of my son out there in the middle of the ocean, knowing what Walter had been through. I often wish he'd never gone into lighthouse keeping but they both saw it as their duty to keep people safe.'

'They were incredibly brave people,' Levan said, and Eden had an instinct he wasn't merely being polite.

'They were. You imagine being stuck out in the middle of nowhere, with two other men, sharing a tiny bunk room and a sitting room, for months on end – especially if you didn't get on with the people you were living with.'

Levan frowned and picked at the label on his bottle. 'It must have been a living nightmare . . .'

'At times, but Walter and Roger were used to it in the end. They said it had its consolations: the views, being away from the city.'

'Dad always used to say it was worse for the families left behind . . .' Eden said, noticing the goosebumps on Levan's own arms. It wasn't cold, so what had given him the chills? Was it the mere idea of being cast away on a rock lighthouse – or a more personal memory that it had evoked?

Not seeming to have noticed Levan's discomfort, Iris continued. 'We had to do the waiting. Waiting for them to come home, waiting to see if the weather would turn and the relief boat couldn't reach the tower, then waiting to see if they were safe and hadn't been drowned or crushed during the transfer.'

'Then waiting for them to have to leave again,' Sally said, with a shudder. 'I hated that last week before they were due to go back again. Roger was always on edge, couldn't relax or sleep properly. We all were.'

'Walter was the same,' Iris said. 'He tried to hide it, but I knew. He couldn't settle to anything. It was as if we were always living half a life: either worrying they had to go or that they wouldn't come back.'

'It was hard to plan anything,' Sally said. 'I was glad when the lighthouses were all automated.'

'When was that?' Levan asked.

'They were all automatic by nineteen ninety-eight,' Eden said. 'This one was automated in ninety-five.'

Iris chipped in. 'Walter was retired by then and we'd already got the bungalow in Penzance. Eden was at primary school and Roger and Sally decided to stay here and buy this place. They didn't have very long to enjoy it though.' Iris's voice faltered and Eden patted her hand. 'Roger passed away a few years after he retired.'

'I'm so sorry to hear that. You must all miss him very much,' Levan said carefully.

'We do.' Eden still did but they'd had no choice but to

carry on with life and her main concern had been – would always be – for her mother and grandmother.

Levan's gaze swept over them, and Eden guessed what he was thinking: how sorry he was for this mother, wife and daughter grieving their beloved family member.

The atmosphere had dipped and, sensing it, her mum became brisk and cheerful. 'Come on inside. This roast beef won't wait much longer.'

After demolishing lunch, everyone was in need of a break before pudding and Sally suggested they return to the garden to eat it.

Fluffy clouds and a fresh breeze prevented it from being too warm, and Eden fetched a fleece for her grandmother.

'So, Levan, what made you decide to come all the way down here for work?' Sally asked, her voice deceptively light. 'I'm sure IT specialists are in great demand everywhere.'

Observing him keenly over the last of her wine, Eden saw no sign of awkwardness at the question.

'I'm in a specialist line of work and there aren't as many jobs as you'd think. When a friend offered me an IT contract that I could mostly do from home, I decided to take the opportunity to move out of the city.'

'The city?' Sally said. 'Eden mentioned you were living in London?'

'Yes.'

'It's still a long way to Land's End,' Eden said, unable to resist knowing more herself.

'It is.' He smiled. 'About as far as you can get in one direction and although I do work mainly from home, the company I work for has a couple of clients down here.'

'Including the one at Jackdaw Farm?' Eden suggested innocently.

'Isn't that one of those data centre places?' Sally put in.

'Yes, it is. Dion – my friend – is a cyber security specialist and he asked me if I'd like to work for him. In fact, he was with me the other night in the Last Chance Saloon.'

'That was him?' Eden said, also recalling the confused frown on Levan's face when he'd seen Joe put his arm around her. It had been a fleeting look, but had said everything: Levan obviously thought they were an item.

'Cyber security. Sounds very mysterious,' Iris said. 'Very John le Carré. He used to live round here, you know. He had a holiday home on the cliffs. You probably pass it on your run. Oh, I loved *Tinker, Tailor*. George Smiley is my hero.'

'My life's not as exciting as that,' Levan said swiftly, exchanging an amused glance with Eden.

She smiled back but still wasn't quite satisfied with his explanations, and decided to press him. 'How did you know Longships was for sale? Because we didn't.'

He gave an apologetic grimace. 'I'm sorry they kept you in the dark, though I didn't realise they had, of course. I heard about the cottage from my mate – Dion, the guy who gave me this job. Well, Dion went to uni with the Yarrows' son-in-law, and happened to hear they were thinking of selling, knew I wanted a place to live and so I pounced. You know how hard it is to find property down here.'

'We do,' said Eden, thinking how lucky he had been to simply drop on Longships and to be able to afford it just at a time when his mate had a job going for him. Still, IT was probably a far more lucrative trade than coffee roasting and she *had* once owned her own place – until Simon had wrecked everything.

Sally got to her feet. 'I think we've grilled Levan quite enough. Shall we all have pudding?'

Levan rubbed his hands together. 'I think that's a very good idea.'

Eden picked up her empty glass. 'I'll give you a hand.'

Iris patted her arm before Eden could move away from her garden chair. 'No, I'll help your mum. You stay here and chat to Levan.'

Eden had no choice but to stay put, stranded with this gorgeous stranger whose chat had raised more questions than answers in her mind. There'd been no mention of partners or family, no specifics. It was early days, however, she reminded herself.

Sally returned with a tray bearing four bowls of summer pudding, Iris following with a pot of clotted cream.

'We don't always have such a feast,' Eden told Levan, after refusing second helpings. 'I'll have to start jogging, too.'

'Rubbish. You have a lovely slim figure,' Iris said.

Eden couldn't meet Levan's eye. 'The roastery keeps me fit,' she murmured.

'I'm sure it does. Those bags were incredibly heavy,' Levan said.

In unison, Sally and Iris glanced up at Eden, their eyes as keen as Sardine's as dinnertime approached.

'Was Eden overdoing it again?' Iris said with a tut.

'I was fine, Granny. Levan only helped me with the bean delivery the other day,' Eden qualified, keen to stop their imaginations running away with them. 'He had a look around the roastery when he brought the sacks inside.'

'Oh, did you show him the secret door?' Sally asked.

'I pointed it out.' Eden recalled the look on Levan's face when she'd shown him. He hadn't seemed too keen to venture through it.

'Ooh, you should have a proper tour of the lighthouse,' Iris said excitedly. 'I can't manage the stairs these days, but Eden would oblige you.'

'I'm sure Levan's not interested, Gran.'

'Actually, I am,' Levan said. 'I'd love to see inside a working lighthouse, but I know how busy Eden is . . .'

'Oh, she can spare half an hour to show you round,' Iris said breezily.

'Well, I think it's for Eden to decide that,' Sally said. 'Or I could always show you,' she added.

Iris pouted and Eden felt sorry for her gran. She didn't want to seem rude to Levan either but understood her mum was trying to be diplomatic.

'I'm sure I'll manage to find some time,' Eden said, trying not to sound as reluctant as she felt about spending more time alone with their charismatic neighbour.

'Of course,' he said with a polite smile. 'If you're sure it's convenient?'

'It's fine,' she said, trying not to focus on how gorgeous his eyes were and how they reminded her – annoyingly – of the merman in the story, luring the maiden to a watery home far away from her family.

She cleared her throat and stood up. 'Now, if you're absolutely sure you don't want seconds, I'll clear away.'

Chapter Ten

A few days later, Eden walked out of the Surf Bar at Sennen Cove, with a mental punch of the air. No matter what was happening in her personal life, business had to come first. With the season kicking off, she had to make the bulk of her profit over the next few months.

She'd been trying to get the manager of the Surf Bar to buy more from her for months. At her suggestion, he'd started serving a wide variety of iced coffees, which had been flying out of the door, and he'd finally agreed to double his order.

She'd decided to celebrate by meeting Wenna on the bar's beachside deck and had settled down at a table to wait for her friend. It was still hot at almost five o'clock in the afternoon and happy hour had just begun.

The hum of chatter and music added a tropical vibe to the scene, with the clientele sitting on the deck, watching surfers ride the waves across the sweep of golden sand.

Eden realised that she no longer missed the buzz of London: where else in the world could you enjoy a view like this? It made her more determined than ever to make a big success of the café.

'Hello, hun!'

Morwenna materialised with a hug for Eden.

In a white kaftan, a pair of aviators and her blonde hair tied back with a silk scarf, she might have just waltzed off the deck of a super yacht. She ordered drinks and insisted on paying.

'How's it going?' she asked Eden.

'Good. In fact, the manager asked me for a much bigger order next time.'

'That's fabulous!' Morwenna's eyes glinted. 'I've got some good news, too. I'd mentioned you to several of the cottage companies. Most of the holiday lets offer a welcome hamper and the luxury places include fresh coffee. They said they'd be willing to trial some of your roast. It could be huge if it comes off.'

'That would mean hundreds of cottages . . .' Eden exclaimed. 'It would be amazing!' *Also quite scary*, she thought. 'Thanks, Wenna. You are a star.'

'I've given the housekeeping managers your email and number so don't be surprised if you get a call this week. Your coffee could be in the hampers before the school hols.'

Eden's mind worked at top speed. 'I'd definitely need help if a deal like that came off. Good job I've already decided to take on Courtney full time and train him up to do the roasting, though I might need an extra part-time barista, too.'

'I thought you might need time to expand, which is why I've kept things low-key – so far.'

'Thanks, Wenna. Can I have the contact details too so I can follow them up?'

'I'll forward them.' After a slurp of her mocktail, she narrowed her eyes at Eden. 'You look a bit tired, hun. I do hope you haven't been losing sleep over Slimeball Simon? He'd better not have sent you any more letters?'

'I've just been super busy with work. I haven't heard from him again.'

'Good!' Wenna fixed Eden with an even harder stare. 'Are you going to answer the creep's letter?'

Eden sighed then said, 'I've been wondering what to do.'

'If you're still wondering, then maybe it's better to ignore him?' Morwenna said, smiling at the waiter as he walked past with a tray of food.

Eden nodded and was about to reply when her phone beeped with a message.

She read it.

'Anything interesting?'

She looked up in surprise.

Morwenna pointed at the phone. 'You're grinning like the Cheshire Cat . . .'

'Was I?' Eden said. 'Oh, dear.'

Morwenna rolled her eyes. 'This is a good thing, Eden.'

'It's only Levan,' she said, slipping her phone into her bag. 'Granny forced me into offering him a tour of the lighthouse. He's texted to make a date.'

Morwenna lowered her aviators and peered at her. 'Iris "forced" you?'

'Kind of. Mum asked him to Sunday lunch and I'm sure he only agreed to come out of politeness. Then Granny tried to' – she wrinkled her nose – 'well, I'm sure she's trying to matchmake the two of us.'

'How embarrassing.' Wenna pulled a face then smirked. 'Though I can think of worse people to be fixed up with.'

'I don't need fixing up with him.'

'Or any man who dares to look at you. Look, even if you're absolutely dead against any kind of relationship at all, you do realise that you don't have to fall in love with him? You could just sleep with him?'

'Wenna! He lives next door and I live with my mum. One, how are we going to find any privacy? And two, it would be excruciating when we split up.'

'You're not a teenager. You can tell your mother to mind her own business, and as for splitting up, what if – wow – it worked out between you?'

'No. No, it wouldn't. I'll admit, he's very decorative, he's a good listener and he's nice to Granny and the cat. Beyond that, no, I'm not interested – and you know full well why.'

'Eden, that was three years ago.'

'Two years and three months, though the length of time doesn't matter.'

'I hate to say it . . .'

'But you're going to anyway?' Eden offered.

'I do hope your reluctance to give Levan a chance hasn't got anything to do with Simon sending that letter!'

'Nothing whatsoever. I just don't think it's a great idea.' Eden snatched up a menu. 'Shall we order some food? As you pointed out, I'm looking frazzled and a large portion of fish and chips is exactly what I need right now.'

'Rather than an entanglement with a handsome, enigmatic next-door neighbour?'

'Exactly,' said Eden with a smile and a wave at the waiter

to come and take their order. She'd answer Levan's message later when Wenna was safely out of sight.

It had been a while since Eden had been inside the lighthouse. In fact, she'd been wracking her brains to work out when the last time was. Certainly a couple of months; since the coffee business had taken off, she'd been too busy.

The lighthouse was still a working one, run by the lighthouse authority, and generally speaking holiday guests were told that visitors weren't allowed; otherwise the family would have been expected to show tourists round every day of the week. There were health and safety issues involved, not to mention security.

So, when Eden met Levan by the roastery in the evening sun, she had to issue a warning to keep his visit to himself.

He zipped his lips. 'Your secret's safe with me.'

She laughed. 'Thanks, and I do feel bad telling people we can't let them inside the tower, even if it is true. Some arrive on holiday thinking they can use the lighthouse as a playground. They're not even aware that it still works to actually help the shipping, not as some kind of theme park landmark.'

He rolled his eyes. 'Jeez. Some people.'

'I know. Now, I'll let you in by the inside door. We could use the front steps, but it's more discreet this way. You know, you really don't *have* to have a tour at all . . .' she said, deciding to give him a get-out clause after his reaction in the roastery. She'd been wondering if he suffered from claustrophobia or had a fear of heights. 'It's quite confined inside and the stairs are very narrow. At the top, we're high, too. It's not everyone's cup of tea. I just thought I'd give you an escape route . . .'

'No escape is needed,' he said. 'Though thank you for giving me the opportunity.'

The glint in his eye and the tilt of his mouth made his words seem like a joke, but Eden wondered whether he was teasing her or not. At times, she sensed deeper layers under his chilled-out exterior.

His accent was non-existent, his manners impeccable, with the easy-going, natural charm of someone who'd been brought up to do and say the appropriate thing for every situation, be it meeting the King, being trapped in a bomb shelter or having Sunday lunch with three women he barely knew. A thread of quiet confidence ran through him that made Eden think it was not just assumed, but inherited.

Was that warmth a carefully cultivated facade? Or was it genuine?

Her experience with Simon had left her suspicious about everyone, paranoid even, and for that, she could never forgive him.

She tried to rationalise how she was feeling, and realised that it was the very careful drip-feeding of details about himself that made her wary of Levan; the almost-too-keen willingness to listen to other people and ask them questions that niggled at her.

She'd almost rather he started boasting about himself, like many men did.

'Do *you* need an escape route?' Levan's voice echoed, cutting into her thoughts. 'I'm sure you're very busy and you don't have to show a strange guy round the lighthouse.'

'No. No, I mean, yes, I'm busy, but this isn't a chore.'

'But not a pleasure?'

She laughed. 'How about somewhere in between?'

His eyebrows lifted though he didn't seem the least offended. 'I admire your honesty.'

'I'm joking. Believe me, I wouldn't do it if I didn't want to.'

'I'm pleased to hear it. Life's too short to do things just to please other people, isn't it?'

Wondering if he was referring to any specific 'things' or simply using a phrase, Eden wasn't quite sure how to respond. She decided to treat his words as merely polite chit-chat. 'Come on,' she said, eager to move on. 'I hope you're fit.'

Although she watched him carefully, he showed no sign of being uncomfortable about ducking under the low door.

Once inside, the space opened out into a high-ceilinged room full of machinery. 'This is the engine room,' she said, her voice echoing.

He exhaled. 'Wow. I hadn't expected *quite* so much kit.'

'It's not needed now. It was when the place was electrified in the nineteen-thirties, but most of the equipment you see is redundant now the lighthouse is automated. It's hard to believe that was in our lifetimes, isn't it?'

'Hard to imagine it was once lit by oil lamps, too.'

'Yes, that was not long before Granny was born so almost in her lifetime. You can take a closer look, if you like.'

Eden wandered around with him, pointing out the old batteries and electrical equipment. She'd felt rusty, or perhaps a little nervous because it was Levan she was showing around, but she'd soon got into her stride again and was enjoying reeling off the facts and figures about the lighthouse.

They reached the far end of the room where a door had a sign saying: 'Private. No entry'.

'What's through there?' Levan asked.

'Ah, that's the west wing. No one is allowed in there.'

'Like in Bluebeard's Castle?'

She laughed. 'Something like that, though I hope there's nothing more horrible behind it than the odd dead mouse.'

His eyes twinkled. 'Maybe we should have brought Sardine for protection?'

'He might not be much use. He's too well fed. It's actually the door to the tower. I have the key . . .' She met his amused gaze with a challenge. 'If you dare.'

'Oh, I always dare.'

Amusement melted into something far more intimate: a look that sent a ripple of desire right through her.

'I'll – um – open up, then.'

She turned her back and pushed the old-fashioned key into the lock, hoping he wouldn't notice that her hands weren't quite steady.

'I haven't been up here for a while. No one has since the spring and that was Mum. I've been too busy with the business.'

She wiggled the key, willing it to open. If it wouldn't she'd feel such a fool.

'Ah.'

Finally, the key turned and she pushed at the door. With a groan, it opened.

'Good,' he said with a sigh of relief. 'I'd have hated to miss out now you've whetted my appetite.'

'I wouldn't get too excited,' Eden muttered. 'Please, come in and mind the step.'

Tilting his head backwards to look high above him, he exhaled. 'Now, that is one hell of a staircase.'

The dizzying snail-shell spiral wound upwards around the edges of the tower.

Levan patted a large brass tube that ran up the middle. 'What's this for?'

'It's the weight tube. That's how they used to keep the light turning. It's like a pendulum on a clock and the keepers used to have to wind it up every hour.'

'Every *hour*?'

'Oh yes, day and night,' Eden said, starting to enjoy sharing her experience, now that Levan was obviously intrigued.

He blew out a breath. 'I can see why they automated everything.' Still gazing up, he spoke into the echoing space. 'I thought there would be floors. I never expected it to be this . . . exposed.'

'There would be floors in a tower lighthouse and it would be even higher than this one. Everything you needed – the kitchen, the bedrooms, a tiny sitting room – would be packed within these walls.'

'Sounds like fun. Not.'

'It's not for the faint-hearted.' She pointed to the spiral staircase that had a brass handrail, and back at Levan. 'Are you ready?'

He met her gaze head-on, as if relishing the challenge she'd thrown his way. 'I can't wait.'

'Great,' she said, sensing a crackle of attraction between them that was impossible to deny. 'Um. I think it's best if you go first.'

'Of course, you're in charge,' said Levan without a trace of irony before setting foot on the stair.

Feeling very much not in charge of the situation, Eden followed him up the stairs that wound their way up to the lantern room. They'd already come dangerously close to flirting . . .

With her bringing up the rear, at least he couldn't see her

and she kept her own eyes on the metal steps, unwilling to be distracted by the muscular bum encased in denim ascending before her. She'd have been horrified to think of him looking at her in that way . . .

There was a degree of satisfaction in hearing him breathing a little faster by the time they reached the top. Her own heart was beating hard.

Levan's attention, if it had ever been on her, was now on the glorious panorama laid out before him, like a feast of views waiting to be gorged on.

'Wow . . .'

As ever, the light was on, sweeping its circular path over the Cornish landscape.

'How far can you see?'

'The light's visible for almost thirty miles.'

'That's incredible. Tell me what we're looking at.'

Eden pointed out the sights. The view stretched from over the wave-capped Atlantic. Eden had always thought of Land's End as the toe of Cornwall, kicking at the sea yet always in danger of being overpowered.

'I'd forgotten how special it is,' said Eden wistfully. 'Dad used to let me come up here when I was little. I'm not sure he should have. I used to skip up the stairs then. Or at least, that's how I remember it.'

She'd had to stand on tiptoe to see the view. Sometimes, her father would lift her up – until she grew tall enough to see for herself. She remembered how safe she used to feel with him, and what a treat it was to have him home and his attention to herself for a little while.

She turned back to Levan and caught a look of concern for her, or possibly compassion.

Brushing aside her wistful mood, she focused on showing Levan the sights. A circle around the lens to the landward side revealed fields and rugged moorland, dotted by the odd church spire stretching all the way to the north coast of the peninsular.

He walked back around the lantern and leaned on the rail. 'I can see two other lighthouses out to sea.'

'The coast around here is so dangerous, we need three lighthouses to warn the shipping of all the reefs. That's Longships to the west off Land's End and the Wolf Rock is eight miles out in the Atlantic. Dad served on that for two years before I was born, and Grandad did a stint as well.'

'All that way out . . .' Levan murmured, transfixed by the lonely tower so far off the coast, it looked like a needle amid the vast ocean. He turned to Eden with a furrowed brow. 'And Wolf Rock isn't a very friendly name.'

'No. Some say it's because of the noise the wind makes when it howls around the rock. In fact, hundreds of years ago, they did put up an iron beacon with a bronze wolf head on it. The waves soon tore it down and the stone one you can see was built in eighteen sixty-four.'

He trained the binoculars on the tower for a closer look. Eden picked hers up too and saw that the waves were breaking over the base and steps even on this balmy June day.

He lowered the glasses, disbelief in his eyes. 'And your father actually lived inside *that*?'

'Yes . . . he always told us the Wolf was the station he dreaded most. In a storm, the waves would batter the windows and even shake the structure.'

'Yet you live in a cottage named after a place he hated?'

'When our lighthouse was automated and the cottages

were turned into houses, Dad suggested naming them after lighthouses.'

'And he chose Wolf Rock?' Levan looked incredulous. 'Why?'

'Because he knew he'd never have to set foot on it again, and he was now safe at home. So he chose the name – as a kind of joke against the tower. Reclaiming it, as it were.'

'I like his style.'

Levan asked a few more questions about the lighthouse and how it operated now. He seemed genuinely interested and Eden swiftly got back into her stride, telling him about the modern light and how the filament bulbs would soon be replaced by LEDs which meant the sweeping beam would become a static flashing light.

'Are you sad about that?' he asked, obviously picking up on her mixed feelings about the change.

'The LEDs will be better for the environment, but the lanterns are so iconic. I'll be sorry to see them go. My dad and grandad tended them for so many years, keeping the oil lamps burning and then the bulbs operational, I almost feel as if *their* light will have gone out.'

Catching Levan watching her intently, she felt awkward and laughed it off. 'But I don't believe in clinging to the past. It's not healthy.'

'No . . . but sometimes it can be difficult to shake off the shackles.'

He met her gaze and, this time, she didn't look away. 'Almost impossible, but we have to try.'

The sunlight gleamed in his dark-blond hair and he held her gaze a second too long for comfort. Her stomach did a flip as alarming as it was exciting.

They spent a few minutes exploring the tower and the horizon, where everything from lobster boats to shipping containers as tall as apartment blocks bobbed and steamed past. Eden knew some of the smaller craft by name, and in answer to Levan's questions told him who the skippers were and what they were fishing for.

'The engineers do still have to visit the rock and tower lighthouses to do maintenance. They obviously get dropped off by helicopters but they still have to stay on them.'

'On their own?'

'Yes. But only for a couple of weeks, not two months like the old keepers. I couldn't have done what they did, what my father and grandfather did. They used to be called the "silent service", you know. I think they were all heroes, devoting their lives to keeping others safe, risking their own safety and sacrificing their family time.'

He nodded. 'You all made a lot of sacrifices too. You and your mum and Iris.'

'I never thought of it like that. We just got on with it. There were upsides. In many ways, it was an idyllic way to live. I only ever knew life on a land lighthouse, where Dad worked a few moments away. I didn't have to endure his absence all the time, like Mum and Granny did.'

'Living here?'

'You can see how beautiful it is, and we had those views every day of our lives. There weren't quite so many people about then. Even as I've grown up, it's become busier in high summer. The rest of the year, even now, it's blissful.'

'I hardly see anyone on my morning jogs.'

Eden gave a knowing laugh. 'Wait until the height of the season, but even then, when the day-trippers have gone home, you can almost have the place to yourself. It's definitely a place to escape to, in some ways.'

He exchanged a glance with her. 'But also very lonely?'

'Sometimes, in a way. I couldn't stay here forever. I wanted to see the big wide world and that meant moving. So after I'd gone to college I went to London and did a hospitality degree before moving into a shared house with some colleagues. I landed a job in a hotel and eventually managed a swanky bar . . . and that's where I met Simon.'

She became aware of him listening intently, almost too intently, and she felt embarrassed and annoyed at herself for giving so much away. Why did she have the urge to go all confessional in this man's presence?

'Do you still have your parents?' Eden said, determined to even up the score by drawing him out of himself and asking some questions of her own.

There was a pause and when he did answer, his eyes rested on the horizon rather than on her. 'Yes. My mother and father live in Hertfordshire.'

'That's a long way from here,' she said lightly. 'Will they be coming for a visit?'

'I've no idea.' It was an uncharacteristically blunt response before he qualified it. 'My father's not always . . . in the best condition to travel too far.'

Eden felt sorry for him. 'That's a shame,' she said. 'But at least you can go back and see them.'

'If I need to, yes.'

If he needed to see them. Not *when* he wanted to visit. Eden thought it was a strange answer and an odd attitude towards his parents. Then again, not everyone had a good relationship with their family. She was very fortunate, and so was Simon, she thought before angrily dismissing him from her mind.

'It's a real pity, though, that they can't see Hartstone for themselves,' she went on. 'What about your other family and friends?' she persisted and said, with a warmth she hoped would encourage him to say more, 'Most people who move here are inundated with mates and relatives wanting a free holiday.'

His own smile was fleeting and held no warmth at all. 'I have an older brother but he lives abroad. As for friends, even if they wanted to visit, I don't have much room. I turned my spare bedroom into an office.'

Although he spoke in a polite, half-amused tone, Eden was beginning to suspect that there was a different person under Levan's veneer of laid-back charm. No matter how much she'd opened up to him, he rarely let the mask slip.

Or, she thought, remembering something her gran had once said: she was definitely overthinking things. *Or . . .*

It suddenly occurred to Eden that Levan might be trying to field questions about his personal life because he was in a relationship that he wanted to keep private. He'd mentioned the mysterious Dion a couple of times so maybe he was more than a friend?

Even though she knew she was probably being a bit cheeky, she pushed a little harder. 'I wondered if your friend Dion might be staying over . . .'

Levan frowned then broke into a grin. 'He didn't stay with me. After he brought me home, he went to see a colleague near St Ives. They've got a big place with masses of spare rooms. He's bound to have enjoyed five-star treatment there.' He looked directly at Eden. 'You were with a *friend* too,' he said, taking Eden aback. 'The tall baker,' he added.

'Oh, you mean Joe? Yes, he's lovely. He's a film and TV extra too. He's been in *Poldark* and a couple of movies.'

Levan laughed softly. 'I can see why.'

'Can you?' she prompted, seeing if he'd mention the fact that was obvious to everyone on the planet: that Joe was extraordinarily good-looking.

'Yes. I had a friend who was an actor. She had the same – aura – as your Joe. You wanted to look at her all the time. She was mesmerising.'

'Mesmerising'. Such a specific word – and said in such an emphatic way. Eden's instincts told her that Levan's feelings for this actress must stretch beyond mere admiration.

'So,' he said, returning the conversation to her. 'We were talking about your Joe . . .'

Eden laughed. 'He's not my Joe and he never will be, because he's the Joe of a property developer called Ravi. They live in a seafront pile in Lamorna and they're engaged.'

Levan's lips parted, understanding gleaming in his eyes. 'Ah.'

'Joe and I went to school together. Almost everyone had a huge crush on him.'

'Including you?'

'I tried not to, because I knew I'd only have my heart broken.' She laughed. Having offered enough – more – of her own personal life, Eden was now determined that Levan would reciprocate. That's how communication worked, wasn't it? You shared some personal detail and the other person empathised and gave you something in return? Like casting out a line with a nugget of bait in the hope you'll catch a tasty fish.

'This actress,' Eden said, determined not to be put off. 'Was she a school friend?'

'Ah.' His smile was wry, sad even. 'No. I went to a boys' boarding school. She'd never have been allowed within a mile of the gates. I met her later at university.'

'Oh? Which one?'

'It was in Cambridge,' he said before his eyes widened and he pointed over her shoulder. 'What's that in the sea? That huge, dark shape?'

He clamped the binoculars to his eyes and Eden took up her pair. She didn't need help to guess what the two dark shapes were. They were moving gracefully through the emerald water around thirty metres from the base of the cliffs.

A closer inspection brought a ripple of excitement. 'I'm pretty sure they're basking sharks.'

'Sharks?' He lowered the binoculars with a look of disbelief at her. 'They're huge.'

'They are, but also harmless. You're lucky to see them. They don't visit every year. They'll probably hang around for a few days now. See, they turned up specially for you.'

He turned to her, his eyes holding an excited gleam that mirrored her buzz of sharing this experience with him. He was wearing the white linen shirt again, this time with the sleeves rolled back to expose his tanned forearms and an Apple Watch. The buttons of the shirt were open just enough to reveal a leather cord with a silver disc on it. She thought she saw initials: 'H' and something else. She felt an unexpected stab of jealousy. Were they the ones of the 'mesmerising' actress?

'Wow, I obviously turned up here at exactly the right moment,' he said. His eyes were lit with a sexy gleam that made her stomach do a little flip and heat rise through her. 'Perhaps it's fate.'

From a flip of desire, her stomach knotted with unease.

'I don't believe in fate,' she said coldly. 'Shall we go back down again?'

With a nod, he set off ahead of her, with Eden preoccupied by his smile, the look – and the words.

'Perhaps it's fate.'

Those were exactly the ones Simon had used the day he'd first chatted her up over a cocktail at the counter of a Soho bar.

Chapter Eleven

Levan swiped his card over the reader by the door of the centre and stepped out into a pool of bright sunlight. He screwed up his eyes and let the warmth wrap around him after an afternoon in the centre's shuttered, air-conditioned interior.

It had been a very intense week since Eden had shown him around the lighthouse. He'd been working at the centre a lot and then late into the night at home.

He pulled his aviators from his laptop bag and was in the process of putting them on when he spotted a familiar pick-up in the car park, with a man leaning on the bonnet scrolling through his mobile.

'Ah, the man of mystery,' Dion said when Levan reached him.

'There's nothing mysterious about me,' Levan said. 'But you've turned up out of the blue. I wasn't expecting you to be here.'

'I didn't expect to be here.'

'Oh? Trouble?'

'Most probably not, but it pays to err on the safe side.'

'"Safe side"?' Levan echoed. 'Sounds ominous.'

'Like I say, it's probably nothing but security have flagged up something.'

Despite Dion's chilled-out demeanour, the hairs on Levan's arms stood on end.

'And?'

Dion toed the dust. 'There's a guy watching the centre.'

'And? People always watch the centre.'

'Yeah, but this guy has done it three times this week.'

Levan shrugged. 'Probably some conspiracy theorist with a YouTube channel or data centre obsessive. They're like train spotters, collecting alleged "secret facilities". Remember the guy who made a video of alleged spy installations that turned out to be a nail bar and an old Tesco click-and-collect hut?'

Dion smirked. 'Maybe there's nothing in it – apart from the fact that this really is a secret facility.'

Levan nodded. 'Could be a journalist?' he offered.

'Possibly. The thing is, he seems to have been watching *you* specifically. I can show you the footage from the cameras.'

Although he was careful not to show any reaction, Levan's pulse quickened. 'Go on then, let's have a look at my "stalker",' he said in a world-weary tone.

In silence, he watched the video on Dion's phone, which seemed to have been compiled by the security staff from a number of camera angles. It showed a hooded man standing on a public footpath on the far side of the fence from the data centre. He had binoculars trained on Levan as he stood outside making a call, then walked to his car and got inside. The hair stood up on the back of Levan's neck. It didn't seem like the behaviour of wannabe James Bond YouTube nerds . . .

'Do we know who it is?' he asked.

'Not yet,' Dion said, switching off the video. 'The database isn't bringing up any of the usual suspects. Can you think of anyone?'

'No . . . I suppose it could be a journalist who's found out I'm working here, but I don't know how and why they would even be interested in me these days.' Even though Levan kept his tone light, his brain was working overtime and his stomach tightening with anxiety.

'It does seem unlikely, I admit.' Dion left a significant pause before asking, 'Is there anything I should know?'

'You mean anything that you don't know already?'

He smiled. 'Anything . . . new? Any concerns about your neighbours for example?'

Levan sighed. 'Well, Iris worries me. She had Dostoyevsky on her bookcase. She told me she couldn't get past the first few pages but that could be a bluff. She could be a sleeper.'

Dion laughed. 'Very funny. I'm not expecting her to try and break into the building with her walking stick.'

'I wouldn't bet against it. She's a feisty woman. Courageous . . . In her youth, I can imagine she'd have been rather a good asset to the security services. She did live through the war, even if she was very young and she's served her country in a different way.'

'Oh?' Dion's interest was piqued.

'She kept her family together while her husband and son were stationed in the middle of the Atlantic, and she's survived the death of both. She, Sally and Eden are all strong characters, and have been through the mill.'

Dion eyed him. 'This Eden . . . you like her,' he said shrewdly.

Levan wasn't about to deny it. Despite Eden growing cold on him at the end of the lighthouse tour, he'd felt they'd really connected. Maybe she had too and that's why she'd backed off, scared of becoming too involved again. It was frustrating that he hadn't seen her since.

'I like all three of them,' he said.

'Let's focus on Eden for now,' Dion said firmly. 'Do you think that this man watching you could be a rival?'

He snorted. 'A rival for what?'

Dion tutted. 'Her affections, mate. The usual thing. He could be an old boyfriend. An ex.'

Levan was about to scoff and deny such a thing was possible but then he thought about the letter Eden had received and how persistent Simon must be, to harass her after so long.

'Oh, shit . . .' he murmured.

Dion raised his eyebrows. '"Oh, shit", *what?*'

Levan shook his head, wanting to laugh at the idea that had weaselled its way into his thinking. 'No, it can't be. It's ridiculous. I hardly know her.'

But it was too late. Dion was like a dog with a bone. 'Come on, let's hear what's bugging you, however ridiculous.'

'Simon, her ex, is a conman and a Grade A bastard, though I have no idea why he'd be watching me.'

Dion raised an eyebrow. 'Maybe he thinks you're trying to move in on her.'

'He'd be wrong,' Levan said firmly. 'But he has been in touch with her again and asking to see her.'

Dion nodded. 'OK. It may not be him but, nonetheless, I think we'd better try to find out.'

Levan drove home, mulling over his conversation with Dion. He was a little disturbed over the 'stalker', wondering if it was someone – possibly a journalist – who'd discovered he'd moved to Cornwall. His trial and conviction had been reported in the media but had merited only a few column inches on the inside pages.

Even so, the fact he'd made it into the press at all had added a fresh layer of torment and misery to his family, who were already incandescent with shame and anger at him.

'*Career officer dismissed with disgrace from the army and jailed for two years.*'

Seeing those words written in the kind of newspapers his family called 'the gutter press' – and, even worse, the newspapers they did read – had destroyed any shred of sympathy they had for him.

No, Dion was probably right: no journalist would be bothered about him now.

As for Simon, Levan felt slightly foolish for even mentioning him as a possible suspect. It signalled how involved he'd become with the Carricks in such a short space of time. Maybe he should back off . . .

If he even could. The Carricks represented the warm family life he'd never experienced, a fresh start in a community where no one cared about wealth, rank or status. He felt more like the person he wanted to be than he had in his whole life, and he wasn't going to let go of that lightly.

*   *   *

Levan had discovered that each cottage had a small allotment patch on the headland in front of the cottages, where the keepers could grow fresh food. They were protected from the worst of the winds by thick white walls and each had a gate, painted green like the rest of the woodwork on the cottages.

Most, like his own, had been turned into chic sunbathing areas for guests complete with barbecues, wooden furniture and tubs of agapanthus, whose green leaves and flower stalks danced in the breeze. However, the Carricks' patch, the largest, was still used for its intended purpose.

When he was young, he'd have laughed at anyone who'd told him he'd find comfort and solace in digging someone else's garden. But it turned out he did.

'Are you sure you don't mind doing this?' Eden's mother stood by the gate, with an amused look.

'As long as you don't mind me invading your garden.'

Smiling broadly, she walked onto the plot. 'I said I didn't. You seem to know what you're doing and anyone who wants to do some of the heavy work is fine with me.'

Like her daughter, she was keen-eyed and tanned from the Cornish outdoor lifestyle, though markedly more at ease with herself. Eden was a restless soul, but that was hardly surprising after what she'd been through. Levan knew she didn't trust him and, while his instinct was to change her mind, part of him thought it was probably for the best.

'Where did you get your love of gardening?' she asked.

Levan hesitated. He could tell her the truth, or he could lie. He decided on something in between.

'From a friend. He had an allotment and I wanted to see him. He was busy and told me the only time he had to talk was while he was planting up his vegetable plugs one spring. So I had no choice and I told him I felt guilty for watching while he worked.' He smiled at the memory. 'He handed me a spade . . .'

'I'd have done the same!' In Sally's laughter, Levan glimpsed and heard Eden – an Eden before she'd been battered by the sheer bloody unfairness life could hurl at you.

'I do appreciate the help,' Sally said. 'I love the garden, and so did Roger and my father-in-law, Walter. It keeps me fit and my mind off darker things. If that doesn't sound maudlin.'

'Not at all. You can't think about too much when you're planting and weeding and harvesting. Circle of life and all that stuff.' He waved a hand towards the sea. 'Especially not with that view. Give me this patch over some stately kitchen garden, any day.'

Her eyes lit up. What was she – just sixty, possibly? The same age as his mum yet, even devoid of make-up, bronzed by the sun and in shorts and a T-shirt, she looked years younger. His own mother wouldn't be seen out of her bedroom without a rock-hard blow-dry and heels. Levan checked himself. His mother had her own burdens to endure, but she hid those deep beneath her armour. She wouldn't even register Sally Carrick's existence if she passed her in the street.

'Have you gardened in a stately home then?' Sally said, amused.

'Not really,' Levan said truthfully, declining to add that his family had had gardeners to get their hands dirty. He would never have been allowed to join them, anyway.

'Roger always said he could forget his troubles when he was in here. Obviously, he grew our own food out of necessity when he was on an island lighthouse where there was room for a small patch. When we married and moved around to different places, I got into the habit too, because even though I could drive, it seemed mad to get the car out and drive miles for a bunch of carrots or some spuds.'

Two gulls landed on the wall, squawking at each other.

Sally laughed. 'Hartstone was always our favourite station. We were all so relieved when we heard the lighthouse would be automated and we'd be able to stay here. We jumped at the chance to buy the cottage . . . it's just a shame that we had so few years here as a family. I always thought we'd grow old here and end up being carried out of the cottage feet first.' Her eyes glistened.

'I'm very sorry,' he said gently. 'You must have all been devastated.'

'Yes. Yes of course . . . I was but I had Eden to support, and Iris too, so I couldn't fall apart, even though at times I felt like I could have jumped off this bloody cliff. I felt the service had robbed me of so much of my married life with Roger. He was away so much.'

Levan's stomach knotted. He knew how it felt to feel your life trickling away, far away from home – from the life you'd dreamt of once.

'You know . . . I've never told anyone this before, but I *almost* felt sorrier for Iris than myself. To lose the son she worshipped when he was still so young. It's a mother's worst nightmare. I don't know how I could go on if I lost Eden.'

'No. I don't either.' Levan suppressed a shudder. The thought of something happening to Eden was not something he wanted to contemplate, even though he'd only known her a few weeks. That in itself alarmed him: that he cared so much after so short an acquaintance. Was it symptomatic of how hard he was falling for her?

'Wow,' Sally said, smiling. 'Where did that come from? It's not like me. I don't like dwelling on the past. God knows, there's been enough hardship for the family already. Eden especially.' She checked herself. 'I'll leave you to do the hard work for me. Can you return the key to the shed door under the pot by the cottage step, please? I daren't leave it open or someone's bound to use it to store their bloody bodyboards. They see fit to wash their wetsuits under my garden tap as it is.'

'I'll charge them a pound a go,' Levan said.

'I like your way of thinking. Don't work too hard . . .' She went as if to leave before apparently changing her mind. 'Oh, Eden might have told you that Iris is going to be ninety at the end of next month. We were thinking of having a little party here, hopefully in the garden, if it's fine. A tea party or barbecue. Nothing fancy, just the three of us, Eden's friend, Morwenna, and Joe and Ravi. Maybe a few of Iris's chums. You're very welcome to join us.'

'That's very kind of you but if it's a family celebration, I wouldn't want to intrude.'

'You won't be intruding. I wouldn't have asked if I thought that.'

Levan hesitated. It seemed an intimate event to be invited to when he was supposed to be trying to keep some distance between himself and the Carricks, and Eden in particular.

'Iris would enjoy having you there,' Sally said. Her voice had a hopeful edge that was impossible to ignore.

How could he snub Iris by not attending? He relented. 'You're only ninety once, and if you're sure, I'd be honoured to come along.'

'Great. I'll let you know more about it closer to the date. She knows we're arranging something, but not exactly what.'

He tapped his lips with his finger. 'Your secret's safe with me.'

'Thanks – though keeping anything from Iris is difficult at the best of times.'

'I bet.'

'I'll let Eden know you're coming. I'm sure she'll be pleased.'

I wouldn't bet on it, thought Levan as he waved goodbye to Sally, remembering how frosty Eden had been when they'd said goodbye at the lighthouse.

Chapter Twelve

'Granny? Are you in there?'

Eden buzzed her grandmother's doorbell for the third time.

Seabreeze Court was a complex of flats and mini bungalows in a cul-de-sac set back a couple of roads from the Penzance seafront. A warden lived on site, and Eden was seriously thinking of going to her accommodation if Iris didn't answer in the next couple of minutes.

Her grandmother was supposed to be coming over to Lighthouse Cottages that afternoon and, from an exchange of messages over WhatsApp, Eden had understood Iris would be in all morning and ready to be picked up at two p.m.

However, she'd had to make an unscheduled trip to the wholesaler nearby and thought she'd surprise her grandmother, take her to lunch and drive her to Wolf Rock afterwards.

Bzzzz.

Holding her finger down on the bell, Eden tried to chase away the grim scenarios filling her mind. What if something had happened? The nameless something she never wanted to think about happening to her beloved almost-ninety-year-old granny.

Of course, her rational side told her that Iris could be round at a friend's – but in that case, why wasn't she answering her phone?

'Mornin'. Are you looking for your gran?'

A man in a cricket hat hailed her from a shady bench by the rose border outside the bungalows. Recognising him immediately, Eden hurried over.

Jim Tresize wasn't really a friend of her grandmother – Iris thought he was 'a bit of a busybody' – but Eden wasn't unhappy to see him in these circumstances and treated him to a smile. Her grandmother wouldn't want Jim to know Eden had been worried about her. She tried not to let her imagination go into overdrive.

'Yes. I came to pick her up but I'm very early. I thought I'd surprise her.'

'Well, you're out of luck. She went out with a young chap an hour since.'

Eden's stomach rolled over. 'A young chap? Who?'

'Don't know him from Adam. I've never seen him before but she was leaning on his arm so she must.'

Stay. Calm, Eden told herself, already itching to dial 999 to report a gran-napping. 'Did she seem OK with this man?'

'OK?' Jim seemed incredulous. 'More than OK, maid. She was giggling.' Jim was relishing every moment. 'Haven't seen her so happy for ages, to be honest with you.'

That must be good, thought Eden, unless this man had drugged her. She tried not to indulge in such wild imaginings. Jim's report was encouraging.

'Um – what did he look like?' Eden said, in case she had to give a description to the police.

'Now, let me see. He was tall, with a ponytail and one of those bloody studs in his eye.' Jim grimaced then realised what he'd said. 'Sorry, lov, but I don't see why anyone has to have a rivet through their face. You're such a pretty maid without that ironmongery.'

'Thanks.' The penny was dropping and her terror subsiding. 'You say he had a stud through his *eye*?'

'Here,' Jim said, tugging at one of the caterpillars over his eyes.

'Oh, through his eye*brow* . . . Was he blond, by any chance?'

'Not 'zackly blond. Not like Princess Di blonde, but I'd say he was fair-haired, yes.'

Eden exhaled and muttered, 'Levan.'

'What?' Jim said.

'The chap. Did he have a van?'

'Oh, yes. A silver Ford. I got the reg, if you want, maid.' He pulled a small notebook from his pocket. 'I keep an eye on anything unusual. Just in case.'

'Thanks,' said Eden, wondering how much use Jim's observations would have been once her gran had been lured away by some kidnapper. 'You've been very helpful, but I don't need his number now. I know who she's with. It sounds very like a – um – neighbour of ours.'

'That's a relief, though she did seem very keen to go off with him.'

Eden had an idea. 'Erm, Jim? You didn't happen to overhear where they were going, did you?'

He grinned. 'I did as a matter of fact. Nothing wrong with

my ears, though it pays to act as if I'm a bit deaf now and again. Iris said something about going to the bank . . .'

'The bank?'

'Yeah. The fair-haired lad said he'd give her a lift there.'

A swirl of unease stirred again. Why was her grandmother going there with Levan? What was going on?

Leaving Jim to his observations, Eden climbed into her own van and called Iris again.

'Oh hello, Eden! What? You're at the bungalow? Why?'

'I wanted to surprise you, Gran, but you weren't here.'

'That's a shame and I am sorry I missed you, but I'm with Levan.'

'OK . . . but why are you out with him?'

'Because I messaged him about some old photographs of mine and he said he'd love to see them and he mentioned he was on his way back from meeting a friend nearby – and so I said to call in.'

Photographs? Eden thought. Why on earth had Iris been messaging Levan about some old pictures? However, her more immediate concern was the issue with the bank – even though she didn't dare mention it specifically because her gran would know she'd been gossiping behind her back.

'So, you haven't been into . . . town?'

'Yes, we've been into town. Levan said he was going to the computer place and so I asked him if he'd mind dropping me at the bank. I had one of those scam texts this morning. Or I thought it was a scam, but it turns out it's all legitimate. I wasn't going to fall for any of it. I always check in person at the branch first if I'm worried.'

Eden exhaled, cross with herself for her wilder imaginings. 'Good decision.'

'And it's such a lovely day that we decided to have a spot of lunch at the Jubilee Pool. I wanted to treat Levan for being so kind and putting himself out. If you come over to the pool now, you'll be in time for pudding.'

'But Granny—'

'Oh, I have to go, Levan's coming back from the gents' and I don't want to be caught talking about him behind his back. Eden . . .'

'Yes?'

'I hope you haven't been worrying about me?' Iris said pointedly.

'No, Granny,' Eden said breezily. 'I'll see you in a few minutes.'

With a huge sigh of relief, she set off. The pool was only a few minutes away, but she needed every second to calm down after allowing her imagination to go into overdrive. Her grandmother was perfectly entitled to live her own life, see who she wanted and take a handsome young man to lunch.

Even so.

Traffic lights on red. She stopped, her mind churning. In her defence, what did they really know about Levan? He'd gained her grandmother's trust very quickly. He was charming, gorgeous and seemed to be an all-round nice guy with a social conscience. As her ex had seemed.

Damn him. Simon had poisoned her faith in half the population and made her lose all sense of perspective.

'You bastard, Simon!' she shouted, smacking her hands on the steering wheel. 'I don't care if you drive off a cliff!'

A glance out of her window revealed an overalled man in the van next to her staring through both their open windows from the driver's seat. The lights changed and he roared off like Lewis Hamilton. Eden just had time to read the sign on the back of his van.

Simon Nancollas
Painter and Decorator
Residential and Commercial throughout
West Cornwall

Praying that the innocent Simon N never turned up to her café for a coffee, Eden parked and walked up the road to the Jubilee Pool. The Art Deco lido on Penzance seafront had been a favourite place of her grandmother's since it was first built in the 1930s. Since its restoration a few years previously, it had become hugely popular with bathers and diners alike, who flocked to swim in the salt water or enjoy a meal in the café.

A couple of times a month, year-round, Iris loved to bathe in the heated smaller pool.

Iris and Levan had bagged a table with a parasol on the front of the terrace, from where they could admire the great sweep of Mount's Bay. The panorama from the Lizard, almost to Land's End, was spectacular enough; add in the fairy tale castle of St Michael's Mount and there could be few better views in England.

Spotting Eden, Iris waved and Levan broke into a smile. Several people looked from him to Eden as she made a beeline for the table. Were they thinking the same as she was? That he was extraordinarily handsome and why was he having lunch with an elderly lady and a woman with a pixie cut, dungarees and DMs?

Eden kissed her gran's cheek and managed a smile for Levan, whose eyes were hidden behind aviators.

'I ordered you a cold drink,' he said. 'Iris said best not to get a coffee.'

Iris lowered her voice, though not quite enough. 'I told him it's not as good as yours.'

'Not yet,' Eden said. 'I'm working on it.'

'Ah, but,' said Levan with mock solemnity. 'It's surely only a matter of time before they see the light.'

Eden winked. 'Of course it is.'

'There was a queue building so we already ordered dessert for you,' he added.

Iris nodded. 'We thought it was best.'

'Good thinking.' Eden noted the 'we'. The two of them were already acting as a team.

'Actually, I think this is our order now.' He nodded at a waitress approaching with a tray of desserts and glasses with condensation on the sides. She put the drinks and lemon tart with clotted cream, a tiramisu and strawberry cheesecake on the table.

'We ordered a bit of everything so you could take your pick,' Levan said, taking off his sunglasses.

Gratefully, Eden selected a glass of elderflower fizz and inhaled the fragrance of sun-warmed strawberries. 'Hmm. Thanks . . . I'll have the cheesecake, if it's OK?'

'I knew she'd say that!' Iris cried in triumph. 'She loves cheesecake. When she was little, I came home to find she'd taken a huge slice out of the fridge. I'd been keeping it for her dad when he got back that night. Eden had scoffed the lot and was sick.'

Eden felt her cheeks going the same colour as the cheesecake. 'Thanks, Gran!'

Levan was making a terrible job of not dissolving into

laughter. The Cornish light danced in his eyes and Eden felt less frosty towards him for kidnapping her gran. Jim was right: her beloved granny looked happier than she'd been in ages.

The cheesecake was delicious and Iris had a smile on her face the whole time they were eating. Her grandmother was a positive and sunny person but there was a perkiness about her that Eden hadn't noticed before. She was waxing lyrical about Levan's travels, which they must have been chatting about before Eden arrived.

'I was telling Levan about the pool here and how warm it is,' she said. 'And he said that swimming in tropical places is like swimming in a warm bath. He's been to so many exotic places, haven't you?'

'Oh?' Eden was even more intrigued. 'That sounds very glam. Like where?'

'Here and there,' Levan said, looking a little embarrassed.

'He's been to Belize and Papua New Guinea and the South Pacific.' Iris sighed. 'I love that film.'

'I think it was actually shot in Hawaii, Granny,' Eden said.

Iris rolled her eyes. 'I know that, but it's *set* in French Polynesia and Levan has been there.'

Visions of Levan skinny-dipping in a turquoise lagoon sprang to mind. Eden pushed them away, her cheeks flushing. 'Um. That sounds very exotic . . . you mean you've been to Tahiti?'

'Yes, and some of the more remote islands . . . the Marquesas, the Gambiers.'

'Wow. Some holiday,' she said.

'A working holiday. I went to help with some conservation projects on a gap year after I left uni.'

'Now *that* is a gap year. I went to flip burgers in a pub kitchen in Bodmin.' Realising she'd sounded churlish, Eden softened. 'It sounds amazing. Tell me more.'

'Believe me, there were many times when I'd have killed for a burger.' Levan laughed and then, at Iris's request, he told them a bit about turtle conservation and shark feeding and the marae temples and churches.

Iris had clearly heard some of this already, and nudged him. 'Tell her about the time you were almost hit on the head by a coconut and the story about the shark.'

Levan laughed. 'I don't want to bore you both and I'm sure Eden has stories of her own,' he said.

Eden wondered whether to share the story about spotting a TV wildlife presenter peeing up the wall at the back of the restaurant she'd worked at in Soho. Perhaps not. Her gran loved the show and it would be a shame to spoil it for her.

'What did you do after your gap year?' she asked.

'Joined the real world. Worked.'

'Which was?'

'Boring IT stuff.' He laughed.

'It still sounds very exotic to me. The opposite of boring.'

He sipped his Coke. 'Not really. Sadly. I was too busy working to get out and see the sights much.'

Iris nodded and sighed. 'Same as Walter and Roger. Some people think lighthouse keeping must have been romantic. Ha! Anything but. Working three shifts round the clock. Cooped up with two other men, who you couldn't get away from – and maybe you couldn't stand. All of 'em chain smoking. Imagine it in the middle of winter with the whole place shaking and dark at four o'clock. How romantic is that!'

'They were very resilient and I don't think I'd have been

able to stand it,' Levan said, catching Eden's eye. She wasn't sure why but she gave him a brief smile then picked up her phone. Levan had her granny spellbound, and Eden even more intrigued than ever.

'I hate to spoil the party but I really need to take Granny to Wolf Rock and I'm sure you have boring IT stuff to be getting on with. Plus those coffee beans won't roast themselves.'

Levan checked his watch. 'You're right, I should be getting back. I have masses to do.'

'You two work too hard,' Iris said. 'And though I've had a lovely time, I wouldn't want to keep either of you any longer. Before we set off, I need to visit the ladies'. I won't be long.'

Picking up her stick, Iris made her way across the sunlit terrace.

Levan waited until she'd gone before speaking. 'Sorry if you were worried about Iris. She said you wouldn't be at the flat until after lunch.'

'I wasn't worried,' Eden said, lying through her teeth. 'A bit surprised she wasn't in but she's obviously had a lovely time and it's very kind of you to think of her. You must be busy.'

'Oh, I'm always busy but I also have the luxury of being able to work when I want.'

'Even so, it's good of you to interrupt your day to take an old lady out for lunch.'

'Iris invited *me*, and I don't think of her as an old lady.'

Eden thought he meant it. 'I don't want to think of her as old, either,' she admitted.

'I don't think Iris does. She jokes about it but inside I think there's still the vibrant woman of her youth. I wish I'd known her then.'

Eden was struck by a rogue thought that she found faintly

disturbing: that her granny might . . . *fancy* Levan. Iris might not think of him as some kind of surrogate grandson or potential partner for her granddaughter but as a young guy who she would have fallen for, had she been Eden's age. In another time, another place . . . and had her grandad, Walter, not been around. She had a sneaking suspicion that the photographs had simply been an excuse to get Levan round to the house.

'These, um . . . photographs . . .' she began, feeling uncomfortable with the idea of her beloved granny having a crush on their neighbour.

'Iris mentioned them to me the other day.' His eyes twinkled. 'Over the garden hedge, as a matter of fact. We were talking about your grandfather's time on the lighthouse and she let slip she'd looked out these old photographs. I'm sure you've seen them, yourselves?'

Eden wracked her brain. 'More than likely, although we haven't had a reminisce for a couple of years.'

'Perhaps this landmark birthday has made her dig them out?' he suggested.

'I'm sure it has.'

'She heard I was going to be really close to her place and asked me to call in and take a look at them, and it seemed to be important to her that I did.'

Eden frowned. She still wasn't certain exactly why grandmother had been so eager to share the pictures with Levan, although he was right: her birthday must have brought up many memories.

'What were they of in particular? Just lighthouses?' Eden said.

'Actually, they were mostly of people. Her husband, and your dad and one of your great-grandparents. They've faded and creased over the years. One's a hundred years old – taken before Iris was born, obviously. She seemed quite upset that a couple of them were almost crumbling away.'

'Poor Granny. I'd like to see them again, I must admit,' Eden said. 'In fact, maybe we could make up some kind of birthday album with them? Maybe even get them repaired?'

'Actually . . .' Levan began with a cautious glance towards the ladies' loo before continuing. 'I had exactly the same thought and I've – er – done something a bit iffy. It was an impulse and I was going to confess . . .'

Alarm bells rang again. 'Something "iffy"?'

'I, er, I kind of borrowed the photographs for you.'

'You borrowed them for me?' Eden exclaimed then lowered her voice. 'How?'

'While Iris went to fetch her cardigan from the bedroom, I took the folder from the dresser drawer and popped out to the car with it.' He stopped, realising Eden was staring at him. 'I know, it was wrong and I regretted it straight away but didn't know how to replace them without her knowing. It seemed a good idea at the time.'

Eden frowned. 'And?'

'Thinking about it now, I know I should have waited for permission first and then asked you to get hold of them. You have every right to be incredibly annoyed with me . . .'

Eden put on her sternest expression, enjoying seeing him flustered for a change.

'Well, it would have been nice to have been asked . . .' she said, still not sure how she felt about him rooting around in the bungalow.

'Of course. I'll come clean immediately and tell Iris the moment she's back.'

'No. No, don't do that!' Eden insisted. 'Even though it wasn't the most honourable thing, you've done it now so we might as well use it to our advantage and keep them.'

'OK.' He sighed. 'Even so, I was worried Iris would miss them and that's why I've told you the first moment I could.'

'Thanks,' said Eden with an eye-roll, then smiled at him. 'Not much gets past Granny, but it's a plan that just might work.'

'I have a scanner. We could scan them in and then maybe you can sneak them back? I've also got a basic photo editing suite that might do a half-decent job, though I'm no expert on photo restoration.'

'Hmm,' said Eden, her mind working overtime. 'You know, I may have a better idea. Why don't I ask Morwenna to help? She has the equipment and the skills.'

'That's a great idea,' he said, sounding relieved. 'I'm sure she'll do a brilliant job. I've seen some of her work.'

'Oh?' Eden said, in surprise. 'When?'

'I bumped into her yesterday while I was out jogging. After I'd *finished* jogging,' he corrected with a smile. 'She was about to call on you, actually, after one of her holiday cottage jobs, and we met in the car park and got talking. She showed me her portfolio – her personal one – on her tablet.'

'Really?' Eden said, clearing her throat. She could picture the scene exactly and the conversation that had followed: Morwenna 'accidentally' getting out of her Mini at the exact time Levan had finished his run. '*Oh, hello again. Fancy seeing you here . . . Oh, you do look fit and you're all hot and sweaty . . .*'

'She's really very talented,' he said with a grin.

'She certainly is,' said Eden with a fresh pang of jealousy that she tried and failed to dismiss.

'So,' he said breezily. 'When do you want to come round to collect these photos?'

'Um. How about tomorrow after work?'

'Good idea. Oh, watch out,' he said with a nod towards the ladies' where Iris was emerging. 'She's on her way back.'

A few seconds later, Iris arrived and encompassed them both with a sunny smile. 'You two look very conspiratorial.'

'We were just talking about how I can get my coffee served here,' Eden said, hoping her nose wouldn't grow like Pinocchio's. 'It would be a good contract for me.'

Levan turned his sexy gaze on her. 'Oh, I'm sure it won't be long before they fall for your charms,' he said then got up to leave. 'Now, Iris, I'm afraid I must be getting back to work. Thank you for inviting me to lunch, I'll see you both later.'

Chapter Thirteen

For God's sake, did he *have* to keep taking his clothes off, Eden asked herself when she arrived back from the Coffee Container the following evening.

Levan was digging the vegetable patch in the evening sunlight, wearing only shorts and hiking boots. He clearly hadn't noticed her watching or he might not have stripped off his T-shirt so extravagantly and tossed it onto the bench like Magic Mike.

As was the way in late June, the end of the afternoon felt like the hottest part of the day, with summer finally in full swing. She hung back as Levan thrust the spade into the soil and turned it over. His torso was glistening with sweat and the muscles in his thighs and arms were flexing and bunching as he worked. The sun shone on his gilded hair and she thought of the merman again.

Cursing her romantic notions, she wiped the dazed look off her face before she pushed open the allotment gate, calling, 'Evening!'

Startled, Levan looked up before breaking into a grin. 'Hello.'

'You seem hard at work,' she said.

'Just thought I'd help your mum out in the veg patch while I waited for you to arrive.'

When she'd first heard that Levan had been 'doing a spot of gardening', Eden had been amazed her mum had let anyone near her precious veg patch. 'I thought she was at home . . .'

'She was in the middle of digging this plot when she was called away to cover for a cottage changeover in St Just. Friend called Shefali? Both their cleaners called in sick and they had no one else, apparently. She really wanted to get these courgette plants in, so I said I'd do it. Do you want to look at the photos now?'

'I wouldn't want to stop you while you're helping Mum,' Eden said, rather reluctant to encourage him to put a shirt on. 'Why don't I give you a hand so we can get the job done quicker?'

He raised a surprised eyebrow. 'I'd love one, but you must have been working hard all day.'

'I have, but I don't mind. The exercise will do me good.' Finally tearing her gaze from his body, Eden headed inside, hoping to cool down – temporarily, at least. Levan obviously spent a lot of time with his top off. When he'd been doing his yoga, she hadn't noticed much of a tan line above the Speedos, either. Inside the cottage, Eden put on her boots and braced herself for an hour or so next to a half-naked Levan.

Sardine sauntered out after her and lay down in a pool of evening sunlight, watching them both at work like a feline chaperone. A welcome breeze stirred and the waves crashed against the cliffs beyond the allotments.

'It's amazing how well these plants do with the salt spray

and gales,' Levan said, stooping over the soil, thigh muscles taut.

Eden averted her eyes from his delicious rear view. 'The thick walls help to protect them and we hardly ever have a frost,' she muttered, wishing for one now to cool her down.

Half an hour later, the job was finished and Eden asked, 'Fancy a beer while we look at these photos?'

'Sounds good.'

She fetched two bottles from home – Iris wouldn't have approved of not bothering with a 'proper glass' – and went inside Longships. Levan had put his T-shirt on, which Eden thought was a mixed blessing.

She joined him in the sitting room where he picked up a cardboard folder from the dresser.

'Here you go.'

Sitting down on the sofa, she slid the photographs out of the folder. They were a variety of sizes, most black and white but a few were colour Polaroids dating from the late sixties and early seventies.

They were all faded or damaged in some way, a couple with ragged holes through them.

'Sad that they're in such a state. I hope Morwenna can work her magic on them.'

'Oh, I'm sure she can work her magic on anything,' Levan said with a glint in his eye.

Eden wasn't sure if he was joking or not. 'She's away on a job at the moment so I haven't had time to ask her.'

She examined the photographs more closely and picked up one of Iris holding a reluctant tabby. 'That was Granny's first cat, Mackerel,' she said and smiled. 'I'm afraid all our cats have been named after fish ever since.'

'What? Like Sea Bass? Monkfish? Whale?' he said with mock solemnity.

She giggled. 'Nothing so exotic. I remember a Tuna though . . . that was my idea.'

One by one, she laid the photos on the table, finding it surreal to see her family's lives frozen in time before her.

Levan sat on the arm of the sofa, sipping his beer. 'I guess you've seen these before?' he said.

'Most of them, though not for years.' She pointed to a very faded and cracked black and white print. 'I don't recall this one at all.'

It showed four figures, two of them her grandparents. All the men were in uniform with jerseys and peaked caps. Grandad Walter had his arm around Iris's waist. The other two men stood a little apart, one with a pipe in his hand, the other holding another cat. Iris looked several months pregnant. It was strange to think that the 'bump' was her father and that one day, that unborn baby's genes would be passed down to her.

'That's Granny and Grandad here at Hartstone Lighthouse. I don't know who the other guys are, presumably the two keepers from his watch, judging by the uniforms.'

'That's what Iris told me,' Levan said.

'I suppose it's not surprising I haven't seen all of her pictures, considering she has boxes of them. When she moved to the Seabreeze Court from her previous house in Penzance after it got too much for her, we didn't have time to go through all her stuff. I don't think she'd have wanted to throw any out, either. These are her only records of the past – not like now, when a digital image is there forever.'

Eden picked up another photo she had seen before. The

picture had a crease that cut across the corner, almost severing it in two. It featured her granny and grandad with a little boy on the beach, squinting into the sun. Iris had a sundress on, her grandad was wearing a flat cap and her dad was in swimming trunks, proudly raising his bucket to the camera.

An unexpected lump rose in her throat and her eyes felt scratchy.

'They all look so happy . . .' she said, her voice cracking. 'I wish I'd known him longer.' Then she smiled up at Levan wryly. 'Sorry.'

'Don't be. You were all so close . . . It must be very hard to have lost your father so young. I think I'd find that tough even though I'm not close to my dad these days. I never was.'

Eden stared at him, amazed he'd let slip such a personal comment. 'It is bittersweet to see pictures of my dad but, as time's gone on, I try to focus on my happy memories – not that I can remember loads about him.'

Levan nodded and she ventured further, sensing this was a moment when he might open up for once.

'Are you sure your parents wouldn't manage to come to visit and see Hartstone? Will you regret not keeping in touch? For all your sakes?'

A small smile crept onto his lips, but so bitter that Eden was filled with sadness. 'If any of my lot want to see me, they know where to find me. We were never a happy family like you clearly are. Let's just say I didn't take the path in life they had planned out for me.'

'What path was that?' Eden said carefully.

'Oh, something important and prestigious.' He rolled his eyes. 'Not a lowly computer geek.'

'I don't think being a cyber security expert is lowly.'

He raised his bottle. 'Thank you. However by their standards, I can assure you it's very lowly indeed.' He hesitated, and his expression held so much turmoil – of struggle, longing and pain. Eden could feel the suppressed emotions and hear own heart beat a little faster.

She held her breath, sensing he wanted to say something important.

'Eden, I . . .' he began.

'Yes?' she said gently.

In a heartbeat, the struggle melted away, smoothed by his easy manner. 'I only wanted to thank you and your family for making me so welcome. It does mean a lot. I hope – I hope I won't let you down.'

She frowned at him. 'Let us down? Why would you?'

'I was joking,' he said, then laughed. 'Although I still feel guilty for taking such precious memories from your gran's house without asking first, even if it's turned out OK in the end.' He picked up the photo of her granny and grandad with the other keepers and said firmly, 'You think Morwenna can restore these?'

'Oh, I'm sure she can,' Eden said, adding archly, 'Morwenna can do anything when she puts her mind to it.'

'I'm sure she'd say the same about you.'

'Maybe . . .' her voice tailed off. 'I'll take these photos with me, then. I need to grab a shower and a bite to eat.'

'Of course,' Levan said. She saw him swallow and a flicker of indecision cross his face. 'Although you could always eat here.'

'Oh . . .' She should really be going now, and she felt torn between wanting to linger and enjoy more time with him – and putting herself out of the way of feeling ever more attracted to him. If she stayed, he might reveal more about his mysterious life before he'd turned up at Lighthouse Cottages. Or she might reveal more about herself than was wise. Attraction and wariness pulled her in two different directions.

'If you don't have plans, that is,' he added. 'Of course, I would have asked your mum, too, if she wasn't working.'

Eden's feelings changed to a mix of relief and disappointment on hearing that Levan would have included her mother in the invitation. His intentions must have been 'honourable' in that case – or at least platonic.

'I don't have plans,' she said. 'Are you sure you have enough food?'

'No worries about that. I bought enough hake and samphire in Newlyn to last a couple of nights. Does that sound OK?'

It was more than OK, and her mouth positively watered at the prospect. All of a sudden, she was starving. Why go home and ping a microwave meal when she could have fresh fish with veggies straight from the earth?

She needed no more persuasion. 'OK. Thanks. I'll pop home, have a shower and bring a couple of beers as my contribution.'

'Great idea. See you when you're ready.'

Chapter Fourteen

Eden wasn't sure how she would ever be ready for an intimate dinner with Levan but, somehow, she showered, dried her short locks and pulled on a T-shirt dress. She almost put some make-up on but then thought it would be odd for a casual impromptu dinner with a neighbour so contented herself with drying her hair and applying a coat of mascara and some lip balm.

Slipping her feet into her sandals, she went round to Longships, two more bottles of beer in hand. Both the front door and porch door were unlocked. Calling out a hello, she ventured through the open front door and into the sitting room. With no sign of him, she carried on through to the kitchen where a pan was bubbling on the stove and the rear door was open.

'Oh!' Levan almost jumped out of his skin when he saw her and Eden's cheeks turned hot with embarrassment when he walked in wearing boxer shorts and nothing else.

'Sorry! I must be early. I'd no idea you were – er – not ready for me.'

Levan grinned and held up a bunch of herbs. 'No problem,' he said with a wry grin. 'I just finished having a shower and popped out to get some parsley from the pot by the back door. The potatoes are on. I'll cook the fish now you're here, though maybe I should put some proper clothes on first.'

Don't bother on my account, she thought, then told herself off again.

'Anything I can do?' she asked, quickly adding, 'With the dinner, I mean.'

'Nope, just chill out. I'll put those beers in the fridge for now.'

Having been a holiday home, Levan's cottage had always been well-maintained and stylish. With its contemporary furnishings and blue and cream seaside colour scheme, it was as brochure perfect as a hundred other Cornish holiday homes. Having never actually been lived in by permanent residents since it was converted, it was all as neat and clutter-free as if it had been brand new, which was what most guests were looking for. It certainly still didn't give any real clue as to Levan's taste and personality and Eden wondered if he'd put his own stamp on it over time, or if he preferred it with the 'everyman' appeal it had now.

'Sorry about that. I'm decent now,' he said, walking back into the room.

Still feeling flushed, Eden wouldn't have described him that way. He might have thrown on a shirt, but in the heat had left it open halfway, which only served to highlight his tanned chest. Barefoot and with his hair loose, there was an untamed air about him that gave her delicious shivers.

When he handed her a beer, his fingers brushed hers and her stomach did a full gymnastics routine. She hadn't wanted to sleep with a man so much in a very long time. Perhaps she'd never wanted a man so much ever.

Every instinct told her to run out of the cottage right that minute, but it was impossible. She couldn't run away from a man who lived on the other side of her bedroom wall.

She was stuck with him, and was glad when the meal was ready so she could at least have the distraction of eating.

She speared a morsel of fish with her fork and dipped it into a homemade salsa. 'You'd pay a fortune for this in a fish restaurant down in Newlyn.'

'Maybe, though I'm sure they actually know how to cook a fish.' He tipped the beer to his lips.

Eden sipped hers, the chilled bottle cooling her warm palms.

Music drifted through the open door. The cottage guests next door were having a barbecue and playing Bruce Springsteen loudly.

Sardine sauntered in and sat by Levan's side, gazing up at the plates.

'Sardine! Who invited you?' Eden said. 'You've had your tea. You're not getting fish too! There won't be any leftovers, anyway.'

Levan swept his hand over the cat's back and Sardine purred. 'I don't mind. He seems to enjoy exploring the cottage.'

She tutted. 'I'm sorry he's so cheeky. I can take him out if he's a nuisance.'

Sardine jumped onto the sofa and started washing his paws.

'He's made himself at home now,' Levan said.

He wasn't the only one, Eden thought. Here she was at Levan's table, eating a meal he'd cooked, with veg her mum had grown. Her grandmother had been to lunch with him and the cat clearly loved him.

After dinner, they sat at the table, finishing their beers. Levan watched her as she drained the bottle and she grew warm under his scrutiny.

Levan had seduced them all, like the merman in the story. He'd bewitched them with his golden hair and his green eyes and his charm. The story ended with him luring the daughter away from her sweetheart and over a cliff to the depths of the sea, where she lived with him forever and could never return home. Actually, she thought dreamily, that didn't sound so bad . . .

Wow. She checked the beer bottle label. This must be a strong brew.

'What are you smiling at?' Levan was watching her, amused.

'That my cat, who doesn't like visitors and dislikes other animals, has decided to sleep in your cottage.'

'Maybe he's a good judge of character?'

'Well, he hisses at the post lady and she's lovely.'

'So, Sardine thinks I'm OK,' he said. 'But I guess the jury is still out on me?' he asked, fixing her with his gaze until she wanted to look away.

It was, but he was winning them over and gaining their trust. She wasn't going to tell him that, though.

She laughed nervously, hoping to avoid an answer.

'Though to be fair,' he added. 'The first time I met you, I was upside down in only my Speedos.'

'Granny made me watch!'

'So, you *were* spying on me?' He gave her a stern look and she wasn't a hundred percent sure he was joking.

'No! Not exactly spying.' She burned with embarrassment.

'It's fine, I'd have looked too. If I'd seen you doing yoga in your swimsuit, I mean.' He wrinkled his nose, and looked a little awkward. 'Sorry, I didn't mean that to sound weird, but I am only human after all.'

Eden realised that her face wasn't the only part of her that was warming. Her frozen heart was thawing a little towards Levan too. Finally, *finally*, he'd shown her the touch of vulnerability she'd been hoping for. He'd lifted the corner on the cloak he'd thrown around himself. She liked him for it, genuinely liked him. And wow, he was so sexy, she didn't know how she was going to cope.

'Oh my God!'

Something skittered over her bare toes. Sardine shot across the room. He had dropped a mouse on the toes of her sandals. 'Oh, it's still alive!'

The mouse darted forward. Sardine pounced but Levan got there first, grabbing a basket that had contained a blanket and throwing it over the mouse.

'I am so sorry! You devil!' She scooped the cat up but he wriggled from her arms while Levan picked up the basket.

'Is it dead?'

'Still alive and very, very pissed off. I'll let it out,' he said.

She could have got rid of the mouse herself but was more than happy to delegate. 'Well away from the cottage, please. Mum hates mice. I don't mind them so much but I don't want them in the roastery. I can't blame Sardine, though, he's only doing his job.'

With the mouse in the basket, Levan hurried outside.

She went to the window to see him heading out of the garden, the basket in his arms. She heard him saying, 'Come on, buddy. You don't want to end up as a gourmet snack for Sardine.' He glanced back over his shoulder at the cottage.

Worried he'd see her watching him, Eden flopped onto the

sofa. Here was a man who knew how to cook a piece of fish, who made her laugh and was happy to scoop up a live mouse and take it outside. Simon would have been standing on the sofa on the phone to Rentokil by now.

Here was a man who she was finally getting to know a little more about. Someone who'd had a difficult relationship with his parents and was seeking some peace in this remote and beautiful location. She understood that desire; she empathised with it.

Could he be any more perfect for her than he was? Had some fairy godmother sent him to live next door specially for her? Or was it a particularly wicked demon who wanted to tempt her?

With a huge sigh, she rested her head back and closed her eyes.

Her whole body yearned to run out and drag him inside his cottage. She'd fling her arms around him and kiss him so hard it hurt. He'd kiss her back as passionately, as if he'd wanted to from the moment he saw her. Then she wanted him to take her hand and lead her up the cottage stairs to the bedroom. She'd kick the door shut and they'd rip each other's clothes off and have wild sex that shook the metal bedstead in his room.

Then, exhausted and unbearably smug, she'd slink off home to her mum's . . .

Oh wait, that part didn't fit with the rest. Forget that.

She refined the fantasy slightly. Her mother would be away for some reason so, at some point, she'd leave his cottage. It might be days later and everyone would wonder why she hadn't opened the container or delivered any orders and Morwenna would have left a hundred messages on her phone . . .

'Are you OK?'

Her eyes flew open. She scrambled up from the sofa.

'Fine. Fine. I was having a little rest, that's all. Busy day. The beer . . .'

'Don't apologise. Stay there as long as you like.'

'No, I'm fine.' She stood up straight, hoping he wouldn't notice the flush in her cheeks. 'How was Mr Mouse?'

'Fine. As fine as you can be when you've escaped death by a whisker. He'll live to fight another day unless Sardine gets to him again.'

'Good. Great . . .' Eden feigned a yawn.

His eyes shone with amusement. 'You must be tired.'

'Yes. It's been a busy day and I still have paperwork to do. I should go home.'

'OK. Don't work too hard and have a safe journey.'

'Ha ha.' She smiled. 'Thanks for dinner and saving the mouse. I'll – um – see you very soon.'

'You will.'

Eden scuttled out, inexplicably feeling like the mouse under Sardine's paw. Yet not hating it. Wanting to be swallowed up.

'Shit.'

Back in her own cottage, she went up to the bathroom and splashed her face in cold water. The bathroom window was open and she looked outside towards the sun sinking to the horizon. There were several other cars in the car park, all belonging to guests.

A couple were heading out for a meal, by the look of their smart clothes. They got into a people carrier and drove off.

She was about to turn away but something made her look back towards the car park.

Her heart beat faster.

It *couldn't* have been.

When the Merc had driven away, she'd thought she'd seen a man standing by the door of a BMW, staring up at Wolf Rock. He must have been hidden by the people carrier . . . but he wasn't there now. She pushed open the window a little more and squinted into the sun to see if he was back inside the BMW, but it was impossible to tell behind the reflections on the car windows.

No. There was no one there and the man – if he had been outside the car – could not be Simon, even though she'd thought it was him for a split second. She was being paranoid. Simon's letter had thrust him into the forefront of her mind again. He'd never had a BMW, he always sneered at people who owned them, and besides, he had no money left to buy one now.

Most of all, there was no way he'd have dared to come down to Land's End to confront her.

And yet . . . a tiny voice nagged at her . . . Simon would dare anything.

Chapter Fifteen

'I feel like a spy,' Eden said, as Levan let her into Longships Cottage evening after next.

'Maybe a new career?' he joked, with an eyebrow raise. 'I think you did incredibly well to get the photos back to Iris without her noticing.'

'Granny popped to the loo so I whipped them out of my carrier bag and put them back inside. I was so worried she'd ask me to look at them while Morwenna was scanning them, or notice they were gone. Thank goodness it only took a couple of days.'

'Well, you can relax, now,' he said, handing her a beer.

'Hmm,' Eden said. 'Maybe . . .' She rubbed her finger around the rim of the bottle.

Sensing her tension, he placed his beer on the table. 'What's up? Have you had another letter from Simon?'

'No. Nothing like that. It's probably my mind playing tricks on me but . . .'

'But, what?'

'Last night, after I left yours. In the twilight, I thought I

137

glimpsed something – a person – possibly – hanging around by my van.' She laughed nervously. 'I half expected to find a note tucked under the wipers.'

'You haven't, though?' Levan said, trying to sound calm while raging inside.

'No. Look, forget I said it. I'm hyper aware these days – since the letter. I'm sure it's nothing to worry about. It probably wasn't him and, don't forget, I'd had a couple of beers during dinner. This guy was most likely a nosy tourist and I was fooled by a trick of the light.' She took a gulp of beer and cradled the bottle.

'You're probably right.' He smiled. 'But if you ever need me, you know exactly where I am.' He became far more serious. 'You can call me any time night or day.'

'I know that, thanks,' she said, touched by his strength of feeling. 'Though I doubt very much I'll ever need to call on you to ride to my rescue.'

'I lost my white charger long ago, if I ever had one . . .' He sipped his beer. 'Have you made a decision about answering his letter?'

'Yes. I'm not going to. Actually it was while I was lying awake wondering if I had glimpsed him that I made my mind up. He's dominated my thoughts far too much lately, so I'm going to ignore him.'

'Good,' he said. 'It can't have been an easy decision.'

'No, it wasn't. It's been driving me mad, to be honest. Everything seemed to be flowing along nicely for me again and he hurls this big boulder into the river and now I have to choose which way to go. I really wish people wouldn't present you with choices. Does that sound weird?'

'Not at all. Especially when it's a choice you didn't ask to have to make. That's what people like Simon try to do: gaslight you into wondering if you're wrong and they're right. Try to manipulate you into thinking you're in the wrong.'

'That's just how it was. I've tried to tell myself that a hundred times but still felt I was to blame by being naïve . . . but it is hard.' Her voice faltered and she downed a large glug of beer. When she looked up at him, he was horrified to find her eyes glistening with tears.

'I think it's time you knew the whole story of what happened between us and why I am so wary about letting him anywhere near my life or the people I love.'

Levan wanted to throw his arms around her and hold her, but he didn't dare.

'Go on,' he said softly.

She took a deep breath before continuing. 'The long and the short of it is that Simon went to jail for fraud. He scammed two women out of their life savings, but that's only half of what he did. He spent our money and he raised loans on the house behind my back. He had a mistress and he was planning to marry her too.'

Levan swore softly. 'You mean he was actually going to commit bigamy?'

'Oh, yes,' Eden said, with the kind of bitter smile that had clearly come from harsh experience. 'It all came out during the investigation. He planned to stay married to me, presumably so he could leech off us both. His mistress had even booked a venue – the date was less than a month away when it all came out.'

'Jesus. He went that far?'

'Believe me, there are *no* limits to Simon's lies,' she declared, then seemed to deflate before Levan's eyes. 'Now he claims he's on the straight and narrow, that he's changed and might die, but I don't believe it. People like Simon don't change. Ever. And I still don't know whether to believe him because I still . . .'

'Because you still care about him?' he murmured, on the verge of telling her he felt her pain, and knew how impossible it could be to let go of feelings for someone you'd once thought was your life, your future. But this moment was hers.

She heaved a big sigh. 'Sometimes, a tiny chink of my armour lets him in. Most times I hate him for what he did to me and other people but, annoyingly, I still care whether he lives or dies. Like I said that first day I told you about him, I might feel like pushing him off a cliff, but I don't want him to be ill or in pain. He doesn't deserve that.'

'Then that's not hate. You don't hate him,' he said, knowing what real hatred looked, sounded and felt like. 'Though it sounds like he's cut you too deeply to ever be forgiven.'

'Yes. He has. The money and the other women – well, the money's gone and I've made a new start. As for the women, I realised long ago that they were victims, too. They were taken in by him as well and suffered. Anyway, even if I could forgive him for hurting me and them, there's something else that I will never be able to forget and always blame him for.'

Levan's stomach swirled with unease because he sensed he'd hate what she had to say next. 'What happened?' he said, making his words as gentle as he could.

'I was ten weeks pregnant when the police knocked on the door to say he'd been arrested.'

Levan's shock was replaced by anger at the pain Simon had inflicted on Eden, but he spoke as gently as he could. 'I am so sorry that you went through this.'

All she seemed able to do was nod, though the nervous swallow was unmissable. 'I'd wanted to start a family,' she said. 'Simon hadn't discouraged me. Knowing that he planned to somehow live this double – triple – life with other women, he still let me believe that we could bring up a child together.

'We'd never been happier. He'd been working away a lot – a lie of course, as he was leading a double life – but he'd said he'd try to get a job that didn't involve so much travel.

'A few days after I found out, I miscarried. The doctors had said it was impossible to say if the shock had caused it; I might have lost the baby anyway. The house was repossessed and I had to come back here to Mum's.'

'Even though you were the innocent one and didn't do anything to deserve your suffering.' Levan's loathing for Simon intensified by the minute.

'Yes. I lost my baby on top of my independence . . .' Eden faltered. 'Anyway, I found out he'd been away and, during that one night, he drained our current and savings accounts. Unbeknown to me, he'd bought first-class tickets to Panama.'

'So he was actually planning to flee to somewhere with no extradition treaty?'

'The police thought so.' She laughed bitterly. 'It's crazy, isn't it? Little Eden from the lighthouse involved with a master criminal.'

'Except he wasn't a master criminal, because he got caught,' Levan said contemptuously. 'Thank God.'

'The judge said he was a narcissist and a fantasist, a sociopath with no real concept of the consequences of his actions on those around him. So,' she took a breath, 'he was convicted of fraud. As he hadn't *actually* married the mistress, the police decided he couldn't be charged with bigamy though

I'm convinced he would have gone through with the marriage if he hadn't been caught.'

She had to pause for breath again before she could go on. Levan could feel her reliving the pain and shock of that time and he raged inwardly at Simon.

'He got three years in prison though he only served eighteen months. Then six months ago he was released for "good behaviour" and ended up back at his parents'. He's been there for a few months since. I'm not sure exactly how long . . . I'm never sure what to believe with Simon. Even at his trial, he was insisting he hadn't really done "serious" damage with his lies. He was so deluded and convinced that his multiple lives were all valid – normal for him.'

'Some people cling onto a nugget of truth in their lives and then build a fantasy around it. The core is based on a real experience, and the rest is embroidery and froth but real to them,' Levan murmured.

'You're saying Simon was a fantasist who couldn't help himself?'

'Maybe. Maybe he was just a liar. A champion liar.'

'Yes, that's just it,' Eden said. 'Lying was something he was very good at, like – like baking or playing an instrument. He was the Olympic champion of lying and he liked the feeling. He didn't care who he hurt in the process.'

'Other people only had value for him as far as they could be conned, or scammed, to feed his ego. Maybe some people can't help their lies,' Levan said.

'I don't buy that,' Eden declared. 'You can always choose to tell the truth.'

Levan grew cold, and told himself it was a post-run chill. 'No excuses?' he murmured, his gut tightening.

'I can't think of any.'

There was a profound regret in her tone that resonated with him. He felt they had a deep connection, born of past experience. Was that silly?

However, he was sure Eden didn't share his mystical notions.

'Yet Simon's lies, his deceptions, are history now. I *have* risen after he threw me down,' she declared. 'And it wasn't him the other night, it was just the spectre of him that I've allowed to haunt my life for far too long. I won't answer his bloody letter and he will never hurt me again.'

Chapter Sixteen

'Sorry, Dion, can you say that again? It's blowing a hoolie and I can hardly hear.'

Slipping into a shelter on Penzance seafront, Levan clamped his mobile to his ear.

The waves slapped the sea wall and a mob of angry seagulls was fighting over a chip wrapper. Although it would be July in less than a week, the Cornish weather had clearly decided to revert to April. The stormy skies matched his mood since he'd heard the full story of what had happened to Eden at the hands of that scumbag, Simon.

'Where are you?' Dion shouted down the phone into his ear. 'A secure location?'

Levan almost laughed. He guessed the public would not be impressed to find an alleged cyber security expert using a seafront shelter as a 'secure location'.

'You could say that,' he said. 'Anyway, did I hear right: you haven't seen my mystery stalker again and you don't have a clue who it is?'

'Well . . . if you want to put it like that, yes.'

Apparently, the latest facial recognition software had failed to identify a man loitering outside a building that monitored information of potentially national significance.

'I'm not that surprised. The guy was a long way from the cameras and looking down, with a hood over half his face. The tech can't work miracles.' Levan pressed the phone to his ear as the gulls screeched.

'It's frustrating . . .' Dion said, sounding downcast.

'It is, but there's been a potential development,' Levan said.

'What development?' Dion shot back.

'It could be nothing,' Levan said, shirking back inside the shelter as a large wave crashed over the seafront. 'And I can't possibly think this guy, Simon, has an interest in *me*. However, he's been hassling Eden to meet him and she thought she might have seen him hanging around the cottages a few days ago.'

Hassling. Levan felt it was such a pathetic word to describe the torment that Simon had inflicted on Eden, but he wasn't going to reveal her private feelings to Dion. He only needed to know what was strictly necessary.

'Did she, now?' Dion said.

'Possibly. She's been trying to convince herself it wasn't him and I didn't want to worry her but I think it could have been. He's no idea I even exist, though.'

'Unless he saw you with her.'

'What?' Levan scoffed. 'Digging over an allotment?'

'He might think you're doing more than planting spuds.'

'Harvesting them, Dion. You're never going to make a gardener, are you?'

Dion laughed, then was serious again. 'I'm back on

Wednesday. Let's meet then and maybe we'll have more on this mystery stalker – and you can try to find out more about Simon in the meantime.'

'Sounds good. Hopefully Eden's wrong about Simon and the stalker is just some idiot who's watched too many YouTube videos and fancies himself as a keyboard warrior. See you on Wednesday night.'

Having ended the call, Levan emerged from the shelter and grimaced at the leaden skies gathering to the west. Spray was breaking on the sea wall, and he could easily be soaked. He'd better get a move on. He wasn't only heading up into town for the deli; he wanted to visit the bookshop and choose a birthday present for Iris.

A birthday present . . . Once again, he reflected on how entwined he'd become in the lives of his neighbours. However, it was too late to disentangle himself now. He felt he had a responsibility for Eden's safety – perhaps that of her family, too – where Simon was concerned.

It was late afternoon when he returned, having called in at the data centre en route to do some work. The rain was now torrential, and he had to jog from the car park to Longships, a jute carrier bag in one hand.

'Hello!' Standing inside the porch of Wolf Rock, Iris called to him over the hedge.

With his shopping and her present in his bag, Levan was reluctant to stop, but smiled a greeting and spoke to her over the hedge.

'Hi there, Iris.'

She nodded at his bag. 'Dinner?'

Thunder rumbled overhead. Rain ran down his face. 'Yes, I just need to put this stuff into the fridge.'

'You'd better hurry up. You'll be drenched standing out here.'

'Well, I would if my neighbour didn't keep me talking on the doorstep.'

She chuckled. 'If you fancy a chat, I'm here on my own. Sally's working late. It's her turn to be on emergency call at the cottage company.'

Levan was torn. He really didn't want to hang around but he hated the idea of Iris sitting by herself feeling lonely. 'Well, if you're sure, I *could* pop in for a little while. Then I have to get some work done,' he said. He was also conscious of her birthday book, only partially protected from the rain by the jute carrier bag.

'Haven't you been at work already?'

'Most of the day, yes, but I have a deadline on a project . . .'

'Oh, I don't want to interrupt anything important.'

Her face fell and Levan melted. 'I can afford to take a quick break and a coffee, if that suits you?'

Her eyes shone again, and he was reminded of Eden the other evening when they were gardening together and she was relaxed and happy. 'That would be lovely.'

'OK, I'll come over in a couple of minutes.'

When Levan returned, Iris was in the sitting room, having made two coffees and brought them through.

'Horrible weather for the end of June,' she said.

Rain lashed the panes and the wind howled. You could barely see the sea for the clouds and mist. He could well imagine how much the lighthouse was needed on a day like this, even if it was high summer.

'It's pretty grim,' he said.

'Makes me melancholy.' Iris sighed. 'I like my own company

but today has been wearing. I've been on my own all day since Eden dropped me off. Sally was called away and Eden should have been home by now.'

'Is she still at the coffee container?'

'No, she closed early with the weather being bad but she had deliveries to do. I don't think she'll be back until late. Not that you're second best, of course. I wanted to talk to you anyway. On your own,' Iris added. 'About the photographs . . .'

Levan's stomach clenched with remorse. Had she found out about what he'd done? Although Eden had approved it, he still felt awkward about his 'theft' and he braced himself to confess all, even if it meant ruining Iris's birthday surprise.

'Oh?'

Iris unconsciously fiddled with her wedding ring. 'They've brought back memories,' she said wistfully. 'Good and bad.'

He relaxed a fraction. Perhaps she didn't know, after all. 'Old photographs always do that,' he said, thinking of the times he'd scrolled through pictures on his own phone – now deleted – or looked at friends' pages on social media.

'Do you want to talk about them?' he asked. 'If you're worried about anything, I'm a good listener,' he added gently.

She glanced up at him. 'I know you are. You don't let on much about yourself, though, do you?'

He smiled. 'There's not much of interest to tell – not compared to someone like you, who has a lifetime of adventures and experience to share.'

'Pah.' Iris snorted. 'You're a charmer, too. That'll get you into trouble, you know, and if I were you . . .' She stopped again, head shaking. 'No, I mustn't. I'll get myself into trouble too – with Eden.'

Levan's skin tingled and he was immediately on the alert.

148

'Now, why would you get into trouble with Eden for talking to me?'

'Because she'd say I was interfering and she'd be mortified to know I'd spoken to you.'

'I promise I won't tell her if you don't want me to,' he said, lightly.

'I'm sure you won't.' Iris peered at him, her lips pressed together. He felt she could read his mind. 'Soul of discretion, you. Good listener, handsome too . . . *far* too handsome.'

He rolled his eyes. 'Now, Iris, you're making me blush.'

'I'm not sure anything could make you blush.'

He grew uncomfortable. 'Maybe not blush, but I am embarrassed. I can assure you I don't think of myself as handsome. It never crosses my mind. My nose is too big for a start, and I've been told I snore.'

Also that he was a 'soft touch', Levan thought, plus a 'family disgrace' (his father) a 'useless twat' (his brother) and, worst of all, 'weak'. That final insult had been the cruellest blow of all, because it had come from the woman he loved and thought had loved him back.

Oblivious to the turmoil of memories, Iris laughed gently. 'I won't ask who told you that you snore.'

'Various people, actually, male and female,' he tried to smile with his eyes as he spoke. 'I was at boarding school,' he added.

'Well, well.' She scrutinised him so hard he almost had to glance away. 'You're a lovely, clever, kind man, I'm pretty sure of that as far as I ever can be.' She sighed. 'But that's not enough for Eden. You're too – charming – and she'll never trust a man who's a charmer ever again, not after that louse, Simon.'

'Luckily, I'm not trying to gain Eden's trust and I understand her wariness of any new men. She has mentioned Simon to me, briefly.'

'She trusted him, though me and her mother never really liked him. Sally tried to hint to her. You mustn't tell her we said that to you!' Iris said, clasping her hands together and sounding anxious all of a sudden. 'Here I go again, telling you things I oughtn't to.'

'Don't worry, Eden's told me herself that she wishes she'd never met Simon. Perhaps she knows how you and Sally felt and regrets not listening to you?'

'Maybe, but we rarely listen to people trying to stop us from doing what we want to, do we? It's part of growing up and rebelling.'

'That's true.' Levan was thrust back to all the times he'd tried to follow the future his parents had mapped out for him. It had been a path he thought he wanted but had ended in disaster. It was how he'd ended up where he was at this moment: listening to a woman with ninety years of wisdom and secrets of her own.

'Did you listen to your parents, Iris?'

'I had no choice back in those days. What Mum and Dad said, went. I didn't leave home until the day I married Walter.'

'But you were happy.'

'In many ways, though it was a hard life at times. I had to follow where he led. I had no choice. It was later in life that I looked back and regretted not being able to follow my own path.'

'Oh?' he said, glad to keep the conversation about Iris, not himself. 'Where would your own path have led?'

'I don't know for sure, but maybe abroad. I'd like to have travelled the world like you have. You know, I envied some of the older village girls who joined the forces in the war. Even though they were in danger, they had exciting lives. Two of them worked in the wartime telegraph station in the valley. You know the place? It has a museum now.'

'I do,' Levan said, also privy to the fact that the former station still hid its own modern-day communications secrets.

'They went off to Malta and Singapore. That could have been me . . . though one of them lost her life in the Japanese camps, poor thing. Some of the other girls married later in life than me. Some never married at all. When I was older, I began to imagine what a different life I might have had.' Iris looked at the window, into the mist, wistfully. 'It wasn't to be. My path was to marry Walter, that was all there was to it.'

Her path. Strange choice of words, Levan thought, almost as if she'd had no choice. 'For what it's worth, I think you've taken a brave path, Iris, and led a heroic life – you and your family,' he said, feeling sorry that Iris might have felt her life was wasted in any way, even though he could understand her frustrations.

'Hmm. They were saving lives . . . but at the cost of their own and – though I'd never admit to Sally or Eden – of ours. I often wished we'd chosen a different route.' She turned her eyes on him, the same searching brown eyes of her daughter and granddaughter. The same wistful hint behind them, of loss and regret. 'You know what I mean?'

He felt the hairs on his arms rise a fraction. 'Yes, I do . . . but we can't go back and change the past.'

'Do you want to?' she asked.

'No. Not all of it. And if I changed one small aspect, everything else would collapse.'

'Like dominoes?' Iris said. 'Walter and Roger played a lot of dominoes on the lighthouse. No one could ever beat them . . .'

'Exactly like that,' he said.

'You know, I'd like to invite you to our book club,' Iris said.

'That's very kind of you.'

'Don't worry, I'm not going to. It can get very heated. I think you'd be shocked. Two women once almost had a physical fight over *Jane Eyre*. They were standing over each other, waving their copies.'

He laughed. 'Over *Jane Eyre*? Why?'

'Over Mr Rochester of course,' Iris said. 'And whether he was a villain or a hero. I had to break it up and ask them to leave.'

'Wow. Book club sounds dangerous.' Levan was relieved to find her more like her old self again.

'It can be – but only to your faith in human nature. Anyway, it's safer for everyone if you don't come.'

'Oh? Why's that?'

'I've a feeling there would be no reading done at all.'

He was saved from replying by the sound of the door rattling.

'Oh! That sounds like Eden!' Iris pushed herself up. 'I'm glad she's home. I don't like the thought of her out on these wet busy roads, with the tourists driving like maniacs. No patience, some of them . . .'

'I'll head off.' Levan got up.

'No, you stay. I've made a lovely fish pie.'

'It sounds wonderful, but I really will have to pass this time. I've got to prepare a big presentation for tomorrow.' Levan winced. He ought to be good at fibbing by now, but it was getting harder with the Carricks.

Eden walked in. 'Hello, Gra— oh! Hi, Levan.'

'Hi there.'

Iris embraced her. 'You look tired? Has it stopped raining? I've been really worried about you out on those roads. I was just telling Levan.'

Again, Levan was seized by guilt. Iris had been telling him far more than her fears for Eden on the roads. He felt he'd been privy to some secrets that he oughtn't to know about. The past few days had reminded him how quickly and deeply he'd been drawn into the lives of the Carricks – of Eden especially – when he should have tried much harder to avoid that. But he just couldn't seem to stay away. He cursed his lack of willpower once more.

He exchanged a glance with Eden and gave her a smile, but she didn't smile back.

'I'm absolutely fine, Granny,' she said, with a kiss on the cheek for her grandmother. 'How have you been here on your own? Mum said she'd had to stay at the office to cover emergency duty.'

'I've been OK. I made a fish pie and read my book and then Levan arrived and we've had a lovely chat.' Iris pouted. 'He won't stay for dinner though.'

'Oh?'

The knot of guilt in his stomach tightened further. 'I mustn't intrude any longer.'

Iris turned to him in dismay. 'Oh, you aren't intruding! You're practically one of the family, isn't he, Eden?'

He decided not to catch Eden's eye, wondering what her response might be.

'I'm not sure Levan wants fish again,' she said evenly enough, perhaps not wanting to give away any hint of what her feelings towards him might be.

'Again?' Iris said with a keen glance at both of them.

'I really am supposed to be working . . .' Levan cut in quickly, feeling he might be outstaying his welcome.

'But you have to *eat*. You told me so yourself and I bet you were planning on having some rabbit-food salad or cheese on toast. You need a proper meal, and my fish pie is the best, if I say so myself. Isn't it, Eden?'

'I can't argue with that, Granny,' Eden said, in a tone that let Levan know she would have liked to argue with everything else Iris had said about him staying and being one of the family.

'It's settled then!' Iris declared. 'It only needs twenty minutes in the oven. I'll go and pop some of your mum's spinach in to go with it while you two relax and have a good chat.'

He cringed as he realised what was happening. Iris was matchmaking them.

'I'll get changed,' Eden muttered. 'I'm filthy after working in the container and delivering coffee all day.'

Whereas he, thought Levan, had just been shopping and doing boring computer stuff. But as he was now forced to 'relax and chat' to her, he decided to use the opportunity to find out more about Simon.

She returned in jeans and a top, a glass of lemonade in her hand.

'Granny won't let me help her,' she said, sinking onto the sofa.

'I'd have offered as well, but she seems to want to do it all herself. I actually really didn't mean to stay, but your grandmother is hard to resist,' he said.

'You've noticed?' she said with a wry smile.

'I'll have dinner and then leave you alone.'

154

He saw Eden give a huge sigh and lean back against the sofa with her eyes closed. 'Busy day?'

Eden nodded and downed a swig of her lemonade. Lively chatter outside drew their attention. It was Iris talking to one of the cottage guests.

Levan took his chance while Iris was out of hearing. 'Have you heard any more from Simon?' he said.

'No. No . . .' She hesitated.

'What?'

'It's nothing. He hasn't been in contact and I must be getting paranoid.' She rolled her eyes.

'I'm sensing a "but" on the way. What's this "nothing"?'

'As I was packing up tonight at the container, a car passed by. They do all the time, of course – but this one slowed down for no reason. I thought it must have been a customer checking to see if we were open. They didn't stop, though.'

'Why did you think it was suspicious?'

'I could have sworn it was the same car that was in the car park – an old black BMW with a crumpled bumper.'

Levan's skin prickled with unease.

She shook her head as though to clear it. 'After what happened, it's hard to trust people.'

'I promise you, I do know what you mean,' he said. 'When the person you love – loved – lets you down when you needed them most, it's devastating . . .' He leaned forward. She stared at him, while his next words hung by a thread. The urge to confess all, to remove the burden from his chest, was so great.

'Dinner's ready!'

Iris stood framed in the kitchen doorway, red-faced and beaming.

'Smells great,' Levan said, getting to his feet.

Throughout dinner, Levan let the chatter wash over him, his thoughts very much focused on Eden's revelation that the BMW man was back.

Declining a pudding, Levan went back to his cottage, mulling over every nugget of information Eden had revealed. This stalker, the BMW man and Simon could be the same person. He'd never met the man yet he loathed him, but he reminded himself not to judge too harshly. Simon obviously had some kind of narcissistic personality disorder, and mental health problems could seize anyone.

He looked out of the window to see Iris watering her plants.

A chill seeped into his bones at the idea of Simon entering the lives of women he'd come to care about more than he'd ever expected. He resolved to find out what the man was up to – even if wading in on other people's business had already caused him enough trouble for one lifetime.

Chapter Seventeen

'I know something's going on. I do hope you're not planning a big surprise party for me.'

Eden exchanged a glance with her mother as Iris confronted them in the sitting room at Wolf Rock the following morning. For some reason, she had decided that now was the moment for some straight talking. It made a change from worrying that Simon was watching.

Sally peered over her laptop and smiled benignly. 'Iris, you can rest assured that your birthday will just be like any other day.'

'You've told us so often that you don't want any fuss, Granny,' Eden said, feeling slightly guilty. 'We wouldn't dare go against your wishes.'

'Well . . . good,' Iris said. 'Because I wouldn't want a big do or anything like that. I'd be more than happy to have a few friends for tea at Seabreeze then spend the actual day with my family here at Lighthouse Cottages. I suppose you could ask Joe and Ravi if you like, and Morwenna if she's not swanning off up country, and maybe Levan if he's not too busy. I like being surrounded by young people rather than oldies all the time. It revives me.'

'So, a couple of small parties for select friends and family . . .' Sally said, with an amused glance at Eden. 'That would be OK?'

'Yes, but remember, Sonali, the warden at Seabreeze, is organising my do there. The other one *here* would be mainly for you and my friends. Then again, I'd be very happy to spend the day reading at home, of course. It would be a lot of work to organise a do for me, and I know how busy you all are.'

Hearing that her grandmother was already planning a birthday celebration of her own, and that secretly she would rather enjoy a little bit of 'fuss', Eden wanted to laugh, but Sally was poker-faced.

'Note taken,' she said solemnly. 'Um. Eden, would you mind looking at this tax return for me? I just can't get the hang of these new digital filing requirements. I don't know how you cope with all the bookkeeping for the business.'

'It's not easy, let me have a look.'

Eden pulled a chair up next to her mum, while both resolutely avoided Iris's eye. Her grandmother's attitude towards the party both amused and infuriated her. However, one thing was clear: despite her protestations, Granny would most definitely not be very happy to spend such a momentous day at home reading.

Besides, the barbecue at Lighthouse Cottages was already organised. All the people Iris had mentioned had already been invited plus several of Granny's friends from her book and swimming clubs, who were being chauffeured by Joe's partner, Ravi, who owned a people carrier. Joe was making an amazing cake that would be a replica of Hartstone Lighthouse, and was also bringing strawberry tarts and profiteroles for dessert. The fizz and cocktails were going to be rustled up by Ravi.

Presents had also been discussed and planned and purchased weeks before.

Eden and Sally had booked a weekend away for Iris and Sally at a hotel on the Roseland Peninsula, a place Iris had always longed to stay at but always thought way beyond her means. A friend at the cottage company Sally worked for had given them a very special rate.

The thought of Iris's face when she found out her birthday surprises lifted Eden's spirits as she worked hard in the roastery and café over the next couple of days. The season was in full swing, with demand for her products high. She'd persuaded Courtney to work full time for her once he'd worked his notice at the pub.

Being your own boss was amazing in so many ways, but man, was it hard work. At least, she hadn't seen any trace of the BMW man since the drive-by – and was now sure she was just being paranoid.

She was just clearing up after a day at the café when Morwenna sent her a message.

Can we meet tonight? It's about the photos.

With no more information to go on, Eden headed to the Surf Shack where Morwenna was waiting with two drinks and nachos.

'I got snacks,' she said with a grin. 'Thought you'd be starving.'

'Thanks. I am.' Eden scooped up some guacamole with the cheesy tortillas. 'So, how have you got on? Is there a problem with the pictures?'

'No, I just wanted to talk about them. I haven't quite finished the editing yet so I haven't brought them with me, but I'm pleased with the results.'

Eden suppressed her disappointment. 'The software can work wonders. Iris will think the prints are as fresh as the day she first saw them but I want them to be perfect, you know what I mean?'

'I'll do my very best, I promise,' Morwenna said solemnly. 'Do you know who all the dudes in the pictures are?'

'Well, Grandad and Dad, of course. There are two other lighthouse keepers in one of the shots. I can't remember their names, but Granny will.'

'I saw those two . . .' Morwenna dipped a tortilla and said casually, 'What about the cute little picture of your gran and her boyfriend?'

Eden's tortilla hovered above the dip. '*What* cute little picture?'

'The one that was tucked down the back of the group of Iris and the lighthouse keepers. I had to remove some of the pictures from the presentation wallet and it was lodged in the cardboard frame behind the photo. It's only small, not much bigger than a passport photo.'

Wenna popped the nacho in her mouth but Eden's own appetite had momentarily gone.

'I've no idea . . .' she said, wracking her brains. 'I didn't even know there was another photo in there. Why do you think it's Granny's boyfriend? You must mean Grandad Walter.'

Morwenna shook her head. 'No, it isn't him. Your grandad was dark-haired. This guy is blond . . . like Levan. Mystery man also has – sorry – nicer teeth so he must have had access to a much better dentist, or else been very lucky.' Morwenna smiled. 'Actually, he was lucky in every respect. Even with the Brylcreemed hair, he's a bit of a hottie.'

Eden was floored. She had to admit that Grandad Walter, while well-built and pleasant enough, could never have been described as a hottie.

'I haven't a clue who this guy can be. Granny's never mentioned him. Are you sure they're not just friends – they're definitely a couple?'

'Very much so! They're cosied up together and grinning like idiots. I think this blond man must have been an old flame of Iris's.'

'Now you've got me intrigued,' Eden said, while also adding she was a little shocked at the idea of her granny with another man. 'She's never mentioned anyone but my grandad . . .'

'Hmm. Maybe she didn't know that photo was lodged in the folder or didn't want it to be seen. Should I ignore it or restore it along with the others?'

'I don't know, and I don't know if I can ask her. She may not want us to know she had this fling . . .' Eden paused. 'Is she very young in it? Does it look like it was taken before she met Grandad?'

'I don't know, hun. It's hard to say.'

'That photo with the two keepers is from just after they married so we could compare it.'

'Good idea. Tell you what, why don't you come round to mine for a pizza tomorrow and we'll have a look. You can stay over if you like. We both need a girls' night in.'

When Eden got home, Levan was harvesting French beans in the setting sun, which seemed to have gilded his hair and torso.

After debating with herself for a few minutes, Eden took a drink out to him and dropped the photo of Iris and the mystery blond into the conversation.

'Has Granny said anything at all about a picture of her and a blond man that was tucked down the back of the presentation card?'

He frowned. 'No, she hasn't and I don't remember that particular one.'

'OK. Only, I didn't even know Granny had another boyfriend before she met Grandad Walter. I've always had the impression he was her first and only love.'

Levan cast her a quizzical look. 'Maybe she thought you might think less of her if she admitted to other relationships?'

'Of course we wouldn't,' Eden said, a little miffed at the suggestion. 'She's human, and she was young . . .' She hesitated. 'I could ask Mum, I suppose.'

'You could.'

'And Granny's definitely never ever mentioned another man to you?'

'She's hardly likely to,' he said.

'She likes you,' Eden persisted. 'I thought she might have taken you into her confidence.'

'We talk about books,' he replied with unaccustomed firmness. 'Not about her private life.' He smiled. 'Thanks for the drinks. I'd better finish getting in these beans for your mother.'

Chapter Eighteen

The next evening, Morwenna got out the folder on her kitchen table to show Eden.

She pulled out the pictures and laid them carefully on the wooden surface. All were yellowing and faded, some were torn and ripped.

'I've seen them all before, apart from this, of course.' Eden tapped the small photo of Iris with the mystery man. It had a small tear in one corner obscuring a brooch that Iris still liked to wear. She picked up the photo as if closer inspection might reveal the stranger's identity. Even in black and white, she could see he had light-coloured eyes, probably blue, and a not-quite-perfect nose that reminded her of someone else.

'And here are the restored monochrome versions,' Morwenna said, removing prints from another folder. 'Ta-da!'

Carefully, she laid them out next to their originals.

Eden gave a sharp intake of breath and a lump formed in her throat. 'Oh, Wenna. I can't believe it. They're so clear – so real . . . They look like they were taken yesterday.'

'I know. It's uncanny, isn't it? Even in black and white. Of course, it is possible to make colour versions now. In fact, I took the liberty . . .'

From a stool under the counter, Morwenna produced yet another folder and removed another set of prints.

This time, Eden covered her mouth with her hands. Words died in her throat for a few seconds as the people in the pictures leapt from the distant past into the present.

From characters who'd lived in another age, one she couldn't possibly relate to, these vibrant young people – people she'd known and loved – faced her. You could see the details of their features and clothing so much more clearly, the tanned skin, Iris's yellow blouse, her Grandad Walter's shiny buttons on his uniforms.

And the mystery man, with his blond hair and cornflower-blue eyes – the one Iris didn't even know they'd seen . . .

'Oh my God . . . Oh my God, Wenna . . . that is totally amazing.'

'I know. I hesitated over whether to do it. I've had to use my own judgements on some of the colours. I guessed yellow for Iris's blouse because I once saw a sixties picture of her wearing a shirt exactly like it.'

'I can't believe how fresh and modern they seem. Thank you so much for all your hard work.'

'You're welcome, hun. I'm thrilled you love them, but what about your granny? What will she think?'

The same thought had been racing through Eden's mind for the past few minutes. She did feel as if she'd lifted a curtain and taken a peek into a world she was never meant to see. After all, the photos had been removed from the bungalow without Iris's consent. Even if Levan had done the 'borrowing',

Eden had continued the deception. Should she have done that, even for a special occasion?

'Are you worried it might be a bit of a shock?' Morwenna suggested when Eden didn't answer straight away.

'I think she'll adore them, but I don't think we can show her the small one with the boyfriend in colour or black and white yet. Mum suggested replacing it in the folder and seeing if she says anything.' Eden picked it up again. Was that her heart beating a little faster as she stared at the handsome blond man who'd lit up her granny's face with such happiness?

She spoke in a hushed whisper almost as if she didn't want to risk being overheard, despite there being only her and Morwenna in the house. 'Wenna, do you think – am I being crazy – but does the mystery man remind you of anyone?'

'You mean Levan?' Morwenna said.

Eden nodded.

Morwenna smiled. 'I've been thinking that since I first set eyes on the photo.'

'You don't think . . .' Eden began, seeing the handsome blond man through fresh eyes and feeling a little queasy. Today was turning into a rollercoaster that she desperately wanted to step off, yet as soon as she thought it was slowing down, it started climbing up again, plunging down the other side at breakneck speed.

'That Iris and this man had a fling and Levan is their descendant?' Morwenna declared.

'Oh God, no, I hope not. I really hope not, but Granny does *really* like Levan. I'd go so far as to say there's a chemistry between them . . . Not romantic, obviously, but beyond friends. I can't quite put my finger on it. If he was some kind of relative, and she knows it, that might explain why she seems so . . . drawn to him.'

'Perhaps, only it's a bit of a coincidence that he's turned up here to find he's living next door to his grandmother's family – or whatever,' Morwenna said.

'Yet that could be *exactly* why Levan chose to live at Lighthouse Cottages. So he could be close to Granny – and us.' Eden stopped as another thought dawned on her and gave her a shudder. 'He might be my long-lost second cousin, which is seriously weird.'

Morwenna shrugged. 'Actually, although the mystery man and Levan do look similar, I think it's a bit of a leap to conclude they're definitely related. Plus, it's hardly credible your granny had a baby that no one knows about.'

'I guess not. My dad was born in the first year after they were married and they didn't have any other children . . . that I'm aware of.'

'I think you'd have heard by now from someone in the family if Iris had been pregnant again. What's probably happened is that Levan reminds your gran of some lost love and that's why she likes having him around.'

Eden nodded. 'That is so sad, though. I don't like thinking about it.'

'Well, it must have set her off looking back on her life and wondering what might have been. Maybe that's why she started reminiscing to Levan about the photos in the first place.'

Eden thought for a moment. 'I wonder if I should mention the likeness to Mum.'

Morwenna wrinkled her nose. 'Mmm. If she hasn't spotted it yet, we might be reading too much into it. I suppose the

166

resemblance might be more obvious in the colour versions. I guess you could always hold them back?'

'I don't like doing that, not from Mum . . . but I'll definitely show Granny the others in colour and keep hold of the mystery one.' Eden looked heavenwards. 'Has Levan seen these colour shots yet?'

'He hasn't seen any of the restored versions. I wouldn't have dreamt of showing them to him without you seeing them first.' Morwenna raised an eyebrow at Eden, who gave her a grateful hug.

Back home the next morning, Eden showed her mum the restored photo of the mystery man.

Sally's puzzled frown said everything. 'Nope, I've still no idea. He's no one I recognise. It must be someone from the village or possibly a tourist here on holiday. She might have had a quick fling before she met Walter.'

She didn't mention the likeness to Levan, so Eden kept quiet about her own thoughts on it. 'She kept the picture all these years, which makes me think he was more than a fling,' she said

'It sounds as if Iris had forgotten it herself. I shouldn't fret about it.'

'I'm not fretting. It's only that I don't know whether to tell Granny that we found it.'

'Hmm, tricky. Perhaps, to be on the safe side, we'll keep it to ourselves for now. Replace it as it was, and we'll hang onto the photos until the party is over. We'll quietly hand them back, exactly as they were, and see if she says anything then. OK?'

'Yes. I suppose that's a good idea.'

There was concern in her mother's tone. 'Eden? Are you all

right? You seem a little preoccupied at the moment. Not worrying about anything, are you?'

'I'm just knackered,' she said, burying her worries about Simon, and Levan and her grandmother's mystery lover . . . 'It's great to be busy but how I wish we could do it without this crazy summer rush.'

Sally patted her hand. 'Poor you. We both need help!'

'At least Courtney has agreed to join me full time but it's quite scary to take on staff. I'm in that precarious position where I need to invest in the business to grow it but I'm not quite sure I have the revenue to justify it.'

'That's what being your own boss is all about: taking a leap of faith. You should back yourself, Eden.'

'Backing myself hasn't come easy since . . .' Eden refused to say Simon's name out loud and the shadow of his recent letter still hung over her.

'Well, I am *so* proud of you and so is Granny. It takes a woman of steel to pick yourself up and start again and make a huge success of a new venture.'

Eden didn't tell her mum she sometimes felt more like a woman of Plasticine – or chocolate, ready to bend or melt at any moment.

'It must be in the genes,' she said, hugging her mum. 'Yours and Dad's.'

'And Granny's and Grandad's. We're an independent and resilient bunch out here.'

Feeling encouraged, Eden broke into a grin. 'I'll fetch the G&Ts and we'll toast to having survived the week.'

A few days later, Courtney was in the roastery, having worked out his notice at the pub. Seeing him lift the coffee sacks as if they weighed nothing was an eye-opener – to say nothing of a time-saver – and he was really into the intricacies of getting the roasting timing exactly right.

'I think it will help give you a sense of ownership of the Lighthouse brand,' Eden said when they'd bagged up the new roast they'd produced together.

'Agreed. I hadn't realised just how much went into creating the drinks we make.' He grinned. 'There's a lot that can go wrong before the beans even make it to the cup.'

'Tell me about it. It'll be great to have someone else to share the workload with and bounce ideas off.'

'I'm looking forward to it.' He smiled. 'Boss.'

'Oh, don't call me that, please! I feel like something off *The Apprentice*. Now that the work is done, please come into the cottage and I'll find you something to drink – don't worry, it won't be coffee!'

Eden returned to find Courtney standing by the wall of the garden, looking out over the sea. It wasn't the clearest night, and clouds had rolled in but it was still and warm.

'That is one hell of a view.' After sipping his drink, he smacked his lips. 'And that's great lemonade. Tell Iris I'm impressed. Almost as good as my grandmother's ginger beer. She always makes it for us when we go back to Jamaica for the school holidays. Maybe I can give Iris the recipe?' While Courtney was a second-generation Cornishman, his grandmother still lived in Montego Bay and he visited a couple of times a year.

'I'm sure she'd love that. You're coming to her birthday party, aren't you?'

'Wouldn't miss it for the world. Do you need any contributions in the way of food?'

'There's no need but if there was something special you wanted to bring, then do feel free.'

'I'll see what I can rustle up. Or what my mother can!'

'That's cheating!'

'I don't care.' He laughed. 'If it's a buffet and barbecue, maybe my mum's special coleslaw and some beef patties. I could bring some jerk chicken and hot pepper shrimp too as we're by the sea.'

Eden's mouth watered. 'Stop it. I want some right now but don't overload your mum with cooking for someone else's party.'

'I won't, and I can do the pepper shrimp on the day. I'll bring the marinaded prawns and the pot.'

'Thanks, Courtney.' Eden wanted to hug him but contented herself with a handshake. 'And welcome to the team.'

Drinks finished, Courtney had a go at programming a batch roast on the computer under Eden's watchful eye. Time flew by and soon it was the end of his shift so he changed into his leathers and helmet and roared off on his Harley, passing Morwenna's Mini on the track to the lighthouse.

A few seconds behind was Levan's car, and the two vehicles parked side by side.

Levan unfolded himself from the driver's seat and joined Morwenna in the car park where they stood chatting. Looking rather cool in his aviators, Levan was laughing out loud at some quip of Morwenna's. She was rocking white capri pants, kitten heels and huge shades. With her hair tied back with a scarf, she looked like a blonde Audrey Hepburn.

Eden wiped her sticky palms on her stained dungarees and tried to stifle an unpleasant pang of jealousy.

She didn't think Wenna would try to make a move on

Levan, but she couldn't blame her friend if she *did*. She'd insisted numerous times that she wasn't interested in him romantically – not that she had any real idea he was interested in *her*.

Her hopes of not being spotted before she could nip inside and have a shower evaporated. Morwenna waved madly and hurried over, Levan sauntering behind with the nonchalant grace of a young Steve McQueen – one of her mum's youthful crushes.

'Hello. You look hot,' Morwenna said.

Feeling a trickle of sweat run down her back, Eden's heart sank. 'Not in a good way?' she asked in dismay.

'You look fine, just a tad on the warm side.'

'I've been in the roastery with Courtney, showing him the ropes . . . Hello, Levan.'

He tipped the shades down. 'Hi.'

'My assistant barista, Courtney, is now full time and a trainee coffee roaster,' Eden explained. 'You both passed him on his Harley as you drove down here.'

'I saw the bike,' Levan said. 'Nice one. And I've seen him in the container when I've driven past.'

'Well done you on expanding,' Morwenna said. 'You'll have a chain of cafés soon.'

'First things first.'

'Next stop the world, but what you really need right now,' Morwenna said, 'is the image to go with it.'

Eden swallowed hard. 'I do need a shower and some clean clothes . . .'

'No, not *your* image, hun!' Morwenna cried. 'You're perfect as you are. It's your *business* image, the website, your socials. They need sharpening up. Don't they, Levan?'

'Um . . .' Admittedly, Levan seemed lost for words, his hands shoved in his jeans pockets, his full expression now hidden by the aviators again. Eden was cringing. She loved Morwenna, but did she have to be quite so unfiltered?

'I made the website myself. Admittedly, it's a bit basic but I haven't had time to redo it.'

'We can help with that,' Morwenna said.

We?

'I can take a whole new raft of photos for your site and show you how to take great pics with your phone for Insta, Facebook and TikTok. I promise that with a few tips, you'll save time in the long run.'

'What about the website itself? I'm so busy.'

Levan spoke up. 'Look, I'm not a graphic designer but I could easily build a site from a template and streamline the sales channels and SEO for you.'

'Aren't you too busy with the day job for helping me?' Eden said, sliding a look that encompassed Morwenna. '*Both* of you.'

'Do you honestly think,' said Morwenna, folding her arms, 'that I'd rather be snapping pictures of welcome hampers and towel art than my best buddy?'

'Plus, it's no problem to help you spruce up your site,' Levan said. 'If that's what you want and it would help. I don't want to muscle in, though.'

It was an unfortunate choice of words, as it drew her attention to the firm, tanned biceps accentuated by his dark grey T-shirt.

'Eden won't mind you muscling in, I'm sure,' Morwenna said with a gleam in her eye. 'Now all we need is to tell the world how a-mazing you are. We'll need shots of the roastery, the container and you and Courtney.'

'Do I have to be in them?'

'Yes, you're the brand. I'll call to set up a time for the photoshoot. No arguments. Bye, Levan.' She swanned off to the Mini, scrolling through her phone – the coolest woman in Cornwall by a country mile.

'You don't have to help with the website,' Eden said as soon as Morwenna had gunned the engine and sped off in a puff of dust.

'I don't *have* to do anything, but if it's what you want, it'd be a pleasure.'

Eden nodded. Pleasure wasn't the word she'd been thinking of. Frustration and jealousy sprang to mind, but she couldn't back out now.

Chapter Nineteen

As promised, Morwenna rocked up at the container – Morwenna always seemed to rock up, rather than simply arriving – to take some shots of Eden and Courtney. The Coffee Container itself had been scrubbed and polished within an inch of its life. The chrome machines gleamed and the countertops sparkled. Everything was neatly stacked and primped.

Eden had ordered new aprons with the Lighthouse logo on them and taken a bit of extra care over her make-up. An SPF moisturiser and mascara were her usual concessions to workday cosmetics, because anything heavy would have slid off in the heat of the container anyway.

'You look fabulous,' Morwenna said when she arrived before opening time to find Eden emerging from the door of the campsite toilet block. She'd been touching up her face and appraising herself critically. She wasn't vain, at least she hoped not, but she owed it to her future to present the best face she could for her business.

'That bandana is perfect; quirky but very you,' Morwenna

said, smiling at the fifties-style blue bandana accessorising Eden's short hair, which she'd teased into waves with a load of product and hairspray. A new lip gloss accentuated her lips and, she had to admit, she was looking well despite the hard work. Her cheeks were rosy from her outdoor life – and probably the roasting – and she was leaner and fitter from the physicality of her job too: hefting those sacks had toned her arms faster than any gym routine. Even if she wasn't in Levan's bracket yet, she felt more herself for the first time in years. Not only since Simon had left but perhaps before.

'Shall we do you two first while you both look so gorgeous?' Morwenna said.

'Yes, please. I'd much rather get it over with,' Eden said.

'I'm looking forward to my photoshoot,' Courtney chimed in. 'Morwenna's right. You look mighty fine, boss, if I say so myself.'

'Don't call me boss,' Eden cried, laughing at the same time and giving him a playful push on the arm.

'This is great!' Morwenna cried, holding her camera in front of her face. 'Happy colleagues, happy coffee!'

'Oh, you haven't started already,' Eden protested.

'I certainly have. Natural pics are the best. Keep up the banter, it suits you.'

A few minutes later, Eden's mouth ached from smiling while pretending to make a cappuccino, and Morwenna finally announced that the 'people shots' were done and she could move on to the container and product.

Several campers were delighted to be given free coffees that were now surplus to requirements.

Morwenna seemed pleased with the results and packed her

camera away in the Mini. 'Right, I'm off to snap pics of a pigsty in St Ives.'

'An actual *pigsty?*' Eden said.

'Oh yes. It's been converted into a "quirky bolthole" with a pull-down bed and there's a glimpse of the sea if you're six feet and can peer over the wall around the yard – sorry, "outdoor suntrap for morning coffee or sundowners". Which reminds me, can you sell me a couple of Joe's croissants? I need to dress the table before I do the shots.'

'They're on the house,' Eden declared, packing them up for her. 'Thanks so much.'

'Well, hopefully you'll like the pictures.'

Morwenna left and Courtney turned the board to open. Soon, they had a queue of campers in onesies snaking back in the courtyard, as word had spread about the photoshoot. It was going to be a busy day and if the new publicity shots worked, Eden would be able to breathe a little easier about the risk she'd taken in hiring a new full-time employee.

A burst of pride and emotion filled her. From nothing – almost less than nothing – she'd built up a thriving business and hauled herself up from a dark pit of despair.

As they closed up, she made a decision. Today had been symbolic of how far she'd moved on and that she was once again becoming the strong, confident woman she used to be.

Wow. Just wow. Two days later, the same word repeated itself in Eden's mind as she scrolled through the pictures Morwenna had taken. Her friend had done a fantastic job of showcasing the conatiner. In the distant background, you could glimpse the Atlantic and the red-painted roof of Hartstone Lighthouse.

The real surprise, though, was – *her*. Thanks to Morwenna's photography skills and way of putting people at ease, you'd never know how nervous she'd felt during the shoot. She and Courtney looked happy and relaxed as they brewed the coffee. The roastery, the drinks and Joe's cakes – and the staff – were presented in a tempting way that should make anyone long to visit the container.

Morwenna had also shown her lots of phone camera tips that would help her create day-to-day photos to build her laid-back, coastal, eco-friendly brand.

If only she didn't have to sit so close to Levan as they worked on her website in his sitting room. Sardine had wandered in and settled in a pool of sunlight on the hearth rug as if he owned the place. If they so much as twitched, his eyes would fly open as if to say: 'Don't even think about getting up to any funny business.'

Trying not to think about what 'funny business' might entail, Eden's bare leg brushed Levan's and she shuffled away from him. 'Sorry!'

He tapped away, answering her apology with an enigmatic smile. Her thigh still tingled from the contact.

She cleared her throat. 'Isn't this a bit low-level for an IT expert?' she said while he whizzed through the code on her existing website, tweaking and amending to achieve the changes she wanted and Morwenna had suggested.

'At the risk of patronising you, you've done a great job of designing it already.'

'Morwenna clearly thinks there's room for improvement,' Eden said, leaning over to take a closer look before hastily putting a bit more space between the two of them to avoid another thigh-bumping incident. 'And you know what? She's absolutely right. It could be a lot slicker and streamlined in keeping with my new professional image.' She smiled.

Together, they inserted the new photos of the container, her products and the shots of her and Courtney.

'We look like we're enjoying ourselves.'

'You always look happy when I've seen you working.'

'I am – mostly. Even when I'm tired or rushed off my feet or flustered, there's an underlying core of – not exactly happiness, but satisfaction. Does that sound mad?'

'It sounds great to me. No point wasting your life doing something you don't believe in, is there?'

'No. It felt crazy when I first had the idea but now I think it's one of the best things I've ever done.'

'There. I think that's done.' He angled the laptop towards her and she noticed his jeans tauten across his thighs. She could smell the sharp scent of shower gel and freshly washed hair. Lust, delicious and painful, kicked in.

'I'll send you the link so you can have a look through at your leisure and play with the ordering system to see how it works for you,' he said, seemingly oblivious. 'Let me know any tweaks you want.'

'G-great,' Eden replied, trying not to look at the soft worn patches on the denim of his jeans. 'Thanks for this. I really ought to – er – do something in return for you.'

'There's no need.'

'I can at least keep you in free coffees and pastries for a while . . .'

'You don't have to,' he said with a definite twinkle in those gorgeous eyes. 'Though perhaps I shouldn't turn down such a tasty-sounding offer.'

Her cheeks glowed, and she was torn between wanting to

back away and enjoying their teasing moment. It felt dangerously like flirting. 'I meant it . . .' she said. 'I want to pay you back somehow.'

He laughed. 'Honestly, the odd cappuccino will do fine. You owe me nothing. I'm happy to see you succeeding after what happened with Simon. There's been no contact with him, I'm assuming?'

'No sign at all, or of the BMW man.' She laughed. 'Like I said, I was probably just being paranoid.'

'Don't dismiss yourself,' he said firmly. 'It's what he would want you to do. You are an amazing woman, Eden. Don't let anyone persuade you otherwise.'

In that second, they shared an intense glance that made every nerve ending tingle with desire. Was it possible that he wanted her as much as she fancied him? Was Morwenna right? Was it time to take a chance and forget any consequences? She ached to kiss him, to touch him, and he must know that she was simmering with lust for him.

His watch beeped.

'Shit!' His shoulders slumped.

Eden balled her fist by her side, and couldn't stop her sigh of frustration.

'What's the matter?' she said as he glanced at his watch with a deepening frown.

'It's my mother,' he said. 'She wants me to call her.'

'Is everything OK?'

'Perhaps.' He hesitated. 'I don't know.'

The mood was completely destroyed, but Eden decided she may as well use the moment to dig a bit deeper into his past. 'You must miss your family. You say you can't see much of your parents, and your brother and – friends.'

'I miss seeing my mother, but as for my father . . . we've never had the kind of close relationship you have with your mother, your dad and Iris. That warm, loving thread was missing from my childhood. I went to boarding school – like my brother, like both my parents – and while that shouldn't necessarily mean we're remote now . . . Well, we are.'

'So, should you try again to make your peace?' Eden said. 'Your mother has just been in touch. Even though,' she said, echoing the words he'd once used, 'you didn't follow the path they had in mind and you feel you've let them down.'

'I have let them down by not being the person they'd planned for me to be. I suppose I should thank them, in one way. My upbringing toughened me up for later in life.'

Eden was shocked at the bitterness in his tone. 'Like, how?'

'In all kinds of ways,' he said sharply. 'But please don't worry about me being lonely. Dion's a regular visitor and I have colleagues at the data centre. I get along with most people . . .' Then the brief smile faded into a far more serious expression.

Eden took that as her cue to leave, once more battling her mixed feelings about Levan.

Gorgeous though he was, however attracted to him she was – and however reliable and capable he might prove – Eden didn't want to be hurt by any man ever again.

By the end of the week, Eden was desperate for a break. As July wore on, the temperatures rose and she'd been busy in the roastery during some very humid weather. Most of the schools had broken up, with families were arriving for holidays, so business was building by the day. The decision to take on Courtney was looking better by the minute.

It was almost closing time and she was looking forward to driving straight to Morwenna's and staying over. One customer remained and Eden hoped to turn the closed sign over on the A-board before any more arrived.

'What can I get you?' she said to the customer, a woman whose family were waiting outside a campervan in the car park.

'Two cappuccinos and a decaf mocha, please?'

'Great.'

Eden turned to the machine and started to make the drinks. She made the mocha first and set it on the side.

She glanced over her shoulder. 'Anything—'

Her heart stopped.

Behind the customer was a face she hadn't seen for over two years – and had hoped never to set eyes on again.

Chapter Twenty

Once more, Simon had snatched her choices away from her.

Eden's hands shook as she put the filter onto the machine. She wanted to run. He had made her feel like that.

How dare he? This was her new life, and he'd invaded it. What did he want?

The customer was frowning. 'I think I ordered two cappuccinos and a decaf mocha . . .'

'Sorry. Sorry,' Eden stammered. She'd managed to make two mochas and a cappuccino. 'I'll make a fresh cappuccino. I'm sorry for the mistake.'

'It's OK,' the woman said. 'No rush, I'm on holiday.'

Eden turned back to the machine, making a fresh coffee, knowing Simon would be watching her every move. The stencil shook as she sprinkled it with chocolate powder. It looked a right mess, but coffee art was the least of her worries.

Simon was back.

She tore her eyes away from his face, grinning over the head of the customer.

'H-here you go . . .' She slotted the drinks in a cardboard carrier at the counter and the customer waved her card over the machine.

'Thanks,' Eden managed. 'Enjoy your day . . .'

The lady left the container, beaming at Simon as she passed him. 'It's worth the wait,' she said. 'The coffee is delicious.'

'I'm sure it is,' he said, with the crinkly-eyed smile that had once made Eden's heart flip and now made her stomach turn over.

Before she could move again, he marched up the ramp that led to the counter. 'Hello. Sorry if I startled you. I'd rather hoped you'd be alone.'

Somehow in her mind's eye, she'd expected prison life to have added a gaunt, hard-edged look to the handsome features she'd once admired, but she was wrong. Simon had always had an angular profile and she'd imagined those lines would be accentuated, but the opposite had happened. His cheekbones had all but disappeared in a flabby face and he had a goatee beard, which she hated on sight and made him look as if he was permanently smirking. How had she ever fancied him?

A momentary pang of guilt struck her. Perhaps the weight gain was due to his treatment.

'Simon,' she said, hardening her heart again. How dare he turn up like this? 'What do you want?'

He sighed dramatically. 'Well, I can't decide between a latte and a flat white. What do you recommend?'

'I recommend you turn around, get in your car and never come back.'

'Hmm.' He nodded. 'This is OK. I understand your hostility. I was told to expect it.'

'Told to expect it? By who?'

'My counsellor.'

'Your counsellor?' Eden snorted in disgust. 'Why do *you* need counselling?'

He smirked, which enraged Eden even more. 'Actually, my parents suggested it and they were generous enough to pay for it. I suppose I don't deserve their kindness after all I've put them through but they insisted on it as a condition of me moving back in with them. Now I realise that their tough love was the best thing that could have happened to me.'

'Tough love'? 'Counselling'? Eden was speechless. She hadn't had any counselling, yet *she* was the victim.

'As I said in my letter, I'm not here to make your life worse than I already did. I want to make amends.'

'Great,' she snapped. 'It's still all about what *you* want. You've brought all the money with you then? I will take cash, or you can do a bank transfer.'

His smile faded away. 'That's not possible, I'm afraid. If it's any consolation, I have my punishment. I probably have testicular cancer.'

Momentarily, Eden felt light-headed. He wasn't being overdramatic in his letter then.

Gravel crunched as a campervan pulled up in the car park. She forced herself to remember she was at work, even though she was trembling.

'You—let's not do this here, Simon. I have customers.'

Simon glanced at the van, as the driver and passenger climbed out.

'Look,' she said desperately. 'I'm genuinely sorry to hear your news but we can't talk here. This is my business. I can't have it disrupted.'

'I know,' he said. 'And I'm genuinely impressed.'

'I don't need your approval,' she snapped.

'Of course.' He held up his hands in a gesture of conciliation. Eden felt even angrier at how patronising he was being, but she had to get rid of him somehow.

'Please leave, and don't even think of coming to the cottage. I'll call you – *if* and when I'm ready. Where are you staying tonight?' she asked.

'I've been at the caravan park outside Penzance. My auntie has a static there.'

Her stomach knotted. He had been staying in the area, then. 'How long have you been there?' she asked, half dreading the answer.

'A few days.'

'My God.' She was about to ask him if he'd already been watching the cottage when the two new customers jogged over.

She lowered her voice to a hiss. 'You *have* to go. I'm working.'

He nodded and turned to leave. 'Thanks for not throwing me out.'

'Just leave now, *please*,' she said, then threw on a smile for the couple walking to the container.

'You're lucky,' she said. 'I was about to close up.'

'Oh no!' the teenage girl said. 'I was dying for one of your iced lattes. I follow your account on Insta.'

'Coming up,' Eden said, while her emotions seethed. She was angry, shocked, upset . . .

Meanwhile, Simon walked away – and he hadn't even bought a drink.

It was all Eden could do to engage with the customers and make up their order. By the time she had, Simon had gone. It was quarter to four but she couldn't face any more customers so she turned the closed sign around on the A-board and started to clean up and close up so she could go to Morwenna's.

She could only hope Simon would stay away from Lighthouse Cottages until – and if – she decided to break the news to the family that he was in Cornwall.

'Eden! What's the matter? What happened?'

Eden practically fell inside the front door of Morwenna's cottage. She'd vowed that Simon would never make her cry again but it had been impossible to stem the tears as she'd driven to her friend's.

'It's h-him!'

'Who? Levan?'

'No, not Levan. Not him! Simon. Bloody Simon!'

'Oh for feck's sake. What's he said now?'

'He's *here*, Wenna. He's here in Cornwall. He turned up at the coffee container an hour ago.'

'What?' Wenna covered her mouth with her hand. 'Christ. Look, come in and sit down.' She put her arm around Eden. 'You're white as a sheet, and no wonder.'

Eden went into the kitchen-diner of Wenna's house, a modernised terraced cottage on the outskirts of St Just, a former mining village with an arty vibe.

'Sit,' Wenna ordered and went to the kitchen before returning with a glass of clear liquid with ice and lemon. 'Drink this.'

Eden's eyes widened.

'That's a big gin.'

'It's water.'

'Oh.'

Morwenna grinned. 'Don't look so disappointed.'

Managing a momentary smile, Eden sipped it. 'Thanks.'

'There'll be gin later but, for now, tell me what Slimy Simon has done and said.'

'Not much. I didn't give him a chance because I had customers when he materialised.'

'*Materialised?*'

'Yes, out of nowhere, like some horrible spectre rising from the grave.' The image made Eden shudder.

'And he's claiming he's at death's door?' Morwenna said.

'He said he's got testicular cancer. Probably.'

Wenna gave a short intake of breath. 'If he has, then even I don't wish that on him no matter how much he's hurt you. But the "probably" rings alarm bells. Does he have any proof?'

'I don't know and I didn't want him to hang around long enough to go into details. I told him to keep away until I contacted him.'

Morwenna heaved a deep sigh. 'Why has he turned up now? It seems a coincidence that you're back on your feet and he rocks up with a "life-threatening illness".' She bracketed her fingers around the words.

'That's what I've been thinking,' Eden replied. 'I suppose he must have seen my website and my socials. You know what it's like – they paint a rosy picture of all the success you're having. Maybe he thinks I'm about to turn into a big brand.'

'Then he's an idiot. If he's seen you, he'll know it's only you and the container – for now. Realistically, he can't think you have any spare cash to share with him.'

'I suppose not. He may just want to control and con me again. I think he loves the thrill of getting one over on a woman, of controlling her, as much as the money.'

'It could be that but . . .' Morwenna pursed her lips. 'Are you sure he isn't trying to worm his way into your life – the whole family's lives – because he thinks there's money in it? I hate to say this but he must know that your granny is elderly. Perhaps he thinks you might inherit some money from her?'

'Granny only has her little retirement bungalow and a few thousand in savings. He wouldn't get a penny!'

'I know that, but he's a deluded narcissist. This may be his next scam: persuading you that he's reformed, and about to die, so what have you got to lose by having him back?'

Eden slammed her water glass on the table, spilling a few drops. 'Over my dead body. I will never have him back.'

'But you do feel sorry for him? You don't want him to die?'

'Of course not. I'm not that evil. I don't want him to die. Cancer is a terrible disease.' Eden was on the verge of tears. 'I just want him to go away and leave me alone.'

'I'm fecking furious with him, too,' Morwenna said. 'But now he's here, we have to deal with him somehow and get rid of him.'

'Yes, and I don't want him disrupting Granny's party and I definitely don't want to worry her or Mum again.'

'Honey, he won't get within five miles if I have my way.' Morwenna hugged her. 'So, we'll come up with a plan, but first, I'll fetch that gin.'

Relieved that at least she'd shared the burden and that she had a trusted friend to help, Eden sank back against Morwenna's squishy cream sofa. Her home was as stylish and well-groomed as Wenna herself. Painted in neutral colours with accent touches in earthy tones, it was a contrast with Wolf Rock, where there was a lot of clutter no matter how tidy Eden and her mum tried to be. Wenna also had something that Eden did not: a view from the window of an old tin mine on the cliff edge.

Wenna's black and white photograph of it occupied a canvas on one wall. Taken on a stormy winter's day with a rare sprinkling of snow on the moorland, the dramatic and moody scene had always inspired Eden with admiration. Against the threatening storm, the engine house looked especially sinister – or perhaps her encounter with Simon had infected her view of it.

Wenna returned with two glasses of G&T and a smile. 'I thought we'd get a takeout delivered. My treat.'

'Perfect. Thanks.'

'Tell you what. Shall we come up with a plan?'

'Yes . . . could I just have a few minutes first? I need to calm down and I want to text Mum and Granny just to reassure myself he hasn't turned up there. I'm pleased that Granny is staying over tonight. I don't want Mum in the bungalow alone with Simon around.'

'He wouldn't bother her directly. He might be a liar and a cheating scumbag, but he's never been violent. What could he gain?'

'I don't know but he's been in jail. Who knows what that's done to him? He said he was having counselling.'

Morwenna almost snorted her G&T. 'Counselling? Him? He needs a—' She stopped and breathed in deeply.

'I mustn't let him get to me,' said Eden.

'*If* you meet him . . .' Morwenna said.

Eden sighed. 'I don't think I have a choice, now he's here, if only so I can tell him I'm sorry he's ill and then to bugger off.'

Morwenna snorted. '*If* he is actually ill.'

'Yes, and if he isn't, I might have to throw him into the sea.

But whatever the truth, I'll leave him no doubt that there's absolutely nothing between us and I don't want further contact with him. Hopefully he'll get the idea.'

'I don't see what else he can do if you tell him that. I'm happy to come with you when you meet him. I can wait in the van.'

'Thanks . . . that's really kind of you,' Eden said, deeply touched by her friend's loyalty. 'Can I have a think about it?'

'Of course. Let's have a look at the local menus and order the takeout.'

'I'll just text Mum first and make sure everything's OK.'

Without giving details, Eden sent a text to reassure herself that her mother and grandmother hadn't received a visit from Simon – although they'd have been on the phone like lightning if they *had* seen him. With that weight off her mind, Eden managed to show an interest in the local takeout's offerings, more for Wenna's sake than her own. Her appetite had dimmed since Simon's appearance.

With Wenna sitting by her, she sent him a text saying she would arrange to meet him when it suited her. He texted back to say he wasn't sure how long he could stay in the caravan so it needed to be soon.

That suited Eden because she wanted him gone by the time her granny's birthday party came round.

'Yes. Thanks. Sorry . . . Look, Wenna . . . Can I ask something about Levan and, um – you?'

Morwenna folded her arms. 'Ask away.'

Eden cringed but it was a day for sharing secret thoughts with her best friend. 'You and Levan. You don't – fancy him, do you? As in – want to take things further?'

Morwenna looked at Eden, her expression unreadable. 'You mean, would I ever harbour dishonourable intentions towards a gorgeous blond with piercing eyes and a body to die for?'

'Well, yes!' Eden said, half amused, half embarrassed.

A wicked grin slid onto Morwenna's lips. 'I'll admit that it had crossed my mind for a moment or two when I very first saw him. He's a gorgeous man with a great body, but I also know he doesn't fancy me.'

'I don't believe that.'

'Don't you?' Wenna said. 'You think every man within a hundred miles is just falling at my feet?'

'That's how it seems,' Eden said.

'They aren't. Not the ones I'd like to fall at my feet and, as you pointed out, the bar isn't that high round here at the moment.' Wenna sighed. 'Even if Levan *did* fancy me, I would never sleep with a guy that my best and oldest friend was crazy about. And one that *really* fancies her too.'

Eden gasped. 'How do you know that?'

'He as good as told me when I bumped into him in the post office queue the other week. There was such a long queue that we got talking. Sorry, I forgot to mention it to you.'

'Yeah, you did . . . What did he actually say about me?' she asked, itching with curiosity.

'I can't recall the exact words but they were something like: "Eden is a great person, I wouldn't want to see her hurt by anyone."'

Eden shook her head in disbelief, sure that Wenna was flattering her. 'He must just mean Simon. He's only being polite because he knows what he says might get back to me.'

'I don't think so. He also said that it was very thoughtful of me to agree to help with the photos, because it would mean such a lot to Iris and also to your mum and to Eden. Especially to Eden. There was a definite emphasis on the "*Eden*"."

Eden glowed inside at hearing herself spoken of in such terms, then told herself off. She didn't need Levan's approval, or any man's, to feel good about herself.

Eden thought back to the moment they were working on the website: the shared look that had almost convinced her Levan wanted her as much as she wanted him. His mother's message had interrupted . . . something. But *what*?

'That's, um, nice of him – and of you to tell me – but it still doesn't necessarily mean that he fancies me.'

'OK . . .' A sly smile spread over Wenna's face. 'Well, when we were talking about the photos, he *also* said that Iris was a stunning woman in her youth and she'd clearly passed on her genes to you.'

Eden burst out laughing. Wenna was surely making this stuff up. 'I don't believe he actually said that.'

'He did. I was quite miffed, to be honest. He made it very clear that he wasn't interested in me and very gently but firmly gave me the back-off vibes by letting me know it was *you* he likes.' Morwenna sighed again. 'It's a pity because I do love a guy who can be gentle but firm. It's such a rarity.'

Eden let out a squeal of horror and a drop of gin spilled out onto one of the photos.

'Oh, shit!' she cried but Wenna had already snatched up a tissue and dabbed the drop away.

'No damage done,' she said. 'But that's designer gin, you know,' she added.

'Sorry,' Eden replied, then glared at her friend. 'If Levan's that keen on me, why have *you* been flirting with him, knowing that I liked him?'

Wenna snorted with laughter. 'So you *do* like him! Because I gave you every chance to say you wanted him. I tried and tried and you flat refused to be honest so I took matters into my own hands and tried to fish out how he really felt about you! I also wanted to get close to him – but not for me! I wanted to see what he was like. If he could be trusted.'

Eden was, briefly, speechless and could only shake her head in amazement at Morwenna's nerve, although she couldn't possibly be annoyed for long.

'I hate you, Morwenna Smith. I really do.'

'No, you love me really.'

'I guess so . . . But are you sure that – that he *can* be trusted?'

'*I* trust him,' Morwenna said with unaccustomed solemnity. 'For one thing, he's been boringly honourable and never tried anything on with me, despite me trying quite hard to tempt him – as a test, of course.' She sighed. 'Even if he fancied me, I could never ever start anything, knowing that you had feelings for him. Never. To be honest, it's a huge turn-off.'

Eden begged to disagree. Levan might be a turn-off for Morwenna but hearing that he might fancy Eden was giving her all the feels. 'Oh God, listen to us – to me,' she said. 'This is like being young again. Really young. It's like . . .'

'When you first fell for Simon?' Morwenna suggested softly.

Simon again. The image of him appearing at the café like a vampire risen from his coffin haunted her thoughts again. She swallowed a large sip of gin before answering. 'Yes, and I hate that. I hate feeling not in control. I hate the way I feel when Levan looks at me. I hate the jealousy I felt when I thought that you and he . . .'

Most of all, she hated herself for not being able to avoid

the fact she was falling for Levan so hard. Only a very long drop awaited, with jagged rocks below it.

'What are you going to do about it?' Morwenna asked.

There was no answer to a question that had nagged at her for several weeks now. 'I don't know.'

'Eden?' Morwenna prompted.

'Something. Soon. Talk to him, maybe.'

'Talk to him sooner rather than later. Be brave. Open up and I'm sure you'll find he'll open up too.'

Would he, though? And was it madness to try to move on to another relationship while Simon was back in her space?

Or was that exactly what her ex would want? To dominate her life again and make it all about him?

Chapter Twenty-One

'Levan!'

Levan stumbled to a halt on the coast path, his heart hammering. He'd been for a run that he hoped would shake off the dilemma he was in, a dilemma he couldn't see a way out of without disappointing or hurting so many people, including himself.

'E-Eden?'

'Over here!' she called, waving at him from the middle of the gorse, her small frame almost hidden by the spiky branches and yellow flowers. Her urgent tone and frantic gestures told him she needed him. She hadn't been at home the previous evening and, when he'd casually enquired about where she was, Sally had said she'd stayed over at Morwenna's.

'Coming.'

He forged through the 'rabbit run', cursing silently as the spikes grazed his bare legs and arms.

Eden's jaw dropped when they finally came face to face. 'Oh God, look at you,' she cried.

He looked down and saw that tiny pricks of blood now streaked his calves and forearms. 'It'll be OK.'

'I'm sorry, I should have realised.'

'I should have realised that walking through gorse in running kit is a bad idea.'

'Here. Have this. It's clean.' She handed him a tissue from her shorts pocket, which strangely touched him.

'Thanks,' he said, dabbing at his arms. 'I presume you want to talk if you've called me over here.'

'Yes, can we go to the secret place?' She grimaced. 'My, that sounds dodgy, but you know what I mean.'

Now, he sensed, was not the time for teasing her. 'Eden,' he said sombrely. 'I'm very happy to go anywhere you want.'

A hint of pink stole into her cheeks before she lifted her chin and said almost haughtily: 'Come on, then.'

He obeyed, unable to decide which he found sexier: her blush or her command to follow him. Squeezing through the cleft in the rock, he wondered what could be so important that she'd invited him into so intimate a space. Would it be a secret he was worthy of being told? He'd already been invited into so much of the Carricks' lives.

'Do you want some water?' She pulled a bottle from her backpack.

'That would be a good idea.' Accepting the drink, he was painfully aware that the sweat was running down his brow. He could feel the salt stinging the tiny grazes from the gorse on his arms, too. He dabbed at a few more with the tissue.

'Ouch. They look sore.'

'They'll heal in no time.' He handed back her bottle. 'Thank you. I needed that.'

She nodded and he saw her struggle to compose herself.

'Take your time.'

'I've taken enough time. I need to tell you something. It's Simon. He's back. For definite, this time.'

Levan bit back an expletive, knowing his reaction wouldn't help Eden.

'When? Where?' he said tightly. 'He hasn't—' he was about to say *hurt you*, but he settled for, '—hassled you, has he?'

'He turned up at the coffee container late yesterday afternoon before I went to stay with Morwenna. As for hassle, he's hassling me simply by existing but he agreed not to come to the cottages or contact me until I contacted him.'

'And have you?'

'I sent him a text saying I'd arrange to meet him when it suited *me*. I've decided to tell him that no matter what the situation is, I don't want to be involved with him in any way. And I want this all sorted before Granny's birthday party.'

Reining in his urge to throw his arms around Eden and comfort her, Levan said: 'Do you think he'll keep his word?'

'It would be a first but if I don't see him, I won't even have a chance to find out what's going on. We both know he's a serial liar.'

'Yes, he makes a career of it. I mean, none of us tells the truth the whole time . . .' He stopped when Eden gave him a quizzical look. 'Everyone tells a few white lies,' he qualified, panicking a little.

'Of course, but those are nothing to what Simon has done. OK, we all make up excuses for getting out of dates, and boring parties and difficult phone calls. "Must go, the delivery driver's here again!" stuff, but nothing that involves wrecking people's lives.' She stopped and stared at him hard. 'What about you?'

He swallowed a lump in his throat. 'I haven't always told the absolute truth, no,' he said, his palms growing sweaty. 'It can get you into a lot of trouble. Sometimes telling the truth can wreck lives.'

'Yes, but even then, surely honesty is better?' she said firmly. 'Why would anyone want to live a lie?'

He shivered. 'True . . .'

She shook her head. 'For what it's worth, I give it seventy–thirty that he is actually that sick. The thing is, do I take that thirty percent chance that it's serious?'

'No odds are bad as long as you also believe you have nothing to lose,' Levan said slowly.

'I suppose.' She began. '*If* he really was as sick as he claimed, he just *might* be looking for a chance to apologise – for once in his life he might genuinely want to make amends.'

Levan's stomach contracted, but much as he also despised Simon, he couldn't wish a terminal disease on the man and hoped he was fabricating his illness – for everyone's sake.

'How could he make amends?' he said. 'Repay the money?'

'No. It's all gone and I've accepted he can't do that, but if I genuinely thought he understood how much he hurt me . . . If I believed that, it would give me – I hate the words, comfort . . . closure? It would be a crumb of comfort to know he really had cared about me for some of the time.'

'I get that. I'm happy to come with you, hang around out of sight if you need me to.'

She rolled her eyes, good-humouredly. 'You and Morwenna both. Who do you think you are? Batman and Robin?'

A woman who could joke, even in the darkest of circumstances. She was a tough cookie and he admired her even more. He also loved the way the smile lit up her eyes, chasing away the shadow of Simon. 'We don't have to wear capes and tights to watch over you,' he said.

'Actually, I'd love to see that so I might make it a condition of you being my bodyguard.'

'You're on.' He noticed her goosebumps and realised a chilly breeze had sprung up from the sea. She was cold and he needed to get cleaned up himself. He handed back the bottle and indicated the rocky passage as if it were the entrance to a magic portal. 'After you?'

However, Eden didn't move. 'Levan,' she said 'You asked me if I always tell the truth. I do try, but there's also another kind of deception that maybe we're all guilty of.'

Hope and uncertainty filled her eyes. His pulse jumped. What was she going to say?

'I've held things back that I ought to say,' she murmured. 'I'm not sure if that counts as lying.'

'Neither am I.'

'I'll admit, I have . . . doubted you, but please don't take that personally. Simon's made me wary of every man. Every person who I haven't known forever, but with you, I've been wrong.'

What fears must she have overcome to be this honest with him. He didn't deserve it. 'Wrong in what way?' he said, hardly daring to hear the answer.

'I can see that you're a good friend to Granny. She loves having someone young and someone who – um – shares her taste in books around.'

'Same,' Levan said, though he felt that guilt was seeping into his bones and his lies oozing out of his pores. He suppressed a shudder.

'There's something else,' she murmured and took a deep

breath. 'And in fact, someone I trust has told me to – to be brave and say what's on my mind.'

Moving closer, she looked up into his eyes. She was so gorgeous that he felt shaky with lust.

'Which is?' he replied softly, sensing the moment was so fragile that if he said the wrong thing, he might shatter it and Eden's bravery might evaporate.

Instead, she reached up and touched his bare shoulder, grazed by the gorse. 'Ouch,' she said.

He closed his eyes momentarily as her fingers lingered on his skin and gently trailed down his arm. How he'd longed for that touch and that look in her eyes. He wanted her and she wanted him and they could rip off their clothes right there and then and finally do what they'd both wanted to do since he'd first spotted her spying on him through the hedge.

When he opened his eyes, her face was inches away, her lips parted and he met them. He kissed her and she kissed him back hungrily. She put her arms around his waist, and he felt her fingers pressing through his running vest. He pulled her to him, knowing that it must have taken all her trust and courage to tell him how she felt.

All her trust.

A trust that was so precious to her – so hard for her to give to another person, especially a man. A trust he didn't deserve.

Levan felt as if the heavens had unleashed a sky's worth of icy rain on him. Gently, he stepped back, putting space between them.

'Eden . . .' he murmured. 'I'm sorry, I can't do this.'

Her eyes opened and she stared up at him, her brow furrowed in confusion. 'What?'

He shook his head, feeling physically sick. 'I can't do this.'

'But – we are doing it? We're kissing. You want this, right?'

'Yes, I want this. I mean, I want you as much as you want me. More, so much more, but not now, not until . . .'

'Until what?' she demanded.

'Until – until – everything is sorted with Simon.'

'Simon?' She dropped her hands from his waist, staggered back and threw up her hands in frustration. 'Bloody Simon. What's he got to do with it?'

'Trust me, you don't need another – entanglement – right now.'

'*Trust* you?' Eden snorted, then she seemed to crumple. 'OK. OK. I – must have made a mistake.'

'It wasn't a mistake. I only think we should wait.'

'I've waited a long time already . . . but you're probably right. This is appalling, horrific timing.' She laughed. 'My speciality.'

'No, Eden.'

Levan caught her arm gently with his hand. The angry hurt in her eyes seared into him and she shrugged off his touch. 'I have to go home. You do too. You're bleeding all over my space. It's making a mess.'

There were splodges of red in the granite dust at his feet and on her T-shirt. 'Sorry. Yes. Making a mess is my speciality.'

She didn't contradict him. 'See you around,' she muttered and then she was gone, melting into the dark space between the rocks, leaving him bloodied and alone – again.

Chapter Twenty-Two

After she'd left Levan, Eden had gone to the roastery and worked late until she'd been so exhausted she'd fallen into bed. She hadn't wanted her mother to see that she was upset or even answer Morwenna's calls.

She'd avoided any chance of even seeing Levan – or hearing him in the cottage next door. She had, however, messaged Simon and ordered him to meet her.

The Old Lookout above Sennen. 6pm. Tonight.

It gave her some semblance of control to make him wait and to choose the time and date. What a joke: she had no control, as far as relationships were concerned. Simon had turned up whether she'd wanted him to or not and Levan had rejected her when she'd finally found the courage to overcome her trust issues. Her leap of faith had crashed as hard as if she'd jumped off the cliffs onto the rocks below.

She went straight from work, pulling on a denim jacket over her café T-shirt. When she finally reached the Lookout, the iron-grey waves reflected her mood. Gulls mobbed a fishing boat as it steamed into the tiny harbour below. On this dull, cool afternoon, the holiday hordes had stayed clear of the beach, though there were still plenty of walkers on the coastal path, admiring the views of Land's End and the Longships lighthouse.

She'd chosen the spot because it was a public place but not *too* public, in case things between them turned ugly. She doubted it, but best to be on the safe side. She hadn't told anyone she was meeting him. Morwenna would have wanted to come as her bodyguard – and so, Eden was certain, would Levan. Was there anything more excruciating than a man who rejected your advances out of some misguided sense of chivalry?

Not that he'd rejected them at first. He had wanted her, physically, as much as she'd wanted him. So that was something, at least.

Maybe he'd been right about now being the wrong time. Or maybe it was simply an excuse to avoid a proper relationship with her.

She clearly still didn't know him as well as she thought she did.

She heard heavy breathing and saw Simon hauling his way up the final steep slope and taking the steps to the lookout, where Eden stared down on him.

'W-woah. M-must be out of sh-shape.' Simon was puffing like an old steam train and his face was bright red. Eden was struck by remorse: he used to be a serial gym-goer, although she now suspected that for some of the 'sessions' he'd been engaged in a different kind of exercise to the one she'd imagined. However, if he was ill, wasn't it thoughtless of her to have suggested meeting all the way up here?

'Are you OK?' she asked.

'Y-yes.' He eased himself down onto a bench. 'Though, obviously, I've been better.'

Eden stayed on her feet, forcing herself to look at him. 'It's a steep climb up here. Perhaps it wasn't the best choice.'

'I'll live,' he said and then laughed mirthlessly. 'Well, the climb up here won't kill me, that's for sure.'

'Don't joke,' she said. 'It's not funny.'

'Sorry. Dark humour. I – um – thought you might be sceptical about my diagnosis so I brought a letter from my consultant.' He pulled a crumpled sheet of paper from the pocket of his chinos.

From seeming red in the face, he now turned paler. Her instinct as a decent human told her to refuse to see the letter. Her instincts as one of Simon's dupes told her to examine it minutely.

'Go on, take a look. If I were you, I'd want to. Mum and Dad very generously paid for me to have access to a private consultant.'

Eden accepted the letter, hoping he wouldn't notice the slight tremor in her fingers. Whatever it contained would give her no satisfaction. It also felt unsettling to read such personal details from someone else's medical records. She reminded herself that she had once known Simon intimately, and yet he was also a stranger to her in so many ways. She shuddered for all kinds of reasons.

To all appearances, it was official, bearing the name of a well-known private healthcare provider. It was full of jargon but the upshot was that they'd definitely found a tumour, which would require a course of treatment they'd discuss with him shortly

She was torn between not becoming involved and her

204

natural instincts to feel sorry for anyone who'd had such devastating news.

'It's not good,' she said carefully. 'Have you heard any more about your treatment yet?'

'I'm still waiting for an appointment to discuss the options,' he said. Was it her or did his voice sound . . . small? Even a man like Simon must be genuinely terrified of what might happen to him.

'Shouldn't you be back home so you're ready to start it? I don't understand how coming down here and tiring yourself out helps?' she pressed him. 'And there is hope? I thought testicular cancer had a good cure rate if it's caught early?'

He shrugged. 'That's the thing. I don't know if it's been caught early enough. Mum and Dad are out of their minds with worry,' he added.

'I can imagine.' While not the greatest fan of Simon's parents – she had been shocked at the way they'd been in denial about his crimes – Eden did feel for them.

'I'm very sorry about this,' she said, rereading the letter and making her decision. She was going to tell him she was sorry but it would be best if they had no more contact. It was so *hard* though – she felt so callous. She shuddered. He *did* look ill, albeit not in the way she had expected: more unhealthy than unwell.

She glanced up from the letter to find him sitting with his head in his hands, hands spiked through his hair.

He was obviously crushed by his experiences, however well-deserved they were. Prison must have been very hard for a white-collar conman who hadn't even been able to bear to remove a spider from their room and now he had been dealt this fresh blow.

She refolded the letter, which had clearly been read many times judging by the grubby creases. She had no urge to hug him or comfort him, if that was what he'd hoped. Did that make her a horrible person – or a sensible one?

'What do you actually want by coming here, Simon?'

'Nothing. Nothing material, if that's what you mean. I came here hoping to make amends, or if not, to make peace with you in case . . .' He gave her a desperate look. 'The worst happens.'

Her stomach clenched. Strange, how old feelings lingered no matter how hard you tried to suppress them. However, they were feelings of pity and compassion, not desire and love.

'How can you possibly do that?' she asked.

'I'd like to apologise to your mother and Iris for a start.'

'No!' She shook her head so hard it hurt her neck; she must be so tense and wound up. 'You mustn't come near them,' she added. 'It would worry and upset Mum – and as for Granny, I don't want her to have any shocks at her age.'

'I see. She must have a birthday coming up?'

Eden frowned. 'How do you know that?' she asked sharply.

He rolled his eyes at her. 'We were married, Eden. I can't un-remember family birthdays.'

We aren't your family any longer, Eden wanted to blurt out, but settled for, 'Yes, she's ninety at the end of the month, but you can't be part of that. We have separate lives now, and I hate to use a cliché, but I've moved on.'

'So I hear.'

'What do you mean?'

'I – um – forgive me but I was at a low point and I needed to see something familiar again so I drove to the cottages and I saw you.'

'Oh God, so that *was* you hanging around the other week!'

'I didn't come any closer than the car park. I wouldn't have dared.'

'My God, you've been spying on me?' she said, wondering just how long Simon had been watching her and if he'd hung about on other occasions. If so, it was possible he'd spotted her with Levan too.

He hung his head and made his voice small, which irked Eden even more. 'I'm sorry. I shouldn't have even tried to see you but I was desperate.'

'Well, you've seen me *now* and I'm very sorry to hear your news and wish you well, but I can't do any more. If you want me to forgive you, I'm not sure I can, not one hundred percent.' She took a breath but carried on before he could interrupt. 'I have to get this off my chest. I suppose we could have and would have been happy together until you shattered my trust to smithereens. You hurt me so badly I never thought I'd recover but I have picked myself up, thanks to my family. I can't risk being hurt a second time, and I won't worry them a day longer on your account.'

He stared at his shoes. 'I am so so sorry. There's nothing more I can say.'

'Perhaps you are sorry, but it's too late now. Now please, go home to your own family, Simon, and let them support you.' Eden felt sick: a fresh confrontation with him after all this time was really screwing with her head.

'Thank you for your good wishes. I know you mean them,' he said in a 'humble' way that, unfortunately, made her skin

207

crawl. 'You were always a kind and generous person and, after what I've put you through, I'm sure I don't deserve them.'

'I can't wish illness on anyone, Simon.' She held out the letter. 'Here you go.'

He waved it away. 'No, please, keep it,' he said.

'Don't you need it?'

'They sent me a copy by email. You have it as proof.'

'"Proof"? Why do I need proof?' She thrust it at him again. 'I don't want to keep it.'

'And I don't want it back.' Refusing to take it from her hand, he levered himself up with an audible grunt. 'I'm going now, as instructed. Your advice is as sensible as ever. You always were the strong and practical one. I'll keep you updated.'

Suddenly, a thought struck her and she nodded. 'If you insist,' she said, unwilling to encourage him with any other comment or end up in an argument.

He set off down the steps, shoulders sagging, and she couldn't resist calling: 'Take care, Simon.'

He lifted his hand in farewell but didn't turn round.

Eden herself turned away. The Atlantic stretched before her, and she tried to take solace in the fact there was nothing between her and America: a metaphor that the rest of her life lay before her with nothing to hold her back ever again. Yet the view over that endless sea of possibilities blurred as tears filled her eyes. Her encounter with Simon had been every bit as emotional and distressing as she'd dreaded.

No matter how much her head told her she was right to cut off all ties with him, a part of her wondered if she had made the right decision. Was she being a bad person?

She pulled the letter from her pocket.

She was glad now that she'd agreed to keep it, even though

she was sure he'd given it to her so that he would still be on her mind – and her conscience. However, Eden thought as she walked slowly down to her van, she would make use of it in her own way.

Chapter Twenty-Three

'Hello, love. You've been elusive lately. I wanted a word with you.'

Eden's pulse spiked when she walked back into Wolf Rock after meeting Simon. Her mother had such a serious expression. Surely she hadn't found out about it all? She'd had to sit in the van for a while and calm down before she dared face her mum. Even so, she teetered on the brink of blurting out that Simon was back.

'Oh?' She dumped her handbag on the sofa. 'Sounds heavy stuff,' she said, managing to inject a little humour into her voice and giving her mother her full attention.

'It *is* heavy,' Sally said, before breaking into a smile. 'Because it's about Granny's birthday party. There's now so much going on for this supposedly "small family gathering" that I've had to write a checklist.'

'Of course you have,' she replied, her mood lifting a fraction.

'Don't mock,' Sally chided. 'How do you think we ever went on holiday or managed Christmas without a checklist? Your dad and grandad always had checklists. They had to make sure they had every little item they needed before they boarded the boat for the lighthouse. When you have a family, you'll need them too.'

When she had one? It was only a throwaway remark, but it cut Eden unexpectedly deep given how raw she was already feeling.

Sally groaned. 'Oh, love, I am sorry, that was thoughtless of me. I didn't mean to upset you.'

'You haven't, Mum. I know what you mean, and I hope to be in need of a massive checklist one day, too.' Eden wrapped her mother in a warm embrace, hoping she'd be able to stop her tears from falling. She really was on the edge of breaking down completely after the rollercoaster of the past few days.

She stepped back, her face almost hurting as she forced a beaming smile. 'Now, let's see this list. Even though Granny keeps saying she doesn't want a fuss, she'll secretly be expecting her big day to be planned with military precision.'

Her mother seemed relieved. 'OK. Let's sit down with a cuppa. I also brought some scones back from the office. The hamper company accidentally delivered too many cream teas for the holiday lets so we shared the spares out.'

Eden didn't say no. She'd been so busy in the roastery that she hadn't had time for lunch – plus her stomach had been churning about meeting Simon. Now she was home, the relief at having got the encounter over with was finally sinking in and she was ravenous.

By the time her mum brought out scones, jam and cream, accompanied by two steaming mugs of tea, Eden was ready to devour the lot, tray included. Rain blew against the panes and Sally had to turn the lamps on.

'There's something very comforting about being indoors

while a storm rages outside,' Sally said, as Eden slathered her scone with jam.

'You can say that again,' she replied, dolloping clotted cream on top and feeling her limbs start to relax. She'd been like a coiled spring most of the day.

Her mother extracted an A5 notebook from the dresser drawer and brought it to the sofa.

'I do keep a copy of this plan on my tablet but I find the paper version easier to use,' she said, opening the cover and picking up a pen. 'Now, let's start with the guests.'

There was mutual chuckling as Eden realised that her granny's 'I'll be fine on my own' had morphed into a full evening barbecue for twenty guests.

'The good news is that Courtney's volunteered to be the barbecue chef,' Sally said. 'I called him last night and he insisted on bringing some jerk chicken as well as the buffet snacks.'

'He's a lovely guy,' Eden said, warming further to her new barista.

'And did you know that Courtney's mum, Dorian, is in Granny's swimming group?' Sally said. 'I thought it would be a lovely surprise if she came so I invited her.'

'Good idea. Granny will love that.'

'We also don't have to worry about the cake or baked goods, because Joe has that all in hand,' Sally said, ticking off another item on her list with a flourish.

Eden reached for the other half of her scone, adding a bit of extra cream. She *had* been working hard, she reasoned, and was in sore need of comfort food.

They talked through the rest of the food. With contributions from a variety of people, it looked as if there wouldn't be too much cooking required, which was a good thing because they had to tidy the house, set up the barbecue, chairs and tables and a dozen other things.

'Levan's kindly offered to bring some fizz,' Sally said. 'And to chauffeur Granny.'

Eden paused, a final morsel of scone midway to her mouth. 'Has he?' she said carefully. 'Isn't it out of his way?'

'He says he's set aside the whole day in his diary to help us set up and run errands. I've arranged for all the guests to be here so that when he rocks up with Iris, we can all pop the streamers and sing "Happy Birthday". He is such a thoughtful man.'

'Yes,' Eden said, wondering how her mother would think of him if she'd been aware of the disastrous kiss. Of course, telling Eden to cool things didn't make him a bad person but she hadn't felt the same since it had happened. No matter how sensibly or gently he'd given her the brush-off, it had still been an excruciating moment.

The scone was finished and Eden decided to have another half, almost finishing the clotted cream portion.

Her mother gave an amused eyebrow raise. 'Wow, you were hungry.'

'You know I never could resist a cream tea, Mum.'

'It's in the genes,' Sally said. 'Your dad and Grandad Walter were the same. You know my dad came out in hives if he had too much dairy.'

'That's one gene I'm happy to have inherited from Dad's side of the family, then. Do you think Granny has any idea of what's going on?' Eden asked.

'I'd be amazed if she hasn't been trying to find out every chance she gets. Levan said she sent him a cryptic message

213

about "not getting her a present as she was too old". He hadn't even said he was going to get her one.'

Eden smiled. 'Joe said she called and ordered a tray of cream cakes for her friends at the book club and the bungalows. She said "she didn't want a big fancy cake but she thought she ought to treat people or they'd think she was stingy".'

'She's incorrigible!' Sally cried.

'Joe told her that big cakes were a bit naff and said he'd rather have a cheese.'

'He's so naughty . . .'

'I know.' Eden's excitement bubbled up despite her private worries. 'I can't wait to see Granny's face when she sees everyone. I know she's going to have an amazing time.'

Eden sat on her bed and put her phone on top of Simon's hospital letter, staring at both and at a loss to make sense of the conversation she'd just had.

She'd called the number on the hospital letter and managed to speak to the secretary of his consultant. The secretary had, as Eden had feared, refused to give her any details because of patient confidentiality. She'd said she couldn't even confirm if Simon was a patient at all – but she didn't deny it, either.

'Oh, Simon . . .' she murmured the words out loud and let out a deep sigh.

The letter did seem genuine, with a real number and real oncologist's name on it. Surely that made the rest of Simon's claims more likely to be true?

It didn't, however, make Eden feel any more disposed to staying in contact with him. Though she was sad he was ill, his health problems were not her responsibility and, hopefully, he'd get the treatment he needed and had the support of his parents.

She went to work, determined to refocus her energy on the café, and not on Simon – or Levan's rejection of her.

In fact, she told herself to be grateful to him for putting the brakes on quite so decidedly. The last thing she needed was a distraction from her work, no matter how attractive, especially with the season in full swing. At least that side of her life was on the up: the café looked great, and with Courtney by her side, there was more time to keep it smart and appealing.

If business carried on growing steadily, perhaps she'd be able to set up another branch in an even busier spot. Perhaps she'd be able to boost her savings enough to afford the deposit on a small flat of her own. When they occurred, such musings made her buzz with excitement. However, that was for the future: she had to keep her first café thriving first.

Back at the roastery, she decided to grab a few shots for her social media. With the late afternoon light slanting through the door, the roastery had a mellow, golden aura that made for some great pictures. If only there was a way to capture the aroma in a photo . . .

'Hi there, are you OK?'

Eden jumped and whipped round to find Levan silhouetted in the entrance to the roastery. Her initial alarm melted into frustration. Why did people keep asking her if she was OK? Were her worries showing again? Morwenna had dubbed it Simon Syndrome when Eden had called to tell her about her meeting with him – along with a lot of other less repeatable names.

'Am I interrupting anything?' he said, stepping inside with

the wary look of a man entering a bear's den. 'I don't want to ruin a batch.'

Eden's heart sank, though it was silly to have thought she could avoid him forever. She just hoped he wasn't going to allude to their 'moment' the other evening.

'I've finished,' she said coolly. 'I was tidying up.'

'How are you?' he said.

'Fine.' She met his eyes and challenged him. 'Why wouldn't I be?'

She half expected him to repeat a string of platitudes about the kiss, but he wisely didn't go there. 'What can I do for you?' she asked curtly.

'Nothing,' he said, seeming to debate over whether to say anything else. 'Tell me to shut up if it's not my business, but I wanted to ask if you've made contact with Simon?'

'As a matter of fact, yes, I have.'

Did she glimpse surprise in his eyes – or annoyance?

'Dare I ask how it went?' he said coolly.

'Disturbingly.' She heaved a sigh, realising she didn't mind talking to him about Simon. She'd already had the conversation with Morwenna, who'd urged her to have no more to do with 'the sly git'. Even so, it was comforting to hear the perspective of someone else who she hoped, despite everything, still had her welfare at heart.

'Disturbing in what way?' he said carefully.

'In the same way as always.' Eden sighed again. 'He showed me a letter from his consultant saying he'd been diagnosed with testicular cancer. Even so, I still told him I want no further contact with him.'

'Good,' Levan said, his tone hardening. 'So, he's gone home, has he?'

'Yes. I told him I was sorry he was ill and wished him well but I didn't want him to bother my family and that he should spend the time with his parents.' After a moment's hesitation, she went over to the chair where she'd hung her jacket and pulled the crumpled letter from the pocket of her dungarees. 'He gave me this. I meant to chuck it out, but I forgot.'

Levan frowned. 'What is it?'

'A letter from his consultant. You can read it, though it doesn't really help.'

'Are you sure?'

'Yes. He made me keep it.'

'Made you?' said Levan with a frown, taking the letter.

So many questions, thought Eden wearily, but answered anyway. 'He said he has a digital copy. I think he was keen for me to have some kind of evidence that he was telling the truth. And in fact,' she added, 'I phoned the number on it and spoke to his doctor's secretary.'

'What did they say?' he said more sharply than she'd expected.

'Not much. They wouldn't even confirm or deny he was a patient. I suppose it's what I should have expected, but at least I know the hospital is genuine.'

'Hmm.' Levan sat down on a coffee sack, taking his time over reading the letter. He also held it up to the light and frowned, and eventually he placed it on the sacking next to him.

'So,' Eden said, when he finally returned his attention to her. 'What do you think?'

'Like you say, this does seem to prove he's had a diagnosis for what he claims is wrong with him.'

'*Claims?* You sound sceptical.'

'Letters can be forged,' he said.

'Yes, but it's a real hospital and a genuine oncologist. The thing is, I don't know how to find out if he is receiving treatment there.'

'I understand that but perhaps . . . you could call his parents and ask if he's really ill?' Levan suggested.

'God, no! That would be excruciating. Calling them to see if their – possibly – terminally ill son is lying?'

He gave a brief, wry smile. 'I'm sure they've heard worse from you.'

'They have, though I'm not sure they'll even speak to me now. They supported Simon at his trial. I think they wanted to believe his lies that he'd simply been having an affair and never intended to actually marry his mistress. They seemed happier to think he'd only wanted to scam both of us out of our money than that their son was a would-be bigamist.'

'Parents can have strange priorities,' Levan said, handing back the letter.

'My mum and dad always put me first, as did their own parents,' she replied, putting the letter down on her workbench by the roaster. 'I think that made it worse when Simon chose to betray me so badly. I'd been naïve and assumed that most people have good intentions. He trampled all over that notion and stamped on it for good measure.'

'Most people do have good intentions,' Levan said. 'Most parents, most children, but not *all*. Of course, there can be an even bigger problem when their good intentions are bad for you.'

Intrigued despite herself, Eden sat on the sack next to him. 'Is that what happened with you and your family?'

'Like I said, I decided one day that I could no longer follow the path they wanted for me.' There was almost a sneer in his voice as he spoke and Eden sensed she was peeling back layers on a raw wound.

'Which was?'

'They wanted me to join the army so I did, as an officer. But I hated it and I quit.'

'The army!' It was impossible to hide her amazement.

'You sound surprised?'

'I am . . .' She couldn't imagine it: he was the most un-military-looking man she'd ever met, though she would never say that to him, of course. 'Surely they understood if it was making you unhappy?' she asked, instead.

He gave the bleakest of smiles, filling her with sadness. 'They very much *didn't* understand. They thought I'd let them down, my dad and brother especially. My mother tried to be sympathetic but even she gave up in the end when it became clear I was never going back to that life.'

'Is that why you came down here? To get as far away as possible from them and their expectations?'

'Partly. Also because my friend, Dion, offered me a job I do love and the chance to live in this beautiful place. How could I possibly refuse?'

'Well, I'm glad you did decide to come here,' she said, surprising herself with how heartfelt she sounded despite her anger at how he'd pushed her away previously.

'Me too, though you'd have every right to wish I hadn't. I know you might think otherwise . . . especially now . . . but I *do* care. Please believe me.'

'I don't know what to believe any more,' she said briskly, desperate to avoid a repeat of the excruciating scene between

219

them. 'And thanks for coming to see how I was. I'm fine now Simon's finally out of my life.'

'Good. And Eden . . . if Simon does bother you again, please let me know immediately. I'll do anything I can to make sure he stops hassling you.' There was a core of steel in his voice and perhaps, Eden thought, that *was* due to his military background.

'Thanks, but how can you?' she said. 'And I can take care of myself where Simon is concerned. I'm sure he won't come back.'

'Yes, I know but . . .' he started, but seemed to change his mind. 'You're right. You don't need rescuing, or anyone blundering in and threatening what you've built – least of all a man.'

'No, I don't.' She met his eye, willing him to be gone yet unable to stop herself being touched by his determination to 'protect' her from Simon. She really did believe he cared about her, just not in the way she'd thought. Had hoped . . .

'Of course,' he said. 'Whatever you want . . . but I want you to know that you're important to me. In other circumstances, I—'

Shrivelling with embarrassment, Eden stood up and cut him off with a sharp, 'Sorry, Levan, but I really need to get on with this roast and grab some photos for my socials.'

He gave a curt nod that was almost a parting salute and turned on his heel. She watched him walk out into the sunlight.

He was right: he had blundered in on her life but, until that awful episode the other day, she'd started to welcome – even invite – the intrusion. Now, she wasn't sure whether she wanted him in her world at all.

Chapter Twenty-Four

'This isn't technically legal, you know.'

It was two days later that Levan found Dion standing by his car outside the data centre in the evening sun, scrolling through his phone. His friend had waited for him to arrive before making his comment without so much as a 'Hi, how ya doin'?'

'It's probably not legal at all,' Levan said archly. 'But I need to know the truth about Simon and his "diagnosis".'

'You think the letter is fake then?'

'I'm almost certain of it, but almost isn't enough. I need to be one hundred percent sure.'

'Fine by me.' Dion dropped the phone into his pocket. 'And since we've now established that this Simon is the mystery man who's been hanging around the centre and taking fan photos of you, we could legitimately argue that it's an issue of national security.'

Levan rolled his eyes. 'I'm hardly of national importance, am I, though?'

'Maybe not, but the centre *is*. If this place was offline,

because of a security issue involving a hostile person, it would cause serious disruption to the comms between some pretty big global financial institutions, including the government's own. Come on.'

As they walked towards the centre, Levan was struck anew by how nondescript it was. The modest single-storey brick building had a single grey door and a couple of shuttered windows. It could as easily have been a little-used farm building or an electricity substation. Ivy curled around it and the gorse had encroached, poking its spiky fingers through the metal chain-link fence, as if reaching for the brickwork. Levan's calves prickled; he was still covered in scratches, though they were the least uncomfortable of his wounds from his encounter with Eden.

The sun glinted off the mobile phone mast in the farmer's field on the other side of the fence. Cows grazed near to the rather rundown concrete hut, which concealed considerably more power generation and cooling capability than any dairy farm could ever need.

Few people knew it was there, or what was inside.

Suggesting Simon would have the motivation or capability to breach a highly secure IT facility almost made Levan laugh out loud – yet this whole scenario was surreal. 'Some people wouldn't care about that kind of disruption to finance big boys or the government,' he said.

'And they are perfectly entitled to feel that way. I often do myself. However, the impact would – as always – be greatest on ordinary people like you and me, our friends and families. They would suffer when their salary or benefits weren't credited or a payment was late on their business loan and the lender decided to foreclose.'

'I don't want that to happen,' Levan said.

'None of us do.'

'However, Simon Warrener isn't a threat to national security, and not even to my security,' Levan pointed out.

'I think you're splitting hairs, mate. He is a serious threat to Eden's peace of mind and – though we haven't worked out why yet – potentially to her financial security and that of her family.'

Levan nodded. 'I know, but this is still potentially outside of our remit.'

'Since when has stepping outside of your remit bothered you when you wanted to protect someone you cared about?' Dion gave him a hard stare, waiting for an answer to a question as loaded as the container ships that plied their way past the lighthouse.

'That's the excuse a lot of people make, and most of them are criminals – including me,' he replied tartly.

'Oh . . . so you don't want me to help you find out what this individual is up to?'

'Yes, but I'm not asking for your help. I don't want you to be in any trouble.'

'Oh, I'm always in trouble, the important thing is not to get caught.' Dion grinned cheerfully. 'You don't have to be associated with any of the investigations in any way.'

'That would be the coward's way out.' Levan offered up a grim smile. 'I suppose I could do what *you* tell me though. Wasn't that the condition of you giving me another chance?'

Dion slapped him on the back. 'If you're asking if it's an order, then yes.' He waved his card over the reader on the door. 'Now, if you're satisfied we've discussed the ethics of finding out what the delightful Simon is up to, and if he's telling the truth, shall we go inside? For all we know, he could be hanging around watching us right now.'

Levan nodded. He didn't think Simon was watching him for a moment and if he spent any more time or sleep debating the morality of spying on the man, he'd never rest.

He swiped his card and followed Dion inside. As expected, they were the only people in the building. The other four staff had left for the day.

Dion took a swivel chair in front of one of the terminals, but faced Levan. 'Before I do this, I need you to ask yourself a question. If and when we find out all is not what Simon would have us believe, what are you going to do about it?'

'I've thought about that and until I know, I can't make a decision.'

'How will Eden feel if you find out her ex has been lying – again?'

'Hurt. Humiliated. Again. I'd have to tread very carefully.'

'Because you care a lot about her?'

Levan nodded. 'Yeah. I wish I didn't, but it's too late.'

'You can't stop yourself caring about people, Lev. You can't stop being you. If you thought running away down here would keep you immune from that, then you're wrong.'

'I am *not* running away!' he snapped.

Dion's eyes widened. 'Of course not,' he soothed. 'I apologise. Wrong choice of words. I only meant that putting physical distance between you and the people you love – or loved – won't shield you from the pain, anger, regret, whatever it is you felt or don't want to feel now.'

Pain, anger, regret – all of those emotions simmered away constantly within him. He'd been able to keep a lid on them when he'd first arrived in Cornwall, but lately, they'd bubbled closer to the surface. He met Dion's gaze head-on, unable to express his feelings in words, and received a rueful smile in return.

Dion rolled his eyes. 'Enough amateur psychology. You don't need my advice.' He swivelled round in the chair and faced the keyboard, finger above the start key. 'So, do I press the nuclear button or not?'

Dion had accessed what he needed to access, suggested a few avenues of enquiry, then left Levan alone.

Over the next few hours, Levan pulled up Simon's criminal record, news reports and a whole load of stuff that was available to anyone who searched. He also gleaned some nuggets from a variety of government databases containing financial and health information, which certainly weren't open to the public.

He scrolled through them again, growing angrier every time he read the list of excuses that Simon and his lawyers had trotted out to explain his behaviour. They claimed he was suffering from stress, possibly depression, but no clinical diagnosis had been put forward. They claimed he was a high achiever, an only child driven by wanting to live up to the expectations of his parents.

Levan swore out loud. How dare Simon use that as an excuse!

The contrasting pictures he found on news media sites made him boil with indignation. They showed Simon living the high life and poor Eden, anguished and haunted. There was another news picture of her with Sally, who also looked thin and drawn. Other photos showed the woman whom Simon had proposed to and with whom he was intending to enter into a bigamous marriage.

There were snaps of Simon on a holiday. He was so egotistical, he'd taken selfies on his phone of himself in front of the Statue of Liberty. There was even one of him in a first-class suite on the plane to New York.

The arrogance of the man should have astonished Levan, if not for the fact that he'd seen it before: the entitlement, the harm that could be done by an individual who'd decided to exercise a twisted form of 'power' over other people.

In the last few days when he'd thought his mistress might be onto him, he'd operated a 'scorched earth' policy and spent his remaining money on a first-class air ticket to Panama. He'd also hit the casinos and gambled away several thousand pounds, and spent – according to one newspaper – thousands more on vintage champagne. It struck Levan as vindictive in the extreme. Simon had known he was going down and he'd decided to take as much of Eden's money with him as he could.

Levan no longer cared that some of the databases he was accessing were out of the remit of his day job. He knew no one would find out and Dion would never tell.

He felt fully justified because Simon had sucked Eden's confidence away, with his actions.

He'd wanted to tell her that the strongest and bravest person on the planet could still be a victim, could still be exploited and bullied and harmed by someone abusing their position of power.

If he could do anything to stop Simon doing that again to Eden, he would, no matter what the consequences.

A few hours later, he walked out into the evening sunshine, blinking in the light and trying to calm himself.

What he'd discovered about Simon shouldn't have surprised him, but it had.

Dion was waiting.

'Well?' he said.

'The consultant and the private hospital do exist. I called them but of course they couldn't say if Simon was a patient.' Levan levelled his gaze at Dion.

'Or if he wasn't?' Dion said with a wry raise of an eyebrow.

'It was what I expected but I obviously had other avenues to go down and I accessed his medical records. He is definitely not a patient there. As far as I could work out, he's never been referred for any treatment for testicular cancer either before, during or after his stay in jail. The worst I could find was a visit to his GP with an infected in-growing toenail.'

Dion rolled his eyes. 'I do hope it was painful.'

Levan leaned against his car. 'I took no pleasure in having my suspicions confirmed.'

'I bet. So, what are you going to do about it? Tell Eden?'

'In an ideal world, yes, but how can I tell her I've been spying on him? There's no way I could have found out the information by any normal means. I'll either have to admit I've been doing something secret behind her back or keep a vital piece of information from her.'

Dion grimaced. 'Impossible moral dilemmas are one of the downsides of the job and I can't provide the answer for you.' He patted Levan on the back. 'Come on, let's go to the Last Chance Saloon. Maybe we'll find an answer in there.'

Chapter Twenty-Five

Morwenna had arranged to meet Eden at the Surf Bar after they'd both finished work. It was a cool but bright evening, and they'd nabbed a table right by the glass balcony. As Morwenna was driving she stuck to lime and soda. Eden had an Aperol Spritz while they waited for their meals to arrive.

They were looking at a canvas, which Eden kept well away from her drink.

'Oh, Wenna, this is just amazing . . .'

Catching her breath, she held up the A4-sized print that Wenna had had printed on canvas. It showed Iris and Grandad Walter holding hands with Eden's father, Roger. He must have been around two or three, and was wearing short trousers and a hand-knitted jumper – and all three of them were grinning and squinting in the sunshine outside a lighthouse.

It had been taken in the sixties, as Iris was wearing a miniskirt and a figure-hugging sweater. Grandad Walter, his arm around his wife, was in pleated trousers and a white shirt with the sleeves rolled up, which was probably as casual as he had ever managed.

'Your granny was very on trend. She'd obviously embraced the Swinging Sixties,' Morwenna said.

'Whereas Grandad stayed in the fifties for the rest of his life,' Eden said. 'He was a lovely, kind man but he always seemed from a different age. He was a few years older than Granny, but I think it was all the rules and regulations of the lighthouse service. Maybe he never freed himself from that restrictive life.'

'Perhaps he liked it that way. Some people do like rules to live by.'

'I suppose we all need them . . .' Eden said. 'Apart from people like Simon, who don't think they apply.'

'I wasn't talking about breaking the law, only freeing yourself of some of the expectations the world imposes,' Morwenna said. 'Or that we let the world impose.'

Eden thought about Levan, and what he'd told her about his parents' expectations. It sounded like they'd pushed him to go into the army. She'd have loved to spend more time uncovering the layers beneath the surface charm. Yet after their embarrassing encounter, she'd decided to back off from him.

'True.'

'This canvas will make a beautiful present for Granny, together with the other prints. I'm sure she'll be delighted,' Eden said.

'I hope so. I was going to wrap the canvas up as my gift.'

'Oh Wenna, that's a lovely idea. Mum and I thought we'd wait and let her look through the restored photos in her own time after the party.'

'Great idea.' Morwenna slipped the canvas back inside a cardboard box and took it back to her car for safekeeping.

Eden sipped her drink and watched the surfers riding the evening swell. The car park was full of tradespeople's vans that doubled as surfboard transporters. You probably couldn't catch a wave without running into an electrician or plumber.

She smiled. You couldn't surf after work in London, that was for sure. There wasn't much of an upside to Simon's actions, but she was beginning to think that her move back to Cornwall might turn out to be a silver lining.

Morwenna was back at the table. 'So, any word from Simon since you sent him packing? Tell me more about this letter. Are you sure it's legit?'

'Well, it was from his consultant at a private hospital.'

'But?' Morwenna raised her eyebrows.

'It says he has a lump in his right testicle that's cancerous.'

Morwenna pulled a face. 'Yuk. I wish I hadn't chosen the meatballs now. Sorry, hun, shouldn't joke. I suppose I should feel sorry for him but I'm finding it hard. Go on. Did he ask for anything? How have you left it?'

'I wished him well and told him to go home to his parents.'

'Good for you! That can't have been easy.'

'Nothing ever is with Simon. I *did* love him once.'

'Yes, I know, and it must be impossible, but I'm relieved he didn't want anything and that you made your position clear. Let's hope he doesn't bother you again.' She raised her glass. 'Here's to Simon getting well and, more importantly, keeping the hell away from you.'

Eden chinked Morwenna's glass. 'And to me making a fresh start.'

Wenna raised her eyebrows over the rim of her cocktail. 'Will that fresh start involve Levan?'

'That's a different story . . . It's complicated.'

'It always is with you. Oh look, here are my meatballs.' She pulled a face.

After dinner, Eden wasn't ready to go home so the two of them went for a walk along the beach. Carrying their shoes, with the cool sand under her toes, she was reminded again that her move home wasn't the worst thing that could have happened, even though, raw and in the aftermath of the trial and losing the baby, she'd thought so at the time.

Dusk was falling and she glimpsed the wink of the lighthouse beam. How often had her granny and mother looked out on a dark winter's night and imagined their husbands marooned in the middle of the ocean, with weeks until they saw them again?

'Are you looking forward to the party?' Morwenna broke into her thoughts. 'You won't be working, I hope?'

'We're closing the café at two. I'll be too busy at the cottage so Courtney's in charge until then and coming straight to the party a bit later. His mum's arriving earlier to help with the food, along with Joe and Ravi.'

'Levan's still OK to pick up Iris? I can step in if you want to.'

'It's much further out of your way and Levan said he's happy to collect her.'

'So, everything is tickety-boo.'

'Tickety-boo?' Eden laughed.

'One of my clients said it the other day when I turned up to photograph his cottage. He was only our age. Some Hooray Henry. I almost collapsed laughing but I had to be nice and polite. Trouble is, I was *too* nice, because he asked me out on a date.'

'And did you say yes?'

Morwenna snorted. 'I politely declined and said my boyfriend wouldn't approve. I don't date men who wear snaffle loafers with red trousers.'

Eden giggled. 'Sounds like you had a lucky escape.'

The excitement of the party, and a fun night out with Morwenna, put Eden in a more relaxed and positive mood than she'd been in for ages. There was still an undercurrent of concern about Simon – whether he was telling the truth or not. Levan was an unknown quantity but for now he was helping at the party. What happened between them in the future, happened.

As Granny sometimes said: *que sera, sera* . . . although Eden didn't believe in leaving anything to fate after her experiences in life.

The following day, Eden popped into Seabreeze Court early after picking up supplies from the wholesaler in Penzance. She'd texted first and Iris had obviously been waiting by the window of her bungalow because she opened the door before Eden had even got out of the van.

They hugged and kissed on the doorstep before going inside.

'Hello, Granny, how are you?' Eden inhaled. 'Wow. You smell gorgeous.'

Iris beamed. 'It's a new scent. A bunch of us went shopping after we'd been swimming and they insisted on treating me for my birthday. It cost an arm and a leg, but I do love it.'

'It's divine,' Eden said, filling her nose with the floral perfume again.

'I'm going to wear it every day. No use keeping it for best at my age, is there?'

There was no suitable reply to this so Eden simply rolled her eyes and followed Iris through to the sitting room. A pile of cards lay in neat stacks on the dresser, ready to be opened on the big day.

'I thought we could grab a very quick coffee and make sure everything's OK for tomorrow?' Eden said, noting some fresh flowers arranged in a vase on the dining table.

'I've already made a cafetiere when you messaged to say you'd left the warehouse.'

Eden sniffed. 'Actually I can smell it. The new Guatemalan blend?'

'That's it. The one Levan chose.'

'He didn't choose it, he just liked it,' Eden said.

'Whatever you say, love.'

Iris poured two espressos and handed one to Eden. She noted that the kitchen table was covered in goodies: a traybake, a Victoria sponge and a pile of scones.

'Is this ready for your tea party later?'

'Yes. Everyone's bringing something; savouries, salads and the like. I thought I'd better make the cakes myself. Don't want to be accused of cheating.'

'Who'd dare say that?'

'Jim Tresize and Merryn King from swimming club.'

'They wouldn't, would they?'

'They would!' Iris chuckled. 'Not that I care. I enjoy baking and I suppose they're not a bad lot. I do like most of them.'

Eden laughed again. 'You more than like them. You've told me you couldn't manage without your friends and your activities.'

'No . . . I do have a busy life. I'm no lonely old lady – I'd hate anyone to think that – but it's hard not to yearn for your youth and lost opportunities when you get to my age.'

'Lost opportunities?' Eden said, thinking of the mystery photo. 'What do you mean, Granny? You were happy with Grandad, weren't you, even though it was tough to be apart so much?'

'How could we not be? He was a kind and loving man. He always did his duty too, what was right – and you can't say that about a lot of men, then and now.'

Before Eden could reply, they were interrupted by a loud knock at the front door and a voice calling: 'Hello, Iris . . . it's Sonali!'

Sonali breezed in bearing several quiches and a tray of samosas in a cardboard box and they all started chatting about the tea party. Eden thanked her for arranging it and then made her excuses, reminding Iris that Levan would collect her the following afternoon.

'I won't forget that in a hurry,' Iris said. 'There's nothing wrong with my memory!'

'I know, Granny.' Eden kissed her cheek. 'Enjoy your tea party. See you tomorrow!'

She'd got halfway up the path when Iris called: 'I hope you haven't gone to too much trouble!'

'We wouldn't dream of it!' she called back, before waving and climbing into the van.

She drove off towards the Coffee Container, happy that her granny seemed excited about her birthday celebrations but also wondering about her poignant words:

How could we not be happy? He was a kind and loving man. He always did his duty too, what was right – and you can't say that about a lot of men, then and now.

Who was this man who didn't do his duty? Was Iris actually referring to Simon – or the mystery man in the photo?

'Eden Carrick, I thought you weren't coming into work today?' Courtney wagged his finger at Eden when he found her already at the café on the morning of the party.

She was unpacking takeout cups ready to stack them by the machine when he'd walked in through the rear door. 'I couldn't sleep and there's such a lot to do so I thought I'd get up early and help you open up.'

'Are you trying to say you don't trust me to hold the fort on my own?'

'No! I mean, of course I do, but I know how busy Sunday morning can be at breakfast service, plus I had to drop the pastries off anyway so I opened up. Look, they're like gannets around a trawler . . .'

Through the rear door, she spotted two of the campers eyeing up the container over the top of the hedge, hoping it might be open.

'I could have managed,' Courtney insisted, grabbing his apron from the peg.

'I know but you'd have been rushed off your feet. The party isn't until two and Mum said she has plenty of help from Levan and Joe with the setting up, so I came over. I promise I'll be out of your hair later.'

In the end, Courtney might not have managed because the Sunday morning rush was completely manic. Not only did the campers turn out in force, but the café seemed to have a continuous stream of walkers and people pulling up in their cars.

Eden surveyed the queue again. 'Do you think there's an

event nearby that we don't know about? A festival or end-to-end race?'

Busy at the machine, Courtney shrugged. 'If there is, I've heard nothing about it. I think it might have to do with your new socials. At least two people have mentioned they saw us on Instagram and I can see people holding up their phones as if they're making sure they're at the right place.'

'I wouldn't have thought it would make a difference so fast.'

'It probably shows how few people knew we were here before,' he said, expertly finishing two flat whites.

Eden watched more people join the snaking queue. 'Hmm. Morwenna's done us a big favour . . . I think.'

Half an hour later, the breakfast and coffee time rush had died down. Courtney turned to Eden. 'Right, that's it. You *have* to go home. Aren't you supposed to be setting up and helping in the kitchen? It's past eleven!'

Eden squeaked in alarm. 'Oh my God, is it? Mum will be doing her nut. I need to get changed as well as help. You need to come along too. Close up at twelve. We've done so well this morning, we can afford to.'

She'd started pulling off her apron and heard her phone buzzing. It had cut off by the time she'd reached it but she saw the message.

It was from Iris. It said three words.

Simon is here

Chapter Twenty-Six

Eden's blood turned to ice.

In that split second, she was catapulted back to the moment of shock she'd experienced when the police had arrived at her home to tell her that Simon had been arrested. She felt paralysed, her chest squeezing tightly . . .

A moment later, the adrenaline kicked in. Exhaling sharply, she ripped off the apron and threw it on the floor of the container.

Courtney swung round from the machine. 'What's the matter?'

'It's Granny. My ex has turned up at her place. I have to go!'

Without waiting for an answer, she flew to her van and jumped in, her chest so crushed by panic she could barely breathe. Her brain was scrambled with fear and her fingers had turned into pudgy lumps of dough. It took three agonising goes to find and press the speed dial for Iris's number, punctuated with squeals and swearing.

She turned over the engine, ready to roar off the moment her granny picked up.

Click.

'Gran— oh no!

Her call went straight to answerphone. What if Iris *couldn't* answer? Simon wasn't violent but seeing him out of the blue would be a hell of a shock for her granny – especially on her birthday. Iris didn't need that kind of worry at her age,

Eden thanked every star that she'd invested in a hands-free and skidded out of the car park.

'Call Granny!' she ordered.

The dial tone rang out but once again there was no response. Then there was no signal. Squashing the urge to panic, she told herself to stay calm for Iris's sake – it was no use if she had an accident on the way there. Further down the road, she'd get the signal back. There was always some outside the Co-op.

Hurrah!

She tried again but the call went to Iris's voicemail.

Her mother. She had to call her mother. Her hands-free dialled Sally but went straight to voicemail too. Eden swore before she forced herself to get a grip. Her mother was busy and had probably put her phone away somewhere while she focused on the party.

Levan . . . he would have his phone on him. He had an Apple Watch that alerted him to calls and messages too. It was impossible not to get hold of him.

Eden almost shouted in relief when he answered immediately.

'Hi, Eden.'

'Thank God you answered! I need you!'

'What's the matter?'

'It's Granny. Simon's at her place. I don't know why or how but he's there. I got a message five minutes ago but I don't know how long he has been there or what he wants. If he's hurt her or made her ill, I don't know what I'll do!'

'OK,' he said firmly. 'First, from what you've told me about him, he won't hurt her. It's not his style. And secondly, I'm actually already in Penzance.'

'Are you? Brilliant. Can you get there as fast as you can and see if she's OK? I'll be there as soon as I can. Oh shit, a bloody veg truck just pulled out in front of me. Arghhhh!'

'Try not to worry. I'm sure Iris can handle Simon and I'll be there in ten minutes,' he said calmly. 'Do you have the warden's number to call her?'

'Mum does but I can't get hold of her.'

'Don't worry about it, then. I'll be there just as quickly.'

'Thank you! I'll keep trying Granny, and please let me know how she is the moment you get there.'

'I will . . . and Eden, take care!'

Chapter Twenty-Seven

If that bastard had upset Iris . . .

Levan spun out of the exit from the tech warehouse, forcing himself to focus on the road. He believed what he'd told Eden about Simon not physically harming Iris, but she must have had a shock when he turned up out of the blue.

Since he'd discovered that Simon had been lying, and for whatever nefarious reasons of his own was trying to inveigle his way back into Eden's life, Levan had been in a dilemma. Three days later, he still hadn't decided whether or not to tell Eden the truth.

Now it looked as if he might be too late.

He was silently screaming in frustration by the time he arrived at the bungalow, jumped out of his car and jogged to the front door.

He almost cheered in relief when Iris opened it, beaming.

'Oh, it's you!' she said. 'I was expecting Eden . . . but what a lovely surprise.'

'Are you OK, Iris?' he said, trying to assess if she'd been hurt in any way.

'Oh yes!' she replied breezily. 'I'm fine and isn't this lovely, Simon's here – he's brought me some flowers and a card for my birthday.'

She sounded very cheery – too cheery, considering a ghost from the past had turned up out of the blue. Levan's skin prickled with unease.

'Come in,' she said, ushering him into the sitting room. Occupying one of the armchairs, sipping from a teacup, was a man about his own age.

Levan hadn't met the man in the flesh before and it was safe to say he didn't like the flesh. His heart burned with contempt for Simon Warrener, the man who'd caused the Carrick family so much pain.

Simon put the cup on the table. 'So, you're Levan?' he said, smirking but with a spiteful expression in his eyes.

'I keep telling Simon that Walter will be home in a minute . . .' Iris said. 'But now you're here, so that's fine.' She gripped Levan's hand. 'Simon, this is my son, Roger.'

'I think you're a little confused, Iris,' Simon barged in before Levan could even reply. 'This is Levan, a friend of your granddaughter's. I'm Simon, her husband.'

'Are you?' Iris's eyes clouded.

The *bastard*. Levan stood by Iris protectively. Simon must have shocked her so much, she'd become confused. His stomach turned over: what if it was worse than that and she'd had a stroke?

Ignoring Simon, he kissed Iris's cheek. 'I'm Levan,' he said. 'Your friend,' he added soothingly. 'And Simon was married to Eden once but they're divorced now.' With a hand on Iris's shoulder, he faced Simon.

'What are you doing here?' he snapped.

'Bringing a present and card for my wife's grandmother. Iris and I were close,' Simon said. 'Weren't we?'

'Simon made me a lovely cuppa,' Iris said, indicating a china cup, half full on the coffee table. 'I told him I'm not so good on my pins now so he went into the kitchen and did it.'

Levan almost spoke then saw Iris's expression: she gazed up into his eyes with such trust, his stomach turned over. Iris was perfectly capable of making a cup of tea. In fact, she'd made a load of cakes according to Sally and she'd managed to message Eden. What the fuck had Simon done to her in the time he'd been in the bungalow? Had he put something in her tea?

'That's very nice of him,' Levan said, meeting Simon's eyes. He wanted to throw the man out into the street but he didn't want to aggravate a dangerous and scary situation for Iris. Eden would be there soon. 'However, I'm not sure that you were invited to visit by Iris, Eden or her mother.'

Simon kept on smiling. 'I don't need an invitation. I'm one of the family. Unlike you . . .'

Ignoring him, Levan spoke kindly to Iris. 'Eden will be here in a minute.'

'Eden?' Iris murmured, staring into space. 'I don't know any Eden.'

'Granny!'

Eden's shout preceded her arrival into the bungalow. Red-faced and breathing hard, she exploded into the sitting room.

'Simon! What the hell are you doing here!'

She flew to Iris's side and put her arm around her grandmother protectively. 'Are you OK, Granny?'

'Of course I am,' Iris murmured faintly.

'She's not harmed physically,' Levan said, deeply concerned about her mental state. The main thing now was to get rid of Simon before Eden went for him.

'He was just about to leave,' Levan said, blocking her route to the man who was lounging in the chair like a poisonous lizard.

'Hello, Eden,' Simon said, a nasty smile playing on his lips.

Eden answered his greeting with a look of naked contempt. She switched her focus to Iris, taking her hand. 'It's OK, Granny, I'm here now.'

Iris stared at her and said: 'Who are you?'

Levan's stomach turned over.

'It's me, Eden, your granddaughter,' Eden said with a tremor in her voice that made Levan want to hold her – and kick Simon's arse.

'What have you done to her!' Eden cried, fixing Simon with a murderous glare.

'Nothing. She's clearly lost her marbles, though.'

Only with the greatest restraint did Levan avoid leaping on the smarmy lowlife. By now he was deeply worried about a fight breaking out and thought it was high time Simon left.

'You look after your granny,' he said with a warning glance at Eden. 'I'll deal with Simon.'

'Oh, you'll "deal with me", will you?' Simon's voice dripped with sarcasm. 'Should I be scared?'

Levan's pulse spiked. He wasn't sure what Simon knew about his past or if the comment was just coincidence, but his main concern was to end the situation without further conflict and keep Iris and Eden safe.

'It depends if you've done something you shouldn't have,' he said smoothly. 'However, I think we've had enough drama for one day. Thank you *so* much for delivering the flowers, but I've come to take Iris to her birthday lunch so I'm afraid you're going to have to leave. *Now*,' he added with a glare when Simon showed no sign of moving.

Simon lounged back in the chair. 'Oh, but it would be such a shame if I missed the chance to chat to Eden again.'

'I don't think it would be a good idea for you to hang around,' Levan stepped forward, staring down at the smirking face, and understanding just how much trouble and pain this reptile must have put Eden and his victims through. 'For your sake and hers.'

'Get out of here while you can, Simon,' Eden said. 'Or I'm not sure what might happen next.'

Finally, Levan saw Simon's mask slip and genuine fear in his eyes.

'Wait!' Iris cried. 'Simon hasn't found what he was looking for yet.'

Simon snatched up his jacket. 'I don't know what you're talking about, Iris.'

'You seemed very keen to find it earlier,' Iris said with such innocence that Levan's antennae twitched.

'What do you mean, Granny?' Eden said gently, squeezing Iris's hand.

'I'll be on my way now,' Simon muttered, eyeing the door to the hall as if he was now desperate to escape.

Levan gave Simon a hard stare. 'What *were* you looking for, Simon?'

'Nothing,' Simon blustered. 'Iris must be confused.'

'No . . . I don't think so,' Iris declared with sudden firmness. 'While Simon was making the tea I went to the loo and messaged Eden. Then, I heard him opening and closing

244

drawers in the lounge so I hid in the hallway and I spotted him hunting through my dresser.'

Simon scowled at Iris over Levan's shoulder. 'You must have been mistaken.'

'No, I don't think so,' Iris went on, her voice steady as a rock. 'Were you looking for my cheque book, by any chance?'

'Cheque book?' Simon gave a sneering laugh. 'I've no idea what you're talking about. I think you're rambling, Iris.'

'Granny?' Eden said. 'What's this about a cheque book?'

'I'm not rambling,' Iris said. 'And I knew as soon as Simon turned up that he wanted something and it wasn't to wish me a happy bloody birthday! He came here to see what he could get! But you've no chance of finding a cheque book or cash in the house. I don't keep notes here and I do my banking online now, or in person at the branch.'

Eden's eyes lit up as she realised that Iris had been playing a part.

Levan wanted to punch the air in relief.

Iris grasped her stick. 'And if the little git thinks I'm going to be duped by a smooth-talking snake who thinks he can prey on a vulnerable old woman, he can bugger—'

'All right, all right,' Simon said loudly. 'I'm going!'

Eden rounded on him. 'Simon. You utter bastard.'

'Do you want my stick?' Iris cried. 'Let me at him. Trying to con me!'

With Eden looming over him, Simon cowered in the chair. 'I can see you're angry, but I can explain . . .'

'Angry? You swore you'd leave us alone. What the hell are you doing here? I'd like to throw you out.'

She grabbed his arm but Levan intervened. 'Let him go. You don't want arresting for assault.'

Eden released Simon's arm and Simon held up a cushion. 'She's out of control,' he whined.

'I'll show you who's out of control,' Iris shouted, brandishing her stick again.

'This isn't helping,' Levan ordered.

Eden stepped back, visibly trembling. 'If he'd hurt Granny, I'd have . . .'

'He hasn't, love,' Iris said. 'It's all about money and power over us again: over you, me and your mother. I usually believe in giving people a second chance but not him – he's rotten to the core.'

Simon wrinkled his nose. 'I'll hand it to you, Iris, you had me convinced you'd gone senile.' He took his chance to spring out of the chair and run to the door, breathing heavily. 'You lot are pathetic!'

Eden ran after him, with Levan close behind in case Simon turned nasty. He was halfway up the path but Levan could hear every word.

'Wait!' she called. 'I get that you were trying to con us. Bizarrely, I can understand that. It's what I expected from you.'

Levan smiled, quietly and fiercely proud of her despite his anger with Simon.

'Like I said, I expected you to scam me but the one thing that persuaded me to speak to you again was your claim to be sick. So, if it's possible for you to tell a word of truth, tell me this: are you even ill?'

Levan held his breath, his heart beating harder.

Simon shrugged. 'What do you think?'

'Surely you haven't lied about that? About having cancer?'

He gave her a humourless smile and Levan wanted to hit him. 'You'll have to make your own mind up.'

'Simon!'

'Goodbye, Eden. You won't see me again. I've given up on you, as you've clearly given up on me.'

Eden stood on the path, then took a step forward as if she was going to confront or follow him. Levan jogged out to her. 'Let him go.'

She turned to him. 'Can he not even say one true word? I don't think there's ever been anything wrong with him. Yet the hospital letter seems legit.'

'Your granny's right, he thrives on power as much as the scam itself.'

'I know. I *ought* to know. He'd better not come near me again. I might have known he was after money. When I washed my hands of him despite his sob story, he must have decided to see what he could get from Granny. Thanks so much for racing around here to help her.'

'Well, you don't need a white knight . . .' he began.

'No, but occasionally they come in useful.' She touched his hand. 'Thank you, from me and Granny.'

His heart squeezed with emotion at the look of gratitude, and vulnerability, she gave him. It almost made him sweep her into his arms at that very moment and kiss her until she couldn't stand up.

Instead he told her solemnly, 'I promise you, Eden, you'll never owe me anything but I do have a confession to make.'

Her brow furrowed. 'A confession?'

'Yes, and I hope you won't be too shocked but I – I also didn't trust him. I did something that's not technically legal.'

Her lips parted in shock. '*What?*'

'At work, I checked up on his medical records on a central database and, while his hospital and doctor are real, Simon

247

has never been a patient of theirs. He's not ill at all, and I was going to tell you.'

'When did you find this out?'

His pulse skittered. 'Only very recently,' he said, hoping that phrase would encompass anything from a few hours to a few days. 'I was thinking about how to tell you when you phoned to say Simon was at your granny's.'

Eden sat down on the garden bench by the front door. 'Oh, God. I've been such an idiot.'

Levan flew to her side. 'No. No, you haven't! Simon is an accomplished criminal and you phoned the hospital to check. His letter looks so authentic too, anyone would have thought it was real. It's only because I have access to other resources that I was able to check.'

'"Other resources",' she echoed.

'As part of my job. We have to check up on people,' he said limply. 'If they might pose a threat . . .' he hesitated. 'Though it's intended to be a threat to the building, not to people I care about. I'm sorry, I absolutely can't say any more.'

Eden stared at him, and he braced himself for an interrogation. 'Then you shouldn't say more,' she said, at last and much to his relief. 'Perhaps it's best if I don't know how you did it. The important thing is that you did – for Granny's sake, even more than mine.'

He exhaled in relief. 'Good. And would you mind keeping this between us?'

She crossed her heart. 'Of course.'

He'd already gone much further than he'd intended to in revealing he'd investigated Simon. Much further than he should have. He teetered on the edge of another confession, one that was long overdue – and essential if he wanted to tell Eden just how much he felt for her . . .

'Now,' she said with renewed firmness. 'Simon can go away and rot as far as I'm concerned. I've other things to focus on: the people I care about.'

Did that include him? The way she was looking at him, with shining eyes, gave him hope: more hope than he'd ever had before.

'Rest assured, I won't be taken in again.'

'You never were,' Levan said. 'Nor your wonderful granny.'

'She was rather magnificent, wasn't she?'

Just like her granddaughter, Levan wanted to say, but that would have sounded far too much like one of Simon's manipulative compliments so he kept his mouth shut.

'Shall we go inside, make Iris a cup of tea and then take her to Lighthouse Cottages?' he said.

Eden nodded and Levan followed her back into the cottage, making sure the door was shut. He sincerely hoped that Simon would stay away, though he wasn't totally convinced.

Eden and her grandmother were on the sofa, where she was already starting to relate her story of how Simon had turned up, and how she'd realised immediately that he wanted something and how she'd duped him.

'Once I'd got over the shock of him turning up, I actually rather enjoyed myself,' she said. 'Although I was very glad to see Levan. Very glad indeed.'

'Not as glad as I was to see you safe and well,' Levan said.

'Nor me, Granny.' Eden held Iris's hand.

'I'm fine. I can handle the likes of Simon, don't you worry. Now, it's my birthday and I'm more than ready for a good lunch with my family. Shall we not tell anyone about what happened today?'

'I'll have to confess to Mum,' Eden said. 'Or she'll wonder where I am and why I was frantically trying to call her.'

'*I'll* explain to your mother and let her know everything is fine, but I refuse to let that slimy git ruin my special day for a moment longer. Now, I need to put a few things together and then you can take me to this lunch,' she said and turned to Eden. 'Now, you go home, get changed and my Prince Charming here will escort me to the ball.'

Iris linked her arm through Levan's and he smiled broadly.

Eden shook her head. 'Aren't you going to deny being Prince Charming?'

He gave a little bow. 'Certainly not. I like the role too much.'

Eden left with a 'See you later' and Levan was left alone in the sitting room, realising that Prince Charming was the very last role he could ever inhabit. He felt closer to the villain of the piece than the hero, or at least he occupied a spot somewhere along that grey line in between.

Soon, a radiant Iris came downstairs, dressed in an elegant silk trouser suit and smelling of an expensive scent.

Levan took her arm, kissed her on the cheek, whispered: 'You look lovely, Iris,' and escorted her out to his car.

'You know, I really believe you think that, young man,' she said. 'But enough of it. Come on.'

He had a smile on his face but a lump of emotion in his throat. He'd never really known any of his grandparents and all four were dead now. He'd also never known the warmth and unconditional love shared by the Carrick family, or perhaps, he admitted, it was there but his own loved ones were too afraid of seeming weak to show their deepest emotions.

Seeing how Eden had reacted to Simon's betrayal was more than enough for him to keep quiet about his own past – for now. Today was most definitely not a day for shocking confessions of any kind.

Chapter Twenty-Eight

'*Surprise!!!!*'
Noise and streamers exploded into the air as Iris stepped into the garden of Wolf Rock.

'*Happy Birthday to you!*

'*Happy Birthday to you!*

'*Happy Birthday, dear Iris!*

'*Happy Birthday to you!*'

Standing in the gateway, Iris had one hand over her mouth and the other steadying herself on the gatepost.

'Hello, Granny!' Eden rushed forward and hugged Iris at the gate. Sally joined them as everyone tooted horns and shouted greetings. Levan, who'd lingered a few feet behind, followed them, carrying supermarket bags that, Eden assumed, were full of party food.

'Oh my,' Iris fanned herself. 'I suspected you might have invited a couple of friends, but not this many!'

'You're not cross we went to too much trouble?' Sally said, laughing.

'I'm furious, can't you tell?' Iris hugged her. 'No, I'm not cross. It's wonderful to see so many people! I'm only worried about how much work went into this on top of all your other jobs.'

'We haven't minded a bit, Granny. We've loved planning it,' Eden said, delighted at the joy on Iris's face, particularly after such an upsetting morning.

'Have you all been in on it?' Iris's keen eyes picked out the party guests, wagging her finger at them in mock admonishment.

'Oh, yes. Feels like the whole of the county west of Penzance has been in on it,' Eden said.

'Come on, we've got a special seat reserved for you,' Sally said. 'You look fabulous.'

'You do look completely amazing, Granny. I haven't seen that suit before.'

'That's because it's new. I took a risk and ordered it online, and luckily it fit well.'

Eden agreed. Iris must have changed after she'd left the bungalow, and was wearing a shimmering pale lilac suit that looked as if it was silk. In the midst of the earlier drama, Eden hadn't had time to notice that Iris had had her hair done, but she did now. It was beautifully coiffed and her granny had put on some subtle make-up since she'd left.

The colour of the suit brought out Iris's eyes and she was glowing with happiness. Eden could see exactly how her grandad – and possibly other men – had fallen for her.

Soon, Iris was lost amid a throng of friends, all wishing her a happy birthday and telling her how marvellous she looked.

Over by the barbecue, Levan and Courtney were setting light to the charcoal while Joe and Ravi laid out salads and trays of prepared meat on the tables. They were all intent on their tasks and Eden watched them, smiling. Her mother, wearing a new midi dress, was chatting to Courtney's mum. There was only Morwenna to come, after she'd finished a rush job in Lamorna. Everyone Eden knew and loved was safe and well and ready to celebrate, which was more than she'd expected for a while earlier that day.

Not long after, Morwenna arrived, rather breathless. 'Sorry I'm late. Bloody traffic and then I had to whizz home, get changed and call a taxi. Not missed any of the excitement, have I?'

'Nothing too dramatic,' Eden said, deciding to reserve her encounter with Simon until later. 'You're just in time.'

'I've brought the photos in my bag. You still want to show them to Iris in private later, not in public?'

'Yes, Mum and I think it might be too emotional for Granny to look at them in front of everyone, even if we are keeping the mystery man a secret. We'll do it when everyone's gone and if it's too late, we could save them until tomorrow.'

'That's fine with me. Now, where's the fizz? I'm getting a lift home to St Just with Courtney's mum.'

Morwenna flitted off to the drinks table, and Eden found Iris. 'Sorry to drag you away from your adoring public, Granny, but it's time for your presents.'

'What presents?' Iris said innocently.

Eden laughed. 'Come on, this is your seat.'

Levan and Joe carried out a high-backed sunlounger, decked out in balloons and streamers, with a big sign on the back that said 'Iris'.

'I shall feel like royalty,' Iris said.

'You're regal to us,' Courtney replied solemnly.

'Now, put these on, please. No arguments.' Eden handed her a tiara and a sash with 'Nifty Ninety' on it.

Iris chuckled. 'I could get used to this kind of treatment, you know.'

'You deserve it!'

Sally called everyone to order.

'Before Iris opens her presents, I'd like to say a few words. In the old days, it was customary to joke that you didn't get on with your mother-in-law. Those days are thankfully gone. Even if we were in the old days, I'd still tell you that Iris is an amazing mother-in-law.'

A ripple of assent and 'Hear hear's went round.

Iris looked at Sally, with a hint of a tear in her eye.

'Even my own mum and dad tell me I'm lucky to have her.'

'Thank you,' Iris murmured.

'Everyone here knows that the years have, at times, been very challenging. Losing Walter and then Roger were blows we all found hard to bear.'

The backs of Eden's eyes were itchy. She didn't want to cry but it was going to be hard.

'Together we found the strength to continue, helped of course by our wonderful Eden, who was there to help and support us even though she was grieving herself.'

Wow. Her mother rarely spoke of the losses they'd borne and preferred to present a happy, busy face to the world. There were moist eyes all around her and only by digging her nails in her palm could Eden stop the tears from flowing.

'Even when she was experiencing the most testing times herself, she was here for us.'

Iris held out her hand, beckoning to Eden to come near, which she did. She grasped her hand and held it tightly. Levan stood by stiffly, as if he didn't dare to let himself go or he'd cry too.

'Iris has been the bedrock of all our lives, the steady guiding light to her family and friends and all around her. So, this is a toast to her and everyone who loved this place and the friends gathered now to celebrate this milestone. May all our lights shine bright!'

A wobbly but enthusiastic cheer went up. 'May all our lights shine bright!'

'Right, Iris. Time for your presents.'

The next half-hour was taken up with Iris opening her gifts, punctuated by gasps, cries of delight and laughter.

Levan gave Iris a hardback of a new release by her favourite historical author, signed and dedicated to her and wishing her a happy ninetieth birthday.

'How on earth did you get this?' Iris cried when she unwrapped it.

'I made friends with the bookshop owner, who knows the author,' Levan said. 'He arranged for it to be signed to you.'

'It's wonderful,' Iris said, proudly showing it around.

Eden turned to Levan. 'That was a very thoughtful gift for Granny. You couldn't have chosen anything more perfect.'

'Well, she deserves special treatment – especially today,' he said.

'I still don't know how you kept it a secret, knowing how much she'd love it.'

A wry smile crossed his face. 'Oh, some secrets are easier to keep than others.'

In that moment, Eden felt a rush of something beyond friendship and even desire towards him. His willingness to rush to Iris's aid had shown that he truly cared about her granny – and Eden herself. Had he really held back from kissing her because of Simon?

A moment later, she was swept off by Iris so she could

admire the flowers and Cornish champagne from Joe and Ravi, and a silk scarf and luxury chocolates from Courtney and his mum, Dorian.

'And a bottle of spiced rum,' Dorian said, handing over a bottle. 'A friend brought it over specially for you from her last trip to Jamaica. You can't get it here so be careful!'

'I'll have to share this with you,' Iris said. 'I can't drink it on my own or I'll be under the table.'

'It makes great cocktails,' Courtney said. 'I could make you a Mermaid Lemonade.'

'What's that?' Iris said.

'Blue curaçao, lemonade and rum!'

Iris gave a wicked grin. 'I shouldn't, not on top of champagne – but if you'll all join me, I'd be delighted.'

Courtney beamed. 'Of course, I'll go to it.'

'Not too much rum, mind!' Iris called after him.

The tang of the barbecue smoke filled the air. Some of the holiday guests came to see what was happening and wished Iris a happy birthday. One returned with her children, a girl and a boy, and a homemade card that almost made Iris cry again.

'What's it like being ninety?' the little girl asked.

'When you've lived a full life like me, and you have your family and friends round you, it's not too bad at all,' Iris told her. 'In fact, it's pretty marvellous.'

'You don't look ninety,' the boy, around seven, declared. 'You only look eighty-two, like my great grandad.'

His mother shook her head. 'You don't even look eighty, Iris.'

Iris laughed. 'I still feel twenty-one sometimes . . . in my head.'

After the guest had taken the children back to their garden, Iris, Sally and Eden finally had a few minutes to talk, while everyone was chatting, mixing drinks or barbecuing around them.

Courtney appeared briefly with the cocktails, giving Eden a chance to pop into the cottage for Iris's special present.

'This is from us, Granny. Me and Mum.'

Iris was in tears when she unboxed the gift: a glamorous new dressing robe and the voucher for two nights in the hotel.

'Oh, I've always, always wanted to stay there. I never thought I would. Now, we'll all be able to pamper ourselves together.'

Eden frowned. '*All*?'

'Yes.' Iris held up the vouchers. 'We're booked in the Seashell Suite. You, your mum and me.'

'The Seashell Suite?' Eden exclaimed, confused and a little worried. 'The Seashell Suite is the apartment with two bedrooms.'

Eden's mum put her arm around Eden. 'And the sitting room with sofa bed. It overlooks the sea. Like here,' she said. 'Though perhaps a bit more luxurious.'

'And it includes dinner and their food is meant to be fantastic!' Iris said, then her face fell. 'But you shouldn't have done this. It's far too much of a treat for me. I must contribute. I wouldn't go without you both and I wouldn't hear of you paying out for this.'

'Don't worry, Iris. We haven't. OK, we have but, if it makes you feel better, my friend has wangled us a very generous discount.' Sally smiled. 'I know you love a bargain.'

'Yes, but there's no way this is a bargain.'

Eden stood by, confused. Her mother smiled at her. 'And although I was sworn to secrecy, I'm going to set your minds at rest as long as you promise not to let him know I told you. Levan heard that we were going and insisted on contributing to a room upgrade so we could *all* enjoy a touch more luxury.'

The penny dropped. Eden glanced over at Levan, who was with a group of people laughing together by the barbecue.

'That was *very* generous of him,' she murmured.

'He's such a lovely man,' Iris said breathily.

'He is,' Sally said and winked at Eden. 'Please don't tell him you know, though. He wanted to keep it discreet. He said he didn't want anyone to thank him. So, keep my secret, please,' Sally said, her voice serious.

Eden nodded.

Iris zipped her lips. 'I will. I'd better not have another cocktail, though.'

'I think some food would help. I can smell that jerk chicken cooking. Time to start dishing out the hot dogs. Eden, would you mind bringing that sweetcorn relish and the salads outside, please? I think they'll be OK, now we're so close to eating.'

It was all hands to the pump as delicious aromas of barbecued meat filled the air. Plates were piled high and refilled with the chicken, seafood and salads.

Sardine wound his way around the tables, sniffing at titbits, until Eden scooped him up. 'He'll be fat as a pudding hoovering up the chicken and dropped prawns! If he eats any onions, it won't do him any good.'

'I'll take him, inside, shall I?' Levan said.

'You can try and keep him in the scullery for now, with his water and litter tray. I'll have to lock the cat flap.'

'I'll do it.' Levan took Sardine from her. The cat screwed up his face and wriggled. 'Come on, boy. It's for your own good.'

People found seats and drinks and the buzz of chatter grew louder as the sun sank lower. Eden's limbs and mind relaxed, relieved that her granny was none the worse for her ordeal and that Simon would surely now stay away from them all. There were enough bodyguards here to see him off if he did dare to turn up.

Joe and Ravi handed around some nibbles, while Iris chatted. Courtney was showing Morwenna how to make Mermaid Lemonade.

Eden headed into the kitchen to make sure her mother wasn't rushed off her feet, finding the meat and veggies for the barbecue. Levan was already there, removing trays of sausages, seafood skewers and halloumi kebabs from the fridge.

Eden took her chance to speak to him alone. 'It was very generous of you to contribute to the weekend at the hotel.'

He wrinkled his nose. 'That was meant to be a secret. Your mum promised not to let on.'

Eden grinned. 'Well, you just confirmed it for me.'

Levan sighed then shook his head. 'I walked right into that trap, didn't I? I'd be useless under any real interrogation.'

His expression was mock exasperated – and also deliciously teasing. Eden went tingly and reminded herself she had a whole evening to get through, and also that the last time she'd let her feelings for Levan get the better of her, she'd been gently but firmly pushed away.

'Well, thank you again,' she said more stiffly.

'When your mum told me about the booking, I didn't like to think of you missing out.'

'Granny's so happy that the three of us are going,' Eden said. 'It's thoughtful of you to realise that.'

260

'It was also for you,' he said, and he looked at her intensely, almost with longing. 'If anyone deserves special treatment, it's *you*.'

She tried not to react, though her body had other ideas. It was warm in the kitchen so why did she feel shivery?

She picked up a tray and held it to herself defensively. 'I must take this chicken out to Courtney.'

Levan grinned. 'And I ought to bring the halloumi.'

'Guests come first,' Eden said, her voice a little higher than she'd have liked.

'For now,' Levan said, with a wink before sweeping past Eden and out of the kitchen.

Eden managed to keep a safe distance from Levan for the rest of the evening. She was aware that the fizz and the party atmosphere, and the general emotional rollercoaster of the day, had seriously messed with her self-control. At various points she felt like either bursting into tears, dragging Levan off into the night or running for the hills.

The sun sank low on the horizon and the sky turned from blue to indigo, and the lighthouse beam activated.

Those who hadn't been to the spot in the evening before were entranced, whipping out their phones and snapping away. Morwenna had been taking photos from the start and whisked Iris, Eden and Sally away to grab some family groups in front of the lighthouse.

'Everyone's busy eating and drinking so we won't be missed for a few minutes,' she said. 'We should capture this scene for posterity.'

'Will you do me some prints?' Iris asked as they returned to the barbecue.

'Of course,' Morwenna said, exchanging a knowing look with Eden and Sally.

'Lovely.' Iris eased herself into a chair. 'Excuse me, I need a sit-down.'

Eden squeezed her hand. Iris was starting to flag a little and looking tired.

'Just say when you've had enough.'

'I will, but even if I go inside for a nap, you mustn't send anyone home. Party on!'

When everyone had finally finished eating, Joe clapped his hands.

'And now, I hope you've all left room for the pièce de résistance!'

Ravi carried out the cake to gasps and applause.

'Oh my. Oh – oh – that's incredible,' Iris stammered. 'Oh, it's all too much, I really don't—'

'Yes, you do!' everyone shouted as an amazed Iris walked over to the table where the cake had been placed.

The magnificent edible model of Hartstone almost made Eden cry. It was so beautiful. It stretched up four storeys high, with a lantern at the top.

'That's us,' Iris said breathily, pointing to the three female figures made of sugar paste. There was also a jolly keeper in his uniform with a peaked cap and a tiny model of Sardine.

'Where are the candles?' Morwenna said.

'Just you wait,' Joe said.

Very carefully, he removed the top of the lighthouse cake to reveal a concealed holder with a battery tealight within the 'lantern room'. He switched it on and replaced the top. In the fading light, the lantern glowed – and Iris burst into tears.

Eden and her mother stood either side of Iris and put their arms around her.

Joe addressed everyone. 'I want to thank the Carricks for hosting a wonderful party and once again wish Iris a very happy birthday. Now, before you're all far too merry to do it, I think we should have a chorus of "For She's a Jolly Good Fellow"!'

With her arms around the people she loved most in the world, Eden joined in the singing. Out of the corner of her eye, she caught Levan looking at her intensely, with undisguised desire. Tonight might mark a milestone for Iris, yet Eden had a powerful feeling it could mark a fresh start in her own life. Was she ready to embrace it?

Chapter Twenty-Nine

The beam from the lighthouse was sweeping its path across the Atlantic when Levan finally found a moment to talk to Eden. She was standing a little apart by the allotment gate, with her back to him, staring out over the ocean.

Carrying two glasses of champagne, he joined her and spoke softly so as not to startle her.

'Here, you deserve this.' He offered her the fizz, his heart beating a little faster than he'd expected.

Her eyes lit up. 'Thank you. So do you.'

He chinked her glass. 'We both do.'

'I can't thank you enough for going to Granny's rescue earlier.'

'It was an honour . . . I hope you've been able to relax and revel in this evening. I think Iris has had a wonderful time.' They both looked over at Iris, who was leaning on her stick while Joe and Ravi kissed her goodnight.

'The birthday girl is going to bed,' he said, then wished he hadn't used the word with Eden in such proximity. She was wearing a minidress that showed off her amazing legs and she was glowing with a happiness he hadn't seen since he'd arrived. Desire flared and he ached to touch her.

'It's been a long, tiring day for Granny, but I think she's had an amazing time.'

'I think so too. Everyone's enjoyed themselves. It's been a huge success.'

Eden heaved a sigh of relief. 'It could have ended in disaster. I was on edge for ages until I convinced myself Simon would stay away . . .'

'We scared him off, between the three of us.'

'Good.' She gazed up into his eyes, her lips parted, and Levan's stomach flipped as he slipped a little bit further towards the edge of being in love with her. Perhaps, he'd already tipped over the edge; the message his body was sending him was impossible to ignore any longer.

'I'm sorry about the other day at the rocks,' he began, wincing even as he remembered his rejection of her. 'I was an idiot. You must have cursed me after we parted.'

She raised her eyebrows. 'I admit I was pretty annoyed and my pride was hurt.'

'I don't blame you.' He swallowed, before deciding to take a leap into the unknown – and damn the consequences.

'If it happened again,' he said a little hoarsely. 'I *really* hope it would end differently. Is there any possibility I'd get a second chance?'

Her eyes widened in shock.

His hopes tumbled. She must be so angry with him.

'I regret how I made you feel, but can we try again?'

'Here and now?' she murmured.

'Now but not here,' he said, his pulse racing and every pore tingling as he realised that she wasn't pushing him

265

away – that she still wanted him too. 'Is there anywhere we could go?'

Her gaze swept over the remaining guests gathered around Ravi and Joe who were still saying goodnight to Iris. Miraculously, no one seemed to be paying him and Eden any attention.

'It's too risky to go inside either cottage – we don't want to be seen and for rumours to start flying – but I have another idea.'

'Thank God for that!'

She took his hand, and her touch shot electric bolts of desire through him. 'There's always the lighthouse. If we can slip around the back of the cottages and into the roastery, we can go inside.'

'Sounds good to me, but I'm going to have terrible trouble not grabbing you and running there.'

'Me too, but it would be much better if you could restrain yourself.' She stifled her giggles. 'Must be the Mermaid Cocktails.'

'Oh, of course.' He was high as a kite too, ignoring the niggles of doubt that nagged at him. He should tell her so much first. It was so much easier to push those doubts to the outermost corner of his mind. Now was not the time. Tonight was not the time.

Eden abandoned her half-full glass on the gatepost. 'I'll meet you inside the roastery in one minute. Don't get caught on the way.'

'I won't. Don't worry.'

She slipped away along the path, out of the lights from the party and cottages, and vanished into deep shadow. After a quick recce to make sure no one was watching, he followed her into the darkness.

He managed to dart across the courtyard to the roastery door without being seen. It was already open but in deep shadow.

'Eden?' he murmured, walking inside.

'Here.'

He glimpsed her figure in the darkness, closed the door behind him and heard her turn the key.

Warmth enveloped him and the aroma of coffee filled his senses.

Then – a kiss. He wasn't sure who'd moved first and didn't care, abandoning himself to the velvety feel of her lips against his. He explored her mouth with his tongue, holding her in his arms. She fumbled with the buttons of his jeans. He yanked up her dress and his palm settled on her thigh, drawing a sigh of deep pleasure from her.

Her murmurs of desire fuelled his even further and he pressed himself against the soft curves of her body. He almost cried out in delicious agony when she tugged his jeans down his thighs, taking his boxers with him.

They weren't going to make it inside the lighthouse . . .

'Wait!' Eden murmured.

Words tumbled out in his haste. 'Don't worry, I've thought of that. I've got one in my pocket. Unless you're on the pill?'

'No. Of course not. I haven't had sex for ages. Not *that*. There's a noise.'

'Where?'

'Inside the lighthouse. Shh.' She froze.

Teetering close to the edge and still with his jeans and pants round his ankles, Levan strained his ears.

From behind the door to the engine room, he heard faint sounds that could be footsteps. Then a loud clang as if a tool had fallen, followed by swearing.

'There's someone in there!' Eden said.

'Oh God, not now.' With a groan, he pulled his jeans up and fastened a button. 'Wait here. I'll see what's going on.'

With an agonised expression, Eden let her dress fall over her thighs. 'Who is it? How could they have got inside?'

'There are a lot of people here. It could be anyone,' he muttered, cursing inwardly at whoever had interrupted them but knowing that he had to check out the noise. 'How would anyone have got in without the key? I suggest you unlock the outside door and wait outside.'

She pulled a face. 'I'll unlock it but I'm not staying out there. If it's Simon, I'll kill him.'

She was only half-joking. 'Probably not a good idea,' he said. 'Keep back, please.'

While he didn't enjoy going all alpha, Levan didn't want Eden within striking distance on the off-chance her ex was the intruder – for Simon's sake more than hers.

He stood outside the door and said firmly, 'Who's there? We can hear you. Come out now.'

A giggle exploded on the other side of the door, followed by more muffled swearing.

Eden flew to his side. 'There's two of them!'

The door to the engine room began to move with a creak. A light went on and spilled out into the roastery.

'Morwenna!'

'Oh God, this is so embarrassing . . .' Morwenna cried, walking out of the engine room, followed by Courtney. Her ponytail had escaped from its barrette and her mascara was smudged over her face.

'You two!' Eden said.

'We thought you were intruders,' Levan said irritably.

'Sorry, don't blame Courtney. It was my idea. I asked your mum if I could give him a – um – tour and . . .'

'Your mum told us we could borrow the key,' Courtney said.

'Great minds think alike, eh?' Morwenna said. 'Forgive us?'

'You're forgiven,' Eden said, though the glance she exchanged with Levan made him think that she was actually very annoyed with them. Levan tried to think of higher things, but it wasn't easy.

'We – um – didn't interrupt anything?' Wenna asked while Courtney stood sheepishly behind her, trying and failing to pull up the zip on his shorts without anyone noticing. Levan glanced down to check that he'd done up his jeans.

'No . . . no . . .' Eden said hastily. 'We just came in here to check everything was locked up before we went to bed.'

'Oh. That's OK, then,' Morwenna said innocently. 'And we won't tell if you don't,' she added with a smirk.

'There's nothing to tell,' Eden declared, clearly trying to cover up the fact they'd been on the verge of finally having sex.

'Same here.' Wenna heaved a sigh. 'It's going to be one of those nights, isn't it?'

By this Levan understood that Morwenna and Courtney had also been disturbed at a crucial moment. The sensible thing to do would have been to each go back to where they'd been so rudely interrupted but, somehow, he guessed that wasn't going to happen. Everyone was too awkward and embarrassed.

'At least you can go home . . .' Morwenna offered.

Great, thought Levan. After this interruption, who knew what his position would be with Eden?

Morwenna grabbed Courtney's hand. 'We're getting a lift back with Courtney's mum so that's the end of our – um – evening too.'

'I think it's best if you two wander off as if nothing has happened and don't say you've seen us together if anyone asks.'

'Good idea,' Courtney said.

'And Morwenna, you might want to check your mascara in a mirror before you rejoin the party.'

'Oops! Thanks, hun. I'll speak to you tomorrow. I hope Iris loves the pictures.'

'I'll let you know,' said Eden.

'Bye,' said Courtney before adding with a grin, 'Boss.'

They were gone, leaving Levan and Eden in the roastery. Eden switched off the engine room light. They stood in the courtyard. There was still chatter from the party but it was more muted now. A light was on in Eden's bedroom window, showing Iris was probably in there before she went to sleep.

'Damn,' she said.

'Look,' Levan blurted out, 'let's just go to my cottage and sod it if anyone sees us.'

'I wish we'd just done that in the first place,' Eden said. 'Come on then.'

Hastily, she locked the door and they hurried off across the yard to sneak in through Levan's kitchen door.

'Eden!' The call came from Sally, who'd emerged from the kitchen door of Wolf Rock.

'It's Mum,' Eden said with a hiss of despair.

'Is there any chance you can help me in here?' Sally said, stepping onto the terrace in the twilight. She sounded fraught.

Eden groaned softly. 'I can't ignore her.'

'I wouldn't expect you to,' Levan replied, trying to keep a lid on his frustration.

Slipping away, she went over to Sally. 'Mum? What's up?'

'The kitchen is an absolute tip, we've run out of glasses and Ravi and Joe are busy packing up the food for the fridge. The downstairs loo won't flush, and I need to try and find a taxi for one of Granny's friends and I could *really* do with a hand if you don't mind?'

'Of course,' Eden said, feeling guilty for having abandoned her mother.

'I can help if you like,' Levan said, torn between wanting to stay close to Eden and keeping away from the urge to drag her away to the clifftop for some moonlit sex.

'No,' Sally said firmly. 'You've done more than enough. You go and relax. We can manage, can't we Eden?'

Eden had no answer to this so Sally went inside, leaving Eden just enough time to speak to Levan.

'I don't think I'm going to be able to get away again tonight, but I've had an idea. Why don't you come round to the café tomorrow afternoon after I close up and we can have all the privacy we want?'

Levan thought it sounded wonderful – apart from having to wait another day, which made him get frustrated all over again. 'I'll hold you to that. I'll be there by five to, um – sample your new roast?'

She gave a gasp of mock horror. At least, he hoped it was mock. 'Such a cheesy line,' she groaned.

'I couldn't help it. See you tomorrow.'

Her eyes sparkled. 'It's a date.'

Chapter Thirty

With the greatest difficulty, Eden hauled herself off the sofa bed at seven and drove off to the Coffee Container. She'd been up until one a.m. clearing up. After that, a combination of frustration, excitement and having to kip in the lounge hadn't been conducive to a good night's rest. Still, it might have been worse: her usual bedroom was slap bang next to Levan's and lying inches away from what she imagined was his naked body would have been torture.

Courtney was a lot livelier than she was, which was a good job because they were extremely busy with campers and walk-ins. Brisk trade was to be expected in the school holidays, but takings were definitely way up on the same period the previous summer.

It had been non-stop from the moment she'd first turned the A-board to 'open', which meant no time for Courtney to make any remarks about the previous evening. That would have been excruciating for both of them.

Now, she could look forward to the evening, when Levan

was going to call round after work. That delectable prospect gave her the shivers all over again.

Eden left Courtney in charge, with his mum helping out, while she went home for lunch with Iris and Sally. The rain was pelting down and the rush had died down.

'Thank y-you for waiting for me.' Eden was still slightly out of breath after dashing from work to her van, and negotiating lanes full of open-top buses, caravans and tourists who couldn't reverse very well. Then she'd had to run through torrential rain from the car park and into Wolf Rock.

'We don't mind. We wouldn't have started without you,' Iris said.

'We're not having a cooked lunch either, not with so many leftovers from the party,' her mum declared.

'That's fine by me. Jerk chicken with salad followed by birthday cake will be perfect,' Eden said. 'However, we have one more birthday surprise.'

Iris shook her head in astonishment. 'What? More presents?'

'Not quite,' Sally said. 'More of a memento.'

'Of your wonderful life, Granny,' Eden said eagerly. 'And we have a confession to make. You know the photos you showed to Levan before we went to the Jubilee Pool?'

'Yes . . .' Iris frowned.

'Well, he – we – borrowed them and we asked Morwenna to restore them on the computer and print them off.'

Iris stared at Eden and Sally for a long moment before saying, 'I'd no idea. Oh my.'

Eden felt her heart beating with excitement and apprehension. Had they done the right thing?

Sally put her arm around Iris. 'We hope you like them.'

She handed the box of photos to Iris. Eden exchanged a look

273

with her mother as they both wondered if Iris would remember or mention the 'secret snap' at the back of the photo card. Eden's stomach swirled with nerves. She was so glad they'd waited to unveil the pictures until a calm and private moment.

'Morwenna digitally restored the pictures and printed them in black and white,' she explained as Iris lifted the lid from the box.

Iris peeped inside, where the photos were nestled in the kind of shiny transparent paper that Eden had seen in her granny's wedding album.

'Oh my . . .' Iris let out a long breath. 'Oh, they look as if they were taken yesterday, only better, if you know what I mean.'

Together, they lingered over the photos, savouring each one, talking about moments captured forever and brought to life again.

Holding Sally's hand, Iris shed a few tears as she recalled each precious memory from her long life. 'Dear Walter. I wish he was here now. And Roger.'

'I know,' Sally said, sounding hoarse. 'I miss him so much too.'

Holding back her own tears was almost painful for Eden.

'These are – well, I don't know what to say,' Iris went on. 'Please thank Morwenna for me. No, I'll call her myself when I've sorted myself out a bit.'

Eden smiled. 'She's a star, ' she said, remembering how she'd once felt a little jealous of her friend. It was clear that she'd had no need. Levan had been interested in Eden herself all along. Her cheeks grew warm at the thought of what had almost happened the previous evening – and what the two of them had planned for this one.

'You've all done an amazing job, haven't they, Sally?'

'Absolutely. I couldn't believe how wonderful they were myself when I saw them.'

'There's more, though, Granny,' Eden said, hoping that the 'more' wouldn't be too much for Iris.

'What?' Iris's eyes were wide. 'Another surprise? I don't think I can cope.'

'Well . . . Morwenna decided to try her hand at making the photos colour. She used a computer program and her own judgement to choose the colours so they may not be right . . . Would you like to see them? They're really quite something.'

'Would I like to? Of course I would.'

'Well, prepare yourself because it's quite intense seeing the pictures brought to life in this way.'

With a quick glance at her mother, Eden presented the folder to her gran. There was no going back now.

Iris opened it and pulled out the first print, showing her and Walter standing in the sunlight at Hartstone, as vivid and fresh as if the picture had been taken that day.

She was silent as she picked out another snap of her, with Roger in her arms.

'Oh dear Lord. Roger.'

She burst into sobs.

Eden was full of dismay. Her mother was crying too.

'Oh no. I didn't mean to upset you both! It's too much, isn't it? Seeing everyone like this. I'm sorry!'

Eden reached for the folders but Iris patted her hand. 'No, it's beautiful. It's like they're here again. What Morwenna has achieved is wonderful. It's only that it's so emotional to see people like this. Don't you worry. I'm fine and so is your mum.'

Eden didn't feel fine.

Sally wiped her eyes. 'It's OK, love. It's no bad thing to have a good cry every so often. Your dad and grandad are in our thoughts every day but we hold back the emotions. Think of this as a safety valve. A lovely way to let all those feelings out.'

Iris dabbed her eyes with a hanky and squeezed out a smile for Eden.

'Look at this picture of Walter with the other keepers. You can see the detail in the cap badges and the colours in their cheeks. All tanned just like they were when they got to work on shore again.'

She held the colour photo made from the original that had been in the presentation card. Eden held her breath, wondering if Iris might mention the snap of the mystery boyfriend.

'What memories . . .' Iris murmured and Eden's heart beat faster. 'Good ones and sad ones.'

Sally exchanged a glance with Eden and, for a moment, Iris was lost in the past, gazing at the people she'd once known, loved and lost.

Then, with a smile, she laid the photo down on the folder. 'I felt I'd stepped back into their world again.'

Eden hugged her. 'I love you, Granny,' she whispered.

'And I love you, more than I can ever say.'

'Shall we have a cup of tea?' Sally said. 'I think we need it.'

'I need a tot of whisky in mine!' Iris declared.

'You can have anything, now you're ninety,' Eden said. 'I can't because I've got to go back to work but I'll make the drinks.'

She put the kettle on, mainly so she could dab her own eyes and have a few moments to herself. While the tea was brewing, she found a cling-filmed tray of leftover meat and salads in the fridge and was arranging them on plates when her mum walked in.

'Mum. I hope that wasn't too much. Poor Granny and poor you,' Eden said.

'We're both fine. A good blub really is cathartic.'

Eden lowered her voice. 'I'm relieved that Granny didn't mention the special photo.'

'No, and I'm rather glad. I think that really would have tipped us all over the edge.'

'Agreed.'

'Granny loved the pictures. She's having another look at them now and she's fine so don't worry. The important question is: how are *you*? Seeing your dad in those pictures on top of all the worry about Simon and organising the party and running the business – it must have been a lot to take on, to say the least.'

'I'm fine. I've survived and I loved last night, though I was worried Simon might try to crash the party for a while. He didn't . . . so I think he'll keep away for good now.'

'Let's hope so.' Sally touched the table top. 'I could tell you were on edge at the start and then you seemed to relax and have a good time. Levan looked happy too. Happier than I've seen him, genuinely content and chilled out as if he felt part of the fixtures – and the family.'

'Yes, I think you may be right.' Eden felt heat rising to her face again.

'He's settled in here, I'm sure of it. I wasn't sure if this was the place for him at first but now – I'm far more hopeful he'll stay for quite a while.'

'Hmm. I know what you mean,' Eden said, not trusting herself to elaborate on her feelings, in case her mother realised exactly *how* keen she was for Levan to stay. 'I'm starving. Why don't you take the lunch through to Granny? I'll lace her tea as requested.'

After a quick lunch, Sally and Iris settled down to look at the photos again but Eden headed out of the back door, meaning to grab an extra bag of beans from the roastery on her way to the van. Levan's bedroom window was wide open.

She glanced up and he appeared, naked – or at least from the waist up – his hair dripping wet.

He stared down at her, with a look of desire that shot hot splinters of desire through her. Work or no work, she ached to finish what they'd started . . . and she didn't think she could wait a moment longer.

Chapter Thirty-One

The stairs creaked as Eden hurried up and she hurtled inside the bedroom to find him standing completely naked, with a towel on the floor beside him. Steam misted the air and he looked every inch the mythical god she'd fantasised about night after night.

'Sorry, I couldn't wait.'

Her gaze seared his body and, through the open window, the sea breeze stirred the curtains with the gentlest of touches.

'You don't object, do you?' she said, stepping forward into the warm air of his room.

'I think you can tell that I don't.' He crossed the room to her in two strides. 'Only a complete madman – or a saint – would object to the perfect woman appearing in his bedroom while he was stark naked.'

'I really should be at work . . .' she murmured as he pulled her into his arms.

'For once, screw work,' he muttered, kissing her so deeply that her head was spinning.

*　　*　　*

'Hello. Earth to Levan.'

Eden propped herself up on her elbow. Levan was lying on his back, staring at the ceiling. He looked completely shattered, and she felt the same.

He turned to her and pushed himself up on his elbow too.

'I absolutely have to go to work,' she said. 'After I've used your shower.'

'Shower?' he murmured.

She laughed. 'The thing that shoots water at you.'

She expected him to laugh in return but, instead, he sat up and swung his legs out of bed and presented her with his back.

Unease stirred in the pit of her stomach. 'Is something wrong?'

She was met with more silence, as if a wall had been built between them.

She knelt up on the bed and took his arm. 'Levan? Don't say you regret what has just happened? I thought – it seemed as if you didn't at the time.'

'I didn't,' he said, touching her face briefly before withdrawing his fingers again. There was no smile, just a sad resignation that sent her spirits plummeting off a cliff. 'It was amazing. You're amazing.'

'Then we should do this again. Soon. In fact, what about this evening after work at the café?'

Finally he did smile, and trailed his fingers down her breast. 'How could I possibly resist?'

Eden inspected her face in the mirror of the campsite wash block. She'd had another quick shower after her shift at the café and thrown on a T-shirt dress. She'd been high on adrenaline and lust all afternoon, hardly able to concentrate on making coffee. Courtney had asked her if she was OK and said she looked like she was running a temperature . . . If he'd only known the truth!

She brushed her teeth, blow-dried her short hair and considered putting on make-up. Probably not if it was all going to come off anyway, along with the rest of her clothes. That thought made her zing with lust and the recollection of the hot sex she'd had with Levan in his bed.

Soon, he'd be back again for another session – maybe two. A quick dab of lip gloss, a spritz of perfume and she was good to go. Goosebumps popped out on her still-damp skin and the shower block felt hot and oppressive.

She exited as quickly as she could and cut through the gate to the café. She let herself in through the entrance at the back and closed the door behind her.

It was warm inside so she opened the little window at the rear, though she knew she'd have to close it again when Levan arrived. She could always switch on the fan if things got too hot . . . the thought made her even hotter so she checked out her practical arrangements. All afternoon, she'd been thinking of how she could make the place more love shack than old shipping container. She hadn't dared tidy anything while Courtney was there but, as soon as he'd left, she'd gone into the rear area and set to.

The back was mostly floor space and storage. She'd moved all the boxes of filters, takeout cups and soft drinks bottles and cans onto the countertop.

She'd brought a roll-up camping mattress in the van but then thought it was ridiculous.

She heard the crunch of gravel as a car turned into the entrance of the container.

She checked the time and slivers of excitement and desire shot through her. It was Levan. A final check in the mirror as his footsteps approached showed flushed cheeks, bright eyes and a woman on the edge of exploding with lust.

'Eden?' A whisper. 'Are you in there?'

'Of course I am! What kept you? I can't wait any longer!'

She opened the rear door and let out a shriek of shock.

Chapter Thirty-Two

'For a moment I thought you were pleased to see me,' Simon said with a leer that turned Eden's stomach. 'Now I realise you were expecting someone else.'

She tried to shove the door to. 'I told you to keep away.'

He put his foot in the gap. 'Hold on, I want to talk to you.'

Her heart sank. 'I don't want to talk to you.' She noticed he was wearing a suit and tie. 'Why are you dressed like that?'

He smirked. 'I had a job interview.'

'What? Here in Cornwall? You can't!'

'Why not? It's a free country.'

'You *can't* move here.'

'Well, that's what I've come to talk to you about.' He took a step forward into the entrance of the container, forcing Eden to step back before anger and adrenaline kicked in. She lunged forward to push him back out of the door.

'Jesus!'

He toppled backwards, fell out of the door and thumped onto the gravel. Clouds of dust puffed up as he lay on the ground writhing like some hideous insect.

'Oww . . .' he moaned, struggling to sit up. 'That's assault. You could have killed me.'

Eden was unrepentant. 'I haven't. You're fine. You tried to break into my business premises.'

'Business premises? An old shipping container. This place is no different to some roadside greasy spoon.'

Eden felt sick. Feelings she'd thought had been buried forever erupted and made her stomach turn over. Feelings of worthlessness and despair from years before.

'If you don't leave, I'll call the police!' she shouted.

'And I'll say you hit me.' He sounded like a whingeing bully trying to blame his victims when they'd finally turned on him.

'I don't care!'

An engine roared then brakes squealed and gravel sprayed up, spattering the metal walls of the container. Simon was on his knees when Levan jumped out of his car and ran over.

'Ah, the cavalry!' Simon sneered. His suit was grey with dust.

'Levan! Don't do anything. I can deal with him.'

'That's what I'm worried about.' Levan placed himself between Eden and Simon.

'She's already assaulted me,' he whined.

'What? A five-foot-two woman attacks her six-foot ex? An ex with a known history of emotional abuse against her, not to mention fraud? Besides, I didn't see anything.'

'You weren't here!' Simon bleated, finally on his feet.

'Oh, I think I was.'

'You two . . . would be willing to swear to that, would you? You'd lie in a court of law?'

'Why not?' Eden said with far more bravado than she

actually felt. 'Lying has never troubled you before.' So many emotions were running through her. Relief that Levan was here, though she wouldn't admit it, of course.

'Eden? Are you OK?' Levan asked, while also glaring at Simon as if daring him to so much as twitch in her direction.

'Yes. I'm OK.'

Simon brushed at his filthy trousers. 'So, as I suspected, this is your new boyfriend, is it? Judging by the greeting I got – presumably meant for him – I take it you weren't waiting here to serve him up a skinny latte.'

'I suggest you mind your own business,' Levan said. His voice was silky smooth yet his eyes held a cold contempt that took Eden aback.

'Stop,' she ordered, meaning both men.

Simon held up a torn button from his jacket. 'This was a new suit.'

'I can see that,' she said, adding sarcastically, 'And you'd hardly be going for an interview if you didn't have long to live, now, would you?'

He laughed but she knew him too well. Under the bravado, the nerves showed. 'Maybe some miracle cure will come along?' he said with a sneer. 'Though if I had been sick, I'm sure you'd have rather I went away and expired quietly and conveniently.'

Levan let out a hiss of contempt, yet stayed silent.

'It's not funny, Simon. I would never have wanted that, but to have pretended to be terminally ill is a new low even for you.'

'I needed you to listen,' he said in a whining tone that grated on her more than ever. 'How else could I have got your attention and persuaded you to meet me?'

Even though she'd known the truth since his visit to Iris's, Eden felt humiliated that even the tiniest part of her had wondered for a while.

'You really are a piece of work.' Levan spoke up. 'Luckily Eden wasn't taken in by your lies.'

Simon curled his lip. 'You're pulling her strings now, are you?'

Levan stepped forward. To Eden's dismay, he stood inches from Simon's face. 'What did you say?'

Simon stepped back, paler in the face. 'I said that you've taken my place. You're controlling Eden now.'

'Ignore him,' Eden said, sensing the situation was spiralling out of control. Levan was on the edge. 'I'm sure Simon is longing to provoke a reaction now we know he's been telling a pack of lies. I bet you haven't even got a job interview down here, have you?'

Levan didn't move. 'No one is controlling Eden. I'm – a friend, and I care about her. More than you ever did.'

'*Care*? That's a strange word for someone who's been lying to her since he got here.'

Levan looked as stunned as if Simon had punched him in the face, which was exactly what Eden was afraid would happen.

She darted to the two men, pulling at Levan's arm. 'Stop this now! I don't need protecting and I don't want anyone fighting over me. You should leave, Simon, or I will call the police and tell them you're harassing me. And Levan – if you carry on like this, I want you to leave too.'

'You heard her,' Simon said. 'I'm going to do as she says. Will you?'

Levan glanced at Eden, who pleaded with him with her eyes. She could handle Simon but she was terrified that another taunt would tip Levan over the edge. Simon was more than enough to drive the mildest, most peaceful person to act out of character and he'd already been pushed to the brink.

'If it's what you want, and you're sure you'll be OK,' Levan muttered. 'I'll go.'

Eden didn't believe for a moment that he'd actually drive off but if he simply stayed out of reach of Simon, it would be a start.

'It is. For my sake.'

With the barest of nods, Levan turned away and strode off towards his car.

Simon folded his arms. 'See he's running. He's a bloody coward.'

'Shut up!' Eden cried, but it was too late.

Levan had stopped walking away and turned around. A switch had been flicked and his eyes blazed with rage. Eden's heart thumped like mad.

He kept coming, heading straight for Simon.

'Levan.'

Simon staggered backwards.

Levan advanced but stopped a few feet away. 'OK,' he said smoothly. 'Did I just mishear what you said about me?'

In desperation, Simon glanced at Eden but she didn't utter a word.

Levan smiled. 'Because for a moment there, I thought you called me a coward.'

Eden froze with panic.

Simon held up his hands. 'Me? No, mate. You must have misheard me.'

For this one time in her life, Eden was glad Simon had told a lie.

'I see. Because the one thing I am not is a coward, and I'd have to have words with anyone who said otherwise.' There was a smile on Levan's face, but his eyes were cold with fury.

Levan looked like a different person and the hairs on her neck stood on end.

He glanced at Eden before addressing Simon again.

'One thing I do know though, and that's that you, mate, are a liar and a cheat, and what you can do is get in your car this second, drive away and never come back to Cornwall. Otherwise, *mate*, I might not walk away again.'

'Go, Simon,' Eden said quietly. Her legs felt like jelly.

'I don't have much choice, do I?' Simon muttered before walking to his car and getting in. He started the engine and wound down the window. 'Just watch yourself,' he shouted at Eden and pointed a finger at Levan. 'He's not what you think. He's dangerous. Did you see the way he looked at me?'

'Go away, Simon!' Eden shouted, shaky with adrenaline.

Finally, he was gone, leaving a cloud of dust.

'My God, are you all right?' Levan said.

She sat down heavily on the step behind the café.

'No. N-not really.'

'I can't believe he turned up.'

'Levan, you have to understand, Simon is a very clever manipulator. Those things he said to you were to goad you. He *wanted* you to hit him so you'd be arrested.'

'I – I did try to ignore it.' Levan's face was pale. 'But he said things that touched a raw nerve.'

'Calling you a coward? That's pathetic. Simon would know I didn't believe that. And as for you lying to me, he's only trying to drag you down to his level. I didn't take any notice of it and neither should you.'

'No . . .' Levan shoved his hands through his hair. Eden had never seen him so agitated before. Bloody Simon must have shaken him to the core.

'Come inside,' she said gently.

He stepped in. Eden reached up and touched his cheek and went to kiss him. After starting to kiss her back he pulled away.

'What's the matter?'

He took a deep breath, looking very shaky himself. Perhaps it was the shock of his close call with Simon kicking in.

'Nothing,' he said. 'Sorry. I'm – not myself.'

'Don't let Simon destroy what we have – are starting to have,' Eden said, feeling desperate. 'It's what he wants. He only turned up to try and take some form of twisted revenge because he knows his plans have failed again. He's pathetic.'

'No. I – look, Eden, I want you so much, but not like this. Not after this. I'm shaken, I'll admit it. I was this close . . .' he held up his thumb and forefinger, 'to actually hitting him.'

'But you didn't and that's what matters.'

'Yes. I guess so, but it scares me,' he said, reaching to touch her cheek. 'I do want you, Eden, and I care about you more than you can imagine.'

Her hopes rose. Simon's visit had done some good; made her and Levan admit how they felt. 'Me too,' she said.

'Can we go back to mine?' he said. 'I want to talk.'

She laughed and wound her arms around his neck. '*Talk*? Is that all?'

He managed a faint smile. 'Let's go home.'

Chapter Thirty-Three

Eden was like a cat on a hot tin roof when Levan let her into the cottage. The adrenaline of the past hour had been replaced by excitement and lust. She baulked in surprise when, instead of heading straight for the stairs, he ushered her into the sitting room.

'Do you want to sit down?' he said, standing on the rug apart from her.

'Not really,' she said. 'I rather thought we might be going upstairs . . .'

His smile was non-existent and Eden suddenly grew cold despite the warmth of the evening sun filtering into the room. 'You said you wanted to talk?' she said. 'But I thought it was something that could wait?'

His body stiffened and she saw him swallow. 'Eden, no matter how many times I've run through this moment in my mind, I haven't been able to find the words . . .'

Her stomach knotted tightly. 'I don't understand.' She frowned. 'Why not?'

'Because I ought to have done the right thing, the thing I

ought to have done when I first moved in.' His words sounded so formal and stilted: not like 'her' Levan at all.

'What do you mean?' she said, confused and seriously worried, though still trying to keep things light. 'What is this mysterious "right thing"?'

'I should have told you the truth. Simon was right.'

Her skin crawled with foreboding. 'Simon?' she scoffed. 'He's just full of bullshit. He's really bloody got to you, hasn't he?'

'Yes, he has, and I ought to thank him for that.'

His expression was tortured. It was as if Eden had slept with one man a few hours previously and he'd now been taken over by a different person: a stranger.

Her stomach turned over. 'What on earth are you talking about? You're scaring me.' She pulled herself free of him.

'Don't be scared. For God's sake, don't be that. I never want any woman to feel that about me. I – I care about you deeply and I want to make you happy and I fooled myself that I could. That's not possible.'

She moved a little further away. He was a haunted man. She wrapped her arms around herself. 'Then, tell me why.'

'I want you to hear it all and I'm begging you not to say anything until you have. And that's going to be hard because what I have to say might be a shock. And after I've finished, I'll answer anything you want to know. Anything.'

Even though she was shaky with dread, she sat down, feeling sick.

'Go on. I'm listening.'

He took a breath and then lifted his chin and looked her in the eye with quiet and determined resolution.

'First of all, my name isn't Levan. It's Harry Bancroft. My father is a brigadier, my grandfather was a general and my mum is a professor. I went to public school and to Cambridge, where I got a first and did a PhD in Computer Science. I was offered a fellowship and I wanted to be a computer academic but I couldn't take it up. Or rather I *didn't*. It was my decision. I was weak.'

She clenched her hands in her lap, hardly able to speak for shock.

'I didn't because I decided to do what everyone expected. And what they expected was for me to join the army. That much is true. Generations of Bancroft men have been distinguished career officers. One of my ancestors was killed in the Charge of the Light Brigade, another at Gallipoli. Serving our country is in our DNA. Can you believe it?'

Eden swallowed. She did believe it, however she was hearing the story of a different man to the one standing up before her as if on parade.

'What is also true is that my family think I'm a failure, a drop-out and a criminal.'

'And are you?' she burst out. 'A *criminal*?'

'Technically, I suppose. No, let's be one hundred percent accurate. I was convicted of a crime and I did it. So, yes, I am a criminal.'

She closed her eyes as if she could blot out the news she was hearing. Her blood was pounding in her ears.

'You deserve the full explanation. I left university and I was commissioned into the Signals as a lieutenant. I served two tours in Afghanistan, working in a covert communications unit. They made me a captain and I was earmarked for promotion. Everyone seemed satisfied with the path I'd chosen. I won't say proud, because my family don't go in for effusions of affection, or even effusions of anything.'

He spoke mechanically, as if he'd rehearsed the story. Was that because he'd been agonising over when – and if – to tell her everything she thought she knew about him was a lie? She shivered.

'It was never what I wanted to do but I did my duty. Your family know all about that . . . serving their nation is in their DNA, too.'

He stared at her.

'They do but—' She was going to add that they hadn't broken the law. 'What happened?'

'My superior officer and I didn't see eye to eye.' He laughed bitterly. 'That's an understatement. He was a bully. In fact, I'd call him a right bastard, as the men did. He was the son of a friend of my parents and on the fast track to be a general one day. But he hated the men and they hated him.

'He'd single out the ones he saw as weak or vulnerable and expected me to toughen them up. He'd order me to give them humiliating punishments, or to turn a blind eye to bullying by one particular sergeant. When I threatened to make a complaint about him, he told me that he'd ruin my career. I didn't give a fuck about my career by that stage, but if I left then I'd have abandoned the unit to possibly even worse things, so I did everything to avoid imposing these punishments but then he started to pick on me, and call me weak.'

She shuddered, chilled by the shocking story she was hearing and at this new Levan – a stranger – telling it. 'But . . . didn't the army do *anything*? Didn't people complain?'

'No. There was an unspoken code. A conspiracy of silence. I did try to raise my concerns with a friend – Dion – who'd been a captain in another unit. No one listened to him. He wasn't part of the establishment for too many reasons, and after he was invalided out, he became invisible and nothing was done.

'After two years of intimidation, one of the men became suicidal. I tried to speak to my father and brother about it and they told me not to risk my own career and that if I couldn't stand the heat, then I should "get out of the kitchen" and ask for a transfer.

'One day I came into a corner of the camp to find one of the men on his knees in the dirt outside the latrines with the sergeant standing over him. He'd sworn at the sergeant so he'd taken it out on him by giving him punishment drills and calling him a useless—' he took a breath. 'I'll leave the vile things he said to your imagination. They're not fit to repeat.'

'Oh my God. I can't believe this happens in this day and age.'

'Oh, it still goes on, kept under wraps by a conspiracy of silence or code of honour, whatever you call it. It goes on in all big institutions, perhaps most workplaces at some level – maybe not as extreme as in this case. The reputation of that organisation can't be tarnished, the cockroaches stay in the darkness – safe.

'Anyway, I'd had enough and I saw red. I knew I could probably only take down one of them before I was arrested so I chose the major as he was the architect of the whole culture of torment. He was a psychopath who should never have been commissioned in the first place, or anywhere near human beings at all. So, I punched him in the face and he went down like a ton of bricks.'

'And?' she prompted.

'All hell broke loose. The sergeant went for me and I

managed to kick him in the nuts before help arrived. I broke the officer's nose and some teeth and left the sergeant badly bruised. I was court-martialled.'

'What about witnesses?'

'None except me. The soldier was got at, somehow, to stop him telling the court what my provocation was – discharged and paid off or scared shitless. Possibly both. One of my lieutenants and Dion stood as character witnesses but that wasn't enough. I had to plead guilty because I did attack the major and sergeant. It was a pretty serious assault on two long-serving members of the unit – and I also didn't regret it. I showed no remorse.'

Eden could barely grind out a reply. 'What happened?'

'I was dismissed in disgrace and sentenced to three years. I ended up serving just over eighteen months. I was lucky, my brief said, because the maximum punishment for using violence against a superior officer was ten.'

Eden shook her head in horror. 'Are you – are you saying you ended up in a military prison?'

'Oh no, only junior ranks can go to military jail. As an officer, I had the privilege of a civilian prison.'

'Levan . . . I d-don't know w-what to say,' she stammered. 'This is beyond shocking in every way and I – I don't know what to say to you . . .'

'I know,' he murmured, hanging his head in misery. 'I realise I've betrayed your trust every bit as much as Simon.'

He was right. This gentle, kind, handsome man she'd slept with had been convicted of assault, yet in some ways he was a hero.

Except in others, he was exactly like Simon. He'd lied to her, and carried the deception on for months, allowing her to grow to trust him and sleep with him . . . maybe even begin to love him.

'Why did you come here? Didn't your family help you?'

'No. They were devastated. I was the manifestation of their worst nightmares. A son who brings shame on the family. Dismissed with disgrace is pretty rare: it's reserved for the worst kind of people. Imagine how my family felt about that.'

'I can't. I mean . . . didn't they understand why you attacked these people? Weren't they shocked at the cover-up?'

'They only saw – still see – two things: the disgrace and the shame. Even those aren't as bad as me effectively dropping a bomb on their most cherished beliefs. I now represent the shattering of their dreams, the IED that's exploded in the middle of everything they held precious. Honour, duty, service. They didn't want to believe that their beloved institutions – their raison d'etre, the rock at the centre of their lives, that they built their whole selves on – were so flawed. I'd destroyed them.'

'Oh my God.'

'You know what it's like. Your father and grandfather, they served their countries – in a different way.'

'They have served,' Eden replied. 'Though I can't imagine them putting pressure on me to follow the same path if I'd been a boy. I suppose I've been very fortunate that Mum and Granny have always supported me to go my own way in life. Unlike yours,' she added, torn between sympathy and anger with him for deceiving her.

'Before, during and after the court-martial, I turned to my family but they cut me off. I don't want to make excuses – and I don't regret what I did. I bitterly regret having deceived you, though. If I could turn back the clock to the first day we met, I'd tell you everything.'

'Then,' she said wearily. 'Why didn't you?'

'I didn't mean to – to get so involved, but it was impossible. And every day that ticked by, I felt safe, calm, happy. Your family seemed everything that mine have never been. I was addicted . . . and every day the risk of telling you the truth became bigger, and the fallout I'd have to face even worse.'

'Why did you change your name?' she asked.

'Because I wanted a totally new start, almost a new identity – to be born again as the man I ought to have been. Sounds stupid, I know. I changed my surname to my mother's maiden name, and Levan is actually one of my middle names.'

'Born again . . .' She felt completely drained with shock. She sympathised – if what he was telling her was true – but she also felt deeply betrayed. 'I can understand why you stayed quiet, I really can. But I can't *forgive*. I'm sorry Levan, but I'm left wondering which is the real you? The helpful, kind Levan who Granny adores – or the man who lied to me for months and assaulted two people? Even *if* you had a good reason . . .'

'If?'

'Yes. I want to believe you and I probably do, but you've held this back for so long so I just don't know what to think.'

'It is true but I've no excuse for the deception since. That's what I meant when I said that Simon was right – I was a coward in not telling you.'

'I understand why you attacked these men. I do know how it feels to be pushed to the limit, humiliated, wounded and hurt – and more than that I know how I felt when Simon was at Granny's. If he'd tried to hurt her I would have done the same to protect her. It isn't what you've done that's devastating. It's what you *haven't* done. It's not telling me. Not trusting me.'

'Of that, I am guilty as charged. I wanted to tell you so many times. I came up with so many excuses not to. Every time I didn't come out with the truth was a small crime in its own way. At first, I liked you all – your mother, Iris and especially you were welcoming, decent people. You believe in doing the right thing and for the first time in my life, I'd found a warm and loving family for whom family – people – meant everything, not appearances.'

'We aren't your family.'

He flinched.

Eden felt terrible. Never had she been more torn in two. Trust him, forgive him? Or not take the risk again?

'I can't deal with this. I have to go home . . .' she muttered, on the verge of tears.

'I'm so sorry.' He reached out to her.

She darted out of his reach and edged towards the doorway. 'I have to go.'

'Of course,' he said wearily. 'Will you tell your family?'

Her stomach rolled over at the realisation she would have to let her mother and Iris know the truth about Levan. 'I must, but – but not straight away. I need to – to – process it myself first.'

Process? What a cold word to describe the maelstrom of emotions; the battle of counter-instincts raging in her mind. Already she was withdrawing from him; protecting herself by trying not to feel, even though it was impossible.

She did believe him, and in one way she thought even more of him.

Yet even if it was true – he'd told so many lies at the start of their relationship and kept on telling them.

How could she ever be sure he wouldn't do it again? How could she ever trust him one hundred percent? One thing was certain: after Simon, nothing less would do.

Chapter Thirty-Four

L evan woke, or rather opened his eyes and finally decided to abandon his bed, as he'd barely slept all night. Adrenaline darted through his body when his phone pinged with a message from Eden.

I have more questions.
Come to the Secret Cliff after work.

That meant he had a whole agonising day to get through at work, first. Forcing himself to shower and shave, he then drove to the data centre to find Dion inside at a terminal. There was only the two of them. Hearing Levan approach, Dion swung round on his chair and let out a low whistle

'Wow. You look like shit.'

Levan grimaced. 'Good morning to you too, mate. Actually, I have seen myself in the mirror. Let's just say I didn't sleep much.'

Dion raised an eyebrow. 'In a good or a bad way?'

'In the worst way in the history of the world.'

Dion grimaced. 'Wanna tell me about it?'

'No.'

'That crap?'

Levan shook his head, the previous evening's events dominating his mind as they had for most of the night. 'Far far worse. Look, I need to start work and I have to meet Eden afterwards.'

Dion opened his mouth and heaved a sigh. 'I'm guessing she knows, then?'

'Most of it. The part about me, anyway. I don't think she cares about what I do for a living, only that I told her a pack of lies and kept on telling it, even when I knew her ex was a lying scumbag. And didn't tell her the truth before I slept with her.'

'Shit.' Dion winced, getting out of his chair and walking over. 'Is it only Eden who knows at the moment or the whole family?'

'Just her for now, though I can't think it will be long. You know how close they are . . .' Levan's stomach tightened. It was the closeness of the Carricks that had attracted him so much, as well as his feelings for Eden, of course: they represented everything he'd wanted and missed in his own upbringing. In hindsight, it had been ridiculous to think he could live out a fantasy that he was part of the family, like a cuckoo in the nest. He'd only ended up harming Eden with his lies.

'I might be looking for a new place to live,' he said, feeling sick. 'Sooner rather than later.'

Dion lifted his eyes heavenwards in despair. 'Jeez, Levan. The crap you get yourself into.'

'Yeah. I'm a hopeless case.'

'No, I didn't say that!' he said sharply, then in a kinder tone, 'Though it sounds like this particular mess will take some sorting.'

Levan shook his head gloomily. 'Oh, I already know this one isn't fixable.'

Dion slapped his back. 'It's always fixable . . . almost always. I could try and look round for another project for you . . .'

'No way!' Levan snapped. 'God, sorry. I – don't want you moving heaven and earth for me again. It's my mess to sort out.'

'Hmm. I think we need a good heart-to-heart at the Last Chance saloon. I'd take you out tonight but I have to go back up to HQ at Cheltenham; I'll be back here next week. In the meantime, if you need me, call me. Any time, night or day, buddy. If it gets too much, jump in the car and come up north and stay with me. You'll always be welcome.'

Tears threatened but Levan managed a wobbly grin and a quip. 'You should apply for sainthood.'

'Already rejected, mate. Like yourself.' His expression turned serious. 'Don't give up hope and, for what it's worth, I don't think running away from this particular mess is right, either.'

Eden was sitting on a rock, staring out to sea when Levan squeezed through the rocky cleft. Seeing her washed-out face and the dark circles under her eyes delivered a fresh punch of remorse to his gut. He'd found it nigh-on impossible to give his work the focus required, and the tension had built as his meeting with Eden had drawn close.

'Hi . . .' he said.

'Yeah,' she murmured.

Slate-grey clouds had rolled in from the west and thunder

rumbled away over the sea, ominously. He found a rock and perched on it.

'Stupid question,' he began, treading on eggshells. 'How are you?'

'I've had better days,' she muttered without a trace of humour.

'Me too . . . I'm here because you wanted to ask me some questions? I'll answer anything.'

'Anything?' She snorted. 'Or anything you *can*?'

He shifted awkwardly on the granite seat. 'Anything about my past or now – or at least, anything that won't get us both thrown in jail,' he added.

'Isn't it too late for that?' She shook her head. 'Let's try this for starters. Why did you choose to settle here in particular? At Lighthouse Cottages. Near us.'

'Exactly as I told you. I'm a cyber security specialist, which was also my role in the Signals. I served alongside Dion until he was invalided out of the army.'

'Is that something to do with his arm?' Eden said.

'Yes, he lost the lower part when he was working and a booby trap bomb went off.'

She shuddered. 'Poor Dion.'

'He's OK now, and he's the best bloke you'll ever meet. After he left the army, he worked as an information security analyst. Look . . . I genuinely can't tell you too much because almost all of it is classified.'

'I don't want you to break any laws,' she snapped. Her unsaid, 'any more than you already have' hung in the air between them.

'Look, I can tell you this much. Internet traffic arrives in the UK via submarine cables that mostly make landfall on

303

Cornwall beaches: around a quarter of it runs under the cove near to Hartstone. These cables carry all the business and personal data that all of us exchange every minute of every day. Some of them even carry the financial data from the New York stock exchange. You're a Cornish girl. You must have heard all this?'

'I know about the undersea cables and the data centres. Like lots of people round here, I know some of the history from the communications museum but, frankly, I've had other things on my mind over the past few years than national security.'

He nodded. 'Me too. Except I'm paid to have it on my mind.'

Her eyes widened. 'So you *do* work for the government? I thought you worked freelance for Dion? I thought he provided security for the data centre and that it was owned by a telecoms company like all the others round here?'

'Well, most of them are just cable landing stations: places where the undersea cables eventually make landfall and connect to the terrestrial network infrastructure . . . Where the information from the cables is transferred to other data networks.'

She picked up on one word. '*Most?*' she said.

'With the odd exception,' Levan said. 'Some of the buildings have a . . . let's say, a broader role to play. It's true that Dion did find me this job, however he doesn't own the company.'

'I thought that was how you found out about Simon? Illegally hacking into some government database. I didn't know you worked *for* the government!' She stared at him. 'It's GCHQ, isn't it? You really are a spy.'

He might have laughed but he didn't dare. 'I wouldn't call myself a spy, exactly, and I never said it was GCHQ per se . . .'

How far did he dare go? He trusted her, but he still couldn't breach the Official Secrets Act. Hints would have to do. 'Let's just say I work for *a* government organisation. There are several.'

She shook her head. 'But you're saying that the centre at Jackdaw Farm isn't any old cable landing station?'

'Well, it is, of a kind,' he said. It was also an eavesdropping centre where the security services – including him – intercepted certain kinds of Internet traffic from certain kinds of foreign entities in the interests of national security. That, he couldn't tell her, though, no matter how much he wanted to.

'I wish I could say more,' he added, desperate to try to be honest while knowing he really couldn't be. 'I'm aware this sounds like one of Simon's fantasies, but Dion will vouch for me. The rest, while it may seem a huge ask, you will have to take on trust.'

'You don't have to tell me more. I'm not interested in the details,' she said sharply. 'They aren't the thing that really concerns me, or the thing that means *I* can't give you the trust I want to.'

'I understand. Truly,' he said. 'Please ask anything else.'

'Oh, don't worry, I will,' she said sharply. 'You're telling me that your – employer – doesn't care that you have a criminal record?' She sounded incredulous.

He shrugged. 'I'm probably not the only one.'

She opened her mouth. 'Oh my God.'

'The fact I thumped a couple of evil bastards doesn't matter to them. What I did before, and what I can do for them *now*, does. I was fully vetted and Dion vouched for me and his word holds a lot of weight. He's my friend and my saviour, the one who gave me a second chance.'

'Then why won't your family do the same? If they love you?'

'No to the first and, as for the second, I won't say they *don't* love me. They probably think they do – they probably actually do, my mother especially – but they can't bring themselves to forgive me yet and I have tried. My brother has washed his hands of me, my father isn't well and can't tolerate my presence apparently. My mother does call occasionally, when she can find some privacy. In fact, she's asked me to go home and try to make my peace with my father again.'

Eden hesitated before responding. 'And will you?'

'I don't know. Maybe I'll meet her somewhere neutral.' He sighed. 'I do want to.'

'Is there no one else you could turn to besides Dion? Friends? Anyone?'

His fleeting smile was devoid of pleasure. 'I did have someone; in fact, I was engaged . . . but we split up when I went to prison. Actually, we split up when I knew I'd be convicted.'

'She left you too?' she said with a deep frown.

'No, I left her. Or rather, I spared her the embarrassment of breaking off our engagement. She didn't put up much of a fight. She wanted to be married to a career officer and was cut up that I'd thrown away a glittering career. She said I'd hurt her more than I could ever imagine. I make a speciality of it, you see.'

Eden didn't return his rueful smile. He didn't blame her. 'Anyway, everyone was very relieved when I broke it off, her most of all. Her father even visited me on remand to tell me that I'd "finally done the decent thing".'

'This can't be true,' Eden said. 'Parents – families – people can't be this cold and cruel to their own children, and the people they love?'

'I'm not sure my family have any notion that they're being "cruel". As for cold, I'm afraid my father might have invented the concept of the stiff upper lip. It's archaic and ridiculous, but that's how he was brought up himself.'

She rubbed her face with her hands, deeply troubled. 'I just can't imagine a family like that.'

'The thing is, you and your family, you're the real deal. The open, honest, salt of the earth real deal. Hold onto that.' He paused, unsure whether he dared say more, then decided to risk it. 'Moving here as Levan gave me the chance to live as who I want to be. This is the man I am, not Henry Bancroft. Go on, google me. My case was reported widely.'

'I already have.' She looked at him. 'I spent half the night searching for the real Levan.'

He nodded, bereft of answers. 'Do you want me to tell your mum and Iris? Spare you?'

'No, I've decided to tell them later. Mum first, then we'll break it to Granny.'

'OK.' He nodded, his stomach churning at the thought of Sally and Iris hearing the truth.

'What happens next?' Eden said, coolly. 'With you?'

'Dion offered to find me another job if I really want it but I feel I'm helping here, in a small way. Serving my country again,' he said softly. 'Though, I'll probably look for somewhere else to live.'

'I see,' she said tightly. He guessed she didn't want to show too much emotion – or sympathy – towards him. She'd rebuilt a protective wall around her as far as he was concerned.

'Is there anything else you want to know?' he said, his throat turning dry.

She shook her head firmly. 'No, I don't think so. I've heard enough.'

'In that case, I'll go.' He got up, aware that he was standing stiffly, almost to attention. Old habits died hard. 'Please believe that I care about you very deeply, but I know this changes everything.'

'Oh, yes,' she said, and Levan felt the sting of tears in his eyes. 'I'm sorry, but it does.'

Chapter Thirty-Five

How could Eden tell her mother? There was no way, so she waited until Sally came home after work, until after dinner.

Her mum kicked back in the armchair and lifted her feet onto a footstool with a huge sigh of relief. It seemed even worse that Eden was about to lob a grenade into her well-earned rest.

'It's been a crazy day,' Sally said. 'We're short of staff and the traffic is terrible. One of the owners "forgot" to tell us that she'd let the property at short notice so it wasn't clean when the guests arrived and they blamed us . . .'

'Ouch.'

Sally frowned, catching the look on Eden's face. 'You must have had a busy day too. You look worn-out, love.'

'I am very busy.'

'I heard you up and about very early.'

'Yes.' Eden's stomach clenched sharply but she forced a smile. 'Fancy a glass of wine?'

Sally raised an eyebrow. 'Wine on a school night?'

'I think we should.'

'Why? Do you have something to celebrate?' Her mum sat up a bit straighter. 'Is this to do with Levan?' She smiled. 'I do have eyes, you know.'

'Yes, it is . . .' Eden said, her heart sinking further by the moment. 'I'll fetch the wine.'

A few minutes later, she handed a large glass of red to her mother. The situation seemed to call for something robust.

'Are you two seeing each other?' Sally said, taking an appreciative sip of the merlot. 'I must say, it's taken you both long enough. Granny was only saying the other day that she was hoping you'd finally see what was right under your noses.'

'Yes, we were – hoping to get together.'

Sally frowned. '*Hoping* to?'

'Yes, and we do – did –like each other.'

'Eden . . . I'm not getting good vibes around this.' She put her glass down on the coffee table, suddenly alert and tense.

'That's because the vibes aren't as happy as I expected. Not what *any* of us expected. Mum, this might come as a bit of a shock, but Levan isn't who we all thought he was.'

Eden showed her some of the press reports about his case.

With very short hair and bruises on his face, he looked almost unrecognisable. There were pictures of his parents, an upright man with a bristling moustache and an elegant yet brittle woman who looked as if she'd snap if you touched her.

Sally was confused about why, and then – to Eden's surprise – kept saying: 'Poor Levan.'

'Yet he's *lied* to us, Mum,' Eden said, almost as a reminder whenever she felt tempted to forgive him herself.

'I know. I don't think I can forgive him for that. Why didn't he tell us the truth from the start?'

'Because he didn't think we'd want someone with a past like his and because he knew about my experience with Simon. The letter from Simon arrived not long after Levan. He bumped into me when he was running and I was upset and I told him a little about what had happened.'

'I suppose Levan felt he couldn't tell you and then kept digging a deeper hole.'

'Exactly that.'

'His family sound bloody awful.'

'Yes,' repeated Eden. 'And he hit those vile officers to protect a vulnerable man. I understand that and can forgive him. It's honourable and I'd probably have done the same thing, if I'd been that brave. What I can't get over is the continued deception and the fact I don't feel I can ever trust him again.'

'No, I can see that.' Her mum hugged her. 'Why didn't he confess the truth to us?'

'Because he was sucked in, he says. Our family is everything his isn't. He wanted to be part of it, and the longer he kept the truth hidden, the harder it was to reveal it.'

'I also understand that but he must have known how shocked and hurt you'd be when you eventually found out. Was he going to tell you at all?'

'I don't know. I think so. In the end he did, and it must have been hard. There's that but it's too late now.'

'Oh, love, you need time to deal with this. We all do, and I can't tell you how to react because you've been through so much.' She held Eden for a moment. 'What the hell happens next?'

'I'm not sure Levan will stay now.'

'No . . . Are you glad about that?' Sally asked.

'Not glad. I – really don't know how to feel. It's so new.'

'You need time to grieve for the loss of the man you thought he was. We all do.'

'That's exactly how I felt about Simon.'

They embraced and, finally, Eden gave way to the tears she needed to shed.

'The w-worst thing is, I n-need to tell Granny.'

Her mum found her a tissue. 'Hmm. That's going to be difficult.'

'We must, though,' Eden insisted.

'Yes, but not now. Not tomorrow either. Levan's not going to do anything silly like rushing round there, is he?'

'No. He won't dare go near her unless we ask him to.'

'He mustn't, although Iris is going to find that strange. I think I'd better break the news.'

'Or both of us,' Eden said, already dreading the task.

'Yes. Both of us. We'll do it at the weekend and I'll warn Levan of that myself. Now please try and get some rest, love, or you'll be no good for anything. Now's a time you need to be stronger than ever.'

It had been past midnight when Eden had gone to bed, falling onto the duvet in her clothes and staring into space until she eventually dropped off.

The next morning, she got up and went to work, as she had on many difficult mornings over the past few years.

She had to be strong, with a business to run and a living to make. She also didn't want to add any more worry to her mother's burden.

Luck was on her side in one way, as Levan didn't seem to be in for the next day or so. When there were no lights on at his cottage the next evening, she had a slight panic that he'd already decided to move out of Longships.

Wasn't that what she wanted?

If so, why did it fill her with despair?

A WhatsApp arrived while she was at the container, solving the mystery: he was on a 'course'. A course in what, though? Was that even true? How horrible it was when you lost faith in someone and felt you could no longer rely completely on what they said. In that same moment, she told herself that he had no reason to lie any further: the explosion had happened and the damage had been done.

It was a mixed blessing that Morwenna was also up country visiting some mates in Bristol, because Eden was torn about telling her. Likewise, everyone who'd grown to know and like Levan such as Courtney, Joe and Ravi. The mess she might need to untangle felt more convoluted by the second.

Then again, maybe it was up to Levan to tell them. It wasn't Eden's confession to make.

However, Morwenna was different.

Eden felt she had to share the news with her as soon as she could and was dreading her friend's reaction.

Though, before Morwenna heard, the worst was to come: telling Iris.

Sally had arranged for the two of them to take Iris to lunch at the Jubilee Pool and then, once safely in the privacy of the bungalow, to try to break it to her as gently as they could.

'How do you feel about this?' Sally popped her head around the bathroom door, while Eden was getting ready at Lighthouse Cottages on Sunday morning.

Having done a breakfast shift at the container, she'd whizzed home to shower and change. She'd deliberately left it until the last minute so she didn't have too much time to dwell. Her hair was still damp but she no longer smelled of coffee and was in a clean T-shirt dress. She paused, mascara wand in hand in front of the steamy mirror.

'It's not the happiest of prospects but it has to be done.'

'I've not slept well for worrying about it,' her mother said.

'Nor me.'

Sally sighed. 'Well, it will soon be over with. We'll have to put a brave face on over lunch and then do the deed.'

'Poor Granny . . .'

Her mum gave her a brief hug. 'She's a tough cookie, and she'll be more upset for you. I'll go and close the windows and lock up. See you downstairs.'

A few minutes later, Eden considered herself presentable. She dried off the ends of her damp locks, which didn't take long with her short style, and spritzed on some spray, although no product known to man could ever fully counter the effects of the humid Cornish air. It occurred to her that she was putting on armour, ready for the battle to come.

She was taking her denim jacket out of the wardrobe when she heard her mother's voice, loud and panicky from the lounge.

'Iris! Iris. Slow down, I can't follow you.'

Eden shot out of the bedroom and down the stairs.

Her mum clamped her mobile to her ear. 'Iris. Can you call the warden? Or a neighbour? Iris, please try to stay calm. I can't understand you.'

'What?' Eden mouthed.

Her mother shook her head. 'Right, you stay there. Don't move. We're on our way now and we'll try to call the warden from the car.'

Sally threw the phone into her bag.

'Mum?'

'It's Granny. I can't understand what she's saying but it sounds like she's not very well, she's lying on the floor.'

'Shall I call an ambulance?' Eden said, her stomach clenching with panic at the alarm in her mum's voice.

'I'll do it while you drive and then I'll get hold of the warden and ask her to go round too.'

Grabbing bags and phones, they ran out to the van.

'Was Granny able to say anything about how it happened?' Eden said, jumping behind the wheel.

'Not much. She was making very little sense. I don't know if the fall has made her dazed or she fell because of something worse, like a stroke. I just pray it's the first.'

It was agonising to run the gauntlet of tourist traffic, but Sally had managed to get hold of the warden and she'd gone straight round. Half an hour later, they were at the bungalow, where an ambulance was outside, along with several of Iris's neighbours.

Jim Tresize was on the front lawn, looking desperately worried. 'You will let me know how she is? We're all very fond of Iris.'

Eden found a kind word for the poor man. 'Thanks. You're a good friend to my gran, Jim.'

Then she went inside to find that the paramedics had Iris on her chair, with an oxygen mask on her face and hooked up to beeping machines. There was a splint on her left wrist and, for the first time in her life, Eden thought her granny looked her age.

She and her mother introduced themselves to the medics. 'How is she? Do we know what happened?'

315

'Iris seems to have had a fall and hurt her wrist,' the older, bearded paramedic said, while his female colleague soothed and monitored Iris. 'And the warden here thinks the same from what she can glean. Iris was lying on the carpet by her chair.'

'Possibly reaching up to the top of the bookcase?' the warden suggested, indicating scattered books and papers around the shelves.

'Oh, Granny . . .' Eden murmured.

'How is she now? Has she broken anything?' Sally asked.

'Possibly her wrist. Her BP and heart rate are a little faster than we'd like and she also seems a little bit confused, don't you, Iris?'

The other paramedic crouched down and touched Iris's arm.

'Your family are here, Iris, love.'

Eden had to squeeze back the tears when she saw her beloved granny peering over the oxygen mask.

'Granny?' Eden said, stroking Iris's good hand.

'It's Sally,' her mother added gently.

Iris nodded as if she finally knew who they were.

'You've had a little fall,' Sally said.

Iris nodded again and tried to remove the mask.

'No, don't, Granny. You just rest and let us all look after you.'

The female paramedic addressed Iris. 'You know, Iris, I think it would be a good idea if we took you to Penzance hospital to get you checked out. Your wrist must hurt and we can help you with that. Is that OK?'

Iris hesitated and then gave an almost imperceptible nod. While the medics wheeled Iris to the ambulance, the warden spoke to Eden. 'I'll make sure the bungalow is secure and talk to the neighbours. You focus on Iris. She's what matters now.'

Eden had to hand it to the team at the local emergency care centre; Iris was seen straight away.

After X-rays and tests, it was found that her wrist was merely sprained and, although painful, some strapping, rest and painkillers were all that was needed. However, she was still confused and had a raised temperature so, as a precaution, it was decided that she would be kept in for the night.

Eden and Sally were allowed to be with her, and by late afternoon she was settled in a bed, her wrist strapped up.

A doctor arrived with an update. 'The good news is that there's no sign that Iris has had any heart issues or a TIA or stroke. However, she does have a urinary tract infection. It's a fairly common occurrence when you're Iris's age and that could have made her feel unwell and perhaps a little dazed and confused. If she was reaching up to a high shelf, then she probably felt unsteady and fell.'

'A UTI? We didn't realise. We only saw her the other day and she was fine.'

'It might have worsened suddenly and as I say could even have contributed to the fall. They can cause a lot of problems quite rapidly,' the doctor said. 'She's receiving antibiotics and fluids, which should make her start to feel a lot more like herself by tomorrow and able to tell us more. In the meantime, we'll keep an eye on her here.'

'Thank you.'

The doctor barely had time to say 'You're welcome' before

he was called away to another patient, leaving Eden and Sally with Iris, who seemed to be dozing.

Eden heaved a big sigh. 'What a scare. Poor Granny. I'm so relieved it's nothing worse.'

'Me too . . .' Sally sat on the chair next to the bed. She looked exhausted herself.

'Hello . . .' Eden looked down to see Iris gazing straight up at her. 'Why are you here?'

'You've had a fall, Granny. You're in Penzance hospital.'

'Am I?' Iris blinked and looked around. 'Why?'

'Because you had a tumble, reaching for the books,' Sally explained. 'You hurt your wrist. The doctors say you have a water infection that's made you feel poorly but they're giving you antibiotics so you'll feel better soon.'

'I hope so,' Iris muttered, before her eyelids fluttered and she fell asleep again.

Sally and Eden took it in turns to grab a coffee and while Eden was on bedside duty, Iris woke again.

'Water . . .' she murmured and, after Eden had helped her take some sips from a cup, she seemed more alert.

'Where's your mother?' she asked, rather croakily.

'Getting a coffee.'

'She needs a rest,' Iris said. 'You look done in, too, love.'

It was wonderful to see her granny more like herself. 'I'm fine.'

'Are you?' Iris frowned. 'Where's Levan?'

'Levan? I – um – don't know.'

'Is he here?'

'No, Granny. He's been away for a couple of days. I don't know if he's back.'

'Oh. Oh dear.' Iris flapped her hand in agitation. 'I want to see him.'

'What? Right now?'

'Can you call him?' Iris insisted.

Despite her dismay, Eden spoke gently. 'Well, I don't know. He might still be on his training course. I'm not really sure.'

Her grandmother's fingers closed around Eden's hand, tightly. 'Please get him. Not while your mother's here. I want to talk to him.' Iris had never sounded so insistent and her eyes were desperate.

'OK. I'll do my best to find him, but I can't promise.'

'Thank you.'

Iris sank back onto the pillow.

Puzzlement and concern filled Eden's mind. She also had to tell her mother that Iris had asked for Levan, even though Iris had wanted it kept a secret. She couldn't simply go behind her mum's back with such a momentous request. Then it occurred to her that the request was only momentous because of Levan's confession. To her grandmother, he was still the lovely young chap who bought her books and had been so kind to the family.

While Iris dozed off again, Eden found her mother in the café and told her what Iris had said.

'She seemed perfectly lucid for a while but then she was agitated about Levan.'

'The nurse said she might be confused for a while until the meds start to work. Perhaps she'll forget about Levan?' Sally said hopefully.

'I'm not so sure, Mum. She seemed very insistent.'

'We don't know where he is, though, love.'

'No, but I could call him. It's the last thing I want to do but he does genuinely care for Granny and she's so fond of him. She doesn't want you to know she wants to see him.'

Her mother frowned. 'Hmm. Maybe she thinks I won't approve for some reason.'

'You don't think she'd ask him anything personal . . . about me? About the two of us getting together?' Eden said, growing cold at the thought. 'I'd want to sink into the ground if she did.'

Sally shrugged. 'I don't know. We can't stop her having her say if we do call him. It's her life.' She put her arm around Eden. 'It's her decision. Perhaps she'll see him on her own. I think, at her age, she's earned the right to do some things we might not approve of.'

Eden nodded. 'I suppose I've no choice but to call him, then.'

Chapter Thirty-Six

'Levan, it's Eden.'

He knew that. Her name had flashed up on his screen while he was unloading his overnight bag from the car at the cottages.

'Hello.'

'I don't want to worry you but it's Granny—'

'Iris?' His fingers tightened on his phone. 'Is she OK?'

'She's fine. Well, not fine, but on the mend. She had a fall at the bungalow and hurt her wrist and she's been kept in overnight at Penzance hospital.'

'A fall?' Levan said, aghast. 'Oh God, poor Iris. Do you know why she fell? Is she in much pain?'

He fired the questions at Eden without thinking.

'It's not broken, fortunately just a sprain, and she's more comfortable now. She's had lots of checks and they think the fall might have been caused by an infection in her – anyway, by an infection. She's on antibiotics and so I thought I'd call you and let you know.'

He exhaled in sheer relief. 'Yes, thank you. I appreciate it.

I've only just got home after my course when I picked up your call.'

'That's good,' Eden said. 'Because the thing is, Granny is asking for you.'

'For *me*?' He paused before he went on. 'I don't quite understand.'

'To be honest, neither do I. She won't say why but she's very insistent and we don't want to upset her, and so I promised I'd call you and ask.'

There was no hesitation before his reply. 'I'm on my way now.'

Abandoning his unpacking, Levan walked right back to the car and set off for the hospital. Eden's call had been most unexpected, though much dreamed of. It was such a shame it came as a result of Iris's fall; he could not dismiss the picture of Iris lying alone and in pain on the floor. Thank goodness she was now comfortable and being looked after.

The irony was that under other circumstances he'd have been ecstatic to hear from Eden. It had been a long, hard few days.

The course had come at the best and worst of times: the perfect excuse to be apart from the Carricks, for all their sakes. While he was normally a quick learner, it had taken all his powers of concentration to follow the intensive seminars and workshops. He'd had to burn the midnight oil after the day's activities to ensure he'd assimilated everything he was expected to.

All those details had flown from his mind the moment Eden had called him. All that mattered now was Iris. He braced himself: she was ninety.

*   *   *

An exhausted-looking Eden was waiting outside the hospital. Levan was a little out of breath, having parked a long way off and jogged the rest of the way.

'Hi,' she said, and although she didn't smile, she looked visibly relieved as he met her by the entrance. He wanted to hold her but, of course, that was now out of the question.

'I came as soon as I could.'

'I knew you would. Thanks. I'll take you to Granny. Mum's gone into town for a walk and to get something to eat.'

'How's Iris?'

'She's a lot stronger now, though she can get a bit confused. Probably owing to the infection and painkillers.'

'What happened?'

'Still not quite sure but I think she tried to reach for a book off the top of the shelf and overbalanced. She hurt her wrist and couldn't get up.'

'Poor Iris. I am sorry. What a worry for you and your mum too.'

By her stiff manner, it was clear Eden was putting on a brave face though it was etched with exhaustion. 'It was very scary for her and us but it could have been much worse.'

The urge to put his arms around Eden was almost overpowering but he simply followed her into the hospital. He'd lost the chance of any kind of intimate contact with her, physical or emotional. He could hardly complain.

He had to stifle a gasp when he saw Iris lying in the hospital bed. Even though she'd lived a long life and Levan had seen young ones ended in horrific ways – both in the army and in prison – he was shocked and saddened by the sight of her looking so frail.

'Granny, it's Levan.'

Taking a seat next to the bed, he touched her hand. 'Hello, Iris. What have you been up to, eh?'

Eden sat next to him.

'Levan?' Iris gazed at him. 'You're not Levan. You're Tom.'

'Granny, this is Levan, our neighbour. Your friend.'

Even though he was grateful for Eden being kind, Levan winced at the description. Would a friend have continued to lie to an elderly lady?

Iris frowned and then sighed. 'Oh, yes. I was muddled. It is Levan. You bought me the books.'

'I did.'

'I was trying to reach a book and I must have slipped.' Iris glared at Eden. 'I didn't have a "funny turn" or anything like that. The doctors and nurses keep asking me. I was perfectly compos mentis.'

'I wouldn't dare suggest otherwise,' Levan said, and exchanged a glance with Eden. To his relief, she was smiling.

'We're very glad to hear it, Granny,' she said. 'The trouble is that you were a little bit – um – vague when we spoke earlier.'

'Well, I'm not now. I'm not confused, vague and I'm especially not doolally.'

'No one thinks that.'

'Good, because I want you to be absolutely sure that what I'm about to tell you isn't the ramblings of a sick old woman.'

'Iris. I promise you neither of us – Eden nor me – thinks you're rambling.' Levan turned to Eden.

'No, we absolutely don't,' Eden said firmly, but he could see the puzzlement in her expression.

'Iris, are you sure you want to talk about this with me?' he said. 'Don't you want Sally here?'

She grasped his hand with surprising strength. 'No, I don't. I want to talk to you, I need to tell you something. Both of you. When I have, you might not look at me in the same way. I hope you will but . . .' Iris had tears in her eyes. 'It affects you, Eden, and your mother – and maybe Levan. I don't know and I won't until I get this off my chest.'

'Granny, shouldn't we do this when you're home?' Eden indicated the thin curtains around the bed. 'People might hear and surely what you have to say is private?'

Iris frowned. 'Yes, yes it is. But I don't know if I'll make it back home.'

'You will,' Eden said. 'You're going to be fine.' Beside him, she was almost in tears.

'Eden is right,' Levan said. 'And I also have some secrets to share that are for your ears only.' With a smile, he added gently, 'So why don't you get some rest now and tomorrow we'll take you home and we can all share everything.'

A nurse popped her head around the curtain. 'Everything OK? I've come to check on you, Iris. I hope you're behaving?'

Iris rolled her eyes. 'I don't have much choice, do I?'

'Your daughter-in-law is here but I can't allow more than two people by the bed. You look like you could do with some sleep,' the nurse added. 'And your visitors might need some rest. I'll be back soon.'

After the nurse had gone, Iris said, 'That's a hint for you all to go home. Perhaps you're right,' she said to Eden and Levan. 'I am tired. These drugs they're giving me . . . I don't want to be accused of rambling again but I'll say this. I want to tell you everything, and the moment I get out of here, I will.'

Chapter Thirty-Seven

Levan left immediately after the conversation. Sally returned and, after the nurse had done her obs, she said goodnight to Iris before Eden drove them home.

Eden told her mother that Levan had visited and was going to break his own news to Iris the next day.

'Mum, she wants to see us both on her own before she speaks to you. I don't know why.'

'Brace yourself. She probably wants to ask if his intentions are honourable.'

'I hope not. It will be excruciating considering what's gone on, though I think it might be more serious than that.'

Sally frowned. 'Even more serious . . .?'

'Possibly to do with the photos.'

'Oh, I see.'

'I feel bad that you won't be there.'

'Don't, because she must have her reasons and at her age, and with what's happened, we owe it to her to grant her wishes.'

They managed half a ready meal and then spent the evening

326

trying to watch TV. A call to the hospital before bedtime confirmed that Iris was resting comfortably and had eaten some dinner herself. As she'd promised to update Levan, Eden sent him a quick message to that effect.

However, neither Sally nor Eden slept well, always on edge for the phone ringing in case Iris had taken a turn for the worse – and what on earth she would have to say to them the next day. How would she react to Levan's confession?

Eden hoped it wouldn't cause Iris to have a relapse or worse.

By the way she could hear Levan moving about until the small hours, he was probably wondering the same thing too.

'Message me when Iris has finished with you both and I'll come in,' Sally said, outside the bungalow after Iris had arrived home in an ambulance. Eden and Sally and the warden had been there to settle her in and she'd informed Eden that she was now ready to say her piece.

'I will,' Eden said.

Levan arrived, walking straight over to them. 'I'm sorry this has happened,' he said, which could have referred to Iris or his own situation.

'We all are,' Sally said brusquely. 'None of it can be helped now. Iris is what's important. I'm going into town to do some shopping for her. Let me know when I'm summoned.'

'I don't feel I should be here at all,' he said.

'Iris has asked for you, so you should be,' Sally said wearily. 'Drop your bombshell as gently as you possibly can, won't you?' she added, giving Levan a hard stare.

'I'll do my best,' he said meekly.

'Come on,' Eden muttered, reminded anew of his deception. After making cups of tea that neither Eden nor Levan wanted, they sat on the sofa, keeping as much distance as possible from one another, which wasn't easy in the small space.

Though tired and a little bruised, Iris's eyes were as keen as ever and swept them both up in one gaze.

'You two look like you're waiting to see the dentist.'

Levan smiled and Eden had to join in, relieved to see her granny back to her normal self. 'We're wondering what you're going to tell us, Granny.'

'I'm wondering what you have to say to me, too, but someone has to go first and so I will. Call it a privilege of age,' she added.

'Be my guest,' Levan murmured.

'First, yesterday. I may have misled you. I really was winded and confused at first. I think I said I was reaching for a book. I was looking for a box of photographs. Those you had restored – they brought the past to life so vividly. As if I was back there.'

'We didn't mean to upset you with them, Granny.'

'You haven't.' Her gaze encompassed them both. 'Quite the contrary. You brought back so many happy memories. Both of you. In fact, the first moment I saw Levan in his garden, he reminded me of one of the happiest times of my life.'

Eden suppressed a squeak, remembering that moment when she was caught spying on him.

Levan was smiling. 'In my Speedos, upside down?'

'It was impressive, though it wasn't until you were the right way up that I had a proper shock.'

'A shock?' Levan said. 'I hope not.'

'Wasn't your fault. You couldn't help it. You see, you reminded me of someone who I cared for very much. Someone

I loved deeply . . .' She sighed. 'And it wasn't your grandad, Eden.'

Eden was speechless. Even though she'd suspected Iris had had a fling, she hadn't expected her grandmother to admit it so starkly.

'You had a boyfriend before Grandad?' she said softly. 'Was it the man in the photograph? Oh, Granny, we found a snap of a man hidden in one of the pictures we borrowed

With a deep sigh, Iris sank onto the backrest of the chair. 'I guessed as much. I found the snap when you returned the pictures. Yes, it was that man. His name was Tom and I'll say what you're longing to hear: Levan could be his twin.'

'My twin?' Levan echoed. 'I noticed a resemblance but nothing to make me think that.'

'We did,' Eden said. 'Me and Mum and Morwenna.'

Levan exhaled. 'Wow.'

'You can't see what others do,' Iris went on. 'Though of course, it's impossible for you to be his twin and the man – Tom – is probably long gone. He was one of the lighthouse engineers who worked here at Hartstone. He was dashing and – I – fell for him, though I knew nothing would come of it. I never found out exactly what happened to him because he emigrated to Australia not long after that photo was taken.'

'You had a fling with him, before you met Grandad? That's fine. It's normal,' Eden said.

'Ah, but it wasn't fine and it wasn't normal for the times. You see, I didn't have a relationship with Tom before I met Walter. Your grandad was away on a tower at the time while we waited to get married.'

'You mean . . .?' Eden hardly dared ask.

'I was already engaged to your grandad at the time, though

I was in love with Tom. I'm not sure he felt the same about me. I knew he was emigrating and I'd never have the chance to be in his arms again. He knew it too and so we took a risk. I slept with him.'

No matter how hard she'd been braced for her granny's news, Eden could not stifle her gasp.

Levan looked at her and swallowed but was silent.

'Granny . . . I'd no idea.'

'And then two weeks before the wedding, long after Tom had left, I found out I was pregnant.'

'I – I – and you didn't tell Grandad.'

'I agonised over it. I didn't want to deceive him. He was a decent, honourable man and I did love him. He was a steady, loving chap and, God help him, besotted with me. He was ten times the man Tom was, but I was in love with Tom. In love and foolish and very silly, but we can't turn back the clock now. There never seemed a good moment to tell him. I knew it would devastate him and he might call off the wedding. Do you understand?'

'Yes,' Levan murmured.

'So, I was torn in two; until eventually, after we were married, I knew I could *never* tell Walter. So, all these years, I've lived a lie, first with your grandad and then your dad, your mum and you. Can you ever forgive me?'

Eden had tears in her eyes, but her decision was made. 'Granny . . .' She sprang off the sofa and knelt by the chair, holding Iris's good hand. 'Of course I can forgive you. You are so brave.'

'Am I? Sleeping with another man? That's not the word that would have been used about me then. Not now, either. People are still very judgemental and I did do a terrible thing.'

'Not terrible. Human nature.'

'Simon did the same to you and you hated him for it,' Iris said.

'You're not Simon. Nothing like him,' Levan declared, surprising Eden.

'Thank you,' Iris said and then paused, struggling. Eden squeezed her hand in encouragement.

'Once or twice, I *almost* told Walter. I was going to say it was a moment of madness with Tom and would never happen again, but that would have been a lie too. It was true that I only slept with Tom once in the dunes at the beach, but I *was* in love with him.' For the first time, Iris faltered. She'd seemed so determined to 'tell it like it was' until now and, although Eden was shocked, she thought her granny so brave to admit a secret that had burdened her for so long.

'Go on, Granny. It's OK.'

'In the end I decided it was better to stay silent. Easier for me and for all of us. You see, I had to be practical and think about a future for me and the baby – your dad. I *did* love Walter to the end of his days and I'll always love him. What I felt for him was a different kind of love to the way I felt about Tom. Glowing embers that lasted, not a burning passion that was always going to fizzle out.'

'Granny . . .' Eden could hardly get the words out, the shock had forced a lump into her throat. 'So you're saying that my dad was Tom's son, and that he's my grandad?'

'Yes, my love. He is.' She grasped Eden's hand.

Levan shifted in his seat. 'Iris, I'm not sure that I should be hearing this. It's a family affair.'

'Too late now!' Iris said with a sad chuckle. 'And yes, you should. When you, Levan, turned up out of the blue at the cottages, and acting all mysterious, I thought that you might – that you might be a descendant of Tom's, come to find me.'

'Iris, I'd be proud to be a real member of your family but unfortunately there are no Toms in our family,' Levan said gently.

Iris patted his hand. 'Never mind. You being here, looking so uncannily like him, reminded me of him and forced me to confront the truth and be honest with Eden and her mum. I'm grateful for that.'

Eden's eyes flitted to Levan's face, but she couldn't read his expression. His lips were pressed together; perhaps he was feeling guilty at Iris's generous comment.

'Now,' Iris went on. 'I've been waiting for Levan to tell me why he chose to come to Cornwall. I know you're involved in something shady,' she said. 'I've worked that out.'

'Shady?' Levan echoed.

'Oh yes, though you're not the first to be up to shady stuff down here, you know. There's been secret activity going on for donkey's years. It started in the war when I was a little girl, when the authorities took over the telegraph stations. Locals gossip, farmers let things slip in the pub. They suddenly end up with a brand-new barn or a mast on the land and the wife's acting all smug and swanning around in a new car. They'd had a backhander.' Iris fixed Levan with a glare. 'I'm right, aren't I?'

'Nothing gets past you, does it?' He smiled. 'You're right. I do work for the security services and that's why I came to this part of Cornwall.'

'I knew I was right!' She banged the arm of the chair.

'Well, I'm no James Bond!' Levan said with an edge of desperation that almost made Eden smile. 'I really do spend my life doing boring computer stuff. I wish I could tell you more but I'm not allowed to.' He exchanged a look with Eden.

Iris held up her hand. 'I don't want to know. If you're serving your country, that's all I care about.'

'I am. I hope . . . And thank you.'

Iris drew in a breath, as if she had shifted a literal weight from her chest. 'So, now, Levan, what is it you want to tell me . . . Is it all about you being a spy?'

He allowed himself a small smile. 'Iris. I'm not a spy. I promise you.'

'If you say so.' She kept her eyes on him.

'I'm most definitely not a spy, but I'm also not who I said I am . . .'

Chapter Thirty-Eight

'It's always the way,' Eden's mother observed, buttering a slice of toast in the kitchen of Wolf Rock the following day. 'Just at the moment one part of your life is going well, another starts to nosedive. You can't keep every plate spinning at once.'

'A couple of mine have smashed this past week,' Eden murmured, thinking that her trust – perhaps her heart – had suffered the same fate.

'Trust me, mine have wobbled too.' Her mother handed her the toast. 'First, Levan's news and then your granny's. It's been a hell of a week. It's going to take some time to process all of this.'

Iris had called Sally and spoken to her after she'd told Levan. They'd stayed up late into the night talking about it.

'I still can't believe my grandad is someone else – this man, Tom. Will you call Granny later to see how she is? I'll go over after work. Courtney can't manage on his own, we've been so busy since Morwenna gave our social media a makeover. I can barely reply to all the comments these days.'

'I'll call her after breakfast before I go into the office.'

'I hope she's OK after so much turmoil over the past few days.'

'She'll be all right . . . Um, are you going to eat that toast or wave it around all morning?'

Eden stared at her toast. 'Sorry. I'm not very hungry.'

Sally frowned. 'Eat it. How are you going to have enough energy to feed all these customers?'

'I'm surrounded by croissants, Mum. I'll be fine.'

'You may be surrounded by them, but you do need to put something in your mouth.'

Dutifully, Eden managed most of the toast, leaving the crusts as she always did.

Sally watched her over the rim of her mug. 'Your hair will never curl.'

'Just as well I don't want it to.' She smiled then was hit by the reality of having to face Levan again sooner or later. 'I wish there was a way of knowing in advance if you were making the right decision.'

Sally frowned. 'Is this about Levan?'

'Yes, he wants to see me but I'm not sure.'

'Sorry, love,' she said with a rueful smile. 'I can't help there. All I can say is take your time and talk to him.'

'I can't bring myself to have a long conversation with him yet.'

'Well, there's no going forward unless you do.'

When Eden called in to the bungalow later, she found Iris a lot brighter, thanks to the antibiotics. She put away some shopping for her granny, made a drink and sat down. One of Morwenna's photos of Iris, Grandad Walter and baby Roger had been framed and stood on the sideboard.

'That's a nice new frame,' Eden said.

'Morwenna brought it round yesterday. She came to see how I was.'

'That's kind of her.'

'She's a lovely girl. Always makes me laugh.' Iris smiled then became serious. 'Thanks for coming to see me. I want you to say what's on your mind. Everything. Are you very shocked and disappointed in me?'

'I could never be disappointed in you, Granny. I keep having the same thought and it might sound a bit mad. The thing is, I thought that Grandad Walter and his father had handed down so much. Even when everything changed or was crashing down around my ears in my own life, my family were the rock that would never fail.'

'Have I failed you?'

'No! Not you,' Eden said. 'You could never fail me but I've been thinking. When I spoke to Levan, he said something about his own family. He said that they didn't want to believe that their rock – the army and all that tradition – could treat their son so badly. They'd built their identity around being a high-ranking military family and I suppose I've built mine on our family. I'm so proud of Dad and Grandad.' She paused. 'And he will always be Grandad to me.'

Iris's eyes gleamed but her voice was steady. 'Your family *still* is your rock. Nothing can ever change that. I don't believe being a "good" person, who does the right thing, is in your genes. Take lighthouse keeping – Roger went into that because he'd seen the example Walter had set him. It wasn't "in his blood" and neither was being a decent man or having a sense of duty. It's impossible to inherit. It's down to so much more.'

'Oh, Granny, you are so wise.'

'Wise?' Iris huffed. 'My love, I have also been very stupid. What sane woman would have slept with another man six weeks before her wedding? I risked everything.'

'Do you regret it, though?'

Eden noticed Iris touch her wedding ring. 'That's something I've thought about many times over the years and the answer is no, every time. It felt the right thing to do at the time. I balanced the regrets I'd experience about not having that moment, with the guilt I'd feel afterwards, and, no, I don't regret it.'

Eden shivered.

Iris touched her hand. 'What's the matter, love?'

'When you talk about balancing regret with a lifetime of consequences, you could be talking about Levan.'

'I am in a way,' Iris murmured. 'He did the right thing when it mattered. He did what he believed in, knowing the consequences. He became the person he wanted to be.'

'He still lied to us all.'

'So did I, my love.'

'That was different. You—'

Iris shook her head. 'It's closer than you think. I also didn't want my whole life to come crashing down. I also lied to protect what I truly cared about and believed in.'

Eden paused a few seconds before replying. 'So you think I should forgive him?'

'Only you can decide that, because you have more at stake in deciding to trust him again. All I can say is that when he first told me I was shocked, I'll admit. I was angry, like your mother was, though only on your account.' She leaned forward and took Eden's hand. 'His motives were good, and he sacrificed his career, his liberty and his relationships in that

337

moment. He thought he was doing the right thing and could see no other way out. That's why he did it, wasn't it? To help the soldier but also to escape.'

'To *escape*? Levan told you that?'

'As good as,' Iris said. 'He'd reached the end of his tether, pretending to be someone he wasn't, and ignoring injustice.'

'I realise that. It's so – momentous – to trust a man when he's lied to me to gain my trust in the first place. It's as if I attract them.'

'No, you don't. Take some time, think it through,' Iris said and gave Eden a hard stare. 'Would it help you if Levan moved away?'

'No! I mean, maybe.' Eden groaned in frustration, then had goosebumps of fear. 'He has mentioned he might . . . I wasn't sure he was serious. Has he told you he's thinking of moving?'

'If it would help us all, I think he would.'

'Oh God, I don't know. I liked him – liked him very much – and I still do, but can I ever feel the same way about him?'

'Hmm,' Iris said. 'I think you should ask yourself this: would you be happier if you could turn back the clock to the point where he never came into our lives? Your answer lies there.'

Chapter Thirty-Nine

It seemed to Levan that the days were crawling by, as slowly as the lichen growing on the trees in the valley near Lighthouse Cottages. The ticking of the clock in his cottage got on his nerves so much that he took the battery out of it. Funny, it had never bothered him before, but the place seemed too quiet now and, once he'd zeroed in on it, it drove him nuts.

He was waiting for Eden to call him, or ask him to talk to her. Twice he'd seen her while he'd been on a run but both times she'd simply caught his eye and inclined her head in reply to his wave, and carried on walking.

He'd driven past the café most days on his way to work and glimpsed her with Courtney, serving queues of customers. He'd smelt the aroma of the roastery and lain awake at night, listening for her and hoping she might do something magical like knock on his door at midnight or call him on his mobile.

Nothing.

On the fourth day since he'd told Iris who he really was, Dion called him. They'd spoken and emailed over the past few days but Levan was desperate to see his friend face to face. To his relief, Dion said: 'I'm coming back to Cornwall tomorrow for a few days. I thought you could take me surfing.'

'Love to apart from the fact I can't surf and you've only got half an arm.'

'We'll manage somehow. We can hire some wetsuits and boards and fall in together.'

'Great,' Levan said. 'Anything would be better than sitting around here feeling like crap.'

'Really? Things must still be bad.'

'They are . . .' he said. 'In fact, I'm thinking of taking up your offer to arrange a transfer to a different Cornish site.'

A pause, then Dion spoke gruffly: 'OK. If you want me to explore the option, I'll see what's out there, although it could be weeks, months even . . . if you're sure?'

'I think it would be better if I didn't live next door to the people whose trust I've destroyed.'

'Hmm. I never took you for a quitter.'

'Thanks for your frankness, buddy. Leaving seems the honourable thing to do.'

'Sure it is . . .' Dion left another pause, enough to make Levan think he was going to try and persuade him out of leaving. 'We'll talk about it tomorrow afternoon. How about four-ish so we can catch some waves before the pub?'

Levan didn't think he and Dion would be catching anything other than pneumonia, but he was up for any distraction. It was probably a good idea for them to do something active together, before they got down to the business of discussing him moving away from Lighthouse Cottages.

He was packing a rucksack with board shorts and a towel when Eden came to the door.

'Eden?'

'Can I come in and talk?' Her eyes lighted on the rucksack. 'If you're busy, I'll come round later.'

There was no way he was going to miss this opportunity, even if Dion was due in ten minutes. He wasn't even going to tell her. He could only hope Dion would be late.

'Not too busy to talk, come in. Please.'

'Thanks.'

'Um. Why not sit down? Do you want a coffee? Wine?'

The last time she'd been inside his house was when she'd walked into his bedroom. Was she reminded of that moment: the overpowering need to be together and the crash to earth afterwards?

'No, thanks. I won't stay too long.'

This did not bode well.

'I've wanted us to talk,' he said. 'I thought it was better to give you some space, wait until you were ready.'

'Thanks. I needed that space and time. Levan, I've spent so long working out how to say this, but perhaps the best way is to launch right in.'

His heart beat a little faster.

'Since you arrived, my whole world has changed. I've done the thing I never thought I'd do. You made me trust a man again.'

'Then I shattered it?'

'Yes.'

This was the moment when she would tell him to go. This was the moment for him to do the right thing and spare her.

'I've asked Dion about a transfer.' The words gushed out

of Levan as if getting them over with quickly might help. 'It could take a while but I can move out faster. Rent somewhere if needs be, get out of your sight.'

'What? You're *leaving*?'

'If you want me to. Dion's on his way, in fact, to discuss that very thing. He says he can sort something out about a transfer to another site. I thought it would make it easier.'

Eden seemed stunned. 'Easier for who?'

'You, the family. *Us.*'

Noises outside the cottage interrupted them, and then there was a knock on the door and a familiar voice.

'Levan?'

'It's Dion,' he said. 'I'll ask him to wait.'

Eden protested. 'No, don't. We can talk about this another time.'

'Please, no, I want it to be *now*, otherwise neither of us might find the courage to be honest again. Dion will understand.'

Before Eden could insist on leaving the cottage, Levan opened the front door to find not one, but two faces he recognised.

Dion smiled. 'Hello, mate. I've brought you a visitor.'

Next to Dion stood a petite woman in jeans and a black top. Although she was in her late forties, she had a young-looking face, and her hair was scraped back in a ponytail, the grey showing at the roots. She licked her lips nervously before speaking.

'Hello, Captain Bancroft. Do you remember me?'

His palms were clammy. 'Of course, I do, Maddie, and it's good to see you . . . but I go by Levan now.'

'Levan, then.' She sought Dion for reassurance. 'Dion did mention it but I forgot. He asked me to come.'

'I did,' Dion declared. 'And you can be as angry as you like but Maddie has travelled all the way down here and we're not going away.'

'I'm not angry, and I wouldn't dream of sending you away,' Levan said. 'But you need to know I have company.'

'Is it who I think?' Dion asked.

'Yes.'

'Then what I have to say is for her too,' Maddie said, in a firmer voice. 'Dion's also told me what's been going on between you and I think it's high time I spoke up. I'm so sorry for what you've been through, and I can never turn back the clock but I can – me and Rowan – we can try to make amends.'

With great difficulty did Levan avoid his emotions spilling over. 'There's no need, but come inside. I'll introduce you to Eden.'

He wasn't sure what Eden had heard although she must have caught most of the conversation, as the door from the tiny porch was open into the sitting room. He was also doubtful if she would stay and hear what Maddie wanted to say. All he could do was let her have her say.

Eden was standing when he ushered Dion and Maddie into the room. By the look of confusion on her face, she'd heard everything.

'Eden, you've seen Dion before – this is Maddie, she's the mother of one of the soldiers who was in my unit.'

Maddie extended her hand. 'Hello, and sorry for landing on you like this. It must be a shock for you and Levan.'

Eden shook Maddie's hand. 'Trust me, I've had so many surprises over the past few months that I'm almost expecting them.'

343

Levan could have kissed Eden there and then, he was so grateful to her for trying to be kind when she must be wondering what the hell was going on.

'Anyone fancy a coffee?' Dion said.

'I'll make it,' Eden replied.

'Don't worry, we'll do the honours while you and Maddie get acquainted. Levan, I could use the help,' he added firmly.

After they'd returned with a tray of mugs and a cafetiere, Levan found Maddie and Eden deep in conversation.

'That smells great. It's *your* coffee?' Maddie said to Eden when he put the tray on the table.

'Thanks, I gave Levan a packet,' Eden said. 'And to answer your question, it is my coffee, or rather I buy it in and roast here at the lighthouse. I sell it and serve it up at my café near Land's End.'

'Oh yes, we did pass it! What a lovely spot, with the sea in the distance.' Maddie glanced around the cottage. 'It's so peaceful here. Stunning. I can see why you moved all this way, Captain—sorry, Levan.'

Levan found his tongue. 'The distance appealed – and it is very beautiful.'

'You've found peace here?' Maddie asked.

Before replying, he glanced at Eden. 'To a degree.'

A little awkwardly, Maddie nodded. 'And you've always lived here?' she asked Eden. 'Dion told me your family have all been lighthouse keepers? How amazing.'

'I was brought up here,' Eden said carefully. 'I worked in London for a while but I'm back at my mum's now. We live in Wolf Rock, the cottage next door to this one. I'll do the honours, shall I?' she offered.

'Thanks.' As Levan didn't trust his hands to be steady, he

was grateful to Eden for plunging the cafetiere and pouring the coffee. He also thought that he couldn't love her any more than at this moment, which was ironic as he had less hope of his feelings being returned than ever before.

Still, he was ready to face whatever was thrown at him. 'Thank you for coming all this way.'

'I had to,' Maddie said. 'When you said you'd found peace here "to a degree", I think I understand what you mean.'

'I'm guessing Dion's told you the story about me moving to Cornwall?' Levan said, sensing Eden's eyes boring into him.

'Most of it,' Maddie said. 'He called me and said that you'd made a life here but things weren't going smoothly. He said you'd met someone.' She smiled at Eden. 'Someone very special and you'd be devastated if that were to end before it had even begun.'

'Dion said that?' Levan was incredulous.

'More or less, yes.'

Eden cradled her mug, hanging on Maddie's every word.

'This is why I want to speak to you two together,' she went on. 'Of course, I'm not here to interfere in your relationship. It's up to you what decisions you make after I leave but I can't live with myself a moment longer until I say my piece. It's something that should have been said years ago.'

She took a deep breath. 'It was my son, Rowan, who Levan stood up for, although he was only one of many. It was on Rowan's account that Levan was tried for assault and went to jail.'

'I wouldn't change what I did either,' Levan declared, then qualified it quickly: 'I'd still defend Rowan in a heartbeat. I only wish I'd been honest with Eden about what I'd done from

345

the start. I wish I hadn't felt the need to hide my past. I don't know how to make amends for that to the people I care about.'

He exchanged a look with Eden but she quickly glanced away and he felt a wave of despair crash over him. No matter what Maddie said in his defence, how could he ever regain her trust?

Dion listened, his mouth in a line as he kept his own emotions in check.

'I can't solve your problems. I wish I could. All I know is that you are the best man. The kindest, most trustworthy of men.' Maddie addressed herself to Eden. 'Do you know what he actually did when he hit those bastards? He saved my son's life and two others. Not in battle, but by standing up for them, and look what he got for it.'

'I'd gladly do the time again,' Levan declared.

'No, but – afterwards when Rowan was intimidated so badly, he was too afraid to speak up for you at the court-martial. I would have but I wasn't allowed to, they said. They terrified my son into staying silent. They told him he could leave the army "without any trouble" if he kept quiet, and he was at the end of his tether. If he'd gone through the trial, they'd have made his life hell.'

'It's OK,' Levan said, even though he felt like he was in a pit of despair. 'I realised what had happened.'

'It's not OK but you have to understand he *wasn't* paid off. He did it for the sake of his sanity, even if it meant letting you down. He was told he could have an exemplary service record and he could move away and make a fresh start. Even so, he was traumatised by the experience and he had a mental breakdown. He's regretted it every day and now he – we – are going to put it right.'

'It's too late and I don't need you to do that,' Levan insisted. 'I *did* hit the officers; I did do the crime.'

'I explained to Maddie that your conviction will still stand,' Dion said.

'Oh, I'm fully aware of that,' Maddie said firmly. 'But what we *can* do is make a bloody massive fuss and try to get an enquiry into the bullying that was allowed to take place for years. You see, even before Dion contacted me, Rowan had already decided to do something about it. I come here with *his* blessing. He lives in New Zealand now,' she explained. 'He's married and they've just had a baby.'

'I'm very pleased to hear it,' Levan said. 'And he should enjoy his family in peace.'

'Thank you but as for "in peace", he won't rest until he's done what he needs to do. Having a little one has focused his mind. He wants his daughter to know he did the right thing, even if it was late in the day.'

'There's no need.'

Levan felt a hand touch his briefly. Eden's hand. He didn't dare look at her.

'Let Maddie speak,' she said softly.

Maddie smiled. 'Eden knows what's good for you, even if you don't. Besides, Rowan has already contacted some of his former comrades – ones who've left the army. They're all in touch with a journalist from one of the big newspapers. She thinks they have a case to answer and, if they can make enough noise, they can possibly force the authorities to open a public enquiry.'

Levan choked up. 'I don't know what to say . . .'

'Nothing, for now. The enquiry, if it happens, is for the future but you need to know that people who care about you and respect you are fighting for you *now*. And Eden,' Maddie said, 'I was lying when I said I wouldn't interfere, because you two would be crazy to let each other go.'

Chapter Forty

'Goodbye. Have a safe journey.'

Eden hung back in Levan's cottage while he went out to the car park to see Maddie off in case they wanted to talk without her present. Maddie was staying in the same hotel as Dion that evening, then he was taking her home to Wiltshire.

She'd stayed over an hour, during which Eden had heard more of the details about Rowan's experiences at the hands of the bullying officer and during the trial and subsequent cover-up. He'd suffered from depression and severe anxiety for a year after he'd left and Maddie had said it had taken a lot of courage for him to finally speak out. It had been an emotional conversation and Eden had struggled to hold it together.

Finally, she heard the cottage door shut and Levan walked back into the sitting room.

He sat down heavily on the sofa, white-faced.

She let him have a few moments before murmuring, 'Would you like something stronger than coffee?'

'I think that would be a good idea. There's some whisky in the dresser.'

She poured them both a glass and handed one to him, before sitting next to him on the sofa. He seemed surprised to find her so close to him.

'Stupid question but are you OK?' she asked.

'A bit shellshocked but yeah . . . I'm OK.'

'What an incredible woman Maddie is.'

'Yes, she is.'

'And your friend, Dion,' Eden added.

Levan let out a long breath, as if he'd been holding back his emotions for a very long time. 'He's the best.'

'I'm sorry for all you've been through. I can't imagine what it was like.'

'You too,' he said, turning his gaze on her. 'You know, just because Maddie turned up here and said – that stuff about me – doesn't have to change your feelings about me. I'm very happy that she travelled all this way and it's a huge relief to know the truth about Rowan and why he didn't speak up at the time . . . but as for us, it's what *you* think that counts.'

'I know my own mind. I make my own decisions. I always have and especially after what's happened with Simon.'

Finally he smiled and the way he looked at her – with such intense pleasure – made her heart pitter-patter like gentle rain falling. 'That's what I love about you,' he said. 'You are always one hundred percent Eden. You're true to yourself.'

'Love?' she echoed, picking up on the word.

'Sorry,' he said, reddening. 'I shouldn't have laid that on you after what's happened. It's not fair but know this: I do care about you deeply, more than anyone else in my life. But forget I ever said it.'

'That's not going to be easy . . .' Eden said. 'And I'll need time to – to process it.'

'That someone loves you?' he said. 'After what you've been through and what I did to you, I don't blame you. I suppose,' he said warily, 'if I do stick around here, I'll have to pretend we're just neighbours.'

'Probably best,' she said.

'And hope that one day, after a few years, I'll have been able to prove that I really meant it and I'm not going to let you down or ever deceive you again, no matter what the reason.'

'That would take decades,' she said solemnly, though with the smallest of smiles.

He inclined his head. 'Of course.'

She hardly dared to speak for fear of her emotions getting the better of her. 'Like I said, I'll need time. Even if it isn't years . . .' She managed another slight smile for him, torn between wanting to forgive him there and then and her instinct for self-preservation. 'Though whatever happens to us, with us, you should understand this: I don't want you to have to pretend to be anyone but yourself. Whether that's Henry or Levan. Whether it's the hippy who does yoga in his Speedos or the hero who risked everything for what he believed in. Either or both is fine by me.'

'Good.' He reached for her hand and, to his obvious amazement, she let him hold it. 'I've also made up my mind about something else,' he told her. 'I'm going to see my mother – try and reconcile with her at least. It would be a start.'

Chapter Forty-One

A WEEK LATER

Out in the garden, Eden pulled up a few weeds then cursed. Exhausted after the drama of the past few weeks, she'd agreed to take a Sunday off while Morwenna helped Courtney at the café.

After Eden had arrived home that Saturday, she'd told her mum, Iris and Morwenna about Maddie's visit and warned them there might some coverage in the media.

Now, Levan had gone to visit his mother at a hotel near their home. Unfortunately, his father and brother – who was back in the UK – were incensed by his involvement in a newspaper story about the bullying and his case, and had refused to see him or let him come to the house.

He was due back that afternoon and Eden had been trying to relax by pottering around in the vegetable garden but was finding it impossible. Every few minutes, she'd have to look at her phone or strain her ears, hoping to hear the rumble of an engine on the drive down to the lighthouse.

Bzz.

Ripping off her gardening gloves, Eden lunged for her phone, which was resting on the garden kneeler.

However, it was Morwenna's name, not Levan's, that flashed up.

Her words gushed out at top speed, squeaky with panic. 'Eden, get over here now. It's gone crazy!'

'It's only nine-thirty . . .'

'I don't care. We can't cope. Please come now and bring more of *everything*!'

So much for a morning off . . . thought Eden, thinking that a coach party must have landed.

When she arrived at the café, Morwenna was hemmed in behind the counter by a score of people crowding around the container. Some were gazing around in wonder like they'd reached St Michael's Mount. One was taking a selfie of herself with the container in the background. Two more appeared to be rooting in the bins for souvenirs to pose with.

British accents rattled out, as well as German, American, Korean, a smattering of French, and others Eden couldn't place.

Morwenna was behind the counter, looking frazzled as Courtney tried to keep up with all the orders. 'Sorry, *scusi! Pardonnez-moi!* Excuse ME!'

'What's going on?' Eden said, hurrying in through the rear of the container with an extra bag of beans.

'Haven't you seen?' Morwenna said. 'You're the number one coffee outlet in Cornwall on a big travel review site. Some foodie mega-influencer turned up and did a TikTok and an Insta reel of the place. They took the coffee down to a secluded beach, claimed it was the best they'd ever tasted *in the world*, and the clip went viral.'

'Viral!' Eden exclaimed, her mind whirling. 'What do you mean?'

'It had tens of thousands of hits,' Morwenna explained slowly as if Eden were a toddler. 'Your followers have rocketed. The clip's been shared like a zillion times.' She paused, letting the impact of her words sink in. 'Hun, you and your little coffee hut are most definitely on the map now!'

Two people started waving payment cards at Morwenna while chattering excitedly.

'Ah, *merci! Oui!*' Morwenna cried. '*Attendez-vous, s'il-vous-plait! Bitte!*'

The queue was growing longer, as more pictures were taken and people jostled to be first in the queue. Orders for hot chocolates and flat whites, macchiatos and cakes flew from people waving debit cards. It was mayhem.

'Sorry we had to call you,' Courtney said, while Eden fumbled with the ties on her apron, still in shock. 'It's been like this since we opened.'

'It's OK. Looks like we'll need more cups and milk. I'll unload them from my van.'

Over the next couple of hours it felt as if half the holidaymakers in Cornwall under thirty were queueing for her coffee. Eden was worried she might run out of coffee, if she didn't flake out first. Joe's vegan cranberry flapjacks had flown out of the door faster than a 747. Even the 'emergency' biscotti Eden had added as an afterthought had sold out.

Finally, she had to break it to the last customers that everything had gone. The container shelves were also almost empty of take-home roast.

The three of them had hardly drawn breath by the time they had to shut up shop.

'Wow,' Eden said, as Morwenna sank down onto the step at the back of the container with a large glass of iced water. Courtney had already jumped on his bike and hared back to his mum's for lunch.

'Remind me never to volunteer to help again. That was insane!' Morwenna said.

'Insane? It was absolutely amazing!' Eden cried. 'You are a genius, Wenna!'

'Well,' Morwenna giggled. 'Maybe just a *bit* of a genius.'

Eden hugged her. 'Thank you so much for the marketing and helping out today. We'd never have coped without you.' She took a breath and surveyed the empty shelves and general chaos in the rear of the container. 'Looks like I might have to take on another part-timer until the end of the season.'

'I'm just thrilled you're busy,' Morwenna said modestly. 'You deserve some luck . . . all the luck.' She suddenly grew serious. 'Talking of which, is Levan back yet?'

'Hopefully after lunch. It's a long drive from his place. Or rather the hotel near his place.'

'He's still not welcome in his own home?'

'Their home. I'm not sure. I'm waiting to hear.'

'And how about you?' Wenna said. 'Is he welcome in your life as more than a friend and neighbour?'

Eden had thought of little else but that question over the past week or so. She'd told Levan it could take years for her to trust him again, but she'd been having a terrible time keeping her distance from him.

'I'm possibly coming round to the idea.'

'Perhaps you'll never know unless you give him the chance,'

Wenna said. 'And more importantly, give yourself the chance to care about someone again. Maybe, more than care?' she added.

Eden exhaled. 'It's such a risk, Wenna.'

'So was starting your business, but you had faith in it. So is anything worth doing in life, and I love and admire you so much.'

Was that the glisten of moisture in Wenna's eye? Eden almost lost it herself.

'And I love you too, buddy.' She hugged Wenna briefly then clapped her hands. 'Right,' she said. 'I need to clear up and start thinking about how I'm going to cope with my newfound fame.'

Morwenna stayed a while longer to help Eden clear away and close up before she went home 'to collapse on the sofa with a large gin' and Eden headed back to Hartstone.

The moment she turned the final bend in the road that led to the lighthouse, her heart beat a tattoo. Levan's car was in his space and she found herself fighting an insane urge to break into a run – whether toward him or away, though, she didn't know . . .

Instead, she managed to slow her steps, all the time wondering what his visit home might have done to him. A tiny part of her had feared – irrationally – that he might have been tempted to stay away, however unlikely a prospect that seemed given his family circumstances. There was no way she would ever let him know, though.

Morwenna's words hadn't left her. She turned them over and over.

Perhaps you'll never know unless you give him the chance?

And more importantly, give yourself the chance to care about someone again . . . more than care . . .

Eden marched up to the door of Longships and rapped the knocker.

There were a few moments when she feared he might not be inside, then she heard the sound of someone approaching the door. Her heart rate took off like a rocket.

'Levan, I need to speak to you,' she blurted out before he'd barely had a chance to open the door.

'I'm pleased to hear it,' he said, with a somewhat startled expression.

'Can I come in?'

'Of course, you'll always be welcome in here.'

Eden realised she hadn't been inside since she'd met Maddie and Dion. It felt good to be back again.

She sat down and he sat beside her. Courage failed her briefly so she began with his trip to the home that didn't deserve the name. 'So, how was it?'

He sighed deeply. 'Difficult, emotional, but the right thing for Mum and for me. She was relieved I'd agreed to meet her . . . She cried.' He rubbed his hands together unconsciously.

Eden's heart went out to him. He'd been through a hellish ordeal.

'And the rest of the family?' she prompted.

He shook his head. 'Not great. Mum says Dad is struggling to come to terms with the fact his son has "lobbed a bloody great grenade into the heart of a venerable institution".'

'I'm sorry.'

'Me too. He didn't want to see me but Mum has admitted he also asked her if "they" – meaning him and Mum – "might have done more to prevent this disaster". She also found him crying in the garden after she left me at the hotel. She phoned and told me when I stopped for a break

357

at the services. He'd confessed he regretted not agreeing to see me.'

'It must have been hard on you, but it's a step forward,' Eden offered, remembering Morwenna's words again. Perhaps it was time for her to take a step forward too, even though it would take a lot of her own courage to trust him again.

'It is. He's not well and the stress is making him worse. He's hinted he might want to come and see me – here.'

'I hope so. What about your brother?'

Levan snorted. 'Oh, I'm still dead to him. Didn't even want Mum to see me but she basically told him to grow up.'

She winced. 'I can't imagine that kind of stubborn refusal to see the truth. It's an act of self-harm.'

'Please don't worry. It hurt once, but I'm reconciled to it now. He's angry that he'll be tarnished by association. That piece in the newspapers did say that my family disowned me. No wonder he's angry . . .' he took a breath. 'All that matters is that Mum and I are in touch again and that my father's considering building some bridges.'

He gazed down at the floor, seeming overcome by emotion. Eden gave him time to compose himself.

'There's something else I need to tell you, seeing as I swore never to have any secrets again. I saw my ex, Caro, too.'

Eden's pulse beat a little faster. Those words struck fear into her – far more fear than she'd expected or was surely rational.

'Oh?' She squeezed out the word.

'Mum had mentioned she was seeing me and she – well, she "just happened" to turn up in the hotel where we were having lunch.'

Eden gasped. 'You mean your mother engineered the meeting?'

'No. I guess Caro had heard I was back and couldn't resist it. She was with her sister and they made quite a show of telling me and Mum they were out shopping for clothes for her honeymoon. She's getting married next month to a major in the Guards.'

'Is she?' Eden murmured and took a moment to steel herself for the answer to her next question. 'And how do you feel about that? Were you still mesmerised?' she said, remembering his comment.

He frowned. 'That was a long, long time ago. The scales have fallen from my eyes since then. I now know that love isn't sticking with someone for the dazzle of the moment, as I did with her, or for what you think that person will become, as she did with me. It's staying by their side when they need you most. It's putting them first. Which I haven't,' he said, gazing at Eden, 'with you, and I bitterly regret it. I wish so much that I could turn back the clock. This past week or so has been agony and I've tried to give you space so that you don't feel under pressure.'

'Levan . . .' She was unable to bear the pain in his eyes.

'Going back only reminded me of what I've lost here in Cornwall. I wished Caro well and then I left her where she belongs: in the past. This is my home now and I want it to be my future. I love you, Eden, and I have no idea how I'm going to bear waiting decades to show you.'

She reached out to him and took his hands in hers. 'Perhaps you won't have to.'

His eyes lit up. 'There's hope, then?'

'I . . . we need to take it very slowly, but I do want to make a start on us having a relationship – and I don't mean as friends or neighbours.' She smiled. 'It's been agony for me too, you know, with you on the other side of the wall. And even more agony with you not there while you've been away.'

He laughed and the joy in his laughter rang out. 'I'd rather there was no wall at all.'

'We're in the same place now,' she said, standing up and pulling him to his feet. 'Let's make a start on starting again, shall we?'

A second later she was in his arms, kissing him like there was no tomorrow – living for the moment and the sheer bliss of being together, at last.

THE END

Acknowledgements

Readers may think the ideas for books arise in a flash of inspiration that strikes like lightning. The less-than-romantic truth is that this one turned up as the result of a conversation with my cousin, Nick, while he was fitting a new bathroom for us! He'd become interested in the 'communications' sites hidden around my favourite part of Cornwall – the far west. After doing a bit of digging, I was totally fascinated and knew that 'secrets' of all kinds were going to be at the heart of my next book – but in a romantic novel, not a spy thriller.

We have since had great fun driving around the area, spotting old cottages and farm buildings that weren't quite what we thought – however, I must stress that I have *completely fictionalised* all the so-called 'secret sites' in the novel. They have come purely from my imagination and you won't actually find Jackdaw Farm in real life.

At the same time, I found out that one of the members of my Facebook reader group, Jackie Riggs, had been the daughter of a lighthouse keeper, and I also instantly knew that my heroines would hail from a lighthouse family. Jackie has been so generous with her time, sharing her experiences with me to enrich the lives of the characters and the setting.

A huge thank you to Scott, too, who had his own coffee roasting business and spared the time to talk to me about the very complex business of creating the perfect cup of coffee!

A big sparkly thank you goes to the fabulous Thorne Ryan, my editor at Avon, whose insight and hard work made the first draft into a much stronger story. Thanks too to my copy editor Rhian McKay and the Avon sales and publicity marketing teams who work so hard to make sure you can find my books in lots of places.

This year has been an exciting one, largely thanks to my agent, Broo Doherty, who is also a dear friend. I know I can always call on her support, as I can with my friends, the Coffee Crew, The Party People and the Friday Floras, who keep me laughing and sane through thick and thin.

Finally, as ever, I owe my family everything. Mum, Dad, Charles, Charlotte, James and John – I love you.

**If you loved *A Secret Cornish Summer*,
then don't miss this heartwarming read
full of sun, sea, friendship and
romance . . .**

A Golden Cornish Summer

'A warm, beautifully written
tale full of Cornish sunshine'
KATIE FFORDE

Phillipa Ashley

THE *SUNDAY TIMES* BESTSELLER

And explore the beautiful Cornish coast with the rest of Phillipa Ashley's beautifully escapist Falford series . . .

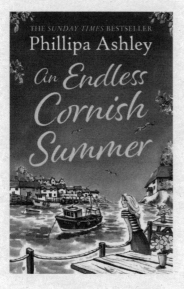

Discover Phillipa Ashley's glorious Porthmellow series . . .

Escape to the Isles of Scilly with this glorious trilogy . . .

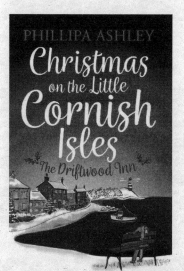

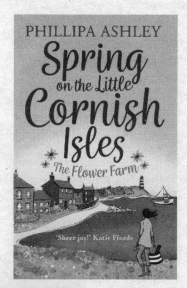

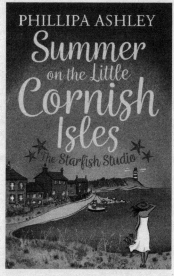

Discover the wonderfully cosy Cornish Café series . . .

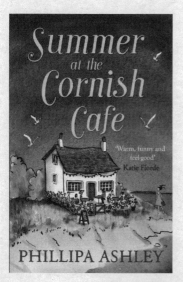

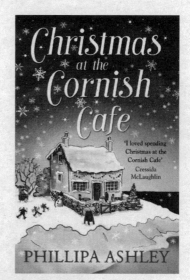

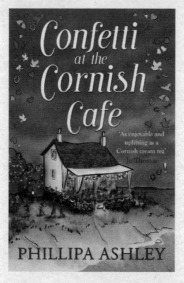

Don't miss these festive romances by Phillipa Ashley, set in the magical Lake District . . .

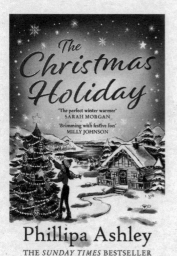